THE SECOND DEATH

Also by Peter Tremayne

Absolution by Murder
Shroud for the Archbishop
Suffer Little Children
The Subtle Serpent
The Spider's Web
Valley of the Shadow
The Monk Who Vanished
Act of Mercy
Hemlock at Vespers
Our Lady of Darkness
Smoke in the Wind
The Haunted Abbot
Badger's Moon
Whispers of the Dead
The Leper's Bell
Master of Souls
A Prayer for the Damned
Dancing with Demons
The Council of the Cursed
The Dove of Death
The Chalice of Blood
Behold a Pale Horse
The Seventh Trumpet
Atonement of Blood
The Devil's Seal

THE SECOND DEATH

PETER TREMAYNE

Minotaur Books
New York

This is a work of fiction. All of the characters, organizations, and events portrayed in this novel are either products of the author's imagination or are used fictitiously.

www.minotaurbooks.com

Library of Congress Cataloging-in-Publication Data

Names: Tremayne, Peter, author.
Title: The second death / Peter Tremayne.
Description: First U.S. edition. | New York : Minotaur Books, 2016. | Series: Mysteries of
    ancient Ireland
Identifiers: LCCN 2016001438| ISBN 9781250081766 (hardcover) | ISBN 9781250081773
    (e-book)
Subjects: LCSH: Fidelma, Sister (Fictitious character)—Fiction. | Women detectives—
    Ireland—Fiction. | Murder—Investigation—Fiction. | Catholics—Fiction. | Nuns—
    Fiction. | Ireland—History—To 1172—Fiction. | BISAC: FICTION / Mystery &
    Detective / Historical. | FICTION / Mystery & Detective / Women Sleuths. | GSAFD:
    Mystery fiction. | Historical fiction.
Classification: LCC PR6070.R366 S43 2016 | DDC 823/.914—dc23
LC record available at http://lccn.loc.gov/2016001438

Our books may be purchased in bulk for promotional, educational, or business use. Please contact your local bookseller or the Macmillan Corporate and Premium Sales Department at 1-800-221-7945, extension 5442, or by e-mail at MacmillanSpecialMarkets@macmillan.com.

First published in Great Britain by Headline Publishing Group, an Hachette UK company

First U.S. Edition: July 2016

10 9 8 7 6 5 4 3 2 1

Et infernus et mors missi sunt in stagnum ignis haec mors secunda est stagnum ignis.
This is the second death, the lake of fire.

Revelation 20:14
Vulgate Latin translation of Jerome 4th century

PRINCIPAL CHARACTERS

Sister Fidelma of Cashel, a *dálaigh* or advocate of the law courts of seventh-century Ireland

Brother Eadulf of Seaxmund's Ham, in the land of the South Folk, her companion

At Cashel

Colgú, King of Muman and brother to Fidelma

Finguine, *tánaiste* or heir apparent to the kingship

Alchú, son of Fidelma and Eadulf

Muirgen, nurse to Alchú

Dar Luga, *airnbertach* or housekeeper to the palace

Brother Conchobhar, an apothecary

Ferloga, visiting tavern-keeper from Rath na Drinne

Ségdae, Abbot of Imleach and Chief Bishop of Muman

Fíthel, Chief Brehon of Muman

Warriors of the King's Bodyguard

Aidan, Acting Commander

Enda

Luan

In Cashel township
Rumann, tavern-keeper
Cerball, Lord of Cairpre Gabra

Among Cleasamnaig Baodain (Baodain's Performers)
Baodain, leader of the Performers
Escrach, his wife
Echdae, a bareback rider
Echna, his partner
Tóla, horse trainer
Ronchú, a conjuror
Comal, his wife

On the marshes in Osraige
Rechtabra, a farmer
Ríonach, his wife
Duach, Rechtabra's friend
Cellaig, Rechtabra's friend

On the Mountains of the High Fields
Brother Finnsnechta, a hermit

At Cill Cainnech
Feradach, *cenn-feadh,* Commander of the township guard
Abbot Saran
Brother Failge, his steward
Ruán, Brehon to Coileach, Lord of the Marshes
Dar Badh, a servant

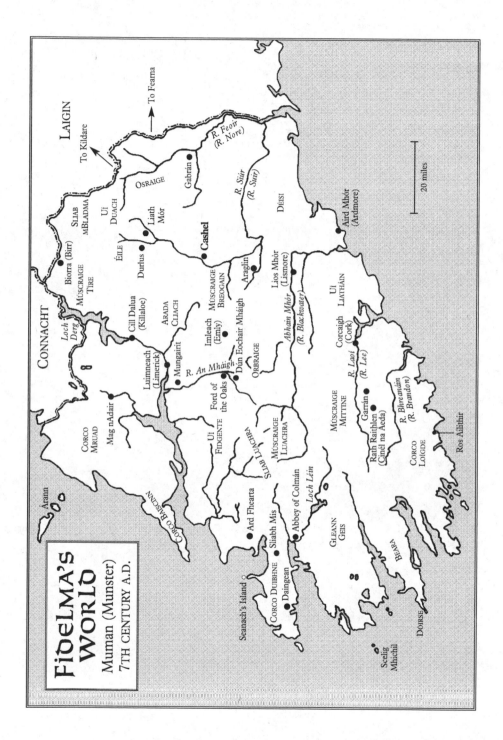

FIÐELMA'S WORLD

Muman (Munster)
7TH CENTURY A.D.

CONNACHT

LAIGIN

To Kildare

To Fearna

Arann

CORCO BAISCINN

CORCO MRUAD

Mag nAdair

Loch Derg

Cill Dalua (Killaloe)

Luimneach (Limerick)

Biorra (Birr)

MÚSCRAIGE TÍRE

SLIAB MBLADMA

Uí DUACH

OSRAIGE

Gabrán

R. Feoir (R. Nore)

Éile

Durlus

Liath Mór

Cashel

R. Siúr (R. Siúr)

ARADA CLIACH

Mungairit

R. An Mháigh

MÚSCRAIGE BREOGAIN

Imleach (Emly)

Dún Eochair Mháigh

Araglin

DEISI

Aird Mhór (Ardmore)

Uí FIDGENTE

Ford of the Oaks

ORBRAIGE

Líos Mhór (Lismore)

Abhán Mhór (R. Blackwater)

Uí LIATHÁIN

SLIAB LUACHRA

MÚSCRAIGE LUACHRA

Corcaigh (Cork)

Ard Fhearta

Sliabh Mis

Abbey of Colmán

Loch Léin

MÚSCRAIGE MITTINE

R. Laoi (R. Lee)

Garrán

Ráth Raithlen (Cinél na Aeda)

R. Bhreanáin (R. Brandon)

CORCO LOÍGDE

Ros Ailithir

Seanach's Island

CORCO DUIBHNE

Daingean

GLEANN GEIS

BEARA

DORSE

Scelig Mhichil

20 miles

AUTHOR'S NOTE

The events of this story follow in chronological sequence those related in *The Devil's Seal*. The year is AD 671, in the last days of the month once called *Giblean*, now April, during the approach of the Bealtaine Fair at Cashel, held on the first day of *Cetsoman*, which is explained in Cormac's ninth-century Glossary (*Sanas Chormaic*) as *cét-sam-sín*, the first weather of summer, which we now call May.

It might add to the reader's appreciation to know that the annals and chronicles of Ireland record, in the period leading up to these events, the burning and destruction of three great Irish abbeys; these were Armagh, Bangor and the 'House of St Telle', the latter being located on the Westmeath border. Although there is a slight variation of dates between the annals, I have accepted the dating wisdom of *Annála Ríoghachta Éireann* (Annals of the Kingdom of Ireland) more popularly known as 'The Annals of the Four Masters'.

It might also interest readers that Clochar (today anglicised as Clogher in Co. Tyrone), the 'place of the stone', was the site of an abbey and later cathedral founded by St Macartan (Aedh Mac Cairthinn), the disciple and friend of St Patrick. The modern church is only a small one. The ninth-century *Félire Óengusso* records that a stone stood on the right hand of the porch of the cathedral. Once covered in gold and silver, it was called the *Cermand Cesiach* and had been worshipped by pre-Christians. *Cermand* was thought to be a local idol, but *Cestach* means 'dark riddles'. The stone was also referred to as the *Cloch Ór* (Golden Stone), said to be a great icon of the Druids, and was noted in the medieval *Vita S. Maccarthinni Episcopi Clocharensus*. The existence of the stone was also mentioned in commentaries even down to the eighteenth century. Today, however, it no longer seems to exist.

And for those who like to know locations, Durlus Éile is Thurles, Co. Tipperary; Cill Cainnech (modern Irish – Cill Chainnigh) is, of course, Kilkenny; Sliabh Ard Achaigh (in modern Irish, shortened to Sliabh Ardagh) are the Slieveardagh Hills – the Mountains of the High Fields. Nearby, you may still find where Brehon Ruán dwelled at Tulach Ruán, which is anglicised as Tullaroan, and Osraige is, of course, Ossory.

CHAPTER ONE

The line of half a dozen or so gaudily painted wagons, some pulled by patient mules and others by oxen, wound its way along the Slíge Dála, the main highway which ran from Tara in the north-east, all the way to Cashel, capital of Muman, the most south-westerly of the Five Kingdoms of Éireann. On a small rise overlooking the 'Way of the Blind' – a road so-called because it was said that it was so well built, even the blind could travel it in safety – two figures on horseback watched the wagons moving slowly along its broad stretch.

'Where are they off to?' demanded Brother Eadulf, surprise in his voice for he and his fellow traveller had only just breasted the rise and spotted the procession.

The young warrior at his side, Aidan, a member of the King of Muman's élite bodyguard, the Warriors of the Golden Collar, replied indifferently, 'To Cashel, I dare say, friend Eadulf. Where else would they be going at this time of year?'

'But for what purpose?' Eadulf was irritated for he knew well where the Slíge Dála ended. Had he not ridden its entire length from Cashel to Tara and back again only a few years before? Yet Aidan's answer implied that he should know something more.

'Have you forgotten that in a few days it will be Bealtaine, the Feast of the Fires of Bel?'

1

Eadulf frowned, still trying to make a connection. 'Therefore?' he prompted.

'Why, it is the day of the *Oenach*, the Great Fair of Cashel, to mark the start of the pastoral summer season.'

A memory stirred. 'I had forgotten,' Eadulf admitted. 'You see, I have never been in Cashel during the festival time. The Fates have always placed Fidelma and me in many other parts of the world when the fair has been held.'

'Then you will enjoy it for the first time,' Aidan said warmly. 'The fair lasts nine days in which there are athletic sporting contests of all sorts, such as archery, and demonstrations of prowess with arms, horse racing, feats of skill from professional entertainers, feasting, assemblies presided over by the King and his Chief Brehon . . . why, even the great fairs of Taillteann, Tlachtga and Carman pale into insignificance compared with *our* fair.'

Eadulf smiled at the young man's boastful enthusiasm and turned his attention back to the line of wagons moving steadily south-west along the great road of timber planking, placed directly over the low-lying and boggy marshlands. On firmer terrain, roads were built differently. They were formed of impacted earth and stone, but through bogland the ingenuity and sophistication of the road-builders was apparent. The road was laid with birch runners traversed by large oak planks, the latters' weight keeping the runners in place and providing a broad and level surface – to the extent that two wagons could pass each other at speed. The road could cross water-logged areas in the manner of a pontoon, or cross streams and rivers by means of wooden or stone bridges. As Eadulf had discovered, their building and maintenance were strictly governed by law, and the responsibility for the upkeep of the roads lay with the local chieftain.

Eadulf knew that from this spot where he and Aidan had halted, the road ran on for another twenty or so kilometres to the great Rock of Cashel, which reared above the plains and on which the fortress of Colgú the King dominated the surrounding countryside. As the road moved through this marshland, here and there little hillocks rose out of the bog, like islands rising from the sea. And the bogland could be just as treacherous and unforgiving as the sea to those who missed their way and were sucked into its greedy maws. And even if he had forgotten that it was soon to be the feast day of the Fires of Bel, the ancient God of Light, he should have been reminded by the mass of yellow flowers, symbolic of 'fire', that were now bursting into life across the countryside: broom, bog myrtle, marsh-marigolds, even hawksweed appeared here and there.

On the far side of the highway stood a bog island that he recognised because it seemed to be a mass of impenetrable oak trees made even darker by the overgrowth of ivy that clung everywhere. It was called Daire Eidnech – the Ivied Oak Grove. He knew that among those oaks was a small religious community which had been established a hundred years before by the Blessed Ruadhán of Lothra.

A series of short sharp bird-calls caused him to glance up at the pale late-spring sun. He saw the small, hovering bird with its familiar grey and russet feathers, as the kestrel began dropping down on its prey. A hare was leaping away at that moment, and even if the kestrel had been large enough to deal with the mammal, its element of surprise was gone. Eadulf noted the animal's escape with a certain amount of satisfaction. He briefly wondered why local hares did not dig burrows as they did in his own land. The hares here made their form, or lair, in an oval-shaped hollow within a moss hummock. Even as he formed the question, the obvious answer came to him: it was impossible to dig a dry burrow in the wet bogland.

'We should join the main highway, friend Eadulf, if we wish to get to Cashel before dark,' Aidan said, interrupting his thoughts, gesturing towards the position of the sun.

Eadulf acknowledged this with a nod of his head and nudged his placid grey-white cob, with its black patch on the forehead, down the rise, keeping to the small dry track that they had been following through the marsh in order to join up with the larger highway. It was not difficult to follow the path which wound its way across the hummocks, but one had to be extra careful in places, since it would be dangerous to miss one's footing, with the marsh-land clawing on either side. Even a path such as this, only big enough for one horse to move in single file, was listed in law, and neighbouring chieftains were deemed responsible for seeing to its maintenance.

It took the two men some time to negotiate their way onto the main highway, where they paused for a moment.

'We should be home well before sundown,' Aidan said confidently. 'The way is easy from here so we can increase the pace, if you wish. The horses won't tire on this firm surface, and it's not far now.'

Eadulf replied with an immediate shake of his head. It was only with extreme reluctance that he made any journeys at all on horse-back, even when the mount was placid of temper, like his cob.

'We'll keep to a steady pace,' he said. 'There's plenty of time.'

They set off, relaxing in the afternoon light for, weak as it was, the sun was still warming to the body. They had soon covered a few kilometres, with the ground rising gradually away from the marshland and the more dominant hills now appearing to the south and west. It was as they were coming through an area of sparse woodland that they saw the pall of smoke ahead and smelled the bitter odour of burning on the faint breeze that wafted in their direction. As they followed the roadway, curving through the wood, they came across a long stretch of the highway. Ahead of them, the line of wagons which they had seen previously was halted to one side of the road.

It was obvious what had caused the pall of smoke. The last wagon in the line was still wreathed in it, although there was no fire. A group of men and women surrounded it; many of them were still carrying buckets, others holding brooms of bound twigs or blankets. The pair of oxen that had been hauling the burned wagon had been unharnessed and led some distance along the road to safety. Now it seemed an argument was ensuing among those who had been putting out the fire. There was shouting and fierce gesticulating.

Aidan increased his horse's pace to a trot to bring him swiftly to the scene. The sound of the approaching horses made the band of people turn and those arguing to fall silent as they watched Aidan and Eadulf come nearer.

'Is anyone hurt?' Aidan called as he halted his mount. The actual fire did not appear to have been a bad one, fortunately.

No one replied for the moment but several people glanced to one of their number, a tall, broad-shouldered man, who was obviously their leader. He looked like a blacksmith, with bare forearms and a leather jerkin which did little to disguise his muscular arms. His pale blue eyes contrasted with his dark, curly hair.

'Who are you?' he demanded rudely. Then his eyes fell on the golden torc around Aidan's neck. 'I am sorry, Warrior,' he muttered, obviously recognising the emblem of the Nasc Niadh, the Bodyguard of the Muman King.

'And you are?' Aidan asked equally curtly.

'I am Baodain, the leader of the *Cleasamnaig Baodain*. You may have heard of us?'

'Baodain's Performers?' Aidan echoed.

'We are entertainers going to Cashel for the great festival.'

'That much I have guessed.' Aidan gestured at the burned wagon. 'I ask again, is anyone hurt? Can we be of help?'

Baodain looked nervously at his companions before replying, 'The driver of the wagon has been overcome by the fumes.'

Eadulf had been gazing at the wagon with interest, since it was an unusual type for the country. It was a four-wheeled, enclosed vehicle with a curving wooden roof of the type he had seen in Gaul. In Rome these wagons, still called by their Gaulish name of *rheda*, were often adapted for carrying entire families to their summer villas outside the city. They could hold six people seated, with luggage. The wagon was not badly burned and, in fact, it seemed that the burn-marks were restricted to the area where the driver sat. The back of the wagon was like a wooden hut on wheels and it appeared to be untouched.

Eadulf turned with a frown to the man who called himself Baodain.

'How badly is the driver injured?'

Baodain shrugged indifferently.

'The driver is dead!' a woman's voice called, and the crowd all turned in that direction. She was standing at the rear of the next wagon, and Eadulf could see that she was young and attractive.

He swung off his horse. 'I will examine his body.'

Baodain immediately blocked his way. 'We want no interference from a foreign religieux,' he grunted, having identified Eadulf's accent as not of the country. 'We will take care of this matter ourselves.'

Aidan leaned forward on his horse, his hand moving to the hilt of his sword and easing it in the scabbard in an unmistakable gesture. 'This is Eadulf, husband to the lady Fidelma, sister to King Colgú of Cashel. You will accept his authority, and if you do not, then you will be answerable to mine. I am Aidan, Acting Commander of the King's Bodyguard.'

Baodain hesitated a moment as if he would contest the order and then, with a sigh, he stepped backwards. At this gesture, the others moved back too, forming a pathway to where Eadulf could see a body stretched out beside the next wagon further down the line. Eadulf walked quickly over to where it lay face down on the muddy path. It was clear that the flames had caught the left side of the body. Trying to hide his distaste at the injuries and the curious smell like roasting pork, he knelt down beside the corpse, which was that of a boy, clad in a rough homespun cloak now partially burned away. The feet seemed quite small, for one leather sandal had come off his foot and now lay by it. The woollen hood was intact and covered most of his head.

Eadulf gently pushed the body over on its back. The hood fell away, and as it did so, he gasped aloud in surprise. The side of the face undamaged by the flames was clearly that of a young woman. Even in death, she was pretty; her face was heart-shaped, the skin pale – but there seemed a faint animation remaining to it as if, at any moment, the dead girl would open her eyes and smile at him.

Eadulf's lips compressed as he sought to control his emotion. That violent death should come to a young girl with such beauty was always harder to take than death in the elderly and ugly. One immediate thing puzzled him. The burn-marks on her left side were not sufficiently bad, in his judgement, to cause death. Pain and shock, yes – perhaps it was shock that had killed her? His keen eyes now examined the body for any other obvious wounds. There were none. Death had certainly occurred very recently yet the lips had already gone purple and the facial muscles exhibited some degree of rigidity. He swiftly checked to see if there were any means of identification on her person. There did not seem to be anything. The clothes told him little, but he did notice something tucked into one of the sandals. It was a small piece of folded vellum, no bigger than one's palm.

Surreptitiously, he unfolded and glanced at it – and immediately felt frustrated. The writing was in the ancient calligraphy called Ogham, consisting of short lines drawn to or crossing, a base line. He had never bothered to learn it as it had long fallen out of general use, and even the language was an archaic one called *bérla na filed*, 'the language of the poets'. He could make nothing from the collection of lines, so refolded the vellum and placed it in the small leather pouch he always carried attached to his belt. Finally he stood up and looked towards Baodain and the others who had gathered around.

'You did not tell me that the driver was a woman,' he said.

Those gathered around let out gasps of astonishment, and Baodain himself moved forward and stared down at the corpse.

'That was because I did not know.' His surprise was undisguised. 'She was dressed as a boy and claimed to be such. She was alone with her wagon.'

'And now she is dead,' Eadulf added in a heavy voice. 'What did she call herself?'

'The boy – girl – gave no name to me.'

'She was part of your troupe,' Eadulf pointed out. 'Are you telling me that you did not even know what name the dead girl went by?'

'He – she – was *not* part of the troupe,' protested Baodain. 'The boy – er, the girl – was a stranger among us. She only joined us at midday today. As for the rest of us, we all know each other, and some of us are related to one another.'

'Where has your band come from?'

'We have been on the road for many weeks now,' Baodain replied evasively.

'From where?' Eadulf pressed.

'We were performing at the Fair of Uisneach.'

Eadulf had heard of Uisneach, which by all accounts was the epicentre of the Five Kingdoms: all borders met at the Aill na Mireann, the Stone of Divisions. The latter was a great standing stone that had been erected there in what was called 'the time before time'. Technically, it was in Midhe, the Middle Kingdom, and the very place where once the High Kings were inaugurated before they moved their capital to Tara.

'So you came south through Laigin before you joined this highway. Did you join at Durlus or come by way of Cill Cainnech?'

'You appear to know the geography of this land well, Brother Foreigner,' Baodain commented rather insolently.

Ignoring him, Eadulf said, 'I am trying to find out where exactly this girl took up with you.'

'As I said, it was about midday, when we were halting to water our animals at the little patch called the Township of Peat. It is not too far from the road that leads to Durlus Éile. It is—'

'I know where it is,' Eadulf said grimly. 'How and why did she join you?'

Baodain's mouth twitched in annoyance, but glancing at Aidan, he continued after a pause: 'We were halted by the stream there and, as I say, were watering the animals, when this wagon . . .' he gestured at the strange vehicle '. . . came through the patch of woodland along a minor track.'

'From which direction?'

'From the north.'

'Did that track lead from anywhere in particular?'

It was Aidan who intervened. 'Any of those tracks would lead across the great marshlands, friend Eadulf. It's not good country to drive a wagon through, as most of the tracks are too narrow. However, a track might lead from Durlus Éile.'

'So the wagon came along this track from the northern marshland to where your wagons were.' Eadulf turned to Baodain for confirmation. 'What then?'

'As I say, the driver gave the impression that he was a young boy. He gave no name, nor did he say from whence he came, but said that he was making for Cashel and could he follow us, for it was better to travel in company than alone. There was no reason to refuse him. It is our custom, where possible, for wagons to band together along the highways in case of robbers. The boy, as we thought him to be, was not overly talkative and, indeed, after we started our journey, there was no need for any conversation. We proceeded at a steady pace along the roadway to Cashel and all was quiet until, a short while ago, the fire halted us and then you came.'

Eadulf stared for a moment towards the driver's seat of the wagon where the fire had taken hold.

'One would presume that she leaped from the wagon when th

flames erupted and must have run several paces to get here, to this point, where she fell and died. Does anyone know how the fire started?'

One of the men stepped forward, a sallow-faced fellow with sandy hair. 'From what I saw, the girl must have accidentally set fire to something and then got caught by the flames. She then had to jump off the wagon to save herself.'

'And what is your name?' asked Eadulf.

'I am Ronchú. My wife and I,' he gave an automatic nod to the attractive young woman who had informed them of the dead driver, 'we were driving the next wagon along. I am merely guessing how the fire began, but it is the logical explanation.'

'So no one saw how it started?'

'I was driving the leading wagon,' Baodain said defensively. 'No one knew anything until those behind alerted us to the fact that this last wagon was on fire. We halted and ran to put out the flames. It was difficult, for water seemed to have little effect. We finally had to beat it out with brooms.'

'When was the body noticed?' Eadulf asked.

Once again it fell to Baodain to offer information. 'I saw the body lying there when I ran back, but thought the boy had merely been overcome by smoke. I shouted for someone to take care of him – but we had only just extinguished the flames when you and the warrior appeared. We did not have time to examine the body.'

Eadulf glanced around and was met by several nodding heads.

'It is as Baodain says, Brother,' said one burly-looking woman. 'Our priority was to put out the fire.'

Eadulf walked over to the last wagon and stood looking at it. The first things that caught his attention were the streaks of black parts of the driver's seat. A half-burned wooden bucket lay by the seat: it had clearly contained the same black minded Eadulf of the glue-like material which sailors planks of their boats to caulk them and make them watertight. He knew that it could be quite flammable. He became aware of the man named Ronchú standing gazing at the wagon over his shoulder.

'Looks like the boy was carrying a bucket of that flammable stuff and it caught alight,' the man observed.

Meanwhile, Aidan was looking at the sky. 'It will soon be dark,' he said 'and a road across the marshland is not the best place to halt a large wagon train to conduct an enquiry.' Seeing a frown gathering on Eadulf's brow, he added: 'I mean that perhaps we should accompany these wagons to Cashel, where a proper investigation can be conducted.'

Eadulf could see the logic in the suggestion. Certainly, some identification of the victim had to be attempted, but at the moment, the tragedy seemed like a straightforward accident.

'The basic frame, the axles and wheels are still strong and undamaged,' Baodain said. 'We could harness the oxen back to the yoke and drive the wagon into Cashel so that it could be examined it there.'

'Very well,' replied Eadulf. 'While you put the beasts back in harness, I shall take a look inside the wagon in case there is a means of identifying who this unfortunate girl is.'

The four-wheeled wagon was familiar to him. He had travelled in one through Gaul when he was journeying to Rome. Usually there was a central door on either side, with open windows on each side of the door. With this wagon, however, the windows had been filled in with fixed wooden panels. Eadulf went to the door on the right side to take hold of the handle. Then he saw that it had been fastened from the outside with a piece of rope secured with a tight knot. He went to the door on the other side and found it fastened even more securely, as if with a carpenter's skill. It seemed a curious thing to do to a good wagon.

He called on Aidan to sever the rope on the accessible door with his sword, then opened the door and hauled himself inside to survey the dark interior. The stench he encountered – a pungent combination of human body odours, stale urine and rotting vegetation – was nauseating. Eadulf stepped back, reaching out a hand to steady himself from falling off the vehicle, and turned away to gulp in fresh air.

Behind him, Baodain uttered a sardonic chuckle at the sight of his ashen face and expression of distaste. 'You look pale, Saxon. Aren't you used to the way travelling folk live?'

Aidan moved Eadulf aside and stepped up in his place. 'She must have kept a pig in there,' he snapped. 'It smells disgusting. Strange, since she did not look like the sort of woman who would live in filth. But with this mess, it's no wonder she kept the doors of the wagon securely fastened.'

Eadulf wore a grim expression. His voice was sombre. 'I am afraid that is the smell of a decaying human body, my friend. I have encountered the same smell in catacombs and graveyards. Someone fetch me a lamp, please.'

There was a silence and Aidan stepped down. Someone appeared with an oil lamp which was handed to Eadulf. Holding the light aloft, Eadulf advanced once more into the gloomy, grime-encrusted interior, while Aidan stood guard on the step behind him. The only word to describe the scene inside was chaos. It looked as if a storm had blasted through it, turning everything upside down. There was a mound in the centre covered by a dark blanket. Eadulf bravely plucked the cover away. Beneath it lay a corpse.

Steeling himself, Eadulf bent down to examine the putrid-smelling body. It was that of a man. Whoever this person had been, he must have died several days ago. The flesh was receding from the bones and the odours of putrescence were almost overpowering. It was that sickly smell that Eadulf had recognised, having encountered it several times before. There was enough of the corpse intact to show that it had been a youthful male, and the bits and pieces of clothing attached to it, revealed that the fellow had been well clad, his leather sandals well made. Eadulf could see that the hairline on the decomposing head was further back than normal, and it occurred to him that it might be the tonsure of the Blessed John; the western churches had adopted this in preference to the *corona spinea*.

For a long time he stared at the hairline until Aidan, peering into the wagon behind him, called: 'What is it, friend Eadulf? What have you found?'

Eadulf began to back out of the wagon. Aidan reached out and helped him down.

'There is a second death,' Eadulf replied. 'A second corpse. There will have to be an investigation when we get to Cashel, but in this case it will not be a matter of death from an accidental fire.'

'Who is it?' demanded Baodain.

Eadulf swung his troubled glance from Baodain to Aidan and then back again. 'This body appears to be that of a religieux.'

chapter two

'It is not fair!'

Colgú, Lord of Tuadmuma, Aurmuma, Iarmuma, Desmuma, King of Muman, the largest and most south-westerly of the Five Kingdoms of Éireann, was sulking. For a moment he looked like a petulant small boy as he sank back in his chair and gazed moodily at his companion.

His sister, Fidelma of Cashel, sighed impatiently.

'Who is to judge what is fair and what is not, brother? You have to accept what fate sends.'

They were seated in the King's private chamber before a crackling wood fire. The conversation had been about the arrival of Eadulf on the previous evening with the wagons of Baodain's entertainers and the news of the dead bodies.

Colgú groaned. 'Please don't enlighten me with one of your favourite quotes from Virgil. I know them all by now. *Fata obstant* – the Fates oppose.'

The corner of Fidelma's mouth twitched irritably but she said nothing.

'It will cast a shadow over the Great Fair of Cashel,' her brother went on in a grumbling tone.

'It will cast an even greater shadow over those who are personally affected by these deaths,' she admonished him.

'You have missed attending some of the Great Fairs in recent years,' Colgú pointed out, ignoring her reproach. 'It is an important event. You should also know that the *Cleasamnaig Baodain* are very well known. They have performed at many of the fairs here.'

'Even I have heard of them, brother,' Fidelma assured him with soft irony. 'I have also heard that they have performed at many of the other great fairs throughout the Five Kingdoms. People speak of their acrobatic feats as being almost miraculous. But no matter their rank and fame, all stand equal before the law when there are suspicious deaths to be investigated.'

'Where is Eadulf now?' her brother asked.

'He has gone for a morning ride with our son. We take it in turns to do so.'

Colgú made an impatient motion with his hand. 'I know, I know. But there are people to be questioned and legal matters to be attended to before we can indulge in our personal life.'

Fidelma's eyes narrowed dangerously. 'When Eadulf returns, we plan to question Baodain's group together under my authority as an advocate of the court.'

Her brother pulled a face.

'Is it wise to delay? From what I hear, it seems a straightforward matter. The girl must have killed the religieux in her wagon and probably wanted to burn the evidence of her crime. She had an accident with the incendiary material and burned herself instead. Then she leaped from the wagon and either died of the shock or injured herself sufficiently to die moments later.'

'Matters that look obvious rarely turn out to be so simple, brother,' Fidelma replied tartly. 'Anyway, Aidan has gone to make sure that Baodain's group are still encamped where they were placed when they arrived last night. He and Eadulf thought it best to leave them in the field on the east of the township rather than allow them to travel on to the site of the fairground at Rath na Drinne. Eadulf insisted on listing all the wagons and their occupants in the order they were in on the highway, and Aidan has placed guards at their encampment overnight.'

'So why the delay? That is, apart from the necessity of taking your son riding.'

Fidelma ignored his sarcasm. 'I decided to wait until this morning before beginning to question them. The delay was deliberate. Guilty people often get lulled into a false sense of security if left alone for a while.'

Colgú stared at her in astonishment. 'Guilty people? Apart from the unfortunate girl, what makes you think that any other member of the group has any involvement in this matter?'

'I think something very strange happened. Until we have the facts, it is best to form no conclusion.'

Colgú looked unhappy. 'Dar Luga has told me there is much gossip and apprehension in the township. It is ill-luck to have entertainers turn up with corpses.' Dar Luga was the plump, middle-aged *airnbetach*, or housekeeper, of the palace. 'The sooner the matter is dealt with, the better for everyone. If only my new Chief Brehon were here.'

Fidelma's eyes glinted ominously; a curious green fire seemed to flicker for a moment. 'Are you saying that you don't trust me to handle this matter? Are you questioning my qualification and method?'

Colgú was immediately contrite. 'No, of course I didn't mean that – you know I didn't. But it seems an extraordinary affair. A strange wagon joins a band of travelling entertainers. It is driven by a girl dressed as a boy. The wagon suddenly bursts into flames. It seems the girl had tried to set it alight, then lost control and had to leap from the wagon to escape. She ran a few paces along the track, then collapsed and died. In the wagon was the body of a man, apparently a religieux. The company that the girl had joined put out the flames. So, what conclusion is there other than that the girl murdered her companion and then set light to her wagon to hide that fact, by accident, killing herself in the process?'

'If it were her intention to destroy the wagon and the body in it, why did she not do so before joining Baodain's group? Why wait until there were plenty of witnesses on the main highway? Why did she ask to accompany them here . . . to Cashel? What was her purpose in coming here?'

Colgú shrugged. 'I don't know. What do you think is the explanation?'

Fidelma exhaled and stretched a little in her chair, telling her brother, 'That is precisely what I must find out. At the moment, we are simply not in possession of all the facts, therefore cannot arrive at an answer.'

'But Eadulf spoke to those nearest the burned wagon and they said . . .'

Fidelma shook her head. 'They told him what they knew, but that doesn't mean to say that they all spoke the truth.'

Colgú sank further back in his seat and resumed his glum look. 'We only have a week before the Great Fair opens. We should have some resolution before then. Don't forget that the princes and their ladies from all the sub-kingdoms and regions of Muman will be attending. All the leading dignitaries of the kingdom and some from beyond our borders will be in Cashel. I just feel that Chief Brehon Fíthel should be here to assuage their fears.'

Fidelma managed to control the irritation she felt at this new evidence of her brother's lack of confidence in her.

'Where is Brehon Fíthel?' she asked coldly. 'If you are so concerned about having him present, why not send a messenger telling him to return here at once.'

Colgú seemed too preoccupied to notice her icy tone. Instead he replied: 'He won't be back for a while. He's gone to mediate in a problem that has arisen with our cousin Olchobur of Raithlinn and his neighbours of the Uí Echach.'

'But it is custom and law for the Chief Brehon to attend the Great Fair because that is the time the *Dál* – the court – sits and dispenses justice for any who wish to appeal to the Chief Brehon and the King,' Fidelma said.

'He will return with time enough to fulfil those duties,' Colgú assured her. 'There are some days left yet but this matter must be cleared up.'

Fidelma sniffed meaningfully as she rose and made for the door. 'As it seems that you only have me to rely on, I had better make a start on finding a solution. I presume that I am given your authority to conduct whatever enquiries that I deem fit?'

Colgú glanced up distractedly. 'What? Oh, of course. You are a *dálaigh*. You don't need my approval to proceed in a matter of law.' He paused for a moment, then said, 'Perhaps it was a mistake that you left the religious and assumed the cares of your office. Life might have been a little less complicated.'

'You know well enough, brother, that life for me was *more* complicated when I was a religieuse!' she replied vehemently.

'But everyone still knows you as Sister Fidelma, and still calls you as such.'

'So long as they also know me as Fidelma of Cashel, a *dálaigh*, I am not concerned what else they think I am. The mistake was for me to have accepted Abbot Laisran's suggestion that I join the religious. At that time, when I left Brehon Morann's school of law, I needed some security in life. But I have learned my lesson.'

'So where are you off to now?' her brother wanted to know.

Fidelma had paused by the door. 'Eadulf had the bodies brought to Brother Conchobhar last night. I intend to hear what he has to say first. I'll keep you informed, brother.'

Brother Conchobhar was the elderly physician and apothecary who had been at Cashel for as long as Fidelma and her brother could remember. He had served their father, Failbe Flann, when the latter was King some thirty years before. Brother Conchobhar had been something of a mentor to both of Failbe's children as they were growing up. His apothecary stood just behind the old chapel on the far side of a narrow flagstone courtyard. Fidelma opened the door and entered. As she had done every time she passed the threshold, she halted and allowed herself to get used to the almost overpowering aromas of the herbs and spices that filled the apothecary's workplace. She found Brother Conchobhar in the rear room where bodies were taken and laid out ready for burial. One of the his main tasks was to wash and prepare the corpse for committal whenever there was a death in the King's household.

The old physician was bent over a body which was stretched on a table in the centre of the room. As Fidelma entered, he glanced up. He was holding an *altan* – a sharp surgical knife – in his hand; it was bloody, and there were bloodstains on the one-piece garment he was wearing over his clothing and which was designed to protect it. He quickly drew a linen cloth over the mid-section of the corpse before turning to greet her. The movement surprised Fidelma.

'What is it, old friend?' she asked. 'Is there something you don't want me to see?'

'There are some things that it is best not to see,' he told her.

Fidelma smiled thinly. 'Not even for the eyes of a *dálaigh* – an advocate who has probably seen more dead bodies than a battle-weary commander in war?'

'There are some things . . .' he repeated, but she cut him short.

'I respect your sensitivity, but a murder is a murder and if I am to resolve this matter then I cannot afford such niceties of behaviour. Come, you are examining the murdered girl,' she gestured at the table, 'so what did you find that you don't want me to know? I have seen people who have died in fires before.'

Brother Conchobhar shook his head sadly. 'It is not that I do not want you to know, nor that I would not tell you, but it is better that you do not see. Anyway, she did not die from the injuries inflicted by the fire. They were bad, especially on her left side, but not bad enough to kill her.'

'Why not tell me first,' Fidelma said quietly, 'and I'll make up my own mind if I need to see afterwards.'

Brother Conchobhar nodded slowly. 'Very well. We will start with the cause of death of this woman. Simply – she was poisoned.'

Fidelma stared at the physician in surprise. 'How could you know that?' she gasped.

'Am I not a physician?' the old man demanded. 'I have examined the blue stain of the lips, the contraction of the muscles of the face – both of which Brother Eadulf pointed out to me last night as being suspicious. I think he suspected poison, but wanted me to come to my own conclusion. Remember, he has studied at the medical school of Tuaim Brecain.'

'Poisoned! But how?'

Brother Conchobhar gave a cynical shrug. 'I can only tell you the what. The how and the why must be left to you.'

Fidelma nodded thoughtfully. 'In telling me the what, perhaps you can suggest what the poison was?'

'One can never be sure in such circumstances. At an experienced guess, however, I would suggest a very concentrated infusion from the plant called the Devil's Bread.'

Fidelma knew the tall plant, its hollow green stem and little white flowers of which children were always told to beware.

'Apothecaries often use it as a sedative,' she protested. 'You have told me that much in the past. It might have been taken as a medication.'

'In very moderate infusions, yes, but this effect, as I say, was caused by a highly concentrated dose. The intent was obvious.'

'It still doesn't make sense. If the girl set light to her wagon, swallowed the infusion, left the wagon and moved to where she was supposed to have collapsed and died, then it would not have caused her death by that time.'

'True enough. I would say the poison would have had to have been imbibed some time before, perhaps even several days before.

Certainly before she reached the stage of death, she would have been showing clear signs of illness.'

'So if she was suffering from the poison, then someone would have noticed?'

'Exactly so,' agreed the old physician.

'But this was not why you were performing a surgical examination?' she said, gesturing at the blood-stained *altan* that he had laid aside.

Brother Conchobhar sighed.

'In truth, I was just about to call the women who, for the proprieties, usually undress and wash female corpses and put them in grave clothes ready for the obsequies, when I realised something. It had been difficult to notice before, for the girl had been wearing a large, flowing woollen robe. As she lay there, however, I saw that the poor girl's *crislach* was swollen.'

The word meant the part of the body enclosed by a *criss* or girdle – which was a polite way of saying the abdomen or belly. Brother Conchobhar was a believer in polite euphemisms when speaking on feminine matters. He paused, but Fidelma said nothing, waiting for him to finish in his own way.

'I removed the clothing and examined the swelling. The only way I could confirm my immediate conclusion was by cutting into the *maclaig*.'

Again, old Brother Conchobhar was choosing a polite euphemism, referring to 'the child's dwelling place' – the womb. Fidelma's mouth tightened and she remained silent, guessing what was to come.

'The girl had been some months pregnant. Perhaps six to seven months. I removed the . . . the growth.' He looked sadly at the shroud-covered corpse. 'I did not think you would want to see it.'

The old man had been right. Fidelma had seen many gruesome sights, but that of a developed unborn foetus was one she would prefer to avoid unless it was absolutely necessary.

'Could anything be discerned from the . . . the infant's body?'

The physician shook his head. 'Only that at the time the mother was poisoned it had been growing naturally and seemed healthy. I cannot guess what the story would have been, had the poison seeped into the growing infant. Now, do you really want to see this?'

Fidelma had changed her mind. 'I will take your word on the matter,' she said. 'So tell me, what of the mother herself? Is there anything to indicate who she was?'

Brother Conchobhar gazed at the uncovered face of the girl who lay before him.

'She was dressed in poor clothing and yet,' he bent over and took one of the girl's stiffened arms from beneath the covering; it was the one which had not been caught by the flames. He pointed to the hand. 'Her fingernails are well cared for. Her hands are soft and there are no calluses. That is an indication that she was of good birth and upbringing. She was certainly not one of these travelling entertainers or someone who worked in the fields or tended a loom.'

Fidelma gave a quick nod of agreement as she examined the hand. 'Anything else?'

'Two things that may be helpful. As I say, the attention to her toilet. Apart from the last day or so, one can see that her skin is fresh and her hair has been regularly washed and dressed with some fragrant-smelling unguent.'

Fidelma bent forward and sniffed at the auburn strands.

'Lavender?' she queried.

'Just so.'

'Then from these observations, we can be assured that this is the daughter of a wealthy house or one of some standing in her community.'

'Exactly,' agreed the old physician.

'Also, if this girl was so fastidious,' mused Fidelma, 'it seems hard to believe that she could accidentally set fire to herself.'

'That is another thing I would like to discuss.' Brother Conchobhar's voice was heavy.

Fidelma gave him a searching glance. 'Go on.'

'A theory has apparently been advanced that the burns on the girl's left side and clothing were caused by accident when she tried to set fire to her wagon to destroy the corpse inside it. However, I noticed an odour about the burns that was unfamiliar. Early this morning, I went to view the wagon. I wanted to see where the fire had started – and the damage. The burned bucket which seemed to be the origin of the fire was still in place.'

'Yes – Eadulf left everything ready for me to investigate. Did you learn anything?'

'Have you ever heard of *Tene Gregach*?'

'Greek Fire? No.'

'It is known by several names; we call it *dergthach*. It is an incendiary material that was used in ancient battles by the Greeks and Romans. A chronicler from Antioch named Malelas once described it as being basically made of sulphur and said that it was fired from giant catapults and caused great damage when aimed at ships in sea battles.'

'Are you saying someone threw this incendiary material at the girl?'

Brother Conchobhar shook his head. 'There were the remains of a wooden bucket, overturned next to the driver's seat. I believe that a mixture had been put in there of *pronnasc*, or sulphur, mixed with *gláed*, or birdlime. That produces something of the sort that I think they would call Greek fire.'

'Birdlime is what our warriors often use to reinforce the seams of their shields,' Fidelma noted. 'It's strong like *sechim* or bitumen.'

'And when mixed with sulphur in the right proportions, it is highly combustible once heated,' confirmed the physician.

'But doesn't that clear up part of the mystery?' Fidelma asked. 'The girl is driving the wagon. She has a bucket of this *dergthach* by her side. It ignites, the flames catch her on her left side – and to escape, she leaps from the wagon and runs forward . . .'

'. . . only to submit to the poison she has ingested days before,' ended the old apothecary. 'There is one problem. Where was her means of lighting the *dergthach*? She would need some agent such as a tinderbox. If by some mishap she caused the flames to spring up unexpectedly, then she would have dropped her tinderbox. Eadulf specifically told me he saw no sign of one.'

'Are you saying the bucket was already alight?' Fidelma asked.

'I can only tell you what I have been told and seen.'

'I will check it out with Eadulf,' affirmed Fidelma. 'Anything else?'

Brother Conchobhar turned to a side table and picked up a small length of plaited hemp rope – about enough to tie around one's wrist. Attached to it was a piece of bronze metal, roughly circular in shape, like a coin, with the cord inserted through a small hole. He handed it to her and she turned it over, examining it carefully.

'It was tied around the wrist of the undamaged arm,' the old man explained, seeing the question in her eyes.

Fidelma moved to the window and held up the bronze disc so that she could see it more clearly.

'It seems to have the image of a bird beaten on it,' she said.

'I would say it was a raven,' the old man said. 'See the stout, heavy bill and pronounced curve at the top?'

'Does the emblem signify something in particular?'

'I have never seen anything like it before.'

'It certainly doesn't indicate wealth or nobility.' Fidelma pondered. 'What of the man who was in the wagon? Did you have a chance to examine his body?' She looked around, wondering where the second corpse was.

Brother Conchobhar nodded and turned to a side door. 'I have already placed it in a coffin outside because of the putrefaction and gaseous smells.'

Fidelma glanced from the girl's corpse to Brother Conchobhar, a question in her eyes.

'The man died several days before the girl,' the apothecary confirmed her unasked question. 'I would say three days. Hence the putrefaction. As you know, when a person dies several changes take place: discolouration, the stiffening of the limbs – and after two to three days the body starts to swell because of gases which emit foul odours. When the body was brought to me last night, these things were already manifest. I made a cursory inspection and had the corpse placed into a wooden box and sealed. He must be buried as soon as possible.'

'Could you tell how he died?'

'I would guess that he had imbibed the same poison as the girl. I saw enough to confirm that he had died in convulsions of the type I have seen when someone has been poisoned.'

'Like the girl?' Fidelma said.

'Yes – but *before* the girl,' Brother Conchobhar said.

'Eadulf believed the man was a religieux wearing the tonsure of Colmcille.'

'I can understand why,' smiled the old man. 'We shave our tonsure from ear to ear at the front of the head. The corpse had a high forehead and, of course, the tightening of the skin that occurs after death accentuated it because it pulls the skin away from the hairline. It is often wrongly thought that hair and nails continue to grow after death. But the tightening and hardening of the skin causes it to shrink back so the hair and nails look longer.'

'So he might not have been a religieux?'

Brother Conchobhar sighed. 'One cannot be certain either way. Like the girl, he bore the signs of being clad in poor homespun.'

'And there is little else that you can tell me about him?'

'Only that he was a young man, probably quite handsome before the disfigurement of death, with fair hair although it had become tangled and dirty.'

'What of the clothing they were both wearing? You say they wore simple homespun.'

Brother Conchobhar pointed to the pile of clothing in a corner. 'There it is. You may examine it for yourself. It could even be the robes worn by a religious community. I found nothing that would give a clue to origin or identity.'

Fidelma turned over the garments but found nothing of particular interest. They were just rough items with linen undergarments of plain quality. Even the leather sandals that both had worn were shoddy. There were no brooches on the female apart from the coin-like piece of metal on the hemp bracelet, and no belt or belt bag on the male. Nothing to identify either victim.

'There is just the piece of parchment that Eadulf found in the girl's sandal,' Brother Conchobhar concluded.

When Eadulf had shown it to her, Fidelma had suggested that he take it to the old physician. Although she had knowledge of the ancient alphabet, and the archaic form of the language which it represented, she had wanted to double-check the meaning with her former teacher, for he had a perfect understanding of it and, what was more important, could recognise any quotations that she might overlook. 'Did you have a chance to look at it?' she asked now. 'I could only make out some name when he showed it to me.'

Brother Conchobhar opened the drawer where he had placed it for safekeeping, and took out the little piece of parchment.

'It was a simple name in Ogham and a location,' he said.

'I read it as Cloch Ór – "Stone of Gold of the graveyard",' she said.

'Ah, but the formation is difficult. I would read it as "Golden Stone is at the graveyard of . . ." But I can't make out the name.'

Fidelma peered at it: she had missed that part of the interpretation. 'It sounds as if it is something set up in a graveyard,' she said thoughtfully. 'A stone of gold?'

'Have you never heard of the Cloch Ór – the Golden Stone?' Brother Conchobhar stared at her in surprise.

'I don't think so. Nothing comes immediately to mind. Why? Am I missing something?'

Brother Conchobhar pursed his lips for a moment and then smiled. 'No reason why you should have heard of it. It's just an old legend. It goes back to the days of the Old Faith, to the time of the Druids.'

'And what is it?'

'It is – or was supposed to be – a sacred stone, encrusted in gold, that stood in some ancient pagan sanctuary.'

'Does it still exist, this Cloch Ór? And which graveyard is it in?'

'I can tell you!' exclaimed a voice. They swung round in surprise, to see the housekeeper of the palace, Dar Luga. The plump-faced, elderly woman stood on the threshold of the room, trying to avoid looking at the shrouded corpse on the table.

'What are you doing here, Dar Luga?' Brother Conchobhar demanded, rather sharply.

'The kitchen has run out of *carlann* and I wanted to prepare some lamb, so I came to ask if you had any that you could spare.'

'Yes, there is some water-mint in there,' he said, motioning her into the next room where he kept his herbs and spices. He ushered both women into the main apothecary, pausing to shut the door behind him. Then he turned to his array of shelves to locate the mint.

Meanwhile, Fidelma was gazing with interest at Dar Luga.

'You said that you knew where this Cloch Ór was,' she prompted her.

Dar Luga smiled. 'Well, not exactly. What I meant was that it was an ancient story.'

'And one that I hope you will share with me,' Fidelma said, smiling back at her.

'Of course, lady. Brother Conchobhar has the right of it. It was an ancient, gold-covered stone, venerated by those who refused to follow the New Faith. It belonged to Mogh Ruith, the Slave of the Wheel, who became a god – one of the sons of An Lair Derg.'

'The Red Mare?' It was a euphemism for the sun. 'You mean that he was a Sun God in the time before the New Faith? I was taught, as a child, that he was supposed to be a blind Druid who dwelled in this kingdom centuries ago.'

Dar Luga nodded slowly. 'There are many stories about him, lady. But the country-folk in the west still believe that he became one of the immortals. If you angered him, he grew to enormous size so that his very breath could create a storm, hurling men, women and children, and all manner of animals, from one end of the land to another, and causing rivers to flood. Those who saw him in anger did not live long.'

'But long enough to recount his amazing powers?' commented Fidelma with some irony.

Dar Luga was not deterred and went on solemnly: 'He wore a hornless bull hide and his face was obscured by a great bird mask, the mask of a raven. His shield was silver-rimmed and studded with golden stars. And he was so massive he carried this golden pillar stone on his shoulder; he could cast it into rivers or lakes, whereupon it turned into a giant poisonous eel and swallowed his enemies.'

'Not a very nice person to argue with.' Fidelma could not disguise the amusement in her tone.

Dar Luga realised that she was not being taken seriously and sniffed in annoyance. 'I'll take my water-mint now, Brother Conchobhar,' she said in a prim voice.

At once Fidelma felt contrite and reached out a hand to touch her arm.

'It is a great tale, and one I have not heard before. I am sorry if I seemed to be making sport of your storytelling. But you said you knew where this magical stone was.'

Dar Luga gave Fidelma a reproachful look.

'They said that Mogh Ruith dwelled on Dairbhre, the Place of

Oaks, which is also called Bhéil Inse, the Island by the River Mouth. It is in the country of the Uibh Ráthach.'

Fidelma frowned as she tried to locate the area. It was Brother Conchobhar who explained: 'That is at the end of the great western peninsula; beyond the territory of the Eóganacht of Locha Léin.'

'Indeed that is so, lady,' confirmed Dar Luga, taking the mint from Brother Conchobhar and, with a quick nod of thanks in his direction, she left the apothecary.

Fidelma paused for a moment and then turned back to the old apothecary and said, 'I've heard of Mogh Ruith, of course, but never knew that he had been transformed into a god.'

'The land of the Uibh Ráthach is a wild and desolate place. It is beyond the great western mountains,' the old apothecary observed. 'In such places tales are told at night that grow into legends, and legends eventually become more certain than history.'

'The closest I've been to the end of that peninsula was to see it from across the sea,' Fidelma said. 'I once journeyed to the monastery on Scelig Mhichil, to the south of it.'

'Dairbhre is even obscured from there as it is on the northern side of the peninsula.'

'Is this gold stone worth pursuing?' she wanted to know. 'I am just wondering why the girl had that reference to it.'

Brother Conchobhar shrugged. 'I think Mogh Ruith was real enough, if we accept the ancient chronicles. According to them, your own ancestor, the King Fiachu Muillethan, called on him for advice when the High King Cormac Mac Airt unjustly marched his army into this kingdom to exact tribute. When Cormac was defeated, Fiachu Muillethan gave Mogh Ruith land to settle on, in perpetuity.'

Fidelma turned to him in excitement. 'Of course! I am stupid. Did he not choose to dwell at Magh-Féne, south of here, and do not those people still regard him as their ancestor?'

'Indeed. They have become the best metal-workers in the entire kingdom,' confirmed Brother Conchobhar.

'Then a stone of gold might even be there?' Fidelma observed thoughtfully.

'That is something I cannot help you with, Fidelma. Perhaps that scratched Ogham name may have no significance regarding the death of these two strangers; or perhaps it does. It is up to you to follow your own course in this matter. Thankfully, I am not a *dálaigh*. I deal with the afflicted and the dead.'

Fidelma smiled wryly. 'I might make a similar claim. But you are right, old friend. We are all beginners at another person's profession. So one more question. Does this stone of gold symbolise anything over and above what Dar Luga was saying?'

'Ah, that is knowledge I do not possess. I suppose you could assume that it was simply regarded as a sacred object under the Old Religion.'

Fidelma raised a hand in farewell to the elderly apothecary and emerged into the small courtyard. She was heading for the stable buildings to see if Eadulf had returned, when at that very moment he rode in through the gates with little Alchú beside him and Luan, the warrior, acting as their escort. The trio halted in the courtyard and Luan jumped from his horse to help the little red-haired boy dismount from his piebald pony. No sooner had his feet touched the ground than Alchú was running, grinning and shouting, towards his mother. She bent down to give him a hug.

'Did you have a good ride, little hound?'

The child grimaced. 'Not really, *mathair*,' he whispered, casting a guilty glance to where Eadulf was alighting and handing the reins over to Luan.

Fidelma was surprised. 'Why not?'

'*Athair* insisted we ride out along the road towards the High Wood. It is so flat and dull there. And he was so quiet and I was so bored.'

Fidelma stared at her son and then turned with a frown to Eadulf as he came to join them while Luan led the horses towards the stables. But before she could say anything to him, old Muirgen the nurse came bustling out of the nearby buildings to take charge of their son.

'Now you run off with Muirgen and have a wash and we will see you shortly,' his mother smiled. 'Then you can tell us more about your morning's ride.'

As Alchú trotted off happily at the side of the nurse, Fidelma turned back to Eadulf. Once again she had barely opened her mouth when there was some shouting at the gate and a mounted warrior clattered inside. He saw them, swung off his horse and marched straight over towards them.

'Aidan sent me, lady,' he gasped, glancing from her to Eadulf. 'You had both better come quickly. Aidan says that he needs you immediately in the town.'

'Why?' Eadulf regarded the agitated warrior in surprise. 'What's the problem?'

'There is a riot . . , or one about to start. It's Baodain and his travellers. Baodain is threatening violence against the guards.'

chapter three

'William you stop trying to hurry us?' Fidelma called out. 'Doesn't Aidan have any warriors with him to keep order?'

Fidelma and Eadulf had mounted their horses and were following the anxious young warrior down the track from Colgú's fortress towards the township below. The young man reined in and glanced back, looking contrite. 'Indeed, lady. He has a company of nine from the *lucht-tighe*.'

The *lucht-tighe* was the name for the household guards of the royal palace and the élite of the forces who guarded the King.

'Then we shall continue at a steady pace,' she replied sternly.

Hardly any time passed, however, before they were crossing the town square, where the sound of shouting came to their ears. On the eastern side of the town was a flat area of grassland where Baodain and his wagons had been placed under guard, with the exception of the strange wagon. This had been taken off to a more secure location in the barn of Rumann the innkeeper. Behind Baodain's wagons, the horses and mules had been turned loose to fodder in a field. In front of the wagons they could see a cluster of men and women. Facing them were Aidan and his warriors, on foot, their shields held protectively in front of them. The position was called the *lebenn sciath*, a defensive form usually assumed when marching to confront enemy warriors. It seemed the action was necessary as some of the women were throwing clumps of earth and even some stones at the warriors, and shouting abuse.

The young warrior accompanying Fidelma and Eadulf immediately leaped from his horse, swinging his shield round for protection, and joined his comrades. Undeterred, Fidelma dismounted slowly and walked towards Aidan. The commander called on her to take care. But she came fearlessly to his side and turned to face the dozen men, women and several children, bunched together in a hostile fashion.

'Stop!' she shouted. 'Put down those missiles. I am Fidelma of Cashel. I am a *dálaigh*. I speak not only in the name of the King, but as a representative of the courts of law. I order you to disperse!'

The answer was an angry muttering and a few shouted insults, but the missile-throwers paused. Then a tall man stepped forward, muscular with dark hair and pale eyes. His expression was hostile.

'This is Baodain,' whispered Eadulf, who had also dismounted and joined her.

'We are simple entertainers,' he told Fidelma. 'We are guilty of no crime and we demand to be released from the constraints put upon us by these warriors.'

Fidelma moved directly towards Baodain so that they were only a single pace apart. Her chin was thrust out to match his aggressive stance.

'Tell your people to put down their weapons and disperse,' she told him quietly but firmly. 'You have a duty to protect your people, for you know the consequences if they continue to hurl stones and clods of earth at members of the King's Bodyguard.'

But Baodain was undeterred. 'We came here to perform at the Great Fair in the Fortress of Contentions, Rath na Drínne, as we have done over many years. We will not be imprisoned or intimidated. We mean to leave here – and if any of these warriors get in the way, *they* are the ones who will be hurt, not us.'

Making no effort to obey her, he continued to stand in his

challenging posture. A growl of approval went up from his followers. Some of the stone-throwers at the edge of their group raised their hands, clasping their missiles.

Fidelma stared directly into the pale eyes of the man. To his surprise her features broadened into a smile.

'Aidan!' she called to the warrior, her eyes never leaving Baodain's. 'Stand by me and draw your sword.'

Aidan did not hesitate. Sword in hand and shield swung defensively to his left side, he stepped forward to stand by Fidelma, as if to protect her from the angry group.

'Aidan.' Fidelma raised her voice slightly. Her words were meant for all to hear her. 'Aidan, if anyone makes a move to throw their missiles, take your sword and strike this man. You need not kill him; just ensure he will never use his right arm again.'

She spoke clearly and calmly, but her words sounded all the more menacing for it. Aidan gave her a startled look, for her order was entirely out of character. But his hesitation was almost unnoticed as he turned to Baodain, his sword raised at the ready.

Baodain stared at Fidelma's determined expression for a moment, then glanced at Aidan's resolute figure and swallowed noisily. Then he cleared his throat. 'Put down your missiles!' he called nervously. His voice even cracked a little. 'Carefully! Return to your wagons. I will deal with this *dálaigh*.'

With some reluctance and many a backward glance, the band dropped their stones and lumps of turf and began to move slowly away, back to their wagons. When she was sure they no longer posed a threat, Fidelma gave an approving sigh.

'Thank you, Aidan. You may sheath your sword and put your men at ease.' Her eyes had remained focused on Baodain. 'A word to the wise, my friend: never challenge my authority again. If it comes to that, never challenge the authority of any Brehon or a *dálaigh*. They may not be as lenient as I.'

There was relief on Aidan's features as he turned to carry out her instruction. As he passed Eadulf, he whispered, 'Do you think she actually meant to do that?'

Eadulf had no idea. He could only shrug as he went to join his wife.

'Now, Baodain,' Fidelma was saying in an easy tone, as if the previous confrontation had not happened, 'let us repair to your wagon and discuss this matter.'

Baodain seemed bewildered by the change in her attitude. With some reluctance he indicated a wagon before which a small fire had been lit with some stools placed around it. A woman and two children stood hesitantly by it.

'Is this your wife and children?' Fidelma asked pleasantly.

Baodain grunted affirmation while the woman scowled. She was tall, with dark hair that was shiny and sleek, its strands covering a broad forehead. The dark eyes seemed menacing.

'What is your name?' Fidelma met her brooding gaze and held it.

'Escrach,' came the belligerent response.

Fidelma looked from Baodain to Escrach and back again with a shake of her head. 'Let me emphasise something to both of you. I am not only sister to Colgú, King of Muman, but I am a *dálaigh*, qualified to the level of *anruth*. Now if that does not mean anything to you, I shall explain . . .'

Baodain interrupted roughly, 'I know well what it means, lady. We are educated.'

'Good,' replied Fidelma with a smile. 'So let me see no more foolish brawling with my brother's warriors. Someone could have been hurt and,' she nodded to his two silent children, 'that would have been regrettable with so many young ones in your camp.'

Baodain and Escrach remained silent.

'Now, let the young ones go to play while we discuss matters.'

Escrach turned and said something to the children, who both went scampering away.

'You have obligations to meet,' continued Fidelma. 'Two deaths have occurred. It is the duty of witnesses to answer all and every one of my questions to my satisfaction. That means you and the members of your company. Is that clear? If you refuse, if you tell me falsehoods, then there will be consequences.'

'But we are not witnesses to anything,' protested Baodain. 'The boy – girl, if you like – simply joined the end of our line. We did not know she was carrying a corpse in her wagon. We knew nothing until the wagon caught fire. *We* put it out. Ask him!' He thrust a finger at Eadulf.

'There are still questions to be answered,' Fidelma replied.

Escrach remained aggressive. 'And if we answer, can we go? Can we get on with earning our living? Our purpose in coming to Cashel was to take part in the Great Fair – and that is our only purpose.'

'The *Cleasamnaig Baodain*,' Fidelma sighed reflectively. 'The Performers of Baodain. I know that you have been here before to perform at the Great Fair. So, if you fulfil your obligations to me under the law, then there is no reason why you should not proceed to the fairground at Rath na Drínne. Are you prepared to answer my questions, fully and without prevarication?'

'Ask your questions, lady,' Baodain bade her. 'The sooner it is done, the better.'

'Then if you will bring seats for me and Brother Eadulf, we can begin.'

Baodain looked at his wife, who took a stool from the wagon and placed it with the others by the fire. They seated themselves on these but Escrach preferred to sit on the steps of the wagon outside the circle. Her expression was still unfriendly.

'Firstly, I would know something of your band. How many are there?'

'We number seventeen adults.'

'And children?'

Baodain glanced at Escrach who answered curtly, 'Seven children.'

'And you travel in six wagons?' When Baodain nodded, Fidelma continued, 'And then you were joined by a seventh wagon, the one driven by a girl, although everyone thought she was a boy, and that wagon contained the body of a man.'

'We keep telling you: we did not know about that.'

'Where exactly did this girl join you?'

'We already told him,' Escrach said, jerking her head towards Eadulf.

'So now tell *me*,' Fidelma instructed.

'We were watering our animals at a pool by the side of the marsh road, the one called the Slíge Dála. It was there that this wagon joined us. I had noticed it came from a side track, from the northern side of the marsh road. It is a small track before you come to the larger road which runs north to Durlus Éile.'

'There's nothing but marshland at that spot,' Fidelma stated. 'So the girl just appeared out of the marshes and asked if she could follow your wagons?'

'Yes. She drove up with her ox wagon and asked if she could follow us to Cashel. I said that as long as she kept up with us, she was welcome. We did not plan to halt, nor were we prepared to slow down for her. You see, we wanted to get here before sundown. In fact, we were delayed a little in moving off because Ronchú had a problem with his wagon harness and had to drop back in the line.'

'Did you not ask this young fellow, as you thought the girl to be, for a name? You did not enquire who he was, nor why he was travelling alone to Cashel?'

Baodain shrugged. 'With the Great Fair coming up, it is not unusual to meet wagons heading for Cashel. No name was volunteered, nor was it asked for.'

'So the first you knew of any problem was when smoke was noticed and you had to stop to put out the fire. How were you alerted? I understand you were driving the first wagon, so five other wagons were interposed between you and the newcomer.'

'We were alerted by Comal blowing her *adharc*.' Eadulf knew that this was a kind of horn. 'Each of our wagons carries a horn which can be used as a warning or simply to keep in contact with one another.'

'Who is Comal?'

'Comal and her partner Ronchú were in the sixth wagon, therefore were closest to the newcomer.'

'What do this couple do in your troupe?'

'Ronchú is a conjuror and Comal is his assistant.'

'So you heard an alarm blown on a horn, stopped the wagons and ran back to see what the problem was?'

'We could see the problem immediately as smoke was billowing everywhere. Then we saw the driver lying by the roadside. I called for someone to attend to them as I believed they had been overcome by the smoke. I then went to unharness the oxen from the affected wagon and lead them to safety. While this was being done, Ronchú and others gathered to put out the blaze. But it produced more smoke than destructive flames.'

'You did not see the cause of the fire?' asked Fidelma.

The man blew out a breath. 'The origin of the fire seemed to be from the black stuff that had been in an overturned bucket by the driver's seat. I think it was Echadae who pointed out that water seemed to have little effect. Several of us took brooms and brushes to beat it out. That was more effective and the flames were soon extinguished, but they produced a great deal of smoke.'

'What had happened seemed obvious enough,' Escrach went on. 'The girl had that bucket of flammable material near her seat at the front of the wagon. She must have tried to light it and the flames became too strong.'

'But why light such a dangerous mixture while driving along a highway?' Fidelma said. 'It makes no sense.'

Baodain and Escrach exchanged a glance and shrugged at the same time.

'The girl was young,' Escrach said. 'Maybe she did not realise her danger.'

'But what would she have ignited this bucket *with*?' Fidelma wanted to know.

'No tinderbox was found on or by the wagon,' interrupted Eadulf, 'and to guide a team of oxen while at the same time trying to strike a spark to ignite the tinder would require an exceptional talent. It just doesn't make sense.'

Baodain struggled with the conundrum and finally gave up. 'Well, there was no other means and no one else to ignite it. It's a mystery. We tried to put out the flames and, having succeeded, were about to turn our attention to the driver when you and the warrior arrived.'

'Very well,' Fidelma said. 'So let us proceed to another mystery: what caused the death of the girl? The wagon that she drove was suddenly in flames, or rather the part where she was sitting. Let us suppose that she jumped down from her seat as the left side of her body was on fire. She manages to run a short distance before collapsing – dead – on the ground. Between where she had been seated to where she was found was little over a *fortach* in distance.'

Eadulf knew that was just less than four metres – or a *fortach* as it was called in Fidelma's language.

'The body was found by the rear wheel of the next wagon,' Eadulf said. 'That would have belonged to Ronchú, the conjuror, and his wife Comal.'

'That is so,' Baodain confirmed.

'So, how do *you* think she died?' asked Fidelma.

Baodain again exchanged a puzzled glance with his wife before turning back to her. 'We assume that she must have been overcome by the smoke, or succumbed to the shock of her burns. Anyway, she was unwell before she joined us.'

Fidelma frowned quickly. 'What makes you say that?'

'When the boy as I thought her to be first joined us, I noticed that his speech was slurred and his breathing quite hoarse and rapid. Comal told me just a while ago that she thought the girl was ill or drunk. Ask her. If anyone can judge if someone has taken too much alcohol, then it is Comal.'

'Why is that?' Fidelma asked.

'On our journey, Comal has become our distiller so that if we camp far from a tavern then she can provide us with a good *braccat*. But she never allows anyone to imbibe too much, for there is always the safety of the wagons to consider.'

'We will question Comal and Ronchú shortly,' Fidelma announced. 'In fact, we shall probably want to talk to everyone. There is a third and possibly even greater mystery, of course. The man in the wagon had been dead for some days when it joined you. So who do you think murdered him?'

Escrach sighed. 'Obviously, the girl did. If she did not start the fire by accident, then she must have been trying to hide the evidence by setting her wagon ablaze.'

'Then who killed the girl? For she died from neither smoke nor shock – but was murdered.'

There was no disguising the shock on both the players' faces. Escrach recovered first.

'Someone else must have been hiding in the wagon, without us knowing. They must have attacked the girl and then ran off,' she said belligerently.

Fidelma smiled softly at her, as if agreeing. 'A good theory – except if they did so, where did they hide afterwards? You were in the middle of the marsh road, with flat bog country on all sides. Did anyone see this mysterious attacker run off? Where would the murderer run to unless it was straight into a bog which would have been certain death unless they were hauled out? I presume no such person *was* rescued at the time? There is one other matter that negates that theory.'

They both stared at her, puzzled.

'When the wagon was opened by Eadulf, both doors were secured *from the outside.*' There was a silence as Fidelma watched their expressions and then she said casually, 'I am interested that neither of you have asked how she was murdered.'

No one answered her.

'I can tell you now that she had been poisoned a few days before, and only at the time of the fire did the poison complete its lethal task.'

Baodain was staring at her as if under a hypnotic spell. Escrach had dropped her eyes and was examining her hands. Fidelma waited, as if hoping that one of them would say something.

'So the deaths are nothing to do with us?' Escrach asked finally. 'She and the man – the second death in the wagon – they were poisoned before they joined us.'

'Yet there is the matter of the mysterious fire,' Fidelma pointed out. 'I have yet to complete my enquiries. Until that happens, you will remain encamped in this spot until I give you permission to move. I have to warn you and your troupe once more, not to create such scenes as I witnessed when I arrived here. You will keep the peace and behave in a manner in which we expect all citizens of Cashel to behave. The warriors of the Nasc Niadh, the King's Bodyguard, will be vigilant, so please do not try their patience. If you co-operate with us, tell the truth and keep the peace, then we will treat you fairly.'

Baodain grimaced. 'We have no option, lady.'

In response, Fidelma's lips formed a thin line. 'That is right. You don't.'

She rose with Eadulf and set off back to where Aidan was waiting for them. After a few paces, she stopped and turned back to Baodain and Escrach.

'I almost forgot . . . *Cleasamnaig Baodain*, the Performers of Baodain. I presume each one of those travelling in your company is a performer of some art or other. What feats do you and your wife perform?'

'I run the company,' Baodain replied with a shrug. 'I tell stories, sing songs, and my wife and I play several instruments. I usually play the *timpan* and the *cuslennach*, while Escrach is wonderful on the *cruit*.'

Eadulf knew the *timpan* was a small three- or four-stringed instrument hit by a bow while the *cuslennach* were pipes, but he found it difficult to envisage the belligerent Escrach playing sweet melodies on the *cruit*, which was a type of harp. He glanced at Fidelma and saw the twitches in the corner of her mouth and realised she was sharing his thought.

As they walked back to Aidan, Eadulf could hardly contain himself, for it was the first he had heard of the girl being the victim of poison.

'So I was right,' he said. 'The girl *was* poisoned. I mentioned my suspicion to Brother Conchobhar.'

Fidelma swiftly told both men of her meeting with the old physician earlier and some of the conclusions that had been drawn.

She turned to Eadulf. 'Brother Conchobhar believes that the girl imbibed Devil's Bread, as you call it, but that would not act immediately even in a massive dose.'

'I was taught some classic symptoms at the great medical school of Tuaim Brecain,' Eadulf replied. 'Baodain has just mentioned two of those symptoms – difficulty in breathing and the slurring of speech as if one was drunk.'

'Which only confirms that the girl had been poisoned before she joined Baodain's travellers,' agreed Fidelma.

'Well, I think the murderer will be found among Baodain's Players,' Aidan said obstinately. 'The fire must have been set to hide the evidence. To me it is clear that the person who killed the girl is either part of this band or is hiding in one of their wagons.'

'The fire is one thing, but the poisoning happened some days before the girl joined Baodain's troupe,' Fidelma repeated. '*That* is the mystery.'

'I still reckon someone in the troupe must be involved,' Aidan said. 'Should I double the guard around them?'

'I don't think they will give you any more trouble,' Fidelma assured him, 'but your company should certainly remain alert.'

'Did Brother Conchobhar agree that the girl was probably poisoned at the same time as the man in the wagon?'

'It seemed a logical assumption but it is an assumption nevertheless.'

'But it shows us that the members of Baodain's troupe are innocent of poisoning them.' Eadulf glanced at Aidan.

'There is still the mystery of the fire.' The warrior was stubborn.

'I agree. Let us ask some questions of this Ronchú and Comal who first alerted the company to the fire,' Fidelma decided.

Eadulf indicated one of the wagons; he had recognised the couple. A young, fair-haired woman stood on the driver's seat, engaged in tying a piece of the canvas covering to a support. A man sat on a camp stool nearby and rose nervously as he saw them approaching, calling to the woman to draw her attention to them. She descended from the wagon with a supple dexterity. The pair stood side by side, waiting as the others approached.

'I am told you are Ronchú and Comal,' Fidelma greeted them.

'We were not part of the protest against your guards,' the man replied immediately. He was a thin individual with gaunt features as if he had never eaten well. His sandy hair was uncombed and his grey eyes had a rheumy quality. This was deceptive, for Fidelma quickly saw how they flickered from side to side and appeared not to miss the smallest movement or expression. He appeared to have a nervous habit of massaging his left wrist with his right hand – and he did so throughout the conversation.

'That is right,' chimed in the woman. 'We want no trouble. That Escrach can be too domineering at times. She has most of the performers under her thumb.'

Fidelma smiled pleasantly. 'But she doesn't boss *you*?'

Comal was young. Fidelma put her at half Ronchú's age, and attractive, with fair hair and violet eyes set in a face that would cause any man to look twice. Eadulf had already formed the theory that she was Ronchú's assistant because audiences would have their eyes focused on the girl and therefore allow the conjuror to perform his sleight of hand. Eadulf was a confirmed cynic about such entertainers as conjurors.

The girl was about to respond to Fidelma when Ronchú interrupted. 'Baodain and his wife are the leaders of our troupe of performers, lady. It is their right to lead while we are with them.'

'And how long have you been with them?' Fidelma asked.

'We joined them at the Oenach Tailtean last summer.'

The Great Fair of Tailtean was held in Midhe, the Middle Kingdom, which was the territory of the High King and regarded as one of the oldest and greatest of the gatherings being held at the ancient Feast of Lughnasa.

'And how long have you been performing together?'

'I joined Ronchú the year before,' intervened the girl.

'And you come from . . . ?'

'We are always between places. Such is the nature of travelling folk performing at the various fairs,' explained Ronchú.

'And you are conjurors, I am told.'

'Ronchú is the conjuror while I assist and help him set out his equipment,' said Comal.

'And what sort of tricks do you do?' Eadulf asked rather contemptuously.

It was evident that neither Ronchú nor the girl liked their act to be dismissed as mere tricks.

'We perform ceremonial magic,' Comal began but Ronchú nervously interrupted her, for he knew that it was ill-advised to speak of ceremonial magic to a religieux.

'We perform many harmless illusions to entertain the ordinary folk, Brother.'

'I am also told that you, Comal, brew *braccat* for the company when you are travelling. That is quite an accomplishment.'

The girl made a dismissive gesture. 'I learned the art of distilling strong drink from my mother. Sometimes our journeys are long and we pass through uninhabited terrain, so my skill comes in handy.'

'I believe that you were the one who sounded the alarm to tell the others that the end wagon was on fire?' Fidelma said.

'That is so. I blew the horn as soon as I noticed the flames and smoke coming from behind. Ronchú brought the wagon to a halt and ran back to see what he could do while I let the others know.'

'Tell us about it . . . no, first tell us what you knew about this strange wagon that had joined you and also of its driver.'

Comal glanced at her partner and then shrugged. 'Neither of us knew anything about it. We were watering our horses at a spring along the marsh road when her wagon joined us. We believed it was driven by a young boy until . . . well, until the Brother here told us differently.'

'You did not notice anything unusual about it or its driver before the fire?'

'We meet so many wagons on the roads when we're travelling,' Ronchù said, 'and there was nothing to distinguish this one from any of the others that we had seen. It was unusual in design, I'll grant you that – but I have seen such vehicles before. Some have been brought over by the Britons who escaped into this country when the Saxons invaded their land. As for the driver, we just thought that he was a boy. That's all.'

'One thing I did notice, and I told Baodain about it because I disapprove of it in such a young person,' the girl put in, 'was that he, or she, seemed to be drunk.'

'How did you know?' Fidelma enquired.

'I was standing nearby when he asked Baodain if he could join us as he was alone and travelling on the road to Cashel. Baodain

45

told him to follow the last wagon in the line, which was, of course, our wagon.'

'But the "boy" was drunk?'

'His speech was very thick and indistinct. He stood unsteadily, and I noticed that he seemed to be breathing very heavily.'

'Did you speak to – him er, her?'

Comal shook her head and Ronchú added: 'No one did. Now Comal reminds me, he *was* afflicted with some breathing problem. He did not say much – in fact, he seemed incapable of saying much. I saw him run his tongue around his lips several times as if they were dry, and he kept sipping at a goatskin water bag on the wagon seat.'

'So no one really had any conversation with the newcomer, apart from Baodain?'

'That is correct.'

'So you set off along the Cashel road and the girl followed?'

'That's right – and we proceeded on for some distance,' agreed Ronchú.

'And then I started to hear a crackling sound,' the girl said. 'You know, the sort that dry wood makes when it is alight? It was that sound.'

'What did you do? Take me through it slowly.'

'Well, I heard it from behind and so I turned. I saw the smoke and flames from the wagon that had recently joined us, but I could not see the driver. I yelled to Ronchú to halt our wagon and reached for the horn that we all carry in case of emergencies. The wagons all stopped and I held the reins while Ronchú jumped off and took our bucket to find water. He was soon joined by others.'

'This is so, lady,' confirmed Ronchú. 'We always carry buckets on the side of our wagons and there was a small stream alongside the road. So I filled it and hastened back . . . others were joining me.'

'On which side of the wagon was the stream?' Fidelma knew already but wanted to make sure of Ronchú's position.

'On the left-hand side, lady.'

'And when was the body of the driver noticed? She would have been lying almost level with your rear right-hand wheel.'

'Baodain came running by and shouted out that the driver was overcome with fumes. Everyone's first concern was to put out the flames because fires can spread on the wind and travel from wagon to wagon.'

'So you went to help the driver?'

'Not immediately. I had to calm our two asses that were pulling the wagon. The oxen behind me were uneasy, and before my team were two very skittish horses.'

'Before?' Fidelma was puzzled.

'I mean the horses attached to the rear of the wagon in front of me. That was Echdae's wagon,' Comal said, as if that explained matters.

'Why would his horses be in front of you at the back of his wagon and not pulling it from the front?'

'Echdae and his wife, Echna, are bareback riders and performers and they have two good horses which are hitched to the back of the wagon when we are travelling. They don't use those beasts to pull the wagon. A moment passed before Echna took charge of the horses while Echdae and Tóla, their groom, ran back to help douse the flames.'

'When did you go to help the driver?' The question was put to Comal.

She paused to think. 'I suppose it was as soon as the asses were under control and Echna had calmed the horses.'

'So, Ronchú,' Fidelma turned to the conjuror, 'you were the first to throw water on the fire. What happened?'

'What happened?' The man looked bemused, as if he did not understand the question. Then his face lightened. 'Oh, yes. When the water hit the burning material, it was not extinguished. I have encountered that material before – I think it is called *picc* or tar

– and realised that we had to smother the flames using sodden rags or beat it with birch-twig brooms. It was not a great fire; otherwise there would have been little hope.'

Fidelma summed up: 'As far as you were both concerned, then, the fire you had to deal with was an accident?'

'What else would it have been?' asked Ronchú, perplexed. 'As Comal says, it did not take long to extinguish the flames.'

At that moment, Aidan came hurrying towards them.

'Lady, one of the performers has fled from the encampment.'

Fidelma whirled around. 'Fled? Do you know who?'

'It is a man called Tóla. One of my men spotted him riding away on horseback and leading a second horse. He was gone before my man could stop him.'

CHAPTER FOUR

Tóla was a small man whose deceptively slender frame carried well developed muscles and strong hands. He was of middle age, with dark hair and eyes that glowered at them all from under bushy eyebrows. His skin was tanned by a life lived mainly out of doors, but the darkness of his skin threw into relief a white scar that ran from the corner of one eye down to his thin-lipped mouth. He stood before Fidelma and Eadulf, with Aidan and two of his men guarding him from behind. Another warrior was holding the reins of two horses – the mounts that Tóla had been riding.

'You thought I was running away?' His voice was sneering. 'Your guards are idiots.'

'You had taken both horses – fast horses,' Eadulf pointed out, 'and were galloping away from the township. Our warriors had difficulty catching up with you before they forced you to return here.'

'Idiots,' the man repeated.

'Then where were you going?' Fidelma demanded. 'We are still waiting for an explanation.'

'I am an *echaire* – a horse groom,' the man said, as if it was the complete explanation.

'And so?' pressed Fidelma.

'I look after the horses of Echdae and Echna. Do you think

such thoroughbreds as they use in their performance can exercise themselves?'

Fidelma's mouth tightened. 'So you are telling us that you took the two horses just to exercise them! Why didn't you seek permission from the guards to do so?'

The man gave a snort of indignation. 'Why should I? Do they not know that horses need exercise? Since we arrived last night, they have had none – the need was obvious.'

'We have given instruction that no one was to leave this site until our investigation was completed. Harm could have come to you for disobeying.'

'The time will *never* come when I will be told when and where I should exercise the beasts in my care!' Tóla proclaimed. 'I know all about horses – could have been a Master of Horses in some noble's stables instead of . . .' He glanced with a sneer towards the wagons on the eastern side of the town square. 'Anyway, animals' needs are more important than the whim of humans.'

'You might know horses, Tóla,' said Eadulf, 'but you do not seem to understand that when you are given orders by the *dálaigh*, you must obey them, or at least seek permission if you need to do otherwise.'

Two people were hurrying towards them from the encampment. Aidan went to stop them but Fidelma called to him to let them through. They were a young couple, moving with the agility of athletes. They both had light brown hair and tanned skin. Their expressions were worried as they approached. Fidelma had guessed that they were the owners of the horses.

'We saw the warriors escorting Tóla and our horses back here,' the girl began breathlessly. 'What's wrong?'

Before Fidelma could reply, Tóla blurted out: 'These idiots thought that I was running away with the horses.'

'Your *echaire* rode off from the encampment without seeking permission,' Fidelma said sternly before they could protest. 'You were clearly told that no one was to leave the encampment until I said so.'

The young man called Echdae frowned. 'But the horses needed exercise. They are not cart horses, you know. They are thoroughbred beasts who have to be treated with care.'

'That's just what I told them,' chimed in Tóla.

'That is not the point,' Fidelma said coldly. 'Had permission been asked, it would have been granted. But the point is that when a *dálaigh* gives an order, it is expected that it will be obeyed. In this case we are investigating two murders. Disobedience could have led to someone coming to harm unnecessarily.'

'Murders?' Echdae looked surprised.

The girl seemed to recover from the news first. 'I am Echna, lady. I am sure it was just a misunderstanding.' She had adopted a coaxing tone.

There was annoyance on Tóla's face. Obviously he felt there was no need for apology for his actions.

'The horses can be exercised in arrangement with the guard and follow a set course,' Fidelma conceded. 'Similarly, any other requests that involve leaving the encampment before you have formal permission to do so must be sought no matter what the circumstances. Is that clear?'

'And next time, when a *dálaigh* gives an order, it is worth your while to obey it unless you wish to face a fine,' Aidan added severely.

Echdae bowed his head. 'It won't happen again, but the horses have to be kept in good condition for our performance.'

Tóla was already moving away, but Fidelma recalled him, saying, 'Before you leave, I have a few questions for you three.'

Aidan had stepped forward to block the groom's path and the man reluctantly turned back.

'A few questions, that's all,' Fidelma repeated. 'It seems your part in the Baodain's Performers is that of feats of equestrianism?'

'That is so, lady,' Echna responded. 'We are bareback riders and perform acrobatic feats while the horses are in motion, dismounting and mounting while they are at the gallop as well as similar feats.'

'And your wagon was in front of Ronchú's when the fire in the stranger's rear wagon began?'

'That is so. Comal gave a blast on her horn,' Echdae said. 'Tóla here peered back and saw the smoke. He shouted "Fire!" and leaped down and ran back. I left the reins with Echna and jumped down from my side, grabbing the bucket we carried, and joined Ronchú who had already started to throw water on the fire. However, the material from which the fire started was something like *picc* – the stuff made from pine resin and beeswax. At least, that's what I thought it was. Water had little effect, so I snatched up a broom and was beating at the flames when others came up and followed my example.'

Fidelma turned to Tóla. 'So you leaped down from the right side of the wagon and ran back?'

The little man shrugged indifferently. 'It happened very fast. I suppose I did.'

'And you saw the body of the driver as you ran by the back wheel of Ronchú's wagon?'

'I could not miss it. The boy . . . well, I am told now it was a girl . . . was stretched out by the wheel. As there was a great deal of smoke, I presumed that he – she – had been overcome with it and collapsed. The clothes were still smouldering.'

'You did not pause to see if you could help her?'

'No, I did not. My thought was to save the two oxen that were yoked to the wagon. I was unhitching them when Baodain came to help me draw them away, out of immediate danger. I told you that animals are my prime concern.'

'So you did,' agreed Fidelma gently. 'And what of your own horses?'

It was Echna who answered. 'The animals pulling our wagon

were calm enough and so I went to quieten down our thoroughbreds, which were skittish, smelling fire and hearing the alarms.'

'So the fire was soon put out. But no one had thought to attend to the driver until that task was accomplished and Eadulf, here, and Aidan rode up. Is that so?'

'It happened so fast,' Tóla replied thoughtfully. 'There was obviously no time to attend to the driver until we had made sure that the fire was not spreading.'

'Comal must have looked after her.' Again it was Echna who spoke. 'I thought Comal had seen her running away from the wagon before collapsing and that she had dismounted and examined her before calling our attention to the fire.'

Fidelma exchanged a quick glance with Eadulf.

'You mean, before she blew on her horn to alert you?' queried Eadulf.

'It happened so quickly, but I just happened to glance round and saw her climbing back onto her wagon before she blew the warning on her horn.'

'Very well, you may return to your wagons,' Fidelma said after some moments of thought. 'Tóla, you may continue to exercise the horses, but . . .' and she glanced to Aidan '. . . one of the warriors will ride with you just to make sure you are safe at all times.'

When she and Eadulf were left alone with Aidan, Fidelma looked troubled. 'I confess that I think this mystery is one that is going to sorely try me,' she admitted. 'A man and a girl are poisoned. The man dies and the girl drives on with his dead body in her wagon before she succumbs to the poison at the same time as her wagon catches fire. Everyone tries to assure me that the solution must be that she did it herself. But why? And why was she making for Cashel?'

'And why was the girl disguised as a boy?' Eadulf reminded them. 'Also, why was she driving a wagon inside which there was a dead man, possibly a priest – who had been dead several days? There are too many questions, and none of it makes sense.'

'It is illogical,' Aidan conceded. 'Maybe there was someone else hiding in the coach who did this.'

Fidelma said, 'As I told Eschrach, according to Eadulf and yourself, the doors of the carriage were secured from the outside.'

Aidan shuddered. 'Maybe someone could pass through closed doors. It is told by the ancients that once there fell into mortal hands a cloak of invisibility and—'

'We have no case of *dícheltair* here,' Fidelma interrupted brusquely. 'There are no incorporeal beings involved with this matter; just as I am certain that the girl herself did not cause the fire. Before we can pursue that matter with confidence, we have much more to do. Before anything further, I suggest we go and thoroughly examine the wagon.'

'After the bodies were taken to Brother Conchobhar's apothecary, I had it removed to a barn at the back of Rumann's tavern and placed under guard,' Aidan said. 'I knew Rumann had an empty barn where it would be safe, and the oxen are in a field at the back of it. I put one of my men there and had him relieved every two hours through the night and day.'

Fidelma did not mention that Eadulf had already explained this.

Rumann's tavern was on the western side of the town's large square. It was a licensed *bruden* whose premises were strictly vetted and governed by the laws administered by a specialist Brehon because it was a large complex, not merely selling drinks and food but offering beds for visitors as well. Next to it was a large brewery, and it was here that Rumann made his ales and stronger beverages. At the back of the complex were stables, barns and fields, all sheltering under the great limestone rock on which the fortress of the Kings of Muman stood, dominating the plains in every direction.

Rumann had observed them coming and met them at the door of the tavern. 'It seems that the only time I welcome you to my tavern, lady, is when a body is discovered or there is a mystery to solve,' he said with a wry smile.

It was only a month or so ago that the body of a visiting religieuse, Sister Dianaimh, had been discovered in one of the vats in
his adjacent brewery.

'I am glad that this visit is not as traumatic as my last one,
Rumann,' Fidelma replied solemnly. 'How are you? And how is your
little boy?'

'We are both well, lady,' the innkeeper told her. 'Already our
business progresses in anticipation of the Great Fair. Many visitors
have started to flock to the town although there is some alarm about
the stories surrounding Baodain's troupe of performers.'

'There should be nothing for anyone here to be alarmed about,'
she said. 'But I agree that the sooner we can resolve the matter, so
much the better.'

'Indeed, lady. The Great Fair is barely a week away and we would
not want any blight to cast itself over it.'

'Then let us examine the stranger's wagon.'

'Will you need to keep it here long, lady?' asked the man anxiously.
'Once the visitors start to come in greater numbers, I will require
the space as well as the fields for their horses and mules.'

'We will try not to inconvenience you for long, Rumann. Do not
worry.'

The innkeeper glanced dubiously across the square towards
Baodain's encampment.

'I saw there was some trouble there a short while ago,' he fretted.
'It is unsettling to my guests and to my business . . .'

'I understand, Rumann,' she said patiently, 'but my brother's
warriors are there to keep the peace. So the sooner I can accomplish
my task, the sooner we can return to normal.'

Rumann took the hint and turned to lead them through the tavern
and out of a back door, across a yard and into one of the barns
there. The main doors of the barn were open and a warrior was
lounging on a bale of hay enjoying the sunshine. He heard them
entering and leaped nervously to his feet.

Fidelma ignored him; her eyes were on the wagon. It appeared as Eadulf had described it to her. It stood on four great wheels; each wheel had six spokes and was rimmed in iron. She estimated the diameter to be over four *troighid* – well over a metre and a half. The roof was slightly curved so that any rain would run off on either side of the wagon, which had a door with a window on both sides and two windows, one each side of the doors, making six windows in all. She noticed, however, that all of them had been covered from the inside with thick hide or wood.

It was a sturdily built wagon, that was for sure, but much discoloured with dirt; while in the front there were streaks of soot and a few scorch-marks. She inspected the conveyance closely and saw that the entire wooden panelling had once been polished and that there were indistinct patterns on it. She walked to the front of the vehicle and noticed the single *sithbe*, a pole or shaft that ran between any two horses or oxen that would be harnessed on both sides of it. She bent closer and noticed that it was made of a hard wood – it looked like tough holly. Immediately before the box-like interior was a small area where the driver would sit. There was room on the bench for three people. This was covered on top and extended to the sides, affording the driver the maximum protection from the elements. The reins were made of leather and the metalwork was of bronze. It had fairly elaborate patterning to it, and it was clear that the wagon's accoutrements, if not the wagon itself, had once been owned by someone of wealth.

She moved back a few paces to look at it, her hands on her hips.

Eadulf was right, she thought, when he had identified it as being an unusual vehicle. No wainwright of the Five Kingdoms had constructed this wagon. However, she had seen the like when in Gaul and, as Eadulf had reminded her, when they had been in Rome. Had the victims been foreigners? Had they brought the wagon over from one of the kingdoms of Britain or even further, from Gaul?

'Shall we examine the inside?' suggested Eadulf, impatient at the length of her examination of the exterior of the wagon.

'Not for the moment,' she demurred. 'I want to see what we can gather from the exterior.'

'Apart from what I have already told you?' he asked, somewhat truculently.

'Let us consider,' she said, smiling a little. 'The wagon is definitely of the style you identified – a *rheda*, and unusual in this country. It is of good workmanship although it appears to have travelled a long distance. Outwardly, it has been well kept, although curiously, the windows and one door have been secured by a trained carpenter. Only one door gives entrance to the wagon. Fortunately, the fire was a poor one or put out too quickly and efficiently for it to have destroyed the vehicle. The flames damaged only the driving seat. It appears that someone had been able to light a bucket of tar, which caused the fire. The driver had sufficient time to descend from the wagon without being overcome by flames or smoke.'

She waited a moment before resuming.

'Yet look at the way the burn-marks are formed. They are on the driver's seat – but also located on the backrest. It is as if someone was holding a bucket of flammable material and then threw the contents of it towards the driver's seat. But to get that angle, that someone must have stood *in front of* the driver's seat, just to the right, facing it. The only problem is, you could not throw burning tar in that fashion.'

'We know the girl was already dying from the poison. She might not have known what she was doing,' Eadulf said, missing her point. 'She could have lit the bucket and overturned it accidentally.'

'Are you suggesting that she could have lit the bucket of incendiary material, dismounted, managed to throw it over the driver's seat of the wagon, turned and run a few paces before she conveniently died?' There was no guile in Fidelma's voice as she posed the question.

Eadulf thought hard. 'If she did not do this, what are we saying?

Are we back to some wraith with Aidan's cloak of invisibility who did this? If we don't accept that, then we come back to a greater mystery. A line of wagons on a long deserted stretch of road with flat marsh all around. Yet someone is able to get to the back wagon, set fire to it, and . . . having already poisoned the girl, let alone the man . . . then disappears as miraculously.'

As he spoke, Eadulf gave an involuntary shiver. He had converted to the New Faith when still a youth, yet had been raised at a time when the gods and goddesses of his people were powerful entities. Somewhere in the back of his mind he had retained a belief in the nature deities of the Angles and Saxons – the *ése*, with the shape-shifting Nixie, the water spirits who could rise out of the waters and marshes and take human form; or, indeed, the elves who used magic to create harm to humans in equal measure as they helped them.

Suddenly Fidelma climbed up onto the driver's seat and bent close to the burned areas, sniffing curiously at them. She glanced firstly at the overturned tar bucket and then at a goatskin water bag; sniffing at both of them. She alighted, looking pleased and holding the goatskin bag.

'That's just a water bag,' Eadulf said as he helped her down.

'Remember the dead girl was observed frequently drinking from it? Comal implied it contain alcohol because she thought the girl was drunk.'

Fidelma gave it a shake and could hear a faint swish of water.

'We'll soon tell if it's alcohol.' Eadulf reached for the bag but she held it back.

'Don't touch it. It might be the source of the poison. We'll let Brother Conchobhar examine it.'

Fidelma handed it to Aidan and told him to tell the nearby warrior to take it directly to Brother Conchobhar and ask him to examine the contents and to be careful in case of poison. As he rejoined them Aidan muttered: 'I say that it was the second body in the wagon that is responsible. Maybe he wasn't dead and—'

'We can forget him as an assailant,' Fidelma said impatiently. 'Brother Conchobhar assures us that he had been dead for two or three days. Nor are we dealing with Otherworld spirits. Aside from that, Aidan, you and Eadulf each bore witness to the fact that both doors were sealed from the outside. The only accessible door was secured – again from the outside – by a piece of knotted rope which you had to cut. The fire was definitely set from outside the wagon.'

The comment she had just made, however, awoke a thought in Fidelma. 'I don't suppose you still have the rope that was cut from the door?' she asked Eadulf.

She was pleasantly surprised when he rummaged in his belt bag and produced a piece of cord. 'I'd forgotten all about it,' he confessed. 'Thank goodness you have taught me how essential it is to keep such things.'

Fidelma stared at it for a moment. The knot was still in place because Aidan had only cut through the strand of the rope.

'The king of knots,' she observed.

'The what?' Eadulf was confused.

'It is an old and simple knot, both easy to tie and to untie. But not many people would have such knowledge.' She sighed and shook her head slightly. 'It's curious that the girl secured the door with it. The catch was not broken, so why secure the door? There must be an explanation.'

'If we can find it,' Eadulf said.

'We shall find it. It is just a question of gathering the facts and applying logic.'

Eadulf sighed a little. 'That is just the problem. We have no real facts about the victims, and no idea why the girl was driving westward for days with a corpse in her wagon and why she was dressed as a boy.'

Fidelma shook her head. 'The facts might not make much sense at the moment, but . . .'

Eadulf's expression was woebegone. 'I have seen you achieve so much over the years,' he said. 'I've seen you unravel a mystery like a ball of thread when there is no obvious start or end to that ball. This is different. There is no thread.'

She did not bother to answer the obvious question but moved to the door of the vehicle instead and opened it, by which time Aidan had rejoined them.

'Best bring a lantern,' she instructed the warrior, who stood looking glumly on. 'The hide blinds are nailed into place covering all the windows. It makes it as black as night inside.'

Fidelma waited until Aidan had fetched a lantern before swinging up into the coach and peering round. The smell immediately caught her throat and she coughed. Even the removal of the putrid body had not improved the stench. She wrinkled her nose in distaste. Aidan, in fact, had positioned himself away from the door and was trying not to breathe through his nose.

'You say that the male body was lying on the floor of the wagon?' she asked Eadulf.

'Under a blanket,' he confirmed, leaning into the vehicle and pointing to the spot.

She looked carefully around. 'There is not much here, apart from the usual things that you'd expect to find. Trunks with clothes for either the girl or the man but all made of simple materials. There is nothing of value, apart from a few religious books.'

Then to Eadulf's surprise she began to knock on the wooden panels of the interior and then bend to examine the wooden seats. Finally she turned, saw his questioning look and shrugged.

'Just a chance there might be some secret place where an important object might have been hidden.'

'I did say . . .' Eadulf began.

'I know what you said,' she snapped back. 'Better two pairs of eyes than one to examine the vehicle.'

Eadulf sighed. He knew that the more difficult she found the mystery, the more irritable his wife could be until she finally found a scent to follow. He had spent most of the night, and even during his ride with little Alchú that morning, turning over the facts; so few facts that they made no sense to him. He now stood silently watching while Fidelma checked and re-checked the interior of the vehicle. She finally gave up and climbed out.

'Now, Aidan,' she said briskly, 'let's look at the oxen.'

The warrior glanced at Eadulf in surprise. 'Look at the oxen, lady?' he echoed.

Eadulf was sure that she was going to stamp her foot.

'Yes, the oxen – the beasts that pulled this wagon,' she explained as if to an imbecile. 'If the wagon cannot tell us anything, then perhaps the beasts that pulled it can.'

Without another word, Aidan led them out of the barn to a field at the back. Eadulf recognised the two oxen – castrated adult male cattle, small in stature, long in back, with wide, slightly elevated, projecting horns. Most people raised among cattle were able to judge the docile beasts and Eadulf had placed them as three year olds.

Fidelma regarded them critically for a moment. 'Worth about twenty-five *screpalls* apiece, I'd say.'

That made them valuable beasts in anyone's terms, Eadulf realised. Even a *Fer Midad*, a clansman without property, could rate an honour price of only twelve *screpalls*.

Fidelma swung over the wooden fence into the field with ease, and began to examine the prints made in the mud in which the placid animals were standing.

'They have been well looked after,' she commented.

Eadulf, who had followed, stared at the ground in bewilderment. 'How can you tell?'

'These oxen are shoed. Since the hooves are cloven, they have to put half-moon shoes on them and you can see the marks distinctly.'

She then walked round to their rumps with Eadulf following at her heels.

'What are you looking for?' he asked, seeing that her eyes were running over the area of the hip joints of the animals. Almost before he asked, he knew the answer.

'The *selaibh*,' she replied.

In a society where the currency was based on the value of cattle, to be a person without any cattle was to be poor indeed, so it was important to keep a record of one's wealth. The *selaibh* was a brand which indicated ownership. Branding to Eadulf, however, implied something different. He shivered, remembering that in Rome he had seen people with the letter 'F' branded on their cheeks or sometimes on their arms. It stood for *fugitivus* and indicated a slave who had tried to run away. Branding slaves as proof of ownership had been the norm in Ancient Rome. And now, in more recent times, the Angles and the Saxons had started to adopt branding as a means of punishment, and had incorporated it into their own law system.

'There!' Fidelma pointed to a distinct brand-mark among the black hairs of the ox.

'Does it mean anything to you?' Eadulf asked.

'As a matter of fact, it does. It is a mark that I have often seen in Midhe, the Middle Kingdom, when I was studying at Brehon Morann's law school.'

When she paused, almost tantalisingly, he pressed: 'And so?'

'The brand is that of the Prince of Tethbae, whose lands are in the western part of Midhe. The head of the family calls himself An Sionnach . . . The Fox. That is his mark, a fox's head. The Prince of Tethbae claims descent from the Uí Néill High Kings, but he is trusted by nobody, especially not the Uí Néill.'

CHAPTER FIVE

R ather than return to the palace, Fidelma suggested that Rumann could serve their *eter-shod*, or middle meal of the day, in his tavern. This was a light meal consisting of cold meats, hard-boiled eggs, *bioror* – a watercress salad – and bread, washed down with *linn*, a light ale. They sat in a quiet corner of the tavern. Ever since they had returned from viewing the oxen, Fidelma had been unusually silent.

Aware of her favourite maxim – no speculation without information – Eadulf decided not to make any comment, although he could tell that she was obviously trying to reason out something based on the information she had recently gathered.

The silence was not something Aidan was used to, however, and so he finally broke it with the question: 'Do you have a theory about these deaths, lady?'

She frowned, annoyed at the distraction for a moment. Then she forced a quick smile. 'Theory? I wish I had!'

'But something about the oxen has caused you to start making some connection,' he said.

Eadulf waited for the irritable response, but to his surprise, Fidelma merely shook her head. He supposed that, as a warrior, she absolved Aidan from a lack of knowledge of her methods.

'As my trend of thought is leading me nowhere, I will share it.

The oxen, as I observed, carry the brand-mark of Sionnach the Fox, Prince of Tethbae, who, by all rumours, is a person one does not want as an enemy. Could these oxen be stolen from him? Or is this strange, foreign wagon also his?'

'I'm sorry,' Eadulf intervened. 'Where exactly is this place – Tethbae? I do not know it.'

'It is in the west of the Middle Kingdom, Midhe,' she replied. The widening of his eyes caused her to ask: 'What?'

'Then it should not be too far north of the Hill of Uisneach?'

'The southern borders of the territory of Tethbae are marked by the River Eithne, a short journey north of Uisneach,' Fidelma confirmed. 'The river actually rises on Sliabh an Caillaigh where you were held prisoner by those conspirators who murdered the High King Sechnussach and tried to seize power.'

Eadulf remembered well enough the time when he feared for his life: imprisoned in an ancient tomb with old Brother Luachan, waiting to be sacrificed to some pagan god.

'It was not a nice place,' he reflected quietly.

'But why did you ask the question?'

'Because I was thinking that if this prince, Sionnach, has a territory close to Uisneach, then we might have a connection.'

'Which is?' Fidelma did not follow his reasoning.

'When I asked Baodain where his troupe had come from, he answered that they were returning after performing at the Fair of Uisneach.'

'But they also said that the girl and her wagon only joined them on the Slíge Dála a short time before the fire,' Aidan reminded them.

'Isn't that too much of a coincidence? She just happens to be driving oxen with the brand of this Sionnach when she joins a troupe that had recently been performing on the borders of Sionnach's own territory.'

Fidelma looked at him sharply. 'What did you just say?'

Eadulf blinked. 'That it was too much of a coincidence . . .'

'No – before that. You said Baodain's troupe had been performing at the Fair of Uisneach.'

Eadulf was puzzled. 'Well, that is what Baodain himself told me.'

'Are you absolutely sure that they had come from the Fair of Uisneach?' she pressed him.

Aidan came to Eadulf's aid. 'He did, lady. I was there when friend Eadulf asked the question and heard the reply Baodain gave.'

Fidelma sat back with a frown.

'Is something wrong?' asked Eadulf.

Fidelma looked from one to another. 'There is something you have both missed. Uisneach is sacred to the old pagan good Bel. We are told that it was Mide, the Druid of the Nemedian, who lit the first sacred fires of Bealtaine there in the time beyond time. So this is why the great Fair of Uisneach is held there . . . at the Feast of Bealtaine.'

Eadulf was still looking puzzled, but Aidan immediately saw the point.

'The Fair of Cashel is also celebrated at the start of Bealtaine, the period of the Fires of Bel,' Aidan said. 'So how could Baodain and his troupe have been performing at the Fair of Uisneach when the fair has yet to be celebrated? There *was* no fair at Uisneach! It is not due until next week, when Bealtaine starts.'

'Exactly so,' Fidelma said. 'I think we will have to have a further word with our friend Baodain. It might not mean anything at all, but it is a curious mistake.'

'So you think there might be some link with this Sionnach of Tethbae, with the murdered couple and with Baodain's troupe?' asked Aidan.

'We can only move forward a step at a time,' Fidelma told him. 'The essence of discovering the truth is to take each fact and double-check it, discarding nothing but adding nothing. I think . . .'

She was interrupted by a commotion at the door of the tavern as several people entered. The leader of the group was a tall, arrogant-looking individual, richly dressed, and it was plain to see that his companions were either in awe of him or were his acolytes. He was bearded, dark-haired and had a hooked nose which at some time had been broken and badly set. It was hard to see whether the leader was a rich merchant or some petty noble. His three companions were equally richly attired. One of them, with corn-coloured hair, carried a sword in the manner of a warrior. He called for the tavern-keeper in a strident tone. Rumann came shuffling forward.

'We need rooms, tavern-keeper,' the newcomer demanded.

'Of course,' Rumann answered. 'For how long?'

The man looked towards the leader, who swivelled his gaze across the tavern, assessing it disdainfully.

'I suppose this dump is the only tavern in this township?'

Rumann's mouth tightened but only for a moment. Business was business, although arrogance was unusual among most travellers to the main township of Muman.

'This is the best and biggest,' he replied without modesty.

The man sniffed derisively, but responded, 'Then I suppose we shall be staying for the course of your fair.'

'For the Oenach Cashel?' Rumann smiled gently at the newcomer. 'Are you participants at the fair?' The tavern-keeper was well known for his sense of humour.

The leader almost spat in anger. 'Do I look like a fairground performer?'

Rumann put his head to one side as if considering the question, but before he could comment further the warrior with the fair hair spoke sharply.

'Show respect, innkeeper. You are addressing Cerball, Lord of Cairpre Gabra.'

Rumann bowed his head with mock obsequiousness which was lost on the strangers. 'I will show you where you and your party may lodge, Cerball of Cairpre Gabra . . . that is, if you do not consider my poor inn too unworthy for you and your companions.'

Only the onlookers in the tavern, who knew Rumann's humour, grinned at one another. The arrogant man, at Cerball's side, frowned and seemed about to say something. His expression told his audience that he was not used to people who did not acknowledge his leader's rank with due humility. However, Rumann had already turned to lead the way from the main tavern room. Cerball and his companions had no option but to follow him.

After they had left, Aidan turned to Fidelma and Eadulf and commented, 'An arrogant man, this Lord of Cairpre Gabra.'

'That is true,' agreed Fidelma. 'But then arrogance is a sign of inferiority, for a true prince of his people is secure enough in his station not to need to assert his rank.'

Aidan was thoughtful. 'I suppose that follows in all stations, from King down to the humblest *flescach*.'

Eadulf knew that a *flescach* was a minor, under the age of choice, which was seventeen years; a *flesach* was therefore of low rank, and his honour price reflected that, rated only at four *screpalls*.

'You are right, Aidan,' Fidelma said philosophically. 'Arrogance is only a mask to hide one's deficiencies.' She stood up. 'Now let us see what Baodain has to say about the Fair of Uisneach.'

Baodain, however, attempted to be condescending.

'The foreigner,' he jerked a thumb at Eadulf, 'misinterpreted me. I merely meant that we had come from Uisneach – *not* that we had been performing there.'

It was Aidan who came to Eadulf's defence again. 'The lady Fidelma's husband is quite fluent enough in our language,' he said sharply. 'And I was a witness to the words spoken. You said you had come from the Fair of Uisneach – but the Fair will not be held until next week.'

Baodain was undeterred. 'Alas, I am not as learned as you both must be in the syntax of our language.' He adopted a patient tone, as if trying to explain the obvious. 'I did not mean that my troupe had been performing there, nor did I mean to imply that I had. I am—'

'You claim that you play music, sing songs and compose ballads,' Fidelma said coldly. 'Therefore one would expect you to have a better command of the language.'

'I am but a simple man, lady. I have not the honeyed tongue to know the deeper meaning of the language of poets. I apologise for my shortcomings. The fact of the matter is that I was hoping to get permission to perform at the fair. After all, the High King himself will be attending this year's gathering. But sadly, the Fair Master told me that they had sufficient performers of the type of entertainment that we offer, therefore they could not employ us. Knowing we are usually welcome at the Great Fair of Cashel, we proceeded south.'

'You must have been several weeks on the road from Uisneach to reach this place with your wagons,' Fidelma observed, sceptically. 'And yet you were told that the Fair of Uisneach was already crowded with entertainers which must have been the case, many weeks before it is due to be held?'

Baodain shrugged. 'It is a popular fair, lady. When we were informed that the entertainers were already engaged, there was little we could do but accept the word of the Fair Master.'

'And who is the Fair Master?'

Baodain raised his eyebrows as if surprised at the question. 'At Uisneach? Why, it is the Lord Iragalach of Clann Cholmáin, cousin to the High King.'

'So, your troupe had travelled to Uisneach with the hope of performing, but he told you that you were superfluous to the needs of the fair.'

'Exactly as I have said it.'

'Was your group of performers complete at that time?'

Baodain frowned. 'I do not understand.'

'All your performers . . . had they been together long?'

'They had – oh, except for Maolán the contortionist and his wife Mealla. They joined us a few days before we arrived at Uisneach.'

'And where were they from?'

'One never asks questions among travelling folk. If information is not volunteered then it is not sought. However, I heard that they had been performing in Connacht before they came to Midhe and asked if they could join up with us.'

'Had any other members of the band recently joined you?' Eadulf queried.

Baodain shook his head. 'The others had been with me a long time.'

'A long time?'

'Well, at least a full season – that is, a year or more.'

'What of Ronchú and his wife, for example?'

'They joined us at Tailltinn last Lughnasa. Why are you asking?'

'Because it is my task to do so,' Fidelma snapped. 'So, you left Uisneach and decided to come to Cashel.'

'As I have said, your brother, the King, has always welcomed us when we have performed at the Fort of Contentions.'

'So, at that time, your company consisted of six wagons with your performers. The only newcomers among you were this contortionist Maolán and his wife. What wagon were they in as you proceeded along the marsh road?'

'They were in the third wagon from the front.'

'Very well. Now I want to be sure . . . at what point along the Slíge Dála did you enter this kingdom? What was your route from Uisneach?'

Baodain had to stop and think for a moment. 'We crossed into the Kingdom of Laigin, into the country of the Loígis, before entering into Osraige.'

Eadulf was struggling to remember the geography of that area, so Fidelma explained quickly: 'The Loígis are a small clan on the borders of Laigin and Osraige.'

'Then we came on the southerly road through Osraige and joined the main marsh road at the crossing of Cill Cainnech on the River Fheoir. There is a ferry crossing there.'

'You said the girl's wagon joined you from the marshlands to the north of the main highway?'

Baodain sniffed. 'It did, but I know little of the country beyond. We stick to the highways which are easier to haul our wagons over rather than small tracks.'

'Had you ever seen any wagon like the one the girl was driving? The shape and design are not often seen in this land.'

The leader of the performers shrugged. 'I have seen all manner of wagons, of all shapes and sizes, in my travels. Why should this one catch my attention?'

'But you did not remark on it to the girl? You did not question her as to where she came from, or what she was doing driving such a wagon alone – alone as you thought, anyway.'

'I did not. As I told you, travelling folk do not ask questions unless information is volunteered.'

'What do you know of An Sionnach?' Fidelma asked suddenly.

Baodain's head jerked back a little. Then he recovered himself. 'An Sionnach?'

'I see you know the name.'

'Most people do who travel through Midhe,' Baodain replied dismissively. 'The Prince of Tethbae has a reputation as someone it is better to avoid.'

'Some might even say that he rules without mercy to those who disobey his wishes,' added Fidelma softly.

Baodain lifted one shoulder and let it fall indifferently. 'I take no interest in such matters. My job is to provide entertainment to whoever pays me for it, even the Prince of Tethbae.'

'Then you have performed for him?' Eadulf asked in a bland voice.

The leader of the troupe shifted his weight as if he were

uncomfortable. 'I'll not deny it. I have performed before many kings and princes, even the King of Cashel,' he added with an attempt at humour.

'But we are concerned with the Prince of Tethbae,' Fidelma countered. 'When did you perform for him? Before or after you had been denied performances at Uisneach?'

'We were not denied!' The use of the word seemed to anger Baodain. 'We were merely told there was no room. There were already too many performers engaged for the fair.'

'Ah,' Aidan commented with a sly smile, 'that sounds like a refusal to me.'

'I am waiting for an answer, Baodain,' Fidelma said.

'Why does it matter?' The man was truculent.

'Because I think it does,' shot back Fidelma.

'The performance took place *before* we were told we would not be taken on at Uisneach. We had been asked to give a performance at the fortress of The Fox.'

'As I recall, the fortress of An Sionnach is situated at Ard Darach, the height abounding in oaks. Was the Prince of Tethbae pleased with your performance? I wonder if he had anything to do with the subsequent refusal you received at Uisneach.'

'I have told you why we were refused!' The words came out in an angry hiss.

'And you had never seen the dead girl or her wagon before you met up on the marsh road?' Fidelma switched subject abruptly. 'For example, you had not seen her in the country of the Prince of Tethbae?'

'Of course not.' Baodain was clearly baffled by the question. 'She joined us on the marsh road exactly where I said she did, and I keep telling you that I thought she was a boy! What are you suggesting?'

'Did you have a look at the oxen that were pulling the girl's wagon?'

Baodain looked astonished. 'Why on earth would I do that?'

'To examine the *selaibh*, the brand on them.'

'I am not interested in brands. I know my own mules which pull my wagon and that is all I need to know.'

'I thought you might be interested in the brand on those oxen, that's all. Because they are the brand of the Prince of Tethbae.'

Baodain sighed heavily. He was silent for a moment or two before stating: 'I cannot tell you more than the truth, and I have told you the truth. No more. No less.'

A short while later, Fidelma and Eadulf were in their chamber in the palace of Cashel trying to gather their thoughts.

'Well,' observed Eadulf, 'there is no doubting that Baodain was surprised when you told him about the brands. But in what way was he surprised? By the fact of whose brand it was, or by the fact that you could identify it?'

'A good point,' Fidelma sighed. 'It doesn't seem to lead us anywhere, though. The fact is, I think he is telling the truth.'

'I don't like the man,' Eadulf said. 'From the very first moment we met, I took a dislike to his arrogance and the fact that he keeps trying to evade answering simple questions.'

'You cannot charge a person with a crime because they are conceited and frugal with their answers,' Fidelma told him.

'More is the pity,' Eadulf said bitterly. Then: 'I cannot see any connection. Unless the whole troupe is lying, we must accept that the girl and her wagon came out of a track north from the marshland.'

'On the contrary, I can see connections but they don't make sense.' Aware that Eadulf was struggling, Fidelma relented and began to explain. 'The girl is driving a wagon hauled by oxen which carry the brand of the Prince of Tethbae. Correct?' Eadulf gave a nod of confirmation. 'The entertainers have performed at the fortress of the Prince of Tethbae. Correct? So there *is* a connection.'

'But the performers deny all knowledge of the girl until she joins on the Slíge Dála,' Eadulf said.

'She could have followed them.'

'True, but why? So far, they have all claimed not to have known her . . . or even that she was really a girl under her disguise.'

'Was there a connection between the girl and the performers? Could the fire have been set by someone in the troupe? Logically, being in the last wagon, only Ronchú and Comal could have done so without being observed by those in the forward wagons. But they gave the warning of the fire, which seems strange if they were trying to destroy the girl's wagon.'

Eadulf pursed his lips for a moment. 'Yes, it would be illogical. But if we reject that possibility, who else is there?'

'My old mentor, Brehon Morann, used to say that if you have eliminated all the other paths, then what remains, even if it seems improbable, must be the answer.'

'There are no other plausible culprits who are supported by the physical possibilities.'

'Except that we have not eliminated all other paths. We simply do not have enough knowledge to do so,' returned Fidelma.

'Then perhaps we should just challenge Ronchú and Comal outright. Isn't there something in your law to say that if there is no direct evidence then one can use indirect evidence as a sign of guilt, and eyewitness proof therefore becomes immaterial? I am sure I have seen that if one is suspected of a crime, then the law says that suspicion can be used to bring about prosecution.'

'There are certain matters where that is so, Eadulf. You remember our law correctly. It is what is called circumstantial evidence – but that has to be very strong, and such indirect evidence in itself is not regarded as conclusive in law. Those accused can demand to make a *fír testa*, an oath in which they formally deny the crime. Only if they are shown to be notorious liars, or untrustworthy, or have any stains against their character, does the law demand what is called *fír nDé*, an ordeal of interrogation, in which reputable persons come forward to say what they know about the person's past – and that past is then used to question their character. I am afraid that we are not in a position to go forward with such a charge based merely on suspicion of Ronchú and Comal just yet.'

Eadulf spread his arms and let them fall in an exaggerated expression of helplessness. 'Then what are we to do?'

'Maybe we need some fresh thinking about this. Let's go and have a chat with Brother Conchobhar. He might have identified the contents of the goatskin water bag by now. If all else fails, I suppose we will have to work our way through all the performers in Baodain's troupe.'

'Including the children?'

'Sometimes children are more prone to indicating the truth than adults,' Fidelma observed thoughtfully.

'Baodain won't like that.'

'It is not up to Baodain what he likes or what he does not like,' Fidelma replied sternly. She then rose from her chair and drew on her cloak, for the day was growing colder with the sun being obscured behind the dark rainclouds that had sprung up from the west.

In the familiar confines of Brother Conchobhar's apothecary with its almost overpowering scents of dried herbs and various plants, they found the elderly physician at work, grinding leaves with a mortar and pestle. He looked up with a wan smile.

'The bodies have been removed and the male has already been interred,' he said. 'I am afraid that after all this time the state of the corpse . . .' He tailed off but they knew what he meant.

'We came to discuss the case,' Fidelma told him. 'I want to see if we are overlooking the obvious.'

Brother Conchobhar set aside the mortar and pestle and motioned them to some chairs, before taking a seat himself.

'The water bag that you sent me contains nothing more than water,' he said before they asked. 'I found no obvious source of poison.'

'Nothing at all?' Fidelma's disappointment was apparent.

'That means that you have met with a blank wall on other matters,' the old apothecary observed cannily.

'It is true that this mystery remains a mystery,' Fidelma conceded. 'I was wondering if you could tell us anything more about the bodies. Perhaps in discussing it, something new might occur.'

Brother Conchobhar sighed. 'There is nothing else. Have you considered the girl's wristband? Did you have any ideas about it, Eadulf?'

Fidelma started in embarrassment, for it was the one thing she had forgotten.

Brother Conchobhar rose and went to a side cupboard from which he took the small section of plaited hemp and the brass disc with the bird's head on it, saying, 'All we know is that it was tied around the wrist of the girl and that it bears the image of a raven. That is really all,' he said.

Eadulf looked at it and then handed it back. 'It simply looks like a small coin with a hole in it so that string can be looped through it.'

Brother Conchobhar replaced it and resumed his seat. 'I can add a little more to the Ogham writing that we discussed earlier . . .' He paused for a moment.

'The Cloch Ór – the Stone of Gold at the graveyard! Whose graveyard?' Eadulf said eagerly. 'Fidelma told me of its meaning.'

'Well, I promised I would ask our Keeper of the Books if he could shed some light on it. We discussed some local legends associated with it but he reminded me of somewhere called Clochar – the Stone Place – where the Blessed Aedh Mac Carthinn set up his abbey on a site that was previously a sanctuary to the old gods.'

'I do not know of it,' Fidelma said.

'No reason why you should. It is in one of the northern Uí Néill kingdoms, Airgialla, in the territories of the Uí Chremthainn.'

'Is that in the north-west of Midhe?'

'Not exactly. The petty kingdom of Bréifne intervenes between Midhe and Airgialla at that point. It is just that some believe that it was that place – the place where Aedh built his monastery – which had been the site of the Golden Stone.'

'Then it has little to do with solving this mystery.' Eadulf sounded disappointed. 'The piece of Ogham writing is irrelevant.'

'We cannot know what it is irrelevant at this stage,' Fidelma said with a reproving look at him. 'We cannot use this information yet, so what else is there? Let us consider the body of the male. There is nothing more you can tell us? We are sure he was poisoned?'

'Poison does not lie to an apothecary.'

'There was no means of identifying him from his robe?'

'No. It was a plain brown homespun of the sort some folk wear on a cold winter's day.'

There was a silence between them as each one retreated into his or her own thoughts.

'I've wondered about the girl,' Eadulf suddenly said. 'What is curious is that we found no *ciorbholg* with her – no comb bag. Even those who work in the fields often carry one and this woman was certainly not of labouring folk.'

'It is true what Eadulf says, Conchobhar,' agreed Fidelma. 'It is a good point. There was nothing else to identify either the man or the girl. The only things in that wagon were old clothes, religious books and papers all but destroyed. Surely there should have been more? How are you going to travel on the roads of the Five Kingdoms without any means of support and, especially, if you are of noble rank?'

'I know that you do not make assumptions, Fidelma,' Brother Conchobhar chided. 'Perhaps the answer is so simple, we have overlooked it. Remember that our victims were both poorly clad – but perhaps they had simply been robbed – robbed and poisoned.'

'A possibility but not a probability,' Fidelma said, and shook her head. 'And robbers do not usually poison their victims. The two of them could just as easily have stolen the wagon and the oxen as to be the victims of robbery. We have discussed their personal state and concluded that neither was used to manual work. Apart from the destroyed books in the wagon, there is nothing to link them with serving the Church – except the poverty of their clothing and what appears to be a tonsure on the head of the male. Even you, Conchobhar, are not certain of that. And if they *were* the thieves, it might account for the girl hiding the dead body in the wagon for several days.'

'You really think they stole the wagon and oxen?' the old physician asked, surprised. 'What makes you come to that conclusion?'

'The brand on the oxen is that of the Prince of Tethbae,' she explained.

Brother Conchobhar sat back in astonishment. 'Tethbae? Was that why you were asking where Airgialla was?'

Fidelma gave a quick nod of the head but Brother Conchobhar was frowning. 'They could have stolen the wagon from Tethbae itself,' she said.

'The distance from Tethbae to Cashel by wagon, even pulled by a good team of oxen, would take a minimum of nearly three weeks. So they had to have been travelling for quite a while before the man was killed. The body of the male had been dead for around three days, but certainly no more than four or five at most. He was certainly not poisoned in Tethbae.'

Fidelma said, 'But the wagon containing the body might have halted for some days before the girl met up with Baodain. I am not sure that your theory helps us.'

'But it does give us an idea of where the man's death might have happened. A sort of minimum and a maximum distance,' Eadulf pointed out supportively. 'However, there is another question that comes to mind.'

They turned to look at him.

'What motive would compel an attractive young girl, who was pregnant to boot, to drive a wagon containing the decomposing body of a dead young man for so many days – if she had been driving it since he had been killed? Why not stop and seek help to bury the corpse?'

'She was taking the body somewhere,' Brother Conchobhar concluded.

'She told Baodain she wanted to reach Cashel,' Eadulf said. 'But she died before she reached here.'

'And why was she coming here?' asked Brother Conchobhar. 'Answer that question and other answers will come flooding to you.'

Fidelma was thinking. 'Perhaps you are right. We may be able to estimate where the man died and, if so, where he was poisoned. We have a timeline to go on – somewhere on a radius of three days' journey from here. Perhaps we should ride out to the marshes, estimating the number of days it would take the wagon to travel.'

'You do not have long,' Brother Conchobhar said, rising from his seat. 'With the forthcoming fair, people will be flooding into Cashel and it will be impossible to keep Baodain and his troupe isolated. I hear that the King, your brother, is quite fretful about detaining them.'

Fidelma looked disheartened. 'I know, I know it. Already some visitors have started to arrive. We were taking the midday meal in Rumann's tavern when the first of the distinguished visitors appeared.'

'An arrogant man and his acolytes,' added Eadulf with a sniff of disapproval. 'What was his name?'

'The Lord of Cairpre Gabra,' Fidelma replied.

They were unprepared for the exclamation of astonishment from Brother Conchobhar.

'The Lord of Cairpre Gabra?' he repeated. 'Are you sure that was his title?'

They regarded him in surprise.

'I am sure,' Fidelma said. 'Why?'

'It is a small territory, that is true but in view of what you have been telling me about the brand on the oxen, then you ought to know that the Lord of Cairpre Gabra owes allegiance to Tethbae. The Place of the Stone – Clochar – that I have just mentioned, is in Cairpre Gabra.'

CHAPTER SIX

'The most interesting point,' Eadulf reflected, once he and Fidelma had returned to their chamber, 'is that the girl expected to meet someone here in Cashel.'

'How do you know that?'

Eadulf smiled briefly. 'Why else was she trying to get here? Her companion is dead. I would say that she probably knew she too had been poisoned and that her fate would be the same as his.'

Fidelma regarded him in approval. 'So you believe that she must have had some pressing information to deliver to someone here? And are you now going to suggest that it is the Lord of Cairpre Gabra she was meeting?'

'Well, her oxen team carried the brand of his master, the Prince of Tethbae. And she had in her possession a note referring to this Golden Stone which is known to be in Clochar, in the territory of Cairpre Gabra.'

'All good points.' Fidelma was thoughtful. 'But what was so important about the girl and her companion that they should have been poisoned and their wagon set on fire?'

Eadulf raised his hands in a dramatic gesture of helplessness.

'I acknowledge that there are far too many whys and ifs. I have no suggestions about how we can start to find out, except that perhaps we should go and confront this Lord of Cairpre Gabra.'

'And if he says that he has no knowledge of what we are talking about? There is nothing to link him with the case – except our suspicion that she was coming to Cashel to meet him.'

'What about the brand on the oxen and the Golden Stone?' Eadulf asked.

'That is not evidence and can easily be dismissed.'

'Then what must we do?'

Fidelma was quiet for a while, thinking deeply. Then she looked up and said, 'Perhaps the body in the wagon is the key?'

Eadulf was puzzled. 'We know even less about that second death than we do about that of the girl. How will that provide us with a lead to unravelling this mystery?'

'I suggest that our next step should be to follow the idea that Brother Conchobhar raised. We start out at the point where she joined Baodain on the marsh road, then proceed back along the track she was observed as coming from. Somewhere along that track we might be able to find traces of her journey and even the point at which her travelling companion died.'

'Three days' journey in the marshlands could cover a long distance, and there are probably several tracks from the north which she might have taken.'

'We know the exact track at the point she emerged onto the marsh road, as observed by Baodain and his friends. Also, we know the maximum distance that a wagon pulled by oxen can travel on these tracks.' Fidelma was growing enthusiastic about the idea.

'But that whole area is Osraige land,' objected Eadulf. 'It is not the friendliest of places.' He had not forgotten how they had barely escaped with their lives from the warlord, Cronan of Gleann an Ghuail, who had styled himself Abbot of Liath Mór, disguising the abbey for a sinister purpose to overthrow King Colgú. Osraige was a border territory, paying tribute to the King of Muman but sometimes siding with the neighbouring Kingdom of Laigin; serving whoever suited it best. True, the current Prince of Osraige, Tuaim

Snámh, had disowned Cronan. Fidelma's brother had allowed him to remain petty ruler of the territory on condition he pay compensation to Cashel.

'I don't think we have a choice if we are to discover more about the curious wagon and its occupants.'

'But it is a lot of territory to cover,' he said. 'True, we can estimate the speed of travel of the wagon – but how do we know how long the girl stopped at any point? Searching for the place he died, let alone the place in which he was poisoned, will be like looking for a beetle in a wheatfield.'

Fidelma was not perturbed. 'It is not impossible that the beetle can be found. We will take a good tracker with us, for among the marsh-tracks there is a lot of mud, and therefore plenty of signs that we may be able to follow.'

Fidelma was rising as if she meant to suit her words to action. Eadulf glanced up at the window in dismay. 'There is not much daylight left today.'

She chuckled. 'I did not mean to start out now. Tomorrow morning at first light is time enough. We'll take Aidan and Enda, who is a good tracker, and be prepared to be away for several days, just in case the search takes that long. But if the girl came out of the marshes and met Baodain just after midday, then she would have only been travelling a short distance that day. She would not have driven a wagon through the marshlands during the hours of darkness. To find where she stopped for the night shall be our first task.'

Eadulf saw the logic of such a search even though he did not entirely agree with it.

'Now we'd better see my brother and tell him what is happening,' Fidelma announced. 'He was worried enough this morning about this matter, so I don't expect him to be happier at our proposed absence now. But he should be informed of our progress . . .'

'Or lack of it,' Eadulf added dryly.

*   *   *

Colgú received them in his private chambers, sprawling in his favourite chair before the log fire. His features were brooding and he had already deduced from Fidelma's expression that she had no good news for him.

'Well, you have brought us a fine mystery, Eadulf,' the King greeted him, waving at them both to be seated.

'There was no other place to take it,' Eadulf replied irritably.

'I suppose not,' Colgú conceded. 'It's just that the timing of this mystery becomes a problem with the Great Fair being only a few days away, and the fact that these people you are holding as suspects are supposed to be there to entertain everyone.'

'That raises a point,' Fidelma remarked. 'Did you know that Baodain and his troupe had been seeking to perform at the Uisnech Fair before deciding to come here?'

Colgú was indifferent. 'You should know that I do not organise the event. That is left to the Fair Master.'

'Who is your Fair Master?'

'It is usually my *rechtaire*, my steward.'

'But you have no steward at the moment,' Fidelma said.

'As you well know,' Colgú sighed. It was only a matter of weeks since Beccan, who had not been long in the position of steward, had been murdered by his co-conspirators. The King had not seemed anxious about appointing a replacement because Dar Luga, the housekeeper, was more than capable of running the household. But a steward had other duties and Fidelma had reminded her brother several times that he needed someone to help him run the affairs of the palace over and above just the domestic arrangements.

'So are we to presume that the Great Fair will be run by itself?' Fidelma's tone was sarcastic.

It was not the first time that Eadulf had witnessed a sibling spat between the two red-haired offspring of King Failbe Flann. They both had short tempers, did not tolerate fools gladly, and the warning signs were the way their eyes seemed to change colour so at one time they appeared cold blue and at others changed to a flickering, fiery green.

The corner of Colgú's mouth quirked in annoyance, and then he suddenly smiled and relaxed. 'I doubt that even the great Druid Magh Ruith could cause that to happen. In spite of what you consider my procrastination, sister, I have actually appointed a Master of the Fair – Ferloga.'

'Ferloga who runs the inn at Rath na Drinne with his plump wife, Lassar?'

'The very same,' Colgú confirmed. 'As a matter of fact he is in the kitchen with Dar Luga at this very moment. He is waiting to see me to discuss some aspects of the Great Fair.'

'Why Ferloga?' frowned Eadulf. 'I thought he and Lassar were happy simply running their inn . . .'

'An inn, my friend, that is placed at the site of the Fortress of Contentions where the Great Fair is always held. Ferloga benefits from the visitors to the Great Fair and has seen enough of the fairs to be able to organise one with a blindfold on.'

'I would like to ask him a few questions before he leaves,' Fidelma said.

Colgú spread his hands with an ironic smile. 'You are the *dálaigh*, sister. But please don't start arresting him. My need for him is desperate, to ensure the Great Fair goes ahead.'

'Do not worry,' Fidelma assured him, taking his response seriously. 'I shall send him to you after I have finished.'

Colgú dismissed the matter with a shrug and then rose to place another log on the fire. 'Tell me then, are these murders connected with the Great Fair?'

'That we cannot say for sure,' she replied. 'Baodain and his fellow performers have not exactly been open in their answers to us. But we must investigate further.'

'Knowing that you have been lied to,' commented the King, 'is a step forward, at least.'

'Speaking of steps forward, Eadulf and I will have to leave Cashel for a few days.'

Colgú was startled. 'With the Great Fair so close? Is that necessary?'

'It is. And I am afraid that we shall need both Aidan and Enda to accompany us. You must insist that whoever is appointed to command your bodyguard will ensure that Baodain and his players do not stir from the confines of the spot where they have been placed under guard.'

'But Aidan is now in command of the Nasc Niadh,' Colgú protested. 'I shall be left without a commander of my bodyguard. 'You propose to take two of my best warriors! Where are you going, or is that a question I should not ask?'

'We are going to the place where the dead girl joined Baodain's wagons. From there we will try to retrace her route to the point where her male passenger was killed. Unless I am much mistaken, the answer will lie somewhere in the marshlands of Osraige.'

'Osraige?' Colgú was even more startled. 'How in the name of all the saints did you deduce that?'

'Simple enough, brother. Old Conchobhar tells us that the corpse in the girl's wagon had been decomposing for about three days. Certainly not less than two. The maximum distance a wagon drawn by oxen of the type she was driving can travel in a day is roughly one hundred and twenty-five *forrach*.'

As she made these swift calculations, Eadulf worked out that this was about seven and a half kilometres.

Colgú thought for a moment. 'Osraige is a country of marsh and conspiracy,' he reflected. 'Remember Cronan?'

'I have not forgotten,' his sister replied grimly. 'But Cronan is dead.'

'Indeed. But I would not trust Tuaim Snámh, the Prince of Osraige.' Colgú grinned suddenly. 'Anyone who does not change his name after his parents have given him that awful name deserves no sympathy.'

Colgú explained for Eadulf's benefit. 'The name means "mound that swims". It must have referred to the sight of the boy's earliest efforts in the water, or his mother swimming when she was heavily pregnant.'

'Have no fear about our safety in Osraige, brother,' Fidelma said. 'Aidan and Enda will protect us.'

'Any idea where in Osraige this girl, her wagon and her dead passenger would have come from?'

This time Fidelma was not quite so confident. 'Well, we know the spot on the marsh road where she joined Baodain, and we can identify the route: the tracks lead from the north.'

Colgú was pessimistic. 'North? There is little there but marshland as far as the eye can see. To the north-east lies Durlus Éile on the border of Osraige. Why not go there, for the wagon might have passed through the town of the lady Gelgéis. I would start with the simple path first.'

Fidelma knew that her brother had developed some attachment to Gelgéis, the Princess of the Éile, thanks to the latter's help in foiling the plot by Cronan. The complex conspiracy to overthrow the Kingdom of Cashel had, it turned out, implicated Dúnliath, whom Colgú had expected to marry.

'You are a king but I am a *dálaigh*,' she reminded him. 'I will start from the point where the girl joined the marsh road. Anyway, the road to Durlus is a long one and there are many side turnings off it. It would take many days to travel from there by wagon if she did not come down the main highway. My hope is to pick up information along the way from the point where we enter the marshes.'

The King shook his head. 'And you don't even know who she is.' It was more of a comment than a question.

'True enough,' she agreed. 'But we do know that the wagon she drove is an unusual one; one that no wainwright in this island would have built. Also, we know that the oxen she was driving bore the brand of the King of Tethbae.'

'The Fox?' Colgú had now ceased being surprised at his sister's revelations.

'The same. And there is an interesting point – well, two interesting points.'

'Which are?'

'The first is that the girl had a piece of parchment on her with the words "Stone of Gold" on it.'

Colgú was unimpressed. 'Stories of stones of gold proliferate all over the Five Kingdoms. There is even a local legend about one of them, mixed up with Druids and the like.'

'Old Brother Conchobhar has told me of the legend of a stone of gold at the place where the Abbey of Clochar was founded by the Blessed Aedh Mac Carthinn. That is in a territory which borders Tethbae, and whose prince acknowledges the suzerainty of Tethbae.'

There was a few moments' silence while Colgú digested this. Then he said: 'You mentioned two interesting points.'

'At this moment, in Rumann's tavern, a new guest has just arrived. His name is Cerball, Lord of Cairpre Gabra. That is the territory which owes allegiance to Tethbae.'

'Both interesting points,' conceded Colgú. 'But what sense do they make? Do they help you to identify the girl and the dead man with whom she was travelling?'

'Not directly,' Fidelma admitted. 'But it is a start. There is also something that Baodain said. The girl asked him if she could join his wagons as she was heading for Cashel. Our theory is that she was coming here to meet someone.'

'You think it was Cerball of Cairpre Gabra? Then why not confront him?'

'I don't want to pre-empt the matter without knowing more,' Fidelma explained. 'He could merely deny it and we would have to accept his word. That is why we shall leave tomorrow at first light to see what we can discover along the marsh road.'

'If the Lord of Cairpre Gabra has arrived in Cashel, and if he believes in protocol, then he will come to the palace to pay his respects to me,' her brother said. The matter of *besgnae*, or protocol and custom, was not one to be disregarded lightly. 'When he does, what shall I say?'

'If he is concerned with the matter, he may well see the wagon in Rumann's barn, which is where Aidan has it placed for safety. He might also recognise the oxen with the King of Tethbae's brand on them. If so, he will certainly question Rumann, who will tell him how they came to be there. There is no hiding the events from him, but the warriors should prevent him from questioning Baodain and his performers. Whether he believes in protocol or not, he will come here to get further information. Tell him nothing, brother, but simply say that I am investigating matters and should be returning shortly.'

'I presume that you have already made arrangements with Aidan and Enda to accompany you?'

'I intend to do so right now,' she replied. 'We leave tomorrow at first light.'

'Then I'll place Luan in temporary command of the warriors.' Colgú sighed. 'I still wish Finguine was here . . .'

'We have to play the *fidchell* pieces as they fall on the board,' replied Fidelma testily, referring to the popular board game. 'Neither your heir apparent, the Chief Brehon, nor Gormán are here. So you had best put up with me, brother.'

Colgú glanced at Eadulf and pulled a face. Eadulf thought he saw a resigned humour in the King's expression.

'You continue to be a *dálaigh*, Fidelma, and I'll continue to be King,' he replied gravely. 'We are both allowed our doubts and questions. So you will leave at first light. You've no idea when you will return?'

Fidelma shook her head. 'It will depend on what we find or what we don't find.'

'Very well. After you have spoken to Ferloga, can he get on with organising the Great Fair?'

'Of course. I'll have a quick word with him now and then send him to you. If we do not return before it is time for the Great Fair . . .' She raised a calming hand as her brother's brows started to knit together. 'I am not saying that this will happen, but if it does, then Baodain and his party may perform but must remain in Cashel until I return.'

'Understood,' her brother acknowledged with a sigh.

'There is another thing that I would like you to do,' Fidelma went on.

'Very well – within reason.'

'Take Alchú riding when you can and also give him a game of *brandubh* or *fidchell* now and then.'

Colgú laughed. 'No need to ask that. I will make sure that my wise little nephew,' he used the endearing term *mo nia cétfadach*, 'is well looked after in your absence.'

'Then we shall be content.' Fidelma smiled and rose. 'And now we shall go to have a few words with Ferloga.'

Colgú rose as well. A slightly worried look crossed his features. 'Look after yourself, little sister,' he said gently as he embraced her. Then, turning to Eadulf with a quick smile, he added: 'Ensure that she does nothing foolish, my friend.'

The couple left Colgú and walked to the great kitchen of the royal house. A few people were there preparing the evening meal while Dar Luga fussed over them, tasting one dish and then another, adding advice or scolding for some mistake. In a corner, sipping at a mug of ale, sat the man they were looking for. Ferloga was the innkeeper from Rath na Drinne – and they knew him of old. The inn itself lay by the great ring whose name meant Place of Contentions, for it was here the townsfolk came to witness contests in athletics and other sports, and where the fairs were usually held. Ferloga had been an innkeeper most of his adult life, and Fidelma and Eadulf had often spent time at his inn for it lay on the road from Cashel across the plain to the Cluain Meala and beyond the mountains of Mhaoldomhnaigh to Lios Mhór. It was only two years ago that Fidelma had been involved in discovering the truth behind the mysterious death of a guest in Ferloga's inn.

As they entered the kitchen, Ferloga caught sight of them and sprang to his feet, setting down his mug on a nearby table. Out of the familiar surroundings of his inn, Ferloga looked awkward and slightly nervous. This was unusual, for during his years as a host, he had had dealings with kings and chieftains, religious of all descriptions and ranks, rich merchants, travelling players passing on their way to market, and even beggars desperate for shelter. He had taken them all in his stride. But here in this royal kitchen, he felt out of place.

'Good day, lady. Good day, Brother Eadulf.'

Fidelma returned his greeting. 'Be at ease, Ferloga,' she ordered. 'I am told you have come to report to my brother about the arrangements for the Great Fair.'

Ferloga nodded jerkily. 'I trust nothing is amiss, lady? I had to leave Lassar in charge of the inn and came as soon as I received the King's summons. He said he needed to discuss the preparations which he usually did with his steward.'

'It is late and already the light has faded.' Fidelma nodded towards the window. 'It was unthinking of my brother to ask you to come here at this time of the day.'

'That's all right, lady. Whenever I am here, Rumann offers me a bed so that I don't have to journey back in the dark. Rumann is a kinsman of mine,' he added, but the look of anxiety did not leave his face.

'Well, there is nothing wrong, Ferloga,' Fidelma assured him. 'I know that my brother is a little anxious about the arrangements of the Great Fair but I know that matters are safe in your hands.'

Ferloga seemed to relax. 'Well, he has no cause for concern. I have been involved in the running of the Great Fair for many years, and have lost count of the times that I have had to help the King's stewards with making the arrangements, especially Beccan. He was always so worried about getting the details right that he often overlooked the wider picture.'

Fidelma remembered how punctilious the late steward of Cashel had been. Punctilious, but weak – and that weakness had allowed him to be drawn into the plot that eventually led to his own murder.

'That is good to hear, Ferloga,' she said kindly. 'It was about the Great Fair that I wanted to talk to you.'

Ferloga's expression was serious. 'Is it about Baodain and his performers?' he said immediately. 'Rumann told me the story when I arrived, or such as he knew it. I saw Baodain and his troupe encamped on the far side of the town square – and under guard.'

Fidelma inclined her head. 'I wanted to ask you what you knew about Baodain, as he has been a performer at previous fairs.'

Ferloga considered for a moment. 'I know precious little, I am afraid. It is true that he and his performers frequent most of the great fairs. Baodain is rather arrogant but not as arrogant as his wife Escrach. In spite of that, he somehow attracts good performers into his troupe.'

'Do you know where Baodain comes from?'

This was met by a quick shake of the head. 'He has the accents of Midhe, the Middle Kingdom. So does she, but whether he has ever called Midhe his home or not, that I cannot say. Oh, he and Escrach play their instruments well enough and have a good repertoire of songs and stories but, begging your pardon lady, they are of a lower class of songs and stories than you would be used to. It is entertainment fit for the likes of farmers and cowherds when drink has been taken. He is certainly not the main attraction at any fair that he attends.'

'But he does get work at the Great Fairs?'

'Oh, that he does surely. I am told he has performed at Tailltenn, Tlachtga, Uisneach, Carman in Laigin, even at Aenach Macha, the ancient fair at Emain in the north country.'

'Then if he and his wife are not good performers, how is he able to entertain at all these fairs?' pressed Eadulf. 'He must have some reputation.'

'Baodain has one great ability,' conceded Ferloga. 'He is able to spot talented performers and recruit them to his troupe. Because he has connections with all the organisers of the Great Fairs, he can assure these performers of work. It is curious . . . because of the talents of his performers, he gets the work and all the glory for the achievement. He is esteemed because of those whose talents he exploits.'

Eadulf chuckled. 'A symbiotic relationship.' When Ferloga looked puzzled he added: 'There is an old conundrum, which comes first – the chicken or the egg?'

Ferloga smiled appreciatively. 'It is true that he provides some pleasing eggs among his performers.'

'Are you saying that he does not always have the same group of players with him?' Fidelma suddenly asked.

'I think it is fair to say that he hardly appears more than two or three times with the same performers. But then we only see him once a year or every other year. I would say,' Ferloga learned forward with a confidential attitude, 'I would say that once his performers have done the rounds of the fairs with him, and made their own contacts for work, they are off on their own if they are any good. I myself would dislike it intensely if I had to be beholden to Baodain for any length of time.'

'He has no regular members of his troupe?'

Ferloga rubbed his chin thoughtfully. 'There is the Strong Man in his troupe . . . what was his name? Barrán. He is getting on in years for a Strong Man these days. One can't go on lifting great weights all one's life without damaging oneself. But he and his wife Dub Lemna have half a dozen kids to feed, as I recall.'

'Five, I was told,' Fidelma corrected him pedantically. 'So Barrán is one of the performers that he has brought with him this time. Can you remember anyone else?'

Ferloga mentioned some names which did not fit in with the ones they had been given for the current troupe, apart from those of the tumbler and jugglers.

'So Corbach and her tumblers were also here last year,' Fidelma noted.

'Yes – and Corbach too is past her prime. Her entire family take part in the act. They are about six adults and three children, as I remember. Probably some of the children are of the age to perform this year.'

'I see.' Fidelma was thoughtful. 'But I was told that only a few of Baodain's performers were new – namely, Maolán and Mealla, the contortionists. But as far as you know, most of them *are* new.'

Ferloga was watching her with a question on his face. 'Is there some significance in this, lady?'

'Perhaps not,' Fidelma replied. 'I am just thinking aloud. How are the performers usually chosen for these fairs? Are they engaged from year to year, or do they just turn up, and if there is space, they are given it to entertain the crowds?'

'You have it exactly right, lady,' agreed Ferloga. 'It is impossible to know the situation from one year to the next. Impossible to know who is available. Indeed, one cannot know the health of the performers and the strength of their acts to be certain they will arrive and be of sufficient standard to perform. Then there is the weather, which can cancel the entire fair. So the players turn up and, as you say, if there is room, they are allotted the land, for which they will pay a tax from the profits that they make. That tax goes to the King to divide among those he has appointed to organise and oversee the fair.'

After a few more moments of polite conversation, Fidelma bade farewell to the innkeeper and left, followed by Eadulf. They still had to advise Aidan and Enda about the next day.

The couple made their way in silence across the courtyard to the *Laochtech*, the Hall of Heroes, which were the quarters of the King's Bodyguard

'What is on your mind?' asked Eadulf, observing his wife's thoughtful expression.

She smiled at him. 'I was thinking that Baodain's performers have a good reputation, according to Ferloga, in spite of Baodain's own, less than excellent contributions. And yet they were turned down by the Fair Master at Uisneach, weeks before the fair was even due to start. So on what grounds were they refused a performance? That is what is bothering me.'

'Baodain says the fair had too many acts.'

'Yet no fair is that crowded so far in advance that the organisers would turn down a troupe which has a decent reputation,' she repeated. 'We can also discount the weather, for no seer could predict the conditions of the ground so far in advance; let alone the health of the performers or the strength of their acts . . .'

Eadulf shrugged. 'Maybe the new acts did not measure up to the troupe's reputation? They had just performed before the Prince of Tethbae. Perhaps he did not like them and said so.'

'You could be right,' Fidelma said slowly. 'We know from Ferloga that Baodain was lying to us about the length of time his performers have been with him. Why would he do that? As Ferloga said: is there some significance in this?'

CHAPTER SEVEN

The day had dawned bright and sunny although there was still a chill in the air. Isolated patches of white cloud hung high and motionless and, even though the marshes spread flat on either side of the great highway of Slíge Dála, the countryside seem verdant, interspersed by patches of bright yellow flowers. They had left Cashel at first light with Fidelma leading the way on her favourite horse, Aonbharr, 'the Supreme One', named after the magical horse of the ancient God of the Oceans, Manannán mac Lir. Aidan rode at her side and behind them came Eadulf on his placid cob with Enda alongside him.

It was not long before Aidan was pointing along the road before them.

'That is where Baodain's wagons halted, where they were fighting the fire. Isn't it so, friend Eadulf?'

'Not much has passed along this way since then,' agreed Eadulf. 'You can still see the tracks and marks where they halted.'

Fidelma paused but remained seated on her horse, surveying the area closely. Looking across the dark, brooding patches of bogland, Eadulf could not rid himself of visions of the *ése*, the water spirits of his own pagan culture, who could shape-shift and appear and disappear at will. It was in just such areas as this that the impossible could happen.

He glanced around the low marshlands with their stagnant pools and low-flying *cuili condae*, the 'fierce fliers' as they were called, the biting insects and midges that spread disease if one was not careful. As a former student of the healing arts, Eadulf always carried his *lés*, a small leather bag containing some medical equipment, and to which he frequently had recourse. The bag contained surgical instruments and *soithech* or containers for ointments or salves; on crossing marshland, he always ensured that some honey and a container of apple-cider were among them. He had found that some solace from the biting midges could be obtained by their application.

He realised that Fidelma was looking round at him curiously.

'There are a lot of midges around here,' he said feebly, to explain his woebegone expression.

'You are right, there are. Come, there is nothing to be learned here. We should not tarry.'

They rode on until Aidan interrupted the silence by pointing towards the part of the highway where the ground started to rise into the hills.

'It was from those hilltops that Eadulf and I first noticed the wagons of Baodain,' he announced.

'Therefore it will not be far before the road from Durlus Éile joins this one from the north,' Fidelma replied. She used the word *ramut*, which indicated a smaller road than the great *slíge* or highway, of which there were only five connecting the capitals of the Five Kingdoms with Tara, the seat of the High Kings.

They passed the main highway that led off to the fortress and township of Gelgéis, the Princess of the Éile. Some distance beyond, at the righthand side of the road, they heard the gurgling of a stream, splashing down the hills over moss-covered roads and into a large pool that eventually seeped away, dispersing into the low-lying bogland through which they had ridden. There were signs in the surrounding mud of wagons, and of horses and other animals using it as a watering-hole.

'This must be where the girl met up with Baodain's troupe. We'll take the opportunity to rest briefly and water our horses here,' Fidelma instructed.

Before long Fidelma ordered them to resume their journey. Only moments later, Aidan spotted a track leading through the treeline to their left, between high bushes into the marshlands. The warrior took the lead now. They had been riding along it for some time when Eadulf began to have doubts: could a wagon, such as the one driven by the girl, have comfortably traversed this route? The path had become narrow and muddy and the horses were getting fretful at the increased attention of the midges and the sudden appearance and disappearance of small mammals among the swampy sedges.

He decided to voice his concerns. 'This doesn't look like the sort of route that the girl would take with a wagon of that size,' he said mildly.

Aidan was immediately defensive. 'Well, Baodain said that she came from a track from the north, and that it was before the spring and pool, and certainly before the main roadway to Durlus. Where else could it have been?'

'Perhaps there is another path?' Eadulf suggested. 'There is no sign of wheel-tracks here.'

Before he could receive an answer, Aidan gave vent to a loud curse. His horse seemed to move backwards for a few paces and then its hind legs started to sink into the adjacent mud. The animal's eyes rolled in terror as it tried to extract itself from the cloying tentacles of the marsh. It reared and lashed out with its forelegs, but this only resulted in its hindquarters sinking deeper.

Aidan was enough of a horseman not to cling on; instead he launched himself over the beast's shoulder and hit the path with a rolling motion which brought him out of reach of the thrashing forelegs.

Meanwhile, Fidelma had dismounted. Throwing her reins to Enda, she went towards Aidan's mount, all the while talking to it in a soft, calm tone. She did not seem to be concerned that the front hooves of the animal might catch her. Taking hold of the reins, still talking, she stared soothingly into the eyes of the beast. Amazingly, the animal began to settle and then she reached forward, gently rubbing its nose. Once it was truly calm, Fidelma began to move backwards, pulling it gently by the head. Using the strength of its forelegs and its back legs as a means of propelling its great body, the animal came little by little out of the clutches of the marsh, emerging with a squelching sound as if the mud was reluctant to let go.

Aidan moved sheepishly towards the animal, knowing enough to stay calm and also murmuring to it and stroking its muzzle. The horse stood, trembling slightly, and allowed Fidelma to hand the reins back to him.

She returned to her own stallion, Aonbharr, and took the reins from Enda, before swinging herself back up on to the animal's broad back. She stared around with a frustrated expression.

'Eadulf was right. We can be sure that no ox-hauled wagon ever came along this path,' she said. 'You can see that this path ends a short distance further on, after which we would all be floundering in the marsh.'

'It has probably been long disused,' offered Enda. 'Perhaps it did lead somewhere once, but marshland can change and can often swallow a whole area of firm land in its maw. It is easy to make a mistake.'

Fidelma did not even smile at Enda's feeble attempt to offer support to his comrade. In fact, she was chastising herself for not observing the path that Aidan had led them on more carefully. She had been concentrating so hard on running over the facts as she knew them, that for a while she had been blind to her surroundings. Now she was angry with herself and this caused her to be angry at those she had counted on to play their part.

'Marshland does not swallow a track in a couple of days! No one has been down this path in years, let alone a few days ago. We simply chose the wrong path and that is all there is to it. So now we must turn round and as carefully as we can go back to the main highway and search out the right path!'

She swung Aonbharr around, almost on the stallion's hind legs, and began to trot angrily back the way they had come. Eadulf followed after seeing Aidan remount and exchanging a slightly sour grimace with Enda.

The sun was well beyond its zenith when they returned to the Slíge Dála and to the very pool from which they had set out.

Aidan was still clearly upset about what had happened. 'The trouble with those roads across the marshes, they all look alike. You never know where they will lead,' he muttered to Eadulf.

'We'll try further along the road,' Fidelma instructed. 'There must be another small track from which she came and joined Baodain's group.'

Enda coughed nervously. 'We ought to rest and water the horses again before proceeding, lady.'

They had been on the road since first light and were now fairly exhausted. Fidelma wanted to move on as quickly as possible and was about to argue about the lost time. However, as an experienced horsewoman, she knew that the animals in her care should be treated with all due attention. While the mounts were being watered and fed by Aidan and Enda, she sat down on a rock by the pool and stared into it moodily.

Eadulf sat down beside her. 'It's not Aidan's fault that we wasted time following the wrong way,' he said gently.

Fidelma sniffed. 'Did I say that I blamed him?'

'Not exactly, but you made it clear that you did not appreciate his mistake.'

'He was so certain that the path was the right one. Apart from the fact that it became too narrow to take a wagon, he should have observed whether there were any tracks in the mud.'

'I should have spoken up earlier. It was as much my fault,' Eadulf said. He glanced over to where Aidan was washing his horse down with the clean waters from the pool. 'I'd say that he was contrite enough.'

Fidelma's irritation merely increased because she was still inwardly blaming herself for a lack of attention. 'We have lost the greater part of the day when we can ill afford it,' she muttered. 'And who knows where the next track will lead, if anywhere? It might prove to be another dead end.'

'Baodain said she came out of a track from the north and joined them at this pool. I don't think there are going to be too many choices,' Eadulf replied dryly.

Fidelma jumped to her feet, using action to disguise her ill temper. 'Then the sooner we find the right road, the better.'

Eadulf saw Aidan exchange a miserable glance with Enda. He felt sorry for the warrior because he himself would have suggested they try the same track as Aidan had done. Initially the track had looked inviting enough and it was close to the pool so was the logical choice. In hindsight, he accepted that they should have looked for signs of the passage of the wagon in the mud. What was the old saying? 'By time everything is revealed.'

When the horses were ready, the group remounted and set off along the Slíge Dála again. They were upon the next track almost immediately – a large gap among the bordering trees and shrubs where wagon tracks showed that its use was quite regular. This time Enda swung down from his horse and bent to examine the tracks. It was not long before he stood up with a smile.

'Well, lady, I cannot be absolutely sure, but a team of oxen has used this road and they were pulling a four-wheeled wagon, the wheels being rimmed with iron and of good quality The beasts themselves were shoed.'

'There's many four-wheeled wagons pulled by oxen, even wagons with iron rims on the wheels.' Fidelma was still in a sour mood.

'I am fairly sure that these tracks were produced by a wagon similar in size to the one that the girl was driving.'

'Then we will try this path,' she conceded grumpily.

The word 'path' was not an exact description because it was not a narrow and isolated track. Eadulf knew that this would be classed as a *tuagrota* under the laws on highways, for the Brehons were very strict about the size of roads, how they should be made, maintained and by whom. The *tuagrota* were classed as farmers' roads and used as such; a means of moving from one farmstead to another. Had it been more carefully maintained, this route was more of a main road between settlements. Perhaps it was still used as such.

However, it plunged straight through the marshland – flat, apparently verdant areas, except that to wander off the hard mud-baked tracks would be dangerous. A man and his horse could easily be swallowed by the sucking mud that lay beneath the innocent-looking verdure; such a fate had nearly overcome Aidan a short while before.

Fidelma and Aidan took the lead again. Most of the countryside was flat and peat-covered, but now and then little hillocks rose, like islands, and there were clumps of trees. Oases of firm land dotted the landscape. Wild brambles edged the track, barricading it from the bogland beyond.

Enda was examining the surroundings closely. 'I believe that I recognise this track, lady,' he announced suddenly with a smile of confidence. 'I remember riding along this way from Durlus Éile several years ago.'

Fidelma swung round. 'Are you saying that this track leads all the way north to Durlus?'

'Yes. It is a long road and fairly deserted, but I remember a tavern some distance ahead where we can rest for the night.'

'That is good news,' Fidelma replied, although her tone did not express much gratitude. 'If the girl came this way with the wagon, then the tavern-keeper should be able to give us information.'

They rode on in silence. The road was long and empty. Only the screech of birds, or the sudden movement of animals crossing their path, interrupted the monotony of their journey.

They came round a slight bend in the track where the bushes were low and they could see across the marshland to the distant eastern hills. Eadulf had spotted a fairly large hillock some way off to his right. There seemed to be a building there, half-hidden by trees.

'What place is that, Enda – the building up on that rise in the distance?' he asked, drawing rein. 'Any idea?'

Enda glanced in that direction. 'It is years since I rode here, friend Eadulf, but I think it is an abandoned farmstead.'

They were passing a gap in the hedge of wild brambles; it appeared to be the beginnings of another track.

'This gap is wide enough for a wagon to have passed through,' Eadulf called out.

They halted, while Enda dismounted and had a look. 'The hard stones here make it difficult to see any signs of the passage of a wagon,' he reported.

Fidelma examined the entrance and then gazed into the bogland beyond. 'Look at the size of that track,' she said, and pointed. 'It starts off looking broad enough but – see, beyond – there is a *tóchar*, a narrow causeway, before the track narrows even further. That's too small for a wagon to pass along.'

Eadulf looked again. Not far along, the bog became a richer green, darker and therefore more dangerous. Someone, at some time, had built a causeway to span the impassable patch. Tree branches, bushes and earth had been laid down to create a base, and planks of wood overlain on top. But it was clearly of old construction, for it was almost overgrown, with green shoots poking up between the planks, several of which were split.

Aidan was nodding in agreement. 'Even if you could negotiate a two-oxen wagon over that, it is true that if you look beyond, the track becomes no more than the size of a *sét*.'

Eadulf knew this was one of the smallest classes of track along which a horse or ox could move in single file, certainly not a team of oxen and a four-wheeled wagon. Nevertheless, he had a curious sense of premonition about the distant building.

'But shouldn't we have a look at it?' he asked stubbornly. 'It seems just the sort of place where the girl might have spent the night before joining Baodain.'

'We do not have time to spare,' snapped Fidelma. 'You can see there is no room for a wagon along that path. It will soon be dusk anyway. Time to press on to this inn Enda has talked about. By the time we ride to that deserted farmhouse and back again, it will be nightfall.'

'I still think that we should not ignore any possibilities.' Eadulf suddenly dug in his heels. 'You have always said that many things seem impossible until they are accomplished. If the girl *could* negotiate that path, then a deserted farmstead would be an ideal place to hide a wagon if a person did not want to be observed.'

'The track tells its own story,' Fidelma said impatiently. 'The wagon could *not* have passed along it. Also, this is too close to where the girl joined Baodain's troupe for that place to be where she stayed.' She added forcefully: 'We will press on.'

'It would have taken her two days, perhaps three, in an ox wagon from Durlus Éile to reach here,' Enda agreed, 'so I think it is unlikely that this place would have any relevance, friend Eadulf.'

In normal circumstances, Eadulf would have accepted the logic of their arguments. Perhaps it was the growing exasperation he felt with Fidelma and her churlish attitude to Aidan earlier. 'I am still of the opinion that we should examine all possibilities,' he said quietly but with determination.

Fidelma glanced at the sky. 'It will be dark shortly. And it will be a wasted journey.'

Eadulf's jaw thrust out. 'Well, *I* shall go and examine the place and then I will rejoin you on the road – unless you reach the tavern first. In that case, I'll join you there.'

Fidelma felt her temper rise. She had begun to have second

thoughts about the wisdom of trying to trace where the girl and her wagon had come from. She now believed that they were wasting their time and had spent long enough already on the venture. Eadulf might have been right when he suggested they should remain in Cashel and confront Cerball, Lord of Cairpre Gabra, as well as questioning Ronchú and Comal on their story.

'If you want to waste even more time, go ahead and look,' she said curtly. 'Take Enda with you.'

. Eadulf, equally stubborn, made a cutting motion with his hand. 'I have no wish to waste Enda's time or anyone else's. I will go on my own.'

Without waiting for any response, he turned his horse and trotted through the gap towards the causeway beyond. Fidelma hesitated and then gave an exasperated sigh, before turning northward along the road towards the inn. Aidan and Enda exchanged a wry glance before following after her.

Eadulf found that the track to the causeway consisted of hard, sunbaked earth reinforced with stones. Many of the ruts and wheel-tracks were obviously quite old. When he came to the causeway, the planks creaked a little as he crossed, and his usually placid cob faltered a few times. Eadulf grew slightly nervous, but it was not long before he reached the far side. He was not a good horseman, as he had so often pointed out to people, therefore he was grateful to the more knowledgeable among them who had recommended his small horse, stoutly built and strong-boned, with its steady disposition. Not for the first time, he was able to trust the animal not to panic as he might do.

It was here that the path narrowed – or seemed to. From the hedge where they had viewed it, it did indeed seem to be wide enough for only one animal to move along it at a time. But now that he was on it, Eadulf realised it was merely that the path was overgrown. It was broader than met the eye from a distance and, more importantly, something of width had recently moved along it. To one side, the grasses and tufts of moss had been partially crushed.

He had half a mind to call the others back to examine this. But there was no sign of them; they had already moved on. He wavered for a moment – then the stubborn streak in his character rose in him once more. A wagon *had* passed here recently. It might not be the girl's wagon but he would find that out for himself. Then he would show Fidelma that he did not make suggestions without a reason. He would teach her a lesson in humility!

Setting his jaw, he urged his cob forward. It was not long before he found himself crossing a patch of slightly raised firm ground with some woodland on it. It was one of the curious islets in the great marshland. Once through this area, no more than a copse, the vista gave way to a large expanse of verdant greenery through which the tiny, hard-earth track meandered. He had to keep reminding himself that the flat stretches, so green and inviting as a short cut, were treacherous. He also began to realise that, while the rise on which the building was silhouetted looked near, the meandering track increased the distance three-fold. The reason why the path moved in serpent-like twists and turns was obvious, and now he reflected that perhaps it had not been such a good idea to refuse Enda's company. But he had set out to prove a point.

A rocky hillock thrust up from the side of the track. He had observed it from some distance back as so much else was flat. He had not even thought that he would pass it, so confusing was the route to the buildings. But now he realised that he was going to pass near it – and behind it, he could see another patch of woodland. It seemed ages ago since he and Aidan had been looking down at these little hillocks rising out of the bog like islands from the sea. That was before they had encountered Baodain and his wagons on the highway. Now he reminded himself that the marshland was just as perilous as any sea.

As he turned to follow the path, he almost halted in shock for, hidden behind the rocky thrust, by the woodland was a second bog road which joined it from the south. Moreover, a man was seated on a fallen tree apparently resting. He was clad in muddy clothes of the sort a farmer or his labourer might wear, and was of middle years, with weatherbeaten skin and bright blue eyes. In his hand was a shepherd's crook but there was no sign of any sheep. A dog sat by him and, seeing Eadulf, the beast rose and let out a low, menacing growl.

The man looked up and said something to the dog in a curt tone. The beast abruptly sat down, but kept cautious eyes on the stranger. Observing Eadulf clad as a religious, the man came awkwardly to his feet.

'God's peace on you, Brother,' he greeted him respectfully.

'And His blessings on you, my friend.'

'Are you lost, Brother?' went on the man. 'This is a curious and deserted spot to find a stranger. You are a stranger to this land, aren't you?'

Eadulf grinned. 'How did you guess?'

The man grinned back. 'How do I know my sheep from my neighbour's? By sound, by look, by smell.'

Eadulf chuckled. 'Well, by whatever means, I am an Angle.' He decided not to say more. 'And you find me on this marsh road because I was interested in that distant house, over there on that rise. Will I find hospitality there?'

The man turned his head to follow the direction of Eadulf's outstretched hand.

'That's been deserted for some years, Brother. Once it was a thriving farm. They called it the Homestead by the Crossing, because there is a small river beyond. It was a prosperous place, but no longer.'

'Why is that?'

'The Yellow Plague, many years ago. It penetrated even these inaccessible marshlands.'

Eadulf knew that the plague had been one of the most devastating diseases to spread through every kingdom in the world. It spared no one – from princes down to the poorest of the poor.

'So all the people at that farmstead died?'

'It was the will of God,' the man said quietly. 'There were seven in the family who worked it. Was not Learghusa, the farmer, my own cousin? All were dead within a week of its visitation, all with the yellowing of their skins.'

'Is there no one there now?'

'It has remained deserted ever since.'

'Does anyone ever go there at all?'

'Only the wild beasts have reclaimed it. You'll get no hospitality there – but there is still plenty of time before nightfall, so you could join the western track when you get there. It will eventually take you to woodland on the borders of this marshland. Beyond that is another farm. That one is inhabited but it is a long way from here.'

'And do you farm near here?'

The man shook his head. 'I am a shepherd and tend my flocks on the low hills south of the great highway. My dog and I were chasing a wandering ewe but I have seen no sign of her. I fear she belongs to the mire now.'

'I hope you are wrong and that she comes back safely to you,' Eadulf said encouragingly. 'God bless your work.'

'May the road rise with you, Brother.'

Eadulf raised his hand, half in acknowledgement and half in blessing before he turned and continued his journey along the dirt track.

Fidelma stood before the log fire of the tavern gazing at the flickering flames which were enveloping the logs. Behind her, in a corner, Aidan and Enda were chattering and chuckling softly about something that had caught their attention. They were the only guests in the tavern. Out of the corner of her eye she noticed the tavern-keeper polishing some *lestar* or drinking vessels. He seemed typical of his calling, a short, rotund man with sloping shoulders, muscular arms and thinning fair hair; a fresh-complexioned fellow with inquisitive grey eyes.

She became aware that he was examining her nervously while trying to give the appearance of polishing the drinking vessels. She realised that she must present a forbidding exterior when she was angry, and she was angry now – angry with herself more than anyone. She should not have behaved to Eadulf as she had in front of Aidan and Enda. She should not have implied criticism of Aidan. In fact, she should probably not have embarked on this journey at all without giving it more thought. True, there were strange coincidences that had to be checked out and which might lead somewhere, but nothing really fitted together. Nothing at all. She acknowledged that it was her own ego which had made her dismiss Eadulf's more sensible suggestion to stay in town.

She turned to the tavern-keeper who almost flinched as she took a step towards him.

'Have you kept a tavern here long?' she enquired, trying to soften her tone.

The man put down his cloth and bobbed his head in a jerky fashion.

'I took over this tavern when your cousin, Máenach mac Fíngin, was King, lady.'

For some reason the remark increased Fidelma's irritation. She had never liked her cousin, who had been the son of her father's brother Fíngin. He had ruled at Cashel for twenty years after the death of her father and, if the truth were known, it was because of him and his arrogant wife that she had sought the security of the religious. Once she had qualified in law, to the level of *anruth* – the second highest qualification given by the secular and ecclesiastical colleges of the Five Kingdoms – she knew it was no use returning to Cashel and throwing herself on the tender mercies of Máenach, so when her distant cousin, Abbot Laisran of Darú, had suggested that the mixed house of Cill Dara needed someone well versed in law, she had joined them willingly.

Ironically, Máenach had died two years after she had entered the abbey. He was unmourned, even by the bards, although he had been twenty years as King. Like his wife he was self-centred and more concerned about gathering tributes than ensuring the welfare of the kingdom. The choice of Cathal Cú-cen-máthair as King instead of Máenach's son, Ailill, who had been fostered outside of the kingdom, was met with relief and celebration. Fidelma's brother, Colgú, had then been named as *tánaiste*, heir-apparent. Ailill had returned to Cashel during the previous year but only to conspire and plot to overthrow Colgú, who had become King after Cathal had died of the Yellow Plague. It was Fidelma who had eventually thwarted the plot, but not before many had paid with their lives, including Ailill himself. Certainly the name of Máenach was no balm to her ears.

'Is something wrong, lady?'

'Wrong?' she frowned, then realised she was being addressed. 'Sorry – what were you saying?'

'You asked me how long I had run this tavern, lady.'

'Oh, yes,' she said a trifle sheepishly. 'You must notice all the traffic that passes up and down this highway.'

The man answered with a shrug. 'I cannot vouch that I know all that pass here, lady. I have to sleep sometimes.' This was said without humour, as a matter of fact. 'I will say that most wagons passing from Durlus will take the opportunity to pause here for refreshment or for a night's rest before moving on to join the main road, which is not far south of here, as you know. But this is only a minor road. It runs parallel to a wider and better maintained road to the west, and that is the usual route taken by those travelling from Durlus to Cashel . . . that is, apart from the river.'

'But people still travel this road?' she asked. 'There are enough passers-by to maintain the inn?'

'Enough to keep my wife and children alive, lady,' replied the man. 'I will not grow rich but I am well content.'

'It seems a somewhat lonely place,' she commented.

'When there are guests, we have our full share of news and

gossip. Also, we have horses and a good cart so we can regularly visit our relatives in Durlus Éile.'

'Are you of the clan Éile?'

'And proud of it. Descendants of Cian, brother of Eoghan Mór.' There was pride in his voice.

'Then tell me this, my distant kinsman,' Fidelma said, trying to adopt a more friendly tone, 'sometime during the last few days, do you recall a foreign-looking wagon passing by here? Perhaps even stopping here? It was drawn by a team of two oxen and driven by a young boy or a girl.'

She added the two possibilities as she was not sure at what point the girl had assumed the identity of a boy.

The man shook his head without hesitation.

'No foreign-looking wagon, certainly not a wagon driven by either a young boy or girl, sought my hospitality nor passed by here.'

'Are you sure?'

'On the heads of my children, lady. You have given a description that is hardly confusing. That would not be a sight seen often along this road.'

Fidelma sighed softly. 'Is there no other way of passing by your tavern?'

'If the wagon came down this road, it would have to pass here. Perhaps it came on the parallel, broader road that I mentioned?'

'There are no other direct roads across the marshlands? Any that would link up with this one and from this road onto the Slíge Dála at the southern end? That would mean it came by here or joined the road at some point from the marshes.'

The tavern-keeper said sceptically, 'There are a few narrow tracks across the marshes, I suppose. None that I would like to traverse with a heavy wagon.'

'Most of the area around here is marshland, isn't it?'

'There are patches where sheep and cattle are grazed by some local farmers,' admitted the man. 'But it is mainly marshland between here and the Osraige territory to the east, and then after that is the barrier of the great river An Fheoir that runs north to south through Osraige.'

'There are no other hard-surfaced roads across the area?'

'Not unless you come through the territory of the Loígis and cross into Osraige. I have heard that the Abbot of Liath Mór had a new road built crossing Osraige, all the way into the Kingdom of Laigin.'

Fidelma could not help but smile grimly for she knew well the reason why Abbot Cronan had built that road. The intention had been to use it for an invasion of warriors from Laigin to cross the plains of Osraige and enter the territory of the Éile in order to launch an attack on Cashel itself.

'But what if somewhat wanted to avoid Durlus? I mean, if you were travelling from the north?'

The tavern-keeper scratched the back of his head. 'From the north? The Slíge Cualann comes from Tara into Laigin and from it you could still cross through the territory of the Loígis and keep east of the River An Fheoir and reach the cross point into Cill Cainnech.'

Fidelma tried to repress her excitement. Wasn't that the very route Baodain said he had taken?

'There is a ferry, so travellers tell me, which connects with the east and west banks,' continued the innkeeper. 'By all accounts the ferry connection has been well developed since the expansions by the new Abbot.'

Fidelma had travelled several times along that route because it was a short distance up the river from Cill Cainnech that An Fheoir turned into a smaller river. Here, the great Abbey of Darú was situated, where her cousin Laisran was Abbot.

Fidelma stared thoughtfully at the innkeeper for a moment. She was not thinking of the ferry crossing but of the fact that the river itself actually provided a quicker route from the north. An Fheoir started its journey to the north of Muman and ran between the mountains and hills through several little ferry points. Cill Cainnech stood right on the river and there was certainly a landing stage there where transports from the north could bring cargoes.

'Is something wrong, lady?' repeated the tavern-keeper wondering why she had fallen silent again.

'There are big barges that ply their trade up and down An Fheoir, aren't there?'

'Of course, lady; big enough to take large wagons on them, if that is what is on your mind. It is now one of the great trading routes eventually linking what they call the Three Sister Rivers – the Suir, An Fheoir and An Bhearú. They all join at the sea port of Laigre.'

'Once across the Sliabh Bladhma Mountains, which border the north of the kingdom, one could get a barge all the way down to Cill Cainnech and join the Slíge Dála there.' Fidelma spoke to herself, but aloud.

'Many barges and boats use the great river, as I have said. In former times, Cainnech was just a small river port, but the ancient settlement has grown quite large since the abbey was built there.'

Fidelma was smiling with satisfaction. Here was a better theory of how this wagon could have reached Muman from the north, than with oxen pulling it for weeks across mountains in inaccessible wild country. She should have thought of it before. After all, the rivers were still the main highways of the Five Kingdoms. She ought to have known from the careful regulations laid down by the laws relating to the *artrach iomchair* or 'carrying ships' which transported cargoes up and down the rivers. Even so, it would be quite a task for a young girl to negotiate with river-men to bring a wagon and a team of oxen from across the northern mountains. Unless, of course, the girl's male companion had still been alive at that time . . . Perhaps the strange wagon had left the river at Cill Cainnech and began its journey from there.

With these thoughts, her mind returned to Eadulf and she stirred uneasily. Perhaps he had been right to check out that abandoned house. She moved across to the window and peered anxiously up at the darkening sky. Nightfall would not be long now.

CHAPTER EIGHT

❧

Eadulf finally reached the large hill-like rise in the verdant marsh. It was larger than he had thought, and it rose to a flat top. In the centre was a rectangular wooden structure that had clearly been the farmhouse itself, but it was clear that the place had been abandoned many years before. The wood was rotting and there was evidence of overgrowth everywhere as Nature struggled to reclaim it. The shepherd had told him no more than the truth.

He identified the main building as once having been a *brugh* or more prosperous house than many of the round *tech-fithi* or wicker-work houses with reed roofs that he expected to find in the marshlands. The roof on this rectangular building was called *slinn* – sloping thin boards of wood that were coated with black *picc* or pitch. He also noticed that the main wood in the construction was yew, which he knew was the hardest and most difficult timber to work. The *ailtire*, the builder in wood, had undoubtedly been an expert at his craft.

The entire broad plateau on which the buildings were constructed was surrounded by a little stone wall, and around the farmhouse were several outbuildings, a few of them of the round wickerwork type that perhaps the farmworkers might have lived in, as well as barns that had once contained animals. These seemed in a more advanced state of decay.

He slid from his horse and hitched the reins to a nearby wooden pole. As he was doing so he glanced at the soft earth nearby and caught his breath. There were indentations in it that showed the recent marks of a wheeled vehicle – a vehicle that had carried some weight, he could tell. The tracks were deep and he estimated that the width between the indentations could easily have been that of the wagon in question. He smiled to himself. If he could find evidence to prove that the girl and her wagon *had* been here, then Fidelma would have to eat her words and apologise to him, while admitting that her irritated outburst had been uncalled-for.

He went to the door of the main house. Close to, he could see that the place had been built with a mixture of woods; the yew had just been employed to anchor deal, which was the main timber used in the building. The door was closed but the latch was easily lifted and he pushed it open. A scampering sound started up as he entered, and some flapping of wings. It was light inside, due to a large hole in the roof where the wooden boards had rotted away and fallen inwards. Obviously, a host of animal life was now reclaiming the place as its shelter.

Whether the house had once been as prosperously furnished as it should have been, judging by the detail of the building, he could not be sure, for the place was empty and covered with dust and dirt. The smell of animals and their excrement caused him to wrinkle his nose in disgust. This was clearly the main room of the house and there were the stone remains of what would have been the central fireplace. The aperture in the roof through which its smoke would have been sucked up was where the rot in the roof had started.

Eadulf was disappointed that he could see nothing that would present a clue as to whether the place had been used. Then he noticed that there were several wooden doors leading off this central room which presumably led to the *imada* or bedrooms. He might as well check everywhere, he decided. There was still plenty of light left. He walked across to the nearest door and pushed it open – it was only half-closed anyway. Once again the room was bare and his entrance caused various scuffling noises and squeaks. He tried another room, with similar results. A third door led off to an area whose wall had crumbled away, and he saw from the stonework in the corner that it had served the function of a kitchen.

Then he uttered a low exclamation as a thought occurred to him. If the girl *had* stayed here, she would not have slept inside the deserted house with its wildlife inhabitants. She would have stayed in the wagon! Almost as soon as that thought occurred to him, he countered it by reminding himself that there had been a dead body in the wagon. But what if the man had still been alive at that stage? Perhaps this was where he had died . . . How could he tell? Eadulf sighed in frustration and decided to go back to the wheel ruts and see if he could find out more.

He came out of the house and went over to the tracks. They led, he saw, to one of the barns. It was a large open affair, little more than a reed roof supported on a frame of oak posts. Certainly the wagon seemed to have rested here for a while, judging by the deep indentations and signs of cloven hooves as well as animal excreta. But the knowledge didn't really help to answer any questions. He stood hesitantly and then decided, since he was here and the girl and her wagon had been here, that he should make a quick inspection of all the other outhouses.

As he suspected, there was nothing to catch his attention in the first two buildings, and he wondered whether to bother with the others. However, Eadulf was nothing if not thorough. He opened the door of a small round wicker construction, finding he had to bend down to look beyond. There was a movement inside – and before he could react, he felt something touch the back of his head. He had not even registered it as a blow before he was swimming in a dark, bottomless pool.

Fidelma went to the door of the tavern and breathed in the night air. She was too restless to think of sleep. A moment later she was joined by Aidan, who said quietly: 'I suppose you are thinking what I am thinking, lady?'

Fidelma's mouth tightened. For a moment she was not sure whether she had forgiven him yet for wasting precious hours of the day by leading them up the wrong road. Her annoyance had caused her to allow Eadulf to go wandering off in these dangerous marshlands all by himself. She silently rebuked herself again for her behaviour. Then she turned to the warrior, saying, 'You are right, Aidan. Dusk is fast approaching and Eadulf has been gone far too long. I am thinking that he might be in trouble.'

'Perhaps I should ride back to that building and take a look,' the warrior volunteered. 'The marshland can be treacherous.'

'I shall come with you,' she decided, turning back into the interior of the tavern. 'Enda, you will stay here while Aidan and I go back to find Eadulf. If we miss him on the road and he turns up here, tell him where we have gone and ask him to stay here with you until we return. We should be back before long.'

Enda was not happy at having to remain behind, but he accepted Fidelma's logic.

Fidelma then turned to the tavern-keeper. 'Do you have a lantern – perhaps two lanterns – in case we are caught abroad by the coming nightfall?'

The man replied that he would fetch the lanterns and was back a short while later. 'I've asked my boy to bring your horses round from the stable,' he said.

The horses arrived quickly and they mounted and set off at a canter to retrace their route back down the road. Night was approaching faster than they had estimated, the darkness increasing with the flood of black rainclouds spreading across the sky. A cold wind began whipping at their faces and they were hard-pressed to watch the landscape with the same ease of earlier. In fact, they almost missed the turning onto the marshland along which the wooden building was situated.

'It's down there!' Aidan suddenly shouted, waving his arm. 'You can hardly see it against the eastern sky.'

Fidelma pulled rein and peered along the path which led towards the building on a hillock.

'Well, we have not missed him on the roadway,' she said. 'We'll have to go and take a look. It'll soon be time to light a lantern at this rate,' she added, glancing at the lowering sky.

Aidan nudged his horse into the lead and moved along the path with Fidelma following. They came to the causeway and crossed it. Then Fidelma gave an angry exclamation. She had seen what Eadulf had seen – the broadening of the track and the signs of a passing vehicle.

'Friend Eadulf had the right instinct,' Aidan could not help commenting, but Fidelma did not reply. She was rebuking herself yet again for having ignored his suggestion.

Twilight was creeping in as they trotted along the meandering track across the marshes. They halted for a moment below the rise, with its trees and manmade structure. Within a few moments they had negotiated the hillock and stood before what seemed to be collection of abandoned buildings surrounded by a low circular stone wall.

Eadulf was swimming slowly upwards out of his black pool, struggling and gasping for air. He tried to move his hands, but his wrists were tied together behind him. Nor could he see, as something was covering his face. It took him a few moments to understand that a hood had been placed over his head. After that, he stopped struggling and tried to relax and breathe more easily.

He knew that he was lying on a cold earthen floor, but his head and shoulders were propped up against a wall, which felt as if it were built of wood. He surreptitiously tested his other limbs. The pressure around his ankles told him that they were also bound, like his wrists.

Lying there, his head aching from the sharp blow, the throbbing in his temples was agonising. He was almost glad of the darkness of the hood and he shut his eyes for a moment to try to block out the pain. It didn't work. The next problem was that every time he inhaled, the hood – a smelly piece of old cloth – was drawn against his mouth, almost causing him to choke.

Only after his assessment of his physical condition did he turn to a consideration of his current predicament and what had been the cause of it.

He could remember the movement behind him as he entered the wicker outhouse. He also remembered trying to turn – but then came the blow on his skull which had sent him spinning into the blackness. So a hood had been placed on his head and he had been tied up. But by whom – and why?

He lay for a while just listening, trying to separate any sounds around him from the drumming in his temples, but could hear nothing. He wondered how long he had been unconscious and whether Fidelma and the others had missed him, by now. Would Fidelma be able to find him? Well, it was no use waiting and hoping. What was the motto that his old teachers used to keep hammering home to him and his fellow students? A line from the Roman Varro – *dei facientes adiuvant* – the gods help those who help themselves. Well, he presumed that one God would do the same as the many pagan Roman gods. So he must help herself. But he must go carefully. He moved slightly, cleared his throat and called softly: 'Is anyone there?'

Almost at once, with a sinking feeling, he heard the catch on a nearby door being lifted.

'So you're awake at last, eh?' The voice was male and harsh.

Eadulf wet his lips, although his tongue was almost dry. 'Who are you?' he managed to reply.

There was a laugh. 'Still causing trouble, eh? Well, you couldn't elude us.'

'My throat is dry. I need some water!' Eadulf countered, not understanding.

This brought forth another sinister chuckle. 'By the powers, you show some spirit. You should have been dead days ago. Go and fetch him and tell him that the man is conscious.' This remark seemed to be addressed to a companion outside. Then the voice sounded closer to Eadulf's ear: 'You will have to wait a while longer, until he comes to have a word with you, so you had better relax or devote the time to praying to your gods.'

The door shut and Eadulf realised that the man had left him alone in the room.

Fidelma and Aidan sat astride their horses peering at the dark outlines of the building and its outhouses.

'There is no sign of his horse,' Fidelma observed. 'Perhaps he did not come here, after all.'

Aidan shook his head. 'It was definitely this building he wanted to see. After all, it's the biggest one so far. Plenty of space for an oxen team and wagon to shelter, and . . .' Then he slid down and bent to examine the ground.

'What is it?' demanded Fidelma.

'Wheel ruts,' the warrior replied. 'The deep impressions of wheels from a wagon of a similar width to the one the girl was driving.' He knelt to look closer. 'Cloven hooves – and ones that were shod at that. Eadulf guessed right. An oxen wagon was definitely here.'

'Then where is Eadulf's horse?'

'Perhaps round the back. He's probably inside. One moment, I'll light one of the lamps because it will be dark in there. I have my *tenlach-teinid* with me.'

Each warrior of the King's Bodyguard carried this 'kindling gear', as it was called, which was stored in a special belt bag so as to be close at hand when needed. Each warrior was trained to produce fire with amazing rapidity. For a warrior of Aidan's experience, it was not long before he had the lamp alight.

Fidelma had dismounted and hitched both their mounts to a nearby post.

'I don't like it,' she found herself whispering as she gazed about her. 'If he is inside, then he should have heard our arrival.'

'Well, there is only one way to find out,' Aidan said, moving towards the door, holding the lamp aloft.

Eadulf came awake with a start, breathing heavily, and cursing himself. He must have fallen asleep due to the pain in his head, the lack of air and the restrictions of his hands and feet. It was the noise of the door opening that had awoken him.

A commanding male voice ordered: 'Get him upright. We don't want anything to happen until he has told us how they survived or where she is.'

A pair of rough hands hauled him up and then pushed him back into a semi-sitting position against the wall.

Eadulf tried to clear his mind, and although the pain was diminishing he felt confused and his thoughts did not come with their usual clarity.

'Good,' said the same voice. 'Now bring the lantern and hold it before his face; then remove the hood so we can see him.'

Behind the darkness of the hood, he saw a dim light coming close and could feel the warmth of its flame against his face. Then the hood was ripped away and the light of the lantern almost blinded him. He blinked several times, then as the lantern was put closer before his eyes he caught a glimpse of the hand adjusting it – a dirty, pudgy hand with thick fingers. He also saw a wristband. It was only a glimpse, but it shocked him into a clarity of thought. The wristband was simply a piece of plaited hemp rope, with something bright and shiny dangling from it, like a polished brass disc.

He tried to open his eyes wider, but the light had been placed in such a way that he could not see his captors. Yet he was still aware of shadows in the room, beyond the lantern's glare.

Then he heard an angry gasp.

'May the Red Screech Owl take you for a fool!' shouted the commanding voice in sudden temper. 'This is not him!'

The light wavered in front of his eyes.

'Keep the lantern where it is, you dolt! Do you want him to recognise us?'

The light steadied, and Eadulf became aware of a face looming close to his. There was an overpowering fragrance, a strong, sweet-smelling scent. It seemed familiar but his thoughts were still chaotic and he could not identify it – yet for some inexplicable reason he associated it with the mead brewed in his village, Seaxmund's Ham, when he was a youth.

'How was I to know that it wasn't him?' Eadulf identified a new, almost whining voice raised in protest. 'I just saw the religious robes. We were told to hunt for a religieux and a girl, who were probably hiding in the marshes. No religieux comes into these parts anyway, so who else could it have been than those you sought? We knocked him on the head, bound him and brought him to this meeting place before sending for you.'

'You idiots!' sneered the man, who was obviously in charge. 'This one wears the tonsure of Rome whereas the other . . .' The scent was strong as the face came closer still. 'Now, who are you?'

Eadulf had recovered some of his equilibrium. He licked his dry lips. 'A better question is who are you and what is the meaning of this?'

'Your accent betrays you as a Saxon . . .'

'I am an Angle,' Eadulf corrected, trying to keep a sense of humour that he did not feel.

'And your arrogance betrays the fact that you have pretensions of authority.' There was a note of derision in his captor's voice. 'Your authority counts for little here. I ask again, who are you?'

Eadulf quickly reviewed his options. The only one he could see that might work was to impress the man enough to release him.

'I am Eadulf of Seaxmund's Ham, in the Land of the South Folk among the Kingdom of the East Angles. I am husband to Fidelma of Cashel, sister to Colgú, King of Muman.'

A silence fell, to the point that even the spitting tallow in the lantern sounded loud. Then a soft whistle was emitted – he presumed it was from the man who was questioning him.

'I have heard of Brother Eadulf,' the voice said quietly. 'I can see that you do not lie. What are you doing in the marshlands?'

Eadulf thought rapidly. 'I became lost. I was following a track to Durlus Éile, to the north and . . .'

'Are you alone?'

The answer came from one of the other men. 'He was quite alone when we found him, lord. . .'

'Shut up!' barked the questioner. 'And cover his head with the hood, you imbecile!'

'Wait!' cried Eadulf, but the hood came down over his head and the lantern was removed so that he was plunged into darkness again. 'Wait! Who are you . . .?'

He was aware of the light being removed from in front of him. Then it seemed the questioner had turned to address his companions. 'You worthless scum! Of all men to mistake our quarry for – a relative of Colgú of Cashel. May the devil choke you!'

'It's not my fault,' the man with the whining voice asserted.

'Not your fault? I put you in charge. Well, now you must repair your mistake. I want no trace of this business to lead to our Fellowship. I shall wait at the usual place. Come and find me when you have done so.'

There was a bang at the door and this time Eadulf heard the whinny of a horse and then receding hoofbeats.

The man with the whining voice seemed to be asking a companion: 'Has he gone?'

'That he has, my friend.' The reply was from the man with the cold tones whom Eadulf had first heard when he recovered consciousness.

'How was I to know?' the other man moaned. 'It was dark and I did not see him well. Anyway, he was wearing religious robes and that was all the description we were told. I am not to blame.'

'Whether you are or not, my friend, he does blame you. What will you do? He placed you in charge. You know what he means by repairing your mistake. It is certainly not *my* mistake.'

There was a moment's silence, which was when Eadulf realised the danger he was in. He hesitated for a moment, trying to judge whether his verbal intervention would do him any good.

'I know well what he means,' the other man was responding. 'But one thing I will not do in conscience is kill a relative of an Eóganacht, even if he is a foreigner. He is husband to the sister of Colgú, no less. Can you imagine the retribution that will fall on us?'

'But how will they know?' demanded the other. 'What's so special about the Eóganacht – even if they are noble?'

'You are a man of Osraige. Doesn't your own prince pay tribute to them?'

'If you are not strong, then you need to be cunning. Osraige accepts the overlordship of the Eóganacht while it is in our interest to do so.'

'Well, you forget that I am from the Corco Loígde,' replied the other. 'You don't know the Eóganacht as I do.'

'They are people like any other.'

'That is where you are wrong,' the other told him in an awed tone. 'They are not only the descendants of the great Eibhear Fionn, son of Golamh, who brought the Children of the Gael to this land in the time beyond time, but they are protected by Mór Muman, after whom their very kingdom is named. You do not insult the goddesses who spawned the kings of the Eóganacht.'

'Our gods and goddesses are just as strong as the brood of Mór Muman,' jeered the other. 'Besides, this man is just a Saxon.'

'You may place your belief in Badh, but I tell you: I will not have the blood of the relative of an Eóganacht on my hands nor on my conscience. Only bad will come of it.'

'So you want *me* to kill him? I shall do so, but I shall tell our lord that I had to do it since you were so afraid. If I don't kill him, then what is your plan? Will you release this Saxon? If *he* finds out, then you will know the worst of it. No Eóganacht deity will protect you then.'

There was a silence. Clearly the man in charge was thinking.

'I am still your superior in the Fellowship. Who says I shall release him? All I have said is that I will not have his blood on my hands nor on my conscience.'

'Then what is it to be? Do you want me to cut his throat for you?'

Eadulf tensed himself, determined – as helpless as he was – to resist to the end.

'You shall not touch him while I command,' snapped the second voice. 'I did not take service with him to fight the gods but to serve them. And if the goddess of the Eóganacht is affronted . . .'

'But you have been left no other course.'

'No one saw us bring him here. He is bound hand and foot, and hooded, with no chance of escape. So we will leave him to the will of his ancestors and of the ancestors of the Eóganacht. If the deities who bred their family will it, then it is their choice whether he lives or dies. His blood will be on their hands, not mine.'

'That is a curious logic,' snorted his companion. 'What if they allow him to escape – what then? Our lord expects the foreigner's death, no less. How will you answer to him?'

'How will he know – unless you tell him? I will not challenge the gods even if our lord claims that he speaks for them.'

'You forget, he is all-powerful.'

'Then let *him* argue with the will of the gods. I prefer to argue with the Lord of—'

'Shut up, you fool. If you are determined not to kill him, what will this foreigner know unless you tell him by using that name?'

'Let us leave him to be disposed of as the gods will.'

'So you are determined to defy our lord?'

'Rather that, than the Goddess of Muman. Since you are so worried, you will leave here first, my friend. I shall be behind you with my sword. We will go as far as your farmstead, where I shall leave you. After that, you may run to him and tell him that I have disobeyed his will. But we will leave the Saxon here unharmed. For the last time I say: *I will not defy the gods.*'

'Very well. But I give you fair warning. His revenge is merciless and his reach is long.'

Eadulf had the impression of renewed darkness, and then he heard the door bang shut. Lying still for a moment or two, he realised that the lantern had been extinguished; quiet had descended. There was a lonely howl of a wolf in the distance and then the movement of horses which receded quickly.

Bound hand and foot and hooded, he was alone and helpless.

Aidan pushed open the door and, holding the lantern high, peered into the darkness.

'Eadulf?' he called. His voice echoed hollowly out of the darkness. There was a smell of musk and decay in the once wealthy farmhouse, and they could hear scurrying noises.

Aidan moved forward with his lantern, with Fidelma following closely behind. 'Friend Eadulf? Are you in here?' he called again.

There was a sudden flapping of leathery wings and something flew across the room to perch beyond their line of vision, presumably on the roofbeams.

'Bats,' Aidan muttered, glancing upwards – and before he could say anything further there was an angry squeaking and the sound of pattering feet 'Shrews,' he identified. 'This house is being reclaimed by the wild animals. Look!'

They caught a sudden flash of chestnut fur in the lamplight and then it was gone, the beast scampering away, up the wall and out the roof.

'What was that?' Fidelma asked. 'It was too big for a shrew.'

'A pine marten,' Aidan said absently, gazing round and holding the lantern higher. 'Well, there is no sign of Eadulf here.'

Fidelma held out her unlit lantern so that Aidan could transfer the flame. When her lantern was alight, she moved to the first door off the main room. 'We might as well be thorough. After all, this was where he came, and the tracks outside confirm that he was correct to do so.'

'I will make a circle of the house,' Aidan announced. 'With the fading light and this lantern I might just be able to see.'

While Fidelma examined all the rooms that led off from the main one, Aidan disappeared outside. It was depressing to see how this prosperous habitation had fallen into such decay.

He went back inside, saying, 'There is no sign of his horse, but I think he has been here.'

'What makes you say that?'

Aidan produced a torn piece of material which, though covered in mud, Fidelma recognised immediately as the brown homespun which was part of the clothing that Eadulf had been wearing.

'Where did you find it?'

'Caught on some splintered wood by one of the outside huts and I think torn off recently.'

Fidelma's lips compressed grimly. 'So if he was here, where is he now?'

'You saw nothing in any of the rooms?' Aidan asked.

'The only things that are moving in here are little creatures on four legs.'

'Could we have missed him in the gloom?' Even as Aidan asked the question, he knew it was a silly one.

Fidelma glanced at the black sky through the hole in the roof.

'One thing is certain, we cannot do anything further now the light has gone,' Aidan went on.

'True enough,' Fidelma sighed. 'We had best find our way back to the tavern. There is a slim chance that Eadulf might have gone there by some other route. If not . . . if not we shall come back here at first light. Enda is a good tracker. We might be able to follow his trail from here.'

As much as he disliked abandoning the place without finding Eadulf, Aidan had to accept that it was the only sensible thing to do. 'Providing those clouds are not bringing rain with them, Enda might be able to spot some tracks,' he said. 'I can't even see the moon now or the stars.'

Fidelma did not reply. She knew only too well the problems of heavy rain washing away any tracks that had been left. What concerned her more was that Eadulf could have wandered off the main path into the marshland, the terrifying quagmire into which numberless humans and animals had been sucked to their deaths.

Eadulf had lain still for a long time, concerned that the departure of his captors might be some trick – and that they were merely waiting for him to move to give them an excuse to kill him. However, it was eventually clear that they had departed, and such a trick he realised would be illogical after what he had heard. It seemed that the man who had been told to despatch him was so bound up in ancient superstition that he had been too afraid to carry out the wish of the mysterious 'lord'. Once more Eadulf strained against his bonds but they were just as tight as before and he had no hope of loosening them by force. In fact, he had little hope of doing anything until he could see again.

He inhaled deeply in annoyance, and once again the linen of the hood was sucked in against his mouth. He spat it out and tried to breathe more gently through his nostrils. It was then that the idea occurred to him. He had once been shown the trick by a fairground performer – ironically, as that now appeared in the light of his current adventure. The performer would have himself blindfolded twice by someone from his audience and then be given a bow and an arrow before shooting at a target held by his assistant. As a little boy, Eadulf had demanded to know how it was done. The answer was simple. The first blindfold totally obscured the vision while the outer hood was of such loose threads they could be seen through. Obviously, when the audience tried both the blindfolds on together, they could not see a thing. When the performer had the hood placed over the first blindfold, this obscured what he was doing to it. Using his mouth and teeth, he was able to manipulate and pull it down from his eyes, so all he had to see through were the loose weaves of the hood.

Now Eadulf wondered whether the same principles would work for him.

He breathed in through his mouth and sure enough was able to catch the fibre of the hood in between his teeth. Trying not to think of the bitter taste, he began to manipulate it as if he were trying to eat it, pulling at it and twisting it. He nearly choked several times, and several times he had to let it out and recover his breath and simply rest his jaws. Then he seemed to find a correct point to pull at. He felt the cloth rising from the back of his head, coming slowly . . . ever so slowly . . . over his head and face. Then the whole hood fell off in front of him and he was blinking into the darkness of a room. He stayed a while, content just to breathe fresh air and recover from his exertions. He did not know how long he had taken to remove the blindfold but it seemed an age.

After a while he started to focus into the shadowy darkness. It was clearly nighttime, and judging by the gloom he did not think there was a good enough moon to help him see. He felt, more than observed, that he was in a circular building and, judging by the texture of the walls, it was of interwoven wickerwork. In that case he was surely in one of the outer buildings of the farmstead. Perhaps even the one he had been examining when he was struck on the head.

If that were so, why had Fidelma and the others not come back to look for him when he had failed to rejoin them? They knew where he had been going. Surely Fidelma would not have been so annoyed at his insistence in coming to the deserted house that she had decided not to bother to look for him until daylight? Surely not!

He stretched and pulled at his bonds – but they were very secure. He needed to free his hands, and his ankles were tied very tightly. He blinked and once more focused his eyes on the shadows. In the darkness he could see nothing that would assist him. The grim thought struck him that he could do nothing until he could see – and that meant waiting until dawn. Yet he had no way of estimating how long that would be. His captors might return at any time to finish their task. What if the superstitious one had been overcome by his companion, who seemed so greatly in awe of the person who gave the orders? Yet there was no alternative. It was with reluctance that he forced himself to lie back in as relaxed a position as possible and close his eyes. There was no one more surprised than he was when, as if a moment later, he beheld the bright light of day. As uncomfortable as he was, and in such a perilous situation, he had fallen fast asleep.

CHAPTER NINE

⌘

Aidan and Enda found themselves hard-pressed to keep up with Fidelma as she trotted her horse along the track that zigzagged its way through the marshes. At first light she had awoken them and had the horses made ready to set out for the deserted farmstead. She had cantered ahead almost at break-neck speed along the road until the turn-off which led through the marshland, and did not slow down until they arrived at the top of the mound.

Enda, who was gifted in the craft of tracking, swung down from his horse and immediately began to examine the ground, while Fidelma and Aidan decided to take another look in the main building to check whether they had missed anything the night before. They had barely begun their search when Enda called to them.

'Here! I have found something.'

The warrior was standing at the entrance of one of the circular wickerwork outhouses. He waved them over and pointed downwards. Just inside the door was a large flat stone.

'What is it?' demanded Fidelma.

Enda bent down and picked up the stone. There was a dark mark on it. Without saying a word, he licked his forefinger and rubbed it on the mark then held it up. There was a dark brown smudge on his finger.

Aidan recognised it at once. 'Blood? This was where I found the torn piece of material last night.'

Enda nodded. 'Yes, it's dried blood but not old. This blood was shed recently.'

'Are there any other signs?' Fidelma had gone pale. 'Any tracks?'

'It's difficult, lady. I have tried to separate the marks of your horse and that of Aidan's where you came last night. There have been several other horses here, and they were certainly here before you came, as your horses' tracks have overlaid them.'

'Can you tell anything else?' Fidelma tried to keep her voice calm.

'Not much at the moment, lady.'

'Then do your best and we will continue with our search.'

But the main building and the outhouses revealed nothing that they could associate with Eadulf. When they returned outside they saw that Enda was on the path beyond the outer wall of the farm-stead. He was frowning and now and then dropping to a crouch as he examined the ground.

'Do you see anything?' called Fidelma.

Enda straightened and shook his head. 'The ground along these paths is too hard, lady. This I can say, however: there seems to have been several horses here. Once they left the enclosure, they started along the path here and were heading south-east.'

'Several horses?'

'I make it three. If Eadulf was here, it seems that he accompanied two others. Whether he went willingly or unwillingly, it is hard to say.'

Fidelma stood undecided. 'Can we even be sure that the bloodstain was Eadulf's blood?' She did not want to accept that conclusion.

'He is not here, lady,' pointed out Aidan gently. 'We must presume that he has gone with whoever rode the other horses and, no doubt, unwillingly. Perhaps he found something that he was not supposed to find. We now know the girl's wagon and ox team were also here. Perhaps whoever it was . . .'

Aidan's voice trailed away when he realised what he was about to say. He looked guiltily at Fidelma, whose expression was grim. She realised that she had to act; that it was no use wasting time speculating about what had happened. Eadulf had been here. The blood might or might not be connected. Some horses had been here and were now gone.

'I suggest that we should follow the tracks as far as we are able. If they head south-east, then that way should eventually meet up with the Slíge Dála. Let us hope that somewhere along the way, we will come across other signs.'

Hearing the resolution in her voice, Aidan and Enda obediently remounted, pretending not to notice the concern on Fidelma's features which gave lie to the confidence in her voice.

When Eadulf came awake, he could hear the cry of birds, and felt softness in the air – a gentle breeze which he later discerned was the wind whispering through the spaces in the wickerwork where the dry wattle had fallen away. He eased himself up into a sitting position. His mouth was dry as sand and his head ached. He felt awful and the blood seemed to have deserted his hands and feet, for they were cold and numb.

He could see that he was in a circular wickerwork hut. He presumed it was one of the outbuildings of the farmstead. In order to survive, he realised that he *had* to get his bonds loosened. But how? He ran his eyes swiftly over the interior of the hut. It was devoid of any furniture although there were several bits and pieces of wood that might well have been a table or a stool at some time.

On the far side was a door and near it stood a tall pole, leaning against the wall. He had no difficulty in recognising a shepherd's staff. Well, that would not help him. He continued to lie still, searching with his eyes around the room. There was a pile of mouldering cloth, or what at first glance he thought was cloth but then realised it was sheep's wool. So this hut had been used by a shepherd at some time. But the condition of the place made it clear that it had long since been abandoned for that purpose. No shepherd would suddenly arrive to help him and, at any moment, his captors might return – having changed their minds or succumbed to the authority of the man who commanded them.

Seeing nothing near him of consequence, he began to painfully manoeuvre his body across the hard earth floor towards the door. Perhaps if he could open the door, get out, he might find a sharp stone outside against which he could use to try to sever the bonds around his wrists. His progress was painful, as there was little or no feeling in his hands and feet.

He was nearing the door when he felt his robes catch on something. He stopped moving immediately. Something dark was half-buried in the earth floor and he stared at it for a moment. Then excitement took hold. He swung himself around so that, in spite of the numbness of his hands, he could attempt to grasp it with his fingertips. It was hard and cold to his touch. He tried to dig his nails into the earth around the object and then worked to pull and push it from side to side, in order to uncover the top part. It felt rusty but sharp.

Sitting with his back to it, he began moving his wrists against the edge. It seemed the work of ages. He had to keep stopping because of exhaustion but slowly, little by little, he felt the bonds loosening . . . and then one of them snapped. It was enough for him to strain and wriggle and eventually loosen one hand. He almost gave a shout of relief. Now he swung round and examined his wrists. They were bloodied and bruised where the rope had cut into them. He saw that the bond on the other wrist could be untied and this he did, clumsily. The blood rushed almost painfully back and he sat for a while massaging his throbbing wrists and hands as the feeling gradually returned.

The next problem was the bonds around his ankles. Whoever had tied him up was no novice at the art. He turned round and looked for the piece of metal that had been his saviour. Carefully, so as not to cut himself, he used a nearby piece of splintered wood to pry the metal completely loose from the earth floor. It took no more than a moment or two before he held it in his hand. He smiled and uttered a silent prayer of thanks to the long-departed shepherd, for what he held in his hand was the rusty, long-discarded blade of a paring knife – a *butún*, the local word came unbidden to his mind. All shepherds carried this type of knife for paring hooves or even stripping the skin off a stillborn lamb to put the skin on a motherless lamb so that the ewe would adopt it for the one she had lost. Eadulf had seen it done many times, but had never thought he would owe his life to such an instrument. Using the knife-blade, it was the work of a moment to sever the bonds around his ankle.

It seemed an age before he felt able to stand. He moved slowly and unsteadily to the door, wondering if his captors – whoever they were – had left his horse behind. That would be wishing for too much. He opened the catch and stepped outside.

That was when he had his first shock.

He was not in one of the outbuildings of the abandoned farmstead. His round wickerwork hut stood by itself within a copse of yews which obscured the surrounding scenery. Only the elevation of the land seemed to indicate to Eadulf that this was also on one of the craggy islets that emerged from the broad sweep of marshlands. He looked about and realised that he had no idea at all of where he was. Not only had his captors taken his horse but also his saddlebag with his goatskin water bag and his *lés*, his medical bag. And his thirst was now almost uncontainable.

Even as this thought occurred to him, he thought he heard the splashing of water. He immediately dismissed the sound as wishful thinking and tried to concentrate his thoughts on estimating where he was, and other mysteries. Who were the two men who had brought him here? Why had they mistaken him for another religieux?

More importantly, who was the 'lord' who could order his death without a moment's hesitation, rather than just releasing him?

He stared out across the flat green plains, so tranquil-looking, but he reminded himself that the green was but a thin covering of the deadly marshland. In most directions, lines of hills of irregular shapes and sizes were just misty marks on the horizon. He wondered how far he would get, feeling ill as he did, with the soreness of his wrists and ankles and the pounding in his head, let alone his incredible thirst. He did not think he would last long in this wilderness. If only he still had his medical bag with him, but everything was gone. That was when he noticed that he was also barefoot.

The sounds of that running water were tormenting him. He started looking for a small pebble. He had once heard that placing a pebble in the mouth caused one to salivate. There was a term for it but his head hurt and he could not remember it. Even as he was looking, the splashing of water became louder. It *was* real. Then something else registered. The shepherd's hut where he had been kept was sheltered by yew trees. It must have been built there for a purpose. The splashing, now that he concentrated on it, seemed to come from behind the trees. He thought there was a wall there but on moving through the thin band of trees he saw that it was a natural rock formation which had been covered as if it were an embankment.

He swallowed with a dry, retching motion. From a hole in this rock edifice, water was gushing into a gully which went down into the verdant covering of the marshland beyond. It was a natural spring – small but more than enough to provide what water he needed. Eadulf almost flung himself at it. On his knees, and using only his hands, he ladled up the water and lapped at it like a dog until he had drunk his fill. Then he lay on his back on the ground, eyes closed and gasping for breath.

Moments later, it came to him that while one immediate problem was resolved, he was faced with others that would soon become crucial. He had to set out to find a habitation – but the first problem was that he had nothing on his feet. He had checked before emerging from the hut in case his sandals had been left there, but everything had been taken, even his belt. The second problem was, which way should he go? The third problem was, he had found water, but how could he carry it to sustain him for any length of time? Each question was one which meant life or death.

Eadulf gave a deep sigh. Sitting here by the comfort of the little spring, he knew that it was high time to become more organised and not waste the day. He went back into the shepherd's hut. The blade of the paring knife would come in useful, and the staff might also help him on the walk he must undertake. But there was nothing else in the wicker hut.

If a shepherd had used the hut frequently, life had taught Eadulf that shepherds usually had four tools of their trade. He had found two of them – the staff and paring knife. He did not expect to find any *loman*, a thin cord or string that shepherds carried, but he was hoping that there might be a *síthal*, a small bucket or vessel for drawing water. All shepherds considered cord or string essential, especially during the lambing season, and a small bucket was often necessary for giving water to distressed ewes. Eadulf was disappointed that there was no sign of the latter item. But then he had no idea how long this place had been deserted.

Luck was with him, however, for in taking a slow walk around the area for one final look, he saw what appeared to be a leather feedbag for a horse or a mule. It was old and discarded, true, and the smell was not enticing but it was better than nothing. Indeed, he recalled something from the writing of the Blessed Jerome – *Equi donatei dentes non inspiciuntur* – one doesn't inspect the teeth of a horse given as a gift. He took the bag into the gully where the spring flowed and started to laboriously wash it out. What came out of it appeared pretty unpleasant and it took him some time to clean it to the point where he felt he might be able to stomach the water it would contain. It was not even completely watertight but it would surely do to help him on the way to some habitation.

He was busy filling it when he heard a faint noise, and looking through the trees, he saw a horse and rider appear in the distance. He was about to run forward, hand rising ready to wave, when some instinct caused him to pause. Was it one of his captors, returning to put him to death?

Without further hesitation, Eadulf turned and ran back to the covering of the yew trees, then flung himself down the bank behind the outcrop of rock. He heard the horse's strenuous breath as it climbed the hillock. There came the familiar commanding tone of the leader of his captors.

'Still alive, foreigner? It seems the lackey I left to make your demise painless was more fearful of shadows than he was of me. Well, he has now gone to meet those gods he feared so much. So I have personally come to put you out of your misery!'

For a moment Eadulf thought the man was addressing him, having spotted him hiding. Then he realised that the man was just venting his anger aloud as he approached the hut.

Eadulf crouched low behind the rocks, eyes searching feverishly for a weapon. A paring knife's blade without a handle was not much protection against an armed man. He heard the sounds of the man dismounting. He must have entered the hut immediately, for a string of profanities filled the air, followed by the banging of the hut door. The man would have assumed that Eadulf had freed himself during the night and long since fled, for he immediately swung back onto his horse. Eadulf could hear the creak of leather as he did so. The man was obviously so concerned about Eadulf's escape that he neglected to search the surrounding undergrowth on the islet but sent his horse at a gallop down to the path and along it – as if he guessed where Eadulf would be heading.

Eadulf waited until he heard the sound of hooves die away. Then he gathered his leaking bag of water, the blade of the paring knife and the old shepherd's staff. He gave a last rueful glance at what had been his prison for the night and made his way down from the hillock to the more level area onto a dry path. Here he stood undecided for a moment. He decided first to make a complete circle of the hillock, following the track to check how many paths led from it and in which directions. There were three. It was then he rebuked his timidity for not trying to get a glimpse of the man and the direction he had taken. At least he would have some means to identify him in future. However, it was too late now.

From the position of the sun he saw that one path went due west; another path led north-east, while the third went towards the south-east. If he recalled correctly, the south-east would bring him closer to the great Slíge Dála and habitation, where he might be able to pick up a horse or at least some footwear. Bracing himself, he began to walk slowly, treading carefully to avoid stones or other sharp surfaces, and with watchful eyes for any cover in case the rider came back.

Fidelma was reluctant to leave the marshland. It seemed to her that she was deserting Eadulf and yet she knew this was emotion speaking, not reason. The marshes encompassed too large an area to spend more time exploring every path that twisted through it. They had done the only reasonable thing, setting off in the direction in which Enda had observed that the three horses were heading. However, after a while the track's surface became harder and the signs that Enda was following petered out. The only course open was to follow the main track and hope to pick up the tracks again. Now, however, they were approaching the borders of the marshland.

'There's a dwelling over there,' Aidan said suddenly.

The ground had been gradually rising from the low-lying bog arca and now they were on more solid but still fertile soil. They had passed through a small wood and now Aidan was pointing towards a collection of buildings – probably a farmstead – with a welcoming wisp of smoke rising from a central chimney. Fidelma was aware of a dog barking, which meant that they had already been seen.

'Do you want to call there, lady, and see if the farmer has news of any travellers?' asked Aidan.

'Perhaps we can ask for the hospitality of a drink,' added Enda. 'It has been some while since we halted.'

'I agree on both accounts,' Fidelma was forced to concede. 'If Eadulf, or the people he was with, came this way, then the farmer would surely know.'

As they approached the buildings, a tall man appeared from the main one and shouted a few commands to the little terrier which was already trotting towards them, barking but in a friendly manner. At the sound of his master's stern voice, the terrier promptly ceased making a commotion and sat with a low whine, watching the farmer with cautious eyes.

The man, Fidelma noted, was of middle years and well muscled, for he wore a sleeveless leather jerkin. His features were fleshy and pock-marked, but tanned as someone used to working in the fields. He wore his sandy-coloured hair, streaked with grey, long and tied at the back, and had a shaggy grey beard. Beneath bushy brows, his brown eyes watched their approach with an unblinking gaze.

'To whose farmstead have we come?' Aidan called as they halted their horses before him.

'You have arrived at the farmstead of Rechtabra son of Fínachta, of the Uí Airbh.'

'The Uí Airbh?' Aidan frowned thoughtfully, identifying the clan. 'So we are in the territory of the Osraige?'

'You are in the Land of the People of the Deer,' the farmer confirmed. Such was the meaning of the name Osraige. Then his eyes widened as he caught sight of the gold torcs around the necks of Aidan and Enda. He obviously knew what they signified because, if anything, his manner became even more guarded. 'You are all welcome to whatever poor hospitality that I can offer.'

'We accept, Rechtabra,' Fidelma replied, speaking for the first time. 'But perhaps you can answer a question first. Have you seen a man in religious robes travelling out of the marsh recently? He wears the tonsure of Rome, and may or may not be accompanied by two others on horseback.'

The farmer was regarding her with a frown of curiosity.

'He would speak with a foreign accent,' Enda prompted.

Rechtabra's features were impassive. He shook his head. 'Few strangers travel into the marshes or, indeed, out of them unless they have cause to be there. Shepherds and the marsh farmers are known to me, but I have seen no strangers. My farm is on the edge of the marshlands and it is not an easy place for travellers to traverse.'

Fidelma dismounted and her companions followed her example.

'We will not tarry long here,' she informed the man, 'but would request water for our horses.'

The farmer examined her for a moment and then, as if remembering his manners, asked: 'Who do I have the honour of welcoming to my unworthy hearth?'

'This is Fidelma of Cashel,' Aidan announced.

'Then you are thrice welcome.' Did Rechtabra have a moment's hesitation before he greeted her? They were not sure. 'Allow me to offer you my humble hospitality. Woman of the house!' The latter was an imperious command.

A woman came out of the building to welcome them. She was much younger than the farmer, hardly a few years more than the 'age of choice'. She had fair hair and attractive features, and her skin was pale, unlike someone used to working outside. Her eyes, a smoky blue colour which contrasted with her naturally red lips, regarded the strangers nervously, and when she saw Fidelma examining her, she shyly dropped those eyes and fixed them on the ground. She was much shorter than the farmer, with a pleasing figure. Side by side, the two of them made an incongruous pair.

'Is this your daughter?' Fidelma asked pleasantly, after the man made no attempt to introduce her.

Rechtabra actually glowered for a moment in response and then he replied tersely, 'Ríonach is my wife. Get inside, girl, and fetch drinks for our guests.'

The girl flushed and then hurried into the house. Rechtabra motioned them inside, allowing them to precede him into the main room of the farmstead. Fidelma noticed that the terrier trotted after them and lay down in a corner of the room with a curious whining sound.

'What may I offer you, lady?' the girl almost whispered. 'We do not have anything grand. We have *nenadmin*, a cider from wild apples, or, if you like something stronger, there is *miodh cuill*, mead made from hazels.'

Fidelma smiled encouragingly at the girl's nervous demeanour. 'I saw a well as I came in. Cold fresh water is often as sweet as wine.'

The farmer seemed disapproving. 'It is no hospitality without a drink,' he muttered the ancient saying.

'Yet water is the original drink of all creatures, and therefore the greater hospitality is preserved,' Fidelma replied gravely.

The farmer looked for a moment as if he would debate the point and then shrugged. 'Hurry, girl,' he hissed at his wife.

She took a jug and hastened outside to the well, while her husband bade them to be seated. He did not offer to provide drinks for Enda and Aidan while waiting for his wife's return. She came with a jug of fresh water for Fidelma and then asked Aidan and Enda if they wanted cider to quench their thirst. They both followed Fidelma's example and settled for the well water. The farmer told the girl to fetch him cider and be quick about it. By now, Fidelma was taking a dislike to him for his bullying attitude to his young wife. He seemed arrogant, and his manner made Fidelma uncomfortable.

'We had not realised that we had crossed into the territory of Osraige,' Aidan said, breaking an awkward silence.

'If you came through the marshlands then there is no way of knowing,' agreed the farmer. 'Coileach is lord of these marshlands and his territory covers the marshes east of the road that runs up to Durlus. Coileach, in turn, pays tribute to the Prince of Osraige.'

Fidelma turned to the young girl. 'And are you of Osraige?' she asked.

The girl blushed and shook her head. 'I was raised further south of here, lady. My parents were of the Déisi. They are now both dead.'

'But now she is of Osraige and the clan Uí Airbh,' the farmer added curtly, causing his young wife to start nervously. 'It is something to be proud of.'

Fidelma felt a growing sympathy for her.

'Where are you heading for?' Rechtabra asked, trying to adopt a more friendly tone when he saw he was making a bad impression on his visitors. But his voice sounded insincere, too suspicious. 'We see few travellers around the marshlands, as I said.'

'We are trying to meet up with our lost companion. Where do those southerly tracks lead to?'

Rechtabra seemed thoughtful for a moment, his expression impassive as he gazed at her. 'Beyond the woodland, it joins the great highway between Cill Cainnech and Cashel.'

'How far is the main highway from here?' Fidelma asked.

'Of *forrach*, no more than two-twenties.'

'A very short distance then,' muttered Enda. 'I did not think we were that close.'

'When you come out of the woodland you will see the Mountains of the High Fields to the south. The highway runs before them.'

'Being so close to the main highway, I am surprised that you do not have much to do with the travellers who pass up and down along the way,' Aidan observed.

'The Fates be thanked that our farmstead is sufficiently hidden from the highway so that travellers pass by without stopping,' Rechtabra replied dourly. 'Some farms that are closer to it have people knocking on their doors at all times of the night seeking a place to stay. There are good hostels and taverns along the highway without honest farmers having their sleep disrupted, their animals disturbed and often no reward for their hospitality.'

'But do you have good fields here? Doesn't the marshland restrict your farming?' asked Enda, who had been raised on a farm.

'We are only a small farmstead,' Rechtabra replied briefly.

'What do you grow here?' Enda pressed. 'The wet ground seems fertile enough.'

'The main crops are *cruithnecht* and *arba*,' the farmer replied. *Cruithnecht* was the native red wheat while *arba* was one of the corn crops. 'We have some animals and get by without having to offer free hospitality to travellers along the great road.'

Aidan and Enda exchanged a frowning glance, wondering if the farmer was hinting that he expected some form of compensation for his meagre hospitality.

If Fidelma felt the same, she disguised it with a sniff. 'This is a time when the great fairs are held,' she commented. 'Particularly the Great Fair of Cashel which will be celebrated soon. There is probably a lot of traffic along the road. I would have thought there would be many wagons of performers passing this way, bound for Cashel?'

Ríonach's mouth opened and she seemed about to say something – but she caught sight of a warning glance from her husband and her jaw clamped shut.

'Well, we have seen no sign of such wagons here,' he said. 'We lead a quiet life, as you can see.'

Fidelma knew there was little point in confronting the farmer further about this. She rose from her seat and stretched; the yawn was, perhaps, a little too over-emphatic. She glanced at Aidan meaningfully, saying: 'Go and check our horses. We must be on our way and join the Slíge Dála ourselves. Oh, and you had best check that the water bags are filled.' She turned to Rechtabra. 'Perhaps your wife could show him where to fill them?'

'No need to give my wife extra work,' the farmer said tersely, to their surprise. Then turning to Aidan, he said, 'You will see the well immediately to your left.'

The girl looked at Fidelma apologetically. That put an end to her idea of hoping that Aidan could ask what the girl had been going to say about travellers before she was forestalled by her husband.

'It is a pity that your visit has been so brief.' Rechtabra spoke politely but without warmth as he rose. It was clearly a hint. 'As I have said, a drink of water is hardly hospitality.'

'It is the degree of welcome that is the essence of hospitality and not the substance,' Fidelma replied quietly as she followed his example.

Rechtabra gave her a quick glance, not sure whether there was a waspish meaning in her reply, but he said no more and moved to the door. There was nothing else to do but to say polite farewells and, once Aidan had filled the water bags, mount their horses.

The farmer stood watching Fidelma and her companions ride slowly out of the yard and along the track which would soon connect with the great highway. The young girl, Ríonach, came to stand at his shoulder, watching their departure with a sorrowful look.

'Do you think the lady suspects anything about your Fellowship?' she asked, as the riders disappeared through the trees.

Her husband's voice was angry. 'It is well you mention the Fellowship only in my hearing, girl. Otherwise you would feel the back of my hand across your mouth.' Then he paused and added: 'She may be a *dálaigh* but she is not gifted with the *imbas forosnai*, the gift of prophetic knowledge.'

'How do you know she is a *dálaigh*?'

Rechtabra chuckled coarsely 'That conclusion needs no illumination from the Otherworld. Who has not heard of Fidelma of Cashel? Did you not see that she rode with men who wore the Golden Collar of the King of Cashel's Bodyguard? Did Fidelma of Cashel not thwart the plans of Osraige's greatest warlord, Cronan of Gleann an Ghuaill?'

Ríonach shivered slightly. 'Then all the more true that your own lord should be alarmed, if you are not.'

'Do not speak of him,' retorted her husband angrily. 'There is no one of mortal flesh that can cause him alarm. The sooner you accept it, the better for you. Otherwise, you will feel the lash of my belt again.'

Eadulf did not know how long he had been walking. He knew he was moving south-east and the stretches of verdant green were now giving way to patches of early blossoming marsh marigolds with their dark green heart-shaped leaves, on long stalks, and the yellow flowers lighting up the dark places. There were now clumps of trees ahead of him, affording him some hope of finding human habitation where he might get help.

He had long since exhausted his supply of water, for the goatskin bag had constantly seeped, spilling more of its content than it had retained. His feet were painful, and even though he tried to avoid the stones along the path, they had soon become cut and bruised. However, he persevered trying to concentrate on other matters.

Then he heard, high above him, the ominous *kraa, kraa, kraa* cry. He looked up and spotted two wheeling birds with their gloss black plumage. His sharp eye spotted the square tail which, apart from size, seemed to be the only thing that differentiated these scavengers, the carrion crows, from the birds of ill-omen and harbingers of death – the ravens. He wondered what dead carcass they had spotted because the circular motions and warning cries showed that they were descending to a spot not far ahead of him.

He grasped his shepherd's staff more firmly as he hobbled towards the trees. It was here that the crows had descended; he saw they had landed at the side of the track and were attacking something with a flapping of their wings.

He was some way off when he realised that the object the scavenger birds were attacking was a human body, or part of one, and obviously dead from the way it lay inert to the crows now pecking at it. He stumbled forward, shouting hoarsely and whirling the shepherd's staff over his head. Why he did this, he did not know, for the man – it was a man's torso – was clearly beyond rescue.

The crows seemed to glance disdainfully at him, but apparently decided some caution was needed before they continued with their feast, so they launched themselves into the sky but did not move far off, simply flying in circles at tree-top height.

Eadulf peered down at the part of the body he could see; it was covered in mud and slime. The man could not have been dead long, for in spite of the mud covering, the cuts and abrasions looked fresh. Much of the lower part of the body was still submerged in the marsh that immediately bordered the path. It seemed to Eadulf that the body had been pushed into the marsh in the hope of concealing it, but the corpse had risen and somehow lodged on the harder earth next to the path.

Eadulf bent forward. The dead man was a thick-set individual, who had no doubt always worked in the fields; a muscular man with callused hands. One arm lay across his chest, a thick arm with a dirty, stubby figures and . . .

Eadulf gasped.

Around one wrist was a plaited piece of hemp rope, and attached to it by means of a small hole, through which the hemp was threaded, was a small disc. Eadulf cupped his hand, scooped up some of the marsh water and splashed it over the disc, which revealed itself to be a shiny metal; it looked as if it were brass. Even before he examined it, he knew that there would be the impression of a bird on one side . . . the image of a raven.

Eadulf bent down and examined the body, trying to ignore the ravages of the carrion. The clothes were torn and ragged, and there was nothing else to identify the man. He carefully undid the knot of the hemp bracelet, and, as he had no bag to place it in, he carefully tied it around his own wrist.

He stood up again and almost missed the mud-covered object that was floating on top of the watery slime not far from the corpse. It was the shaft of an arrow, just the feathered flight and a section of broken wood. Eadulf returned to the body and looked for a wound. There was none on the front. Bracing himself for the distasteful task he seized the corpse by the arms and pulled it further onto the path. He was rewarded for his efforts by the sight of two wooden stubs protruding from the back, indicating where two arrows had snapped off when the man fell.

Eadulf stood up and looked nervously about him. Two things were clear. This had been one of his captors – probably the one who had defied his leader by letting Eadulf live. He had been shot twice in the back with arrows. This was the man's reward for his defiance.

Eadulf wondered whether he should try to fish out the broken piece of arrow from the marshwater. He presumed that it had snapped off as the man was turned over on his back and pushed into the mud. There was no sign of the second broken shaft. But why spend an arduous time searching – since it would tell him nothing in any case? Only someone like Aidan or Enda would be able to identify an arrow and know anything about individual flights.

He gave a final glance at the body. Should he push it back into the marsh? He decided against it. It seemed an improper thing to do even for the body of an enemy, especially when the man had unwittingly spared his life. Eadulf felt he had one duty to perform. He bent over the body and murmured the prayer for the dead.

'*Requiem aeternam dona eis, Domine: et lux perpetua luceat eis, Requiescant in pace.*'

Eternal rest grant unto him, O Lord, and may perpetual light shine upon him. May he rest in peace.

Feeling that he had done his duty as a religieux, Eadulf rose to his feet and gazed around. If there had been some branches handy, he would have tried to cover the body. But there were none. Accepting that there was not much else he could do, Eadulf limped on his way. He had not gone far when he heard the triumphant '*kraa, kraa, kraa*' and glancing back, he saw that the crows had once more descended to their feast.

CHAPTER TEN

As Aidan led the way out of the woodland to join the great road beyond, Fidelma felt a terrible surge of grief, her emotions overwhelmingly telling her that she must turn back into the marsh-land in search of Eadulf. She actually halted her horse and looked back, while Aidan and Enda paused too, their expressions anxious.

'We understand, lady,' Aidan said heavily. 'It is a bad country to be lost in. However, even if we had whole battalions of your brother's warriors at our disposal, we might be looking forever in those marshes and never find him. Who is to say that Eadulf is still there? Perhaps his companions have taken him elsewhere, willing or not.'

Enda felt his comrade had put things a little bluntly and so added more gently: 'At least we know that Eadulf must have been taken captive. Either his captors made a mistake and he will be released, or it might be that he stumbled onto someone who is part of this mystery.' He then realised that his interpretation of the situation was as pessimistic as Aidan's.

'Don't worry, Enda. I know what you mean.' Fidelma forced a smile of thanks at her companions' concerns. 'We know that Eadulf discovered where the wagon had been overnight before it joined Baodain's troupe. So there is a good possibility that he encountered those who had some connection with it and has been taken prisoner by them.'

But what if his captors had killed him? What if they had buried him in the fastness that was the marshland? She tried to push such negative thoughts from her mind.

'We are doing the right thing, lady,' Aidan assured her. 'Eadulf has shown us that the wagon was on the marshland, and by being captured he has also shown us a possible link to whoever poisoned the couple. It is logical that, as you have said, the wagon arrived there from the river-port of Cill Cainnech. It is therefore also logical that Eadulf might have been taken there – because that may be where this mystery started.'

She smiled gratefully at both the young men. They were doing their best to keep her spirits up.

'Besides,' Enda pointed out with sudden enthusiasm, 'friend Eadulf is not a man to be at a loss in any crisis. He has come through many worse situations, as you will recall, and I think he will give a good account of himself.'

It was so reassuring to have their companionship, Fidelma thought, and to hear their belief in her husband.

'You have persuaded me that we should make for Cill Cainnech,' she told them gravely. 'It will be a hard ride if we are to make it before nightfall.'

'The person I am most sorry for is that poor girl,' Enda remarked unexpectedly. 'How can she have allowed herself to be married to that brute of a farmer?'

'You mean the girl, Ríonach?' Indeed, Fidelma also felt sorry for the way the girl had been treated in front of them by Rechtabra. 'She does seem a poor thing – but it must be of her own choosing.'

'Her own choice?' queried Enda. 'She seems intimidated by the man! So how can it be by her own choice?'

'You know the law as well as I do,' Fidelma replied. 'The law allows for separation and divorce in unsatisfactory marriages. She could easily make a complaint to the local Brehon. If the girl is threatened by violence or, indeed, has actually received violence, then she could obtain a separation without penalty and the husband must pay costs and fines. That is clear in the *Cáin Lánamna*, the laws relating to marriage. Therefore, if she has not done so, it surely means that she is content to endure the situation.'

Enda did not accept her interpretation. 'Your forgiveness, lady, if I speak my mind? I observed animals on the farm when I was growing up and I see no difference in the behaviour of some human beings. If you place an animal in a field for a long time, and then leave the gate open, it is often so used to the field that it will remain in it rather than go wandering off to the uninviting countryside beyond.'

Fidelma admitted that the young man had a point but his companion, Aidan, chuckled. 'It is clear that you are smitten with the lass, Enda. But be warned if you pass this way again . . . she is married. And the person who entices a woman away from her marriage contract without sufficient cause is judged as a wandering thief, a fugitive from their kindred with no protection in law.'

Enda grimaced. 'Yes, "without sufficient cause". Well, I believe there *is* sufficient cause, and when this matter we are engaged in is over, I may well come back this way and investigate further.'

Aidan shook his head pityingly. 'A few moments' sight of the girl and you are ready to squander your honour price on her. I have never seen lightning strike so quickly. All I say again, is that she is married.'

Fidelma cleared her throat. 'I am afraid there are more urgent matters to attend to, and it is time we recommenced our journey. Let us leave such discussions until later.'

Eadulf had entered some woodland. He was not sorry to leave the oppressive swamp area behind and enter into the cool of the shrouded forest path. It seemed to be mostly an area of alders, some still with their winter cones, just beginning to green themselves in answer to spring. Indifferent to the alders were great twisted and venerable old yew trees with their poisonous evergreen branches. In such woodland, Eadulf hoped that there would be edible fungi. Apart from a couple of species, most of the plants that appeared so early in the year were either poisonous or inedible. However, he started to look around, now and then seeing stagnant green-covered pools, then clumps of brown plants whose strange brown prongs would soon bloom into enchanter's nightshade, and nearby, the creeping bare roots which would blossom into marsh valerian. It was still damp enough for marsh horsetail and lumps of moorgrass to form tussocks. Eadulf did not want to wander off the path, which had clearly been frequently used. But he was both thirsty and hungry and he looked from left to right for signs of the edible titbits that such woodlands provided.

Abruptly, there came the distant sound of a dog barking. It was clearly a domestic dog and not a creature of the wild nor a wolf, as a moment later came a man's faint answering voice. The sounds were coming from beyond the woodland and he almost broke into a run, stumbling along the path until he burst out into an area of dry land, with some fields containing grazing cattle and – his heart leaped as he saw it – a farmstead, with several outhouses.

He moved rapidly down the small incline to stop at the stone wall which surrounded the buildings. There was no sign of the dog now. It had ceased to bark and all was quiet.

He was about to shout to announce his presence when he heard the sound of a crack. He could not quite describe it. It reminded him of the crack of a drover's whip. There was a faint feminine cry and then a sobbing sound from somewhere in the building.

He hesitated before raising his voice. 'Is anyone there?'

Immediately, a series of short, sharp barks broke the air and a small but muscular terrier came bounding around the side of the house. Although it was small, Eadulf gripped his staff ready to protect himself, for he knew the type of woolly-haired dog which could face a full-grown adult badger, tearing into its sett and drag-ging it out in the fierce grip of its jaws. He was thankful that the wall was between them as the dog leaped up, barking and baring its fangs.

The door of the farmhouse opened and a man appeared, calling curtly to the dog to shut up. In response to his tone, the terrier drew back and actually gave a sound like a whimper, its tail going between its hind legs. The man moved a pace or two forward and grabbed the animal by its collar, almost lifting it from the ground before throwing it into the house and slamming the door. Then he turned to Eadulf and examined him for the first time.

Eadulf was aware that the farmer was staring in surprise at him. He gave the man a brief smile.

'I confess that I must not look a pleasant sight but I have been wandering through the marshland, having been assaulted and robbed. Could you tell me where I am, and then, perhaps, I could use your spring to clean up—?'

The farmer looked at him thoughtfully. 'You are in the Land of the People of the Deer, on the edge of the Great Marsh,' he replied. 'I am Rechtabra, a farmer here. You wear the tonsure of the Roman faction. It is unusual for one such as you to be wandering the marsh. That is why I am surprised.'

Eadulf nodded uncertainly. 'I cannot argue with you on that. The Land of the People of the Deer? That's Osraige, isn't it?'

'Yes. You are in the territory of Tuaim Snámh, Prince of Osraige, and this is my farmstead. What happened to you that you are in such a pitiful condition?'

'I was mistaken for someone else; knocked on the head, left for dead in some shepherd's hut in the marsh, my horse and belongings stolen. I managed to free myself but am lost.'

'Is that so?'

'It is, indeed. Are we anywhere near a church or abbey or a settlement that might give me shelter until I am able to sort matters out? There will be people looking for me, for I am husband to the sister of the King of Muman.'

The farmer's eyes narrowed but he did not seem surprised. 'Is that so?' he repeated. 'And there will be people looking for you?'

'That is so,' Eadulf assured him, echoing the farmer's expression. 'I need to alert my people of my whereabouts – the sooner the better.'

Rechtabra pointed behind the farmhouse. 'There is a stream and pool by those trees that we use for washing. It is unconnected with our well, which we conserve for drinking. I suggest that you first clean off the slime of the marsh and then come beside my hearth while my wife will fetch you food and a drink more worthy than the water from my well.'

'That would be most appreciated and I thank you for it,' Eadulf smiled. 'However, it is water that I immediately crave. I have almost forgotten what fresh water tastes like, having traversed this inhospitable place with scarcely anything to slake my thirst.'

The farmer hesitated a moment and then said: 'Go to the stream and I will bring you fresh water.' With that, he disappeared into the farmhouse. Eadulf could hear the sound of his raised voice behind the door and then, guiltily, he moved in the direction indicated. He had just reached the bank of a small gushing stream when the farmer rejoined him with a jug of water, which Eadulf drained almost in one continuous motion.

'So which way have you come to this spot, my friend?' Rechtabra asked easily when Eadulf handed him the empty jug. 'Not along that track there, surely?' He pointed to the track from which Fidelma and her companions had emerged.

Eadulf turned and pointed to the north. 'I came along a path from that direction. It was a narrow footpath through that wood over there. Whose land would that be, the land beyond those trees?'

The farmer's expression had become slightly tense. 'Beyond the patch of alder and yew trees, you mean?' When Eadulf nodded, the man said, 'The woodland is mine, but the far side is just marshland.'

'I came upon the corpse of a man by the track there,' Eadulf went on more gravely. 'He had been shot twice in the back with arrows. I think someone had pushed him into the marsh, hoping it would swallow him. But it did not. Now the crows are providing an answer to the burial. I said a prayer over him, but could do no more.'

'Is what you say true?' frowned the farmer.

'My word on it. In fact, I will go further and say that the man was one of those who held me prisoner in a shepherd's hut last night.'

Rechtabra looked astonished. 'You recognised him? How can you be sure?'

Eadulf was slightly surprised by the question. 'It is of more import that he was murdered, surely?' he countered.

'Murdered, you say?'

'Two arrows in the back scarcely constitute an accident,' Eadulf reminded him dryly. 'But now I need to wash and change my clothing. Before that, perhaps you will come and view the body with me and see if the man can be identified.'

Rechtabra's thin lips twisted into a smile. 'My friend, it seems that you have been through much. I will do my best to deal with all your concerns. Wash and refresh yourself first – I'll fetch you some dry clothing. As for this corpse, I'll take a walk across to the marsh. Perhaps I will be able to recognise the man and then I'll consider how best to alert our local Brehon.'

Eadulf's eyes widened. 'You have a Brehon here?'

'Not exactly here,' the man replied evasively. 'Proceed with your washing. I will fetch clean clothing for you.'

'I feel better already,' Eadulf assured him, turning towards the stream with its little pool and stripping off his muddied and stained clothing before plunging in. Rechtabra watched him for a moment and then went back into the farmhouse.

Eadulf was still splashing in the chilly waters of the pool, eyes closed as he cupped the water over his face, when he felt the point of cold steel dig into the small of his back.

'Don't move,' was the unnecessary command, given in the cold tones of Rechtabra's voice.

'I don't understand,' Eadulf replied, his back still to his assailant. He had been so intent on his ablutions that he had not even heard the farmer return.

'You don't have to,' Rechtabra assured him in a mocking tone. 'You have had bad luck, my foreign friend. You should have taken some other path out of the marshland rather than the one that led through my farmland. Still, your bad luck is my good luck as you might have found that other path from the marshes and started to spread your tale.'

Eadulf stood quite still, feeling the needle-point in his back. His mind was working rapidly, and now he suddenly recognised the voice of the second captor.

'Say nothing and you may live longer,' instructed the man. 'Now back slowly out of the stream towards me.'

The point dug sharply in his spine. Eadulf obeyed.

'Am I allowed to pick up my clothes?' he asked, shivering, pointing to his discarded clothing.

'You will soon have no need of them,' came the smiling retort. 'Now turn and move towards that small stone hut you see before you.'

Eadulf hesitated a fraction and again the sharp point urged him into movement. The hut was tiny; no higher than a man's shoulder level and so small that two men could barely fit into the interior. There were no windows, not even a small aperture.

'In there!' snapped the farmer. The order was accompanied by another vicious prod with the sword.

Eadulf stumbled in, crouching low, and the door slammed shut behind him. There came the sound of a wooden bar being lifted into place to secure the door. Then there was silence.

Eadulf did not know how long he had been squeezed into his tiny prison. He knew that his limbs were cramped and he was freezing cold. And then he became aware of someone approaching and tensed. He would not succumb to his captor without a fight this time, he vowed, and made ready to strike out as soon as the door opened. Then a feminine voice called softly: 'You in there, don't worry. I am going to set you free.'

He heard the wooden bar being removed and then the door swung open. Eadulf's limbs had been so cramped that he would not have been able to launch himself at his jailer in any case. He crawled in an undignified manner out of the confined space and slowly stood up, forgetting he was unclothed.

The girl who had released him was young and would have been attractive had it not been for the bruise and swollen lip which still showed flecks of blood on it. She gazed on him with an expression of anxiety, almost fear.

'You must leave quickly. He means to kill you.'

'I don't think I would get far in this condition,' he managed to grin, acknowledging his nakedness and attempting to cover himself with his hands.

The girl could not respond to his humour.

'I'll get you something of his to wear, but then you must go. I am not sure how long he will be gone. He went out beyond the woods, saying there was something he had to attend to.'

Eadulf knew exactly what it was the farmer had to attend to. The disposal of the half-drowned corpse.

'Who are you? Why are you doing this?' he asked.

'I am Ríonach. I am his wife.' She said this as if it was some shameful confession. All the while she kept looking around her as if afraid of something terrible about to emerge.

'Well, Ríonach, first things first. Clothes.'

The girl gave a sob of anguish. 'Come to the house, quickly then.'

'What happened to my own clothes?' he asked, as he followed her.

'There is a bonfire out the back. Rechtabra threw everything on it – there was a horse bag and the shepherd's staff that you carried.'

It reminded Eadulf of the piece of hemp and brass disc still tied to one wrist. The farmer had neglected to take it. For some reason he felt glad that he had been able to keep it. But the girl's eyes followed his to his wrist. Her reaction was extreme. She took two steps back from him, hand to her mouth.

'Are you one of the . . . one of the Fellowship?' She stammered.

Eadulf saw that she was trembling so much that she could barely speak and he sought to reassure her. 'I found it on a corpse beyond those trees. Do you recognise its meaning?'

She did not reply but immediately turned, still trembling, and headed to the house. As they entered, Eadulf's heart lurched as he saw the terrier bound towards them. To his amazement, the young woman spoke softly to the animal and patted its head, and it returned to a corner of the room and lay down, its tail thumping the floor.

The girl went into the next room and soon emerged with an assortment of clothing, leather boots and a leather belt. Eadulf turned away to quickly dress himself. She was almost crying as her fear was overcoming her: 'Hurry! Do hurry, he'll be back any moment!'

Eadulf glanced at her. 'You have not told me why you are helping me.'

One hand lifted to show him her swollen features. 'Is this not reason enough?' she asked bitterly.

'He beats you?' Eadulf's eyes narrowed. 'Why?'

'Because he likes it,' she hissed. 'This morning two warriors came here with a young woman. Afterwards, Rechtabra claimed that I was trying to betray him.'

'Two warriors and a young woman?' Eadulf was suddenly excited. 'Did the woman have red hair?'

'She did. The warriors wore golden circlets around their necks.

Rechtabra said that she was Fidelma of Cashel. They asked if we had seen a religieux in the marshland. Rechtabra claimed that he had not, but that was a lie.'

'How did you know?'

'Because yesterday morning I overheard him speaking with someone about the religieux that he had left on the marshes.'

Eadulf was animated with hope now. Only this morning, Fidelma with Aidan and Enda had come here in search of him.

'Where did my wife – I am husband to Fidelma of Cashel – where did the red-haired lady go with the warriors?' he asked.

'Beyond the woods there is the Slíge Dála. They were heading there. But now, please, you must leave here.' The girl was sobbing in her anxiety to get rid of him.

'I can't leave you to be beaten or worse for letting me escape,' he objected.'

'He is my husband. My father arranged the marriage because he wanted the two cows that Rechtabra promised him.'

Eadulf looked sadly at her. 'You don't have to accept this situation.'

The girl gave an anguished sigh. 'Just go, please!'

'I'll not leave you here alone to be beaten,' he said again. Then he looked down at himself. Rechtabra's clothes were not a good fit but he was able to tighten the trousers with the leather belt. At least he felt more in control now that he was clean and decently clothed.

'I can't go without having something to eat and drink,' he told Ríonach then. 'I am half-starved and feeling very weak. Look, I see a jug of cider and some bread there. Give me something to quell my hunger and thirst, and I'll go.'

The girl's shoulders slumped as she realised that Eadulf was being stubborn,

'Then you will go?' she pleaded.

'But I need some information first,' Eadulf said. 'Your husband Rechtabra . . . tell me something about him. And why are you fearful of this emblem?' He held up the brass disc and hemp bracelet on his wrist.

The girl had cut bread, produced some cold meat and poured a mug of cider for him from a jug. 'There is nothing to tell,' she said. 'Rechtabra wears it and so do his friends. Rechtabra has this small farm and that is who he is and what he does. My father used to farm further south beyond the High Hills.'

'Used to?' Eadulf caught the inflection.

'He was killed in a border raid; a cattle raid from Laigin. That was two years ago.'

'And your mother?'

Ríonach shook her head. 'She is long dead.'

'So you have no one you could go to for help?'

'No. Unless it was to old Brother Finnsnechta. He was once a friend of my mother's, but he took to a hermit's life in the hills and I have not seen him since my wedding.'

'Could he give you refuge?'

The girl sighed. 'What would an advocate of the New Faith do but tell me to return to my husband and accept God's will?'

Eadulf paused to finish the last morsel of the bread and cold meat. 'I doubt that he would say that especially if he were told the circumstances.'

'I did once attempt to escape,' the young woman confessed. 'I made it as far as the edge of the forest that borders the Slíge Dála before Rechtabra caught up with me and forced me to tell him where I was going. When I told him, he just laughed. He said that any member of the New Faith would just send me back to him. It was their . . .' she paused, trying to remember the word. 'It was their creed, he said, and that I was his property, nothing more, nothing less. To prove it, he beat me.'

'He told you a lie,' Eadulf protested. 'There are laws in this land to protect you.' He was feeling stronger and more able to confront the burly farmer.

'Now will you go?' demanded the girl.

'A few more questions. Does this farm keep horses?'

'Alas, you will not be able to escape that way. We have some cows, two pigs and an ox for the ploughing. That's all.'

'He didn't come back with any horses the other day?' Eadulf was surprised. He knew his captors had horses, so he assumed they had been kept on the farm.

'Why would he?'

Eadulf had heard his captors ride away; they had taken his little white cob with them. He could also do with his *lés*, his medical bag, which had been in his saddlebags. His skin, now cleansed, was a mass of midge bites that itched and were being rubbed raw by the coarse cloth of the farmer's clothes.

'Did this friend he was talking with yesterday have horses?'

'Not his friend, but . . .'

'But what?' asked Eadulf when she paused with a frown.

'Rechtabra was out all last night. I was awoken just before first light and thought I could hear horses near the wood. That was when I overheard him talking to someone about leaving a religieux on the marshland. The person Rechtabra was speaking to said something about disobedience and punishment, and then I did hear several horses leaving. A little while later, Rechtabra came back to the farmhouse. He took his bow and went out again shortly afterwards.'

'He took his bow?'

'He said that he would try to get a rabbit for our evening meal. Most people in these parts are good bowmen. It is often hard to subsist on the marshlands without hunting.'

Eadulf was beginning to form a picture. The two men had left him to his fate in the shepherd's hut and had ridden back here to the farmstead. Then they had met up again with the leader, their 'lord', who, learning that Eadulf was still alive, had galloped back to finish the task. The man who had disobeyed had been murdered by Rechtabra on the orders of this mysterious lord and dumped in the marsh. That was easy to deduce. But now there were other questions to which he must find the answers.

'Why are you wasting time like this?' the girl wanted to know. She was half-mad with anxiety, aware that Rechtabra could return at any moment.

Eadulf smiled gently at her. 'It is one thing to seize a man when he is unprepared and defenceless, quite another when he is prepared,' he assured her. 'And these questions are of great importance. Who is the lord of this area?'

'Coileach of the Red Hill is lord of the marshland,' she sighed, reluctant to prolong the conversation.

'Coileach, eh? The name seems appropriate.' He knew that *coileach* was the word for a cockerel. 'And the hill where he dwells – the Red Hill – is in which direction?'

'On the way towards the great river; along the road to Cill Cainnech.'

'One more thing. Did you ever see a strange-looking wagon pulled by a team of oxen and driven by a young girl – or she might have been dressed as a boy?'

She stared at him in puzzlement. 'A strange wagon . . .'

'Yes. It might have passed through here in the last week.'

'Passed through the marshland? That is silly. No wagons attempt to travel through the marshland because it leads nowhere.'

'It might be that those in the wagon wanted to hide.'

'There are easier places to hide with a wagon,' the girl asserted. 'Now in the name of all you hold dear, *please go*.'

Eadulf rose reluctantly to his feet. 'I have no wish to leave you here to be beaten by this vile brute you call a husband. You must come with me. I'll make sure I take you somewhere safe out of his reach.'

This time the girl did stamp her foot. 'It is no use, I tell you. No use! Go!'

The terrier was whining and crouching in his corner. Eadulf thought the little animal was merely being sensitive to his mistress's anguished tones. But a moment later, however, he realised just how wrong he was.

The door burst open and Rechtabra stood framed in the doorway, a wicked-looking knife glinting in his hands, his face distorted in an evil smile.

'Well, well, so the foreigner has been released, has he? I should have known you would betray me, girl.'

His wife gave a scream and, hand covering her mouth, she cowered. The terrier trotted over to her side as if to comfort her. It was obvious that he knew his master of old.

The farmer was grinning, his expression malignant.

'I said we should have killed you when we had the opportunity,' he told Eadulf, then he reared up over his wife, trembling in the corner. 'As for you, woman, if you think you have been punished for your disloyalty to me in the past, then you will think again, for you have much to look forward to, once I have dealt with this pathetic creature.' He raised his knife.

Eadulf retreated behind the table that separated them. 'I suppose your master was angry when he discovered that you and your friend had merely left me to the Fates?' he said with a forced smile. 'Angry enough for him to order you to kill your friend?'

'He betrayed us. I killed him. That is simple enough.'

'Very well. Yet why did you obey your friend when he said that he did not want to anger the gods of the Eóganacht? You could have killed him, then me – without all these subsequent problems.'

Rechtabra seemed to take the question seriously. 'I could not do it then. He had been appointed my superior in the Fellowship. I had to wait until my master told me to punish him. Then he had to die. He was stupid anyway. He was the one who mistook you for one of the people that we were told to find.'

Eadulf gave a mirthless chuckle. 'I meant to ask you about that.

Who were you looking for, and how could I have been mistaken for whoever it was? After all, I was clearly a religieux.'

'Fool!' snorted the farmer. 'The person we were looking for was also dressed as a religieux – but you were not him.'

For a moment Eadulf had a vision of the dead body in the wagon. So he had been right – the man *was* a religieux. He then registered the fact that Rechtabra was edging closer.

'Now, my foreign friend,' the man sneered, 'you have to die as it is ordained by the gods.'

'If I have to die for this lord, for this Fellowship as you call it, and for the gods that have ordained it, then perhaps you'll allow me to die knowing who has ordered my death?'

Rechtabra smirked confidently. 'All you need to know, *foreigner*, is that the old powers have returned to reclaim what is rightfully their own.'

'Does Coileach, Lord of the Marshland, believe in the old powers, then?' Eadulf said quickly, hoping for a reaction to put the man offguard.

Rechtabra blinked for a moment, as if in surprise, and then burst out laughing.

'Coileach? May the cat eat his heart and may the wolves from your Christian hell eat the cat! Coileach has departed to the Otherworld by now.'

'That seems a conclusive denial.' Eadulf tried to introduce amusement into his tone. All the while his eyes circled, searching for some weapon with which to defend himself. 'Come now, Rechtabra, you can't let me journey to the Otherworld without knowing who has sent me on the journey.'

'Enough, religieux! Prepare to meet this new God of yours.'

Eadulf was so focused on Rechtabra as the man advanced on him, his glinting knife at the ready, that he had not noticed the movement of the girl until there was a shriek and something hit the side of the farmer's head with a resounding force.

The man seemed to stand stock still for a moment, staring at Eadulf. Then the knife dropped from his nerveless fingers and fell with a clatter onto the floor. It was as if everything was happening silently and in slow motion. Rechtabra began sinking slowly to the floor. Sound came back suddenly to Eadulf and he was aware that the girl was still screaming and raining blow after blow at the farmer's head with a heavy iron object. The man lay motionless on the ground – and still she kept beating hysterically at his bloodied head.

Eadulf moved swiftly to her side and gently removed the heavy iron object from her hand. It was a long-handled cooking pan, a *scillead*. He put it, bloody as it was, on the table before making her sit on a chair. She was still sobbing and screaming. He turned back to the senseless body of the farmer and went down on one knee. In fact, there was no need to examine the man further. He looked up towards the girl.

'You have saved my life, but your husband is dead,' he said quietly. 'I'm afraid that you have killed him.'

chapter eleven

Fidelma halted her horse at the top of the rise and looked down across the broad valley of An Fheoir, the great river which rose in the north to flow south through Osraige, almost dividing it in half. Whoever had named it the 'cold river' had done so because of its cool, pure waters. From her position on top of the cliff-like hillocks, looking south-east towards the river-port, the scene looked quite sparkling and beautiful in the afternoon sunshine. The settlement was on the west bank and clustered around the Abbey of Cainnech which was situated on a hill dominating the township.

The abbey buildings stood imposing, and consisting of a large complex facing towards the river. The western side of the hill was clearly the back of the abbey for there were very few buildings there or on the plain extending from the bottom of the hill. In fact, there was only one group of buildings behind the abbey, which appeared to be a smith's forge. While the forge could be reached by a side track off the main highway, it seemed a curious, isolated place to build a smithy. All the other buildings of the township were placed in front of the abbey, stretching down to the river.

It was some time since Fidelma had been though this settlement and she was surprised at the amount of new building since her last visit, especially within the abbey complex. Her memories of the river-port were of modest wooden buildings set around a rough-hewn local red sandstone church. Now the buildings atop the hill were more extensive, and an impressive mixture of sandstone, with light-coloured dolomite rocks set into the outer walls. They were almost like the walls of a fortress. Some of the buildings along the banks of the river were also solid constructions of locally quarried stones, giving the impression of a place that had developed of substantial a wealth.

Indeed, as confirmation of this, Fidelma could see wooden quays alongside which several barges were loading and unloading amid placidly swimming ducks and even stately gliding swans. It was clear the river was teaming with human activity as well as wildlife.

'It's quite a township now,' said Aidan, articulating her thoughts.

'It could well be that the strange wagon arrived here from upriver or . . . look!' Fidelma pointed to where a ferry was crossing from the far bank with a wagon on it. 'She could have come across that way through Laigin, just as Baodain said his wagons had done so.'

'We can make some enquiries along the quays,' Enda suggested. 'Someone might recall having seen the wagon. It is so distinctive.'

'But we should also find somewhere to eat and arrange accommodation, for there is not much daylight left,' Fidelma cautioned.

'There should be a place near the quays,' Enda said. 'They would provide for passing merchants there.'

Fidelma continued to examine the new buildings with interest. 'It's almost as if this is being built to become the premier seat of the Prince of Osraige,' she commented.

'Except I have heard that Tuaim Snámh has now set his capital in the Sliadh Bladhma, the Northern Mountains, where Ciaran founded his hermitage,' Aidan pointed out.

'Perhaps he has changed his mind?'

'I don't think so, lady,' replied the warrior. 'Tuaim Snámh is a very superstitious man.'

Fidelma frowned. 'I fail to see the connection.'

'The stories go that the hill on which the abbey now stands was a great centre of the Old Faith; it is where the last Druidic priests of the Five Kingdoms retreated when the New Faith gained ascendancy over them. It became the dwelling place of the last Chief Druid of the Five Kingdoms.'

'I didn't know that.' Fidelma was intrigued.

'I heard the stories from my uncle's wife. She came from the vicinity of this settlement many years ago and was of the clan of Máil.'

'What reason would the Prince of Osraige have to avoid this place as a capital?' asked Fidelma. 'The Old Religion was once found everywhere in these kingdoms. It is scarcely more than two centuries since the High King Laoghaire accepted the New Faith, and other kings and princes followed his example. It has taken time to replace the Old Faith, but there are no ancient sites that people shun because of it. There are even some places in the west where you will find people who have still not accepted the New Faith, and other places where the two faiths exist side by side.'

'You are right, lady. But as I said, it was that hill that the Chief Druid of the Five Kingdoms made his last bastion, surrounded by his followers. That was when Cainnech came here to convert the people to the New Faith. Cainnech's method was to arrive with an army and slaughter all the Druids and their followers. He then declared the place Christian and built a church on the very hill where the last Chief Druid and his followers were murdered in their sanctuary.'

Fidelma was surprised by the story for she had always been taught that the change to the New Faith had been a relatively peaceful transition.

'This Cainnech sounds more like an intolerant warrior than a saintly man,' she remarked.

'He was of the Corco Dálainn, raised on a little island off Port Lairge,' Enda replied. 'I know he studied at Cluain Ard, went to one of the kingdoms of the Britons and then to Rome, and even to Iona before returning here. So if travelling is learning, then he was a man of much learning.'

'When did all this happen?' Fidelma was appalled. 'When was this slaughter of the people of the Old Faith?'

'Little more than seventy years ago,' Enda replied after a moment of thought. 'The picturesque settlement you see before you was once awash with blood and consumed by fire.'

'Only seventy years ago? I thought we prided ourselves that our kingdoms had accepted the New Faith without forcing it on the people by fire and sword,' Fidelma muttered. 'This is a very sad history.'

'Well, it is the only instance that I know of such a slaughter,' Enda replied. 'Now it seems almost forgotten and Cainnech's reputation appears to have been restored. His main foundation is in the north of Osraige, at the Field of the Ox. I don't think you'll find many people around here who have cause to remember him fondly nor the slaughter that he brought here.'

'That is not our concern anyway,' Fidelma said firmly. 'We are investigating a more modern slaughter. We must see if we can find some trace of the movement through here of the strange wagon.'

She nudged the flanks of Aonbharr and the stallion ambled carefully down the hill towards the settlement by the river bank, closely followed by Aidan and Enda.

The late-afternoon sunshine dappled the hills which soon gave way to fenland to the north and to cultivated fields to the south. They moved through pink meadowland, the colour made by the finger-long, delicate pink petals of flowers which had just started to blossom in abundance. Fidelma had always thought they were very pretty, but local tradition said that it was bad luck to pick them and especially to take them into the house. They were called *lus sioda* and she found herself wondering what Eadulf would call them. He had taught her much of his language and the names of many plants and animals.

In spite of her outward control, Fidelma was desperate about him. Where was he? Had he been badly injured at the deserted farm? Was he still a prisoner? Why had he been made captive – and by whom? Had he escaped? Was he wandering the marshlands? Above all, was he safe?

At that moment, Aidan went to say something to her and then turned away in embarrassment.

'What's wrong?' she snapped.

He coughed awkwardly. 'Lady, your eyes are watering.'

She put a hand to her eyes. Tears were running down her cheeks.

'Something must have flown into my eye,' she explained tersely.

Aidan was too wise to make a further comment. She had been crying silently without even knowing it.

It seemed to Eadulf that a lot had happened in a comparatively short space of time. His first concern, after he had seen that Rechtabra was beyond all human aid, was to calm the hysterical girl, and in this he was helped by the little terrier who came to her side, snuffling and licking at her hand. It was clear that the dog had been fearful of the farmer and somehow realised that his mistress had sought to protect them both. Eadulf had found some *corma*, the distilled barley drink, and made Ríonach swallow several mouthfuls. This seemed to calm her a little.

Eadulf led her, with the little terrier at his heels, into the adjoining room, which was a bedroom, and told her to lie down and rest for a while.

'You will not leave me alone?' she begged.

He was reassuring. 'No. I have a few things to do, that's all. I'll just be outside, and I won't be long.'

The task he turned himself to was to remove the battered corpse

171

of the farmer from the room. As he knelt beside the man, the first thing he noticed was that, around the man's left wrist was the same piece of hemp from which dangled a small shiny disc that had the familiar bird image on it – a raven. Carefully he untied it and put it on the table before he made a search of the man's clothing. Then, heaving Rechtabra into a sitting position on the floor, he knelt behind him, put his arms under the man's armpits, crossing them and grasping his hands across the chest, then pulled himself upright. Walking backwards in this fashion, he dragged the dead farmer through the door and out of the house. There was only one thing he could think of doing with the body for the time being. He heaved it along the path to the tiny stone shed where he himself had briefly been imprisoned. Panting, he pushed the body inside and secured the door.

Returning to the house, he saw spattered all over blood the wooden boards of the floor and up one of the table legs. Taking a jug of water, he washed the gore away. When he'd finished, he stood in the main room of the farmhouse and peered about to check that all was once more in order. His eyes fell on Rechtabra's bracelet. It was the same mysterious brass disc and raven emblem that the poisoned girl in the wagon had worn; the same as his captive had worn when killed in the marsh. The symbol meant something which had caused Ríonach to tremble in fear.

Time was passing quickly and he could not afford to wait long before moving on. He was about to see if the girl was all right when the bedroom door opened and she emerged, red-eyed but now calmer. The little terrier was still at her heels. She glanced quickly around, as if looking for the body of her husband and then sighed.

'I wasn't sure if you had gone,' she said.

'I promised that I would be here,' Eadulf replied with an encouraging smile.

He crossed to the cupboard and poured another drink of *corma*, for them both this time because he felt the need of a stimulant.

'Are you feeling more able to deal with things?' he asked gently.

She nodded as she sat down at the table. 'What will happen to me?' she asked in a helpless voice.

'Happen?'

'I killed Rechtabra.'

'You did it to save my life. Indeed, from what I heard of his threat he was going to turn on you, so you did it in self-defence. Tell me, does Rechtabra have any kin locally?'

She shook her head. 'His family were wiped out during the Yellow Plague some years ago.'

'And your own family?'

'I told you that I have none now.'

'Then this would be your farm now?'

'I am not even sure that Rechtabra owned this farm. He paid tribute to the Lord of the Marshes. Anyway, I wouldn't want to stay here after . . . after . . .' she ended brokenly, close to losing her composure.

'But there must be someone you can go to for help?'

'I told you before that there is no one.'

'Tell me about this Lord of the Marshes. Is his name Coileach of the Red Hill?'

'Yes, it is.'

'Rechtabra did not seem to have a very high opinion of him. He said he was dead.'

'I've heard him curse him many times,' replied the girl. 'There is a rumour that he is dead.'

'So who is this "lord" that your husband worked for? The one for whom he and his friend captured and tried to kill me?'

'I am not sure. He was always boasting of some great lord who would protect him.'

Eadulf held out his wrist with the brass disc on it. 'When you saw this, you started to tremble with fear. Your husband wore a similar wristband. I picked this one up from the dead body of your husband's companion. You need not fear it now. I just want to know what it signifies.'

Ríonach hesitated, then seemed to summon courage from somewhere. 'It is the symbol of the *Coitreb na Bhran*.'

Eadulf paused for a moment, translating it into his own language. 'The Fellowship of the Raven: what is that?'

'I do not know exactly, except that they frighten me. Rechtabra knew several men who belong to it. They recognise one another by that symbol. There is one man in particular who sometimes came here; he sometimes did work on the farm.'

'What sort of man was he?'

'His voice was whining, almost like a child. I did not trust him.'

Eadulf gave a quick description of the man that he had found in the bog.

'I cannot be sure. I was never told his name but he came from the west.'

'What did he do?'

'Most of the time he was working on local farms, hiring himself out as a day labourer. When he worked here, Rechtabra told me not to leave the house. Occasionally, he also came at night. I know this because I heard his voice but did not see him. Rechtabra would disappear with him. I know nothing except that they both wore that disc, for I saw him once. When Rechtabra was in his cups he talked of this lord who was their master.' The word she used was *coimdiu* and Eadulf knew it was usually reserved for a religious context rather than one like *muiredach*, which meant a lord or master in terms of proprietorship or rank.

'Did he use that exact word?' Eadulf pressed, interested.

The girl confirmed it with a quick movement of her head.

Eadulf was thoughtful. 'Was your husband concerned with any religious group, then?'

'I would have said that religion was the last thing he cared about,' she replied flatly.

'But this *Coitreb na Bhran* . . .'

'I thought it was some hunting fraternity because his friends always came at night. They would all leave and stay out until daybreak. Rechtabra never returned with game, so I do not know what they hunted.'

'I don't suppose that you ever asked Rechtabra where they went during the night.'

The girl gave a shaky snort of derision. 'Not if I valued my life,' she said. 'I was not allowed to even mention it.'

Eadulf sat silently for a while deep in thought. He had been mistaken for someone else, obviously the dead religieux in the wagon. He had been captured by Rechtabra and his companion, who were both working for some mysterious 'lord', or as the girl now indicated 'a religious lord'. What could be the purpose of this Fellowship of the Raven? Why was the same symbol borne on the wrist of the dead girl of the mysterious wagon?

At the behest of this mysterious 'lord', Rechtabra had been ordered to slaughter his companion and bury him in the marsh, simply because he had failed to carry out this 'lord's' instruction to kill Eadulf. And Rechtabra would also have killed him, had it not been for this brave girl, Ríonach. Those were the facts – but what did they mean when put together? Eadulf had no idea.

'What do you intend to do?' The girl's anxious voice penetrated his thoughts.

Eadulf glanced across at her with a smile of encouragement. 'Well, one thing is certain; you cannot be left here on your own.'

She sniffed. 'Neither can I leave. There are the cows and the pigs and some poultry to be attended to.'

Eadulf groaned inwardly. He had forgotten that, apart from anything else, this was still a working farm.

'Are there no neighbours near you?'

'No one that is trustworthy,' replied the girl with a shudder. She gave no other explanation and Eadulf did not ask her for one. He suspected that he knew what the girl meant.

'Is there no local Brehon?' he tried. 'You husband said that there was, when he was pretending to be helpful to me.'

'Coileach, the Lord of the Marshes, no doubt had a Brehon serving him. I suppose there must be a Brehon at Cill Cainnech.'

Another thought came to Eadulf. 'You mentioned a hermit who had been a friend of your mother.'

'Brother Finnsnechta?'

'You said that he had become a hermit in the hills.'

The girl nodded. 'He lives among the trees on the lower slopes of the Mountains of the High Fields.'

'Is that far?'

'It is nearly a day's walk or more from here on the way south.'

'Do you trust him?'

'I told you before – Rechtabra said that he, being of the New Faith, would surely send me back to him.' She paused and swallowed, remembering that much had happened since then. She no longer had a husband to be sent back to.

'It's a long way to travel and leave these farm animals unattended,' Eadulf reflected.

The girl had a further thought. 'There is a shepherd and his family who live nearby, and they never had much to do with Rechtabra. That shepherd and his sons might be persuaded to look after the livestock. But I do not want to remain alone here.'

'I have given you my word that I shall not leave you,' Eadulf promised her. The day was darkening. They would have to remain at the farmstead that night.

Just then, the mournful lowing of a cow came from the distance, and Ríonach looked up, startled. 'The cows haven't been milked today,' she remembered guiltily. 'With everything that has been happening, I have neglected the milking.'

The sound galvanised Eadulf into action. He stood up. 'Then you had better attend to that, while I feed your pigs and the poultry. It will be dusk soon.'

The girl glanced round anxiously. 'Where . . . where is . . . ?'

'Don't open the door of the little stone hut from which you rescued me,' he replied, knowing what question was in her mind. She answered with a nod and took a wooden bucket from a corner of the kitchen. She still appeared hesitant.

'You won't . . . you won't . . .' she stumbled, and he gave her a kindly smile.

'I said that I shall not leave without you,' he assured her gently. 'You have my word.'

She looked at him anxiously for a moment before accepting his vow. Then she opened the door and moved off in the direction of the lowing cow, with the little terrier trotting at her heels, wagging its tail.

Eadulf watched her go and then he raised both arms and let them fall to his side in an expression of mock hopelessness. There was no way they could abandon the livestock for the time it would take to walk to find this Brother Finnsnechta – and even if they found him immediately – after that, what then? He needed to find someone to take care of the farmstead. He hoped the girl was right about the shepherd and his sons. Eadulf knew that conditions would deteriorate quickly unless the livestock were regularly attended to. A curse formed in his throat – until he remembered that he was supposed to be a religieux.

He went out around the farmstead and checked a fenced area where two pigs seemed to be snuffling contentedly at a pile of rotting apples. He made sure there was enough to hand. The distribution of grain for the chickens was also a simple matter. He then decided to look around the farmstead before the light faded entirely. It was a long time since he had done any work on a farm, not since he had helped on his father's farm along the banks of the Fromus, the river that passed Seaxmund's Ham in the Land of the South Folk where he and Egric . . . He caught himself, remembering his brother, and clenched his teeth. Egric was dead. He was alive and had to get on with resolving how he was going to stay alive.

He had to find Fidelma and his companions. That was his first priority. If he could not do that, he must obtain a horse and make for Cashel to seek help from Colgú, although, he did not particularly look forward to facing Fidelma's brother with such bad news.

There seemed no other livestock except for the cows. It was mostly grain crops that Rechtabra had raised on the fields that ran to the east of his farmstead on the slightly higher ground that bordered the marshlands. Having contented himself that he had not overlooked anything that needed attention, Eadulf was returning to the house when he saw the girl approaching from the stream. She was bearing a half-empty bucket and carrying something in a fold of her skirt. The little terrier ambled happily at her heels.

'I put some of the milk in a stone jug and then placed it in the stream to keep it cool,' she told him. 'Also, I've found some fungi. We can have a proper meal.' She showed him a little pile in the fold of her skirt.

'Are you sure they are edible?' he asked anxiously. 'It is surely too early in the year.'

She actually laughed. 'There's beech trees the other side of the stream and I found several oyster mushrooms growing there. Don't worry, they are quite good at this time. I've had them before.'

They turned back to the house as the day was getting chilly.

'We'll have a meal and sort out what best we can do,' Eadulf announced, as he bent to stir the grey ashes of the fire into bright sparks and added some twigs to provide kindling before placing the first log.

'Will I be punished?' Ríonach asked suddenly, her face serious.

'Punished?' Eadulf frowned. Then he realised what she meant. 'Why, no. I am a stranger to your land, but the one thing I have learned in the years I have been here is something about your law. You acted not only in self-defence but in my defence. I will explain everything. My wife is a *dálaigh* and not without some influence.'

'Fidelma of Cashel is very powerful, isn't she?' the girl asked wistfully.

Eadulf chuckled. 'Influential,' he corrected. 'I would not have used the word "powerful" but I am sure, if need be, she will support you. But I do not think it will come to that, once the story is told.'

With a fire blazing, the girl set to work with two hares that Rechtabra had apparently caught on the previous day and stored for use. It was dark, and with the lantern lit, Ríonach set on the table a meal which Eadulf had not seen since he had left Cashel. And there was the cold cider to wash it down. The terrier was left with much of the second hare to gorge on. It seemed a changed animal, no longer nervous and snappish but of even temper.

Suddenly, it occurred to Eadulf that he had never heard the dog called by name and he asked if it had one.

Ríonach said sadly, 'Only I called it by its name. Rechtabra didn't not believe in names for animals. I called it "little king".'

'Rían?' echoed Eadulf.

The terrier looked up at him from its meal and gave a little whine and a thump of its tail. The girl left the table and went across to pat its head. She turned to glance at Eadulf.

'He still knows his name,' she said. 'This little fellow has kept me sane during the dark days. I will not part with him now.'

'No reason why you should,' Eadulf replied. It brought him back to the immediate problem. 'We will have to set off at first light. We must visit the shepherd and ask if he will tend to your livestock, then we will find this hermit where you will be safe.'

Ríonach looked concerned. 'I am coming with you, aren't I?' she said.

'Of course, but only as far as this Brother Finnsnechta's hermitage. I still have to find my wife and my companions. Brother Finnsnechta should be able to look after you, and find a local Brehon who will sort out this problem. You should know your position in law as regards this farmstead. You don't simply want to abandon it – for how else will you live?'

The girl shook her head firmly. 'When we leave here, I hope never to see it again.'

'But,' Eadulf protested, 'you will need some security for the future.'

'I want to come with you.'

'I have to find my wife and companions,' he insisted. 'We were on a commission from the King when I was separated from them and captured by your husband and his companion. I believe it has something to do with this Fellowship of the Raven; of that, I am now certain.'

'Then let me come with you and help.'

Eadulf gave an inward shrug. 'We have a duty to the livestock here and that must be your first priority.'

The girl pouted and tears began to well in her eyes. 'I do not want to live here ever again.'

Eadulf was silent. Then he gave in as she continued to weep, and said: 'I'll tell you what I shall do, Ríonach. I'll promise you that I shall use my influence to find you somewhere in Cashel, something to do there. Why, maybe with such skill as you showed in preparing this meal, you can get work in Colgú's palace.'

She looked hopefully at him. 'You promise? You won't abandon me?'

'I promise,' he said.

Looking much happier, Ríonach began to clear the table.

Eadulf came awake in the darkness. He felt the warm body of the girl pressing against him and was about to react when a soft hand covered his mouth. He felt her lips against his ear.

'Be quiet!' she whispered. 'There's movement outside. Horses.'

He heard the terrier growling softly in a corner of the room and saw the dark shadow of the girl turn and move to the animal to try to quiet it.

Then there was an abrupt banging on the door and a stentorian voice bawled: 'Awake, the house! Rechtabra! Your lord and the Fellowship summon you!'

CHAPTER TWELVE

About the same time that Eadulf was taking the body of Rechtabra to deposit in the stone hut, Fidelma was halting her companions on a deserted stretch of the road just outside the river-port of Cill Cainnech.

'As we are in Osraige,' she said, 'it might be best to remove our symbols of rank and office.'

'Why so, lady?' demanded Aidan. 'Does not the Prince of Osraige pay tribute to Cashel?'

'We might receive more cooperation when we ask questions,' explained Fidelma, conscious of the need for diplomacy.

Aidan and Enda reluctantly removed their golden torcs, the symbols of the Nasc Niadh, the élite Bodyguard to the King of Muman.

'Our presence ought to be greeted with respect,' Enda muttered, irritably.

'So it should,' Fidelma consoled him, removing her own emblem. 'However, reality is sometimes not what it should be. Our purpose is to obtain information and we must consider the best way to succeed in getting it. There is no need to remind you that there has been much hostility in Osraige towards Cashel.'

'At least we should not conceal that we are warriors, surely?' asked Aidan.

She was amused at his words. 'There is no way of concealing

that with you two,' she replied mischievously. 'The only thing I ask is that we should not be too overt about our roles and rank. Often people without rank respond better when they are not confronted by authority. We should be discreet.'

So they had hidden their emblems in their saddlebags and continued down the gently sloping hill into the township.

'So where do we start, lady?' Enda wanted to know.

'We'll start by finding food and shelter for the night as it will be dusk soon,' she answered.

Along the banks of the broad river, An Fheoir, there were a number of wooden quays where boats loaded and unloaded goods. Alongside these stood a line of wagons, ready to deliver goods or transport them to various destinations. Of the two vessels presently at the quays, one surprised Fidelma, for it was a large *ler-longa*, a seagoing ship which could only navigate the river as far as this point. Most seagoing vessels anchored at the southern exit of the river, where it joined the rivers Siur and Barú in the deeper waters around Port Láirge. Such ships usually unloaded there so the goods could be transferred to smaller vessels. It seemed the captain of this ship had chanced the journey up to Cill Cainnech. The other vessel was one of the *serrcinu*, a barge which was taking on cargo, while a smaller river vessel sailed by. Fidelma knew something about the vessels, having studied the *Muir-Brethe*, the 'sea laws', for all matters pertaining to water travel were dealt with by the law.

What had astonished her, as she rode towards the river, was the sight of a newly built ferry landing linking the east and west banks of the river. She examined it for a moment and then made a decision. There was daylight enough to ask a few questions.

'Aidan, you go along the quays and look for a suitable place where we can stay and eat. I'll take Enda and make enquiries at the ferry quay in case the girl's wagon used the ferry to cross from the highway on the far side.'

With this agreed, Fidelma and Enda rode down to the quayside.

It was not busy at that moment. There were a few people, obviously locals, standing around. One man was leaning on the wooden rails. He looked like a warrior, bearing sword and shield, and seemed to be gazing across the river, where Fidelma could see a squat river boat. He straightened up as Fidelma and Enda drew rein, and when Fidelma dismounted and walked over to speak with him, it seemed from his stance that he did not need any emblems to know that she was of the nobility.

'Give you a good day, lady,' the man greeted her respectfully. He was a fellow of average build with fair hair and inquisitive blue eyes. 'If it's the ferry you want, the last trip of the day has left and it won't be back this side tonight. You will have to wait until morning.'

She returned his greeting with a quick smile. 'I am hopeful that you can help me with some information.'

'It depends what the information is that you seek,' the man said guardedly.

'I wish to know about a foreign-looking wagon that might have crossed on this ferry about a week or so ago.' She gave him a quick description.

The warrior examined her suspiciously, and looked up at Enda, still sitting on his horse.

'Why would you be interested in that?' he countered.

Fidelma could have answered by revealing her rank as a *dálaigh*, but she felt it wiser to reason with the man.

'I presume it is the only ferry that crosses the river to join the highway?'

'It is, lady. The ferry has been set up through the good grace of Abbot Saran and the Prince of Osraige.'

'As I said, I need to find out whether this wagon arrived here within the last week or two. If there is normally someone, such as you, in attendance here then I thought you might have noticed it. It was drawn by oxen – a distinctive, foreign-looking wagon with a curved roof.'

The warrior looked uneasy: it was clear that he recognised her description. 'You did not tell me why you want to know about that wagon.'

She took a chance. 'The wagon was expected in Cashel some time ago and has not turned up yet.'

'Why were you expecting this wagon in Cashel?' the man asked.

Enda had sat patiently and silent during the exchange and now he became irritated at the man's intractable attitude.

'Surely that is a matter for us?' he called from his horse. 'We only wish to know if the wagon has crossed here or arrived here.'

Before either Fidelma or Enda had realised what the man was doing, he had a horn in his hand and had blown three shrill blasts.

Almost immediately, two archers appeared from behind a nearby building, their bows tightly drawn and the arrows pointing their way.

'What does this mean?' Fidelma demanded, surprised by the rapid change in the situation.

'It means that you are in Osraige, lady,' replied the man they had been questioning. 'We do not allow suspicious strangers to wander freely here.'

Another warrior came hurrying up. He was tall, an athletically built young man with dark brown hair, handsome features and glinting hazel eyes. Fidelma judged him to be in his twenties. He was clearly someone of birth and rank, for the guard raised his hand in salute.

'Strangers,' he explained briskly. 'They claim to be from Cashel looking for the foreign wagon.'

'This is a public highway,' Enda protested, a wary eye on the bowmen. They appeared professional enough and the arrows were perfectly aligned. 'We have a right to ask questions.'

'The highway is public,' replied the newcomer coolly. 'Questions are not.'

'We were merely asking whether a particular wagon had crossed the river or arrived here recently, as we were concerned about it. It was on its way to Cashel,' Fidelma explained, attempting reason.

'The particular wagon was the foreign-looking one, drawn by a team of oxen and driven by the man and girl,' the guard added.

'Is that so? And you were expecting it in Cashel, were you?' The man, who was clearly the commander of the warriors, scrutinised Fidelma carefully.

'I don't know why this should be of interest to you,' Fidelma said.

'For the time being, that is for us to know and for you to answer my questions,' the man replied. 'Who are you? And why are you enquiring about this wagon?' He suddenly whirled round towards Enda. 'I would remove your hand from your sword hilt, warrior. My bowmen are of a nervous disposition and any threats might cause them to lose their hold on their arrows.'

Enda had sense enough to know when he was not being bluffed. He removed his hand from his weapon.

'Now dismount, and make no attempt to drop your hands near your weapons just in case my men misunderstand your intention.'

With a sigh, Enda did as he was told. 'To whom am I making my surrender?' he demanded, as one of the warriors came forward to take his weapons.

The young man smiled thinly. 'For the moment, I am the *cenn-feadh* of the guard of this town in the service of the Abbot, who also speaks for the Prince of Osraige.'

The rank indicated that he was the commander of one hundred warriors.

'Now,' he turned back to Fidelma, 'you were about to tell me who you are and why were you expecting that wagon in Cashel?'

Fidelma shrugged. 'It is a long story. In the meantime, let me inform you that I am Fidelma of Cashel, sister to Colgú, King of Muman. You should also know that I am a *dálaigh* and I have a right to ask questions. My companion is of the King's Bodyguard.'

A flicker of surprise showed momentarily in the eyes of the commander of the warriors. 'In Osraige, lady, we tend to do things according to our own lights. Here, we do not accept what people tell us just because they wear fine clothes and speak in a haughty manner. And if your companion is of the Nasc Niadh, then I would expect him to be trained to a better standard than he has shown, allowing you to be surrounded by hostile warriors.'

Enda made an inarticulate sound which did not express happiness.

Fidelma eyed the young man coldly. 'In Osraige, where the Prince Tuaim Snámh has sworn fealty to my brother, the King of Cashel, we did not expect to find hostile warriors,' she replied distantly.

'Well said, lady,' replied the man, grinning. 'These are strange times and there is much danger lurking in the most unlikely places. So we must be vigilant and not accept a person's word without proof. Oh, and I presume that it is another of your bodyguards who was wandering the quayside taverns also looking for information concerning this foreign wagon you have asked about?'

Fidelma caught her breath and Enda swore.

Once more their captor chuckled. 'He claims his name is Aidan and he purports to be temporary commander of the King of Muman's Bodyguard. I am wondering how temporary his command will be? Warriors should have brains, as well as brawn.'

'He has not been harmed?' Fidelma demanded anxiously.

'Why would we harm a man wandering along the quayside and asking questions?'

'Why would you object to such questions being asked, anyway?' Fidelma replied.

'As I say, for the moment, it is our business. However, now you must come with me. I will provide some accommodation for you and your companions and, I trust, it will only be temporary until I have made further arrangements.'

The warriors hemmed them in and one of them took charge of

their horses and their weapons. Led by their commander, they walked through the township, along streets where people paused in their business to regard them with curiosity. In the centre of the town was a strong wooden building which Fidelma quickly recognised as the *Laochtech* or warrior's barracks. Once inside, a warrior came forward and ran his hands over their limbs in a quick professional search for any weapon they might have hidden.

Without a further word, they were taken directly to another solid wooden door to one side of the building. The tiny aperture in the centre seemed to serve as ventilation rather than light. The door itself was securely fastened, both with a lock and a wooden bar. One of the warriors removed the bar and turned the key in the lock.

'Inside!' instructed their captor.

Reluctantly, they allowed themselves to be pushed into the darkness. The door was slammed shut and bolted behind them.

A figure emerged from the gloom of a corner. 'I am sorry, lady,' came Aidan's miserable tones. 'I was captured before I knew it. I had no warning.'

'Don't blame yourself,' Fidelma replied resignedly. 'We were taken in the same manner. But the question now is – why? Why this hostility as soon as we mentioned the girl's wagon?'

The banging on the farmhouse door thundered again.

'How many are there?' whispered Eadulf, as he drew on his clothes.

'I heard horses and looked out of the window. I saw only two riders entering the yard,' replied the girl in the same hushed tone.

'Did they see you?'

'No.'

'Wake up, Rechtabra!' cried the harsh voice from outside. 'We have work to do.'

Eadulf thought for a moment. His only course was to respond. He murmured: 'Give me a moment to get behind the door and then open it, stand to one side and be ready.'

'Ready for what?' Ríonach's tone was puzzled.

'Anything,' Eadulf muttered, moving swiftly and gathering Rechtabra's knife with one hand and a heavy blackthorn stick that he had found the previous night. He positioned himself behind the door in the darkness.

'What's keeping you?' shouted the impatient voice from outside.

'Open it!' breathed Eadulf.

The girl bent towards the bolts at the same time, rattling them open and calling out sleepily: 'Patience! I haven't lit the lamp as yet.' She then pulled the door open, yawning and standing to one side as if to invite the man in.

'Where's your husband?' demanded the man who had been knocking, but without entering.

Ríonach jerked her head to the adjoining room. 'Dead to the world. He likes his *corma* too much.' Even in this position Eadulf felt amused that the girl could lie so convincingly. 'Perhaps you would do better than I can in rousing him?'

'Damnation to the man,' muttered the fellow and stepped inside. Eadulf came forward, the movement of his body closing the door a little and thus obscuring the scene from the man's companion who was apparently still sitting on his horse awaiting his comrade. Eadulf's left hand moved the sharp pointed knife into the man's back.

'Not a word!' he hissed.

The stranger stood still; the only sound he made was a long exhalation of breath. Eadulf quietly told him to move to one side, away from the door. 'Now call to your companion to come inside and help you rouse Rechtabra. No tricks, or you are a dead man.'

There was no hesitation. 'Duach!' called the man. 'Come here and help me rouse this drunken sot!'

Eadulf waited, hearing the voice of another man grumbling and the creak of leather as he dismounted from his horse. Then he swung his right hand back and brought the wooden cudgel down hard on the first man's head. The fellow sank to the floor without a sound. Again Eadulf stepped back behind the door as the second man entered.

'It's dark in here. Where is—?' the man began, but before he had finished, the blackthorn stick had rendered him as unconscious as his companion.

Immediately, Eadulf sprang into action. 'Check to see if they were alone,' he said tersely to the girl. Then: 'Have you some rope?'

'I'll need to light the lantern first. It's in one of the cupboards.'

'I'll do it. Make sure there is no one else about, and secure the horses.'

Eadulf knew the oil lamp had been left on the table. In the remains of the fire he found what he was looking for – a half-burned stick – lifted it carefully from the ashes and blew on the end. To his relief the grey turned into a red glow. He took it to the lamp and pressed the stick against the wick, blowing gently upon it. In a moment the lamp had ignited. He glanced at the two unconscious men then went to the cupboards. There were several lengths of fine hemp rope in the bottom of one of them.

By this time the girl had returned.

'There is no one else about,' she reported. 'There were three horses but no other rider. I have hitched the horses to the rail.'

Eadulf looked worried, but the girl told him, 'I think they brought the extra horse for Rechtabra as we do not possess one. There were no saddlebags or equipment on it and I did not see a third rider arriving anyway.'

Reassured, Eadulf said: 'Then bring the lamp while I secure these two.'

He quickly removed the first man's leather belt and the weapons he carried – a dagger and short sword. He then rolled the man on his front and secured his hands behind him, making sure the wrists were tightly bound. He noticed that each man wore the familiar plaited bracelet around their left wrists. He removed them and put them on the table, joking to the girl: 'It seems I am making a collection of these emblems of the Fellowship of the Raven.'

Only when the wrists of both men were bound did he secure their feet. That task accomplished, he examined their weapons and deposited them on the table before returning and making a thorough search of each man.

Ríonach gazed fearfully at the unconscious men. 'What are we going to do with them?'

'You are going to light another lamp, so that I can see them when I talk to them. Is that bucket filled with water from the well?'

When she nodded and bent to the task of lighting the other lamp to provide more illumination, Eadulf picked up the bucket and tossed it over the upturned faces of the two men. They began to groan and splutter, and finally came to consciousness. Their first actions were to struggle against their bonds and curse. They seemed to have a good knowledge of curses and Eadulf finally intervened.

'You will find it as useless to blaspheme as it is for you to struggle,' he assured them jauntily. 'I was taught to tie knots by experts.'

They stopped, suddenly realising they were not alone in the room. The first man, a dark swarthy fellow, stared at him with narrowed eyes.

'Who are you?' he demanded.

'I think etiquette would dictate that you identify yourselves first,' he replied easily.

'Go to the devil!' growled the man.

Eadulf turned to Ríonach. 'Do you recognise either of them?'

The girl was hesitant. 'I have seen him talking with Rechtabra,' she said, pointing to the first man. 'I am not sure about the other.'

'They're not local men?' pressed Eadulf.

'I am not sure,' she repeated.

'So, Duach . . .' The man Eadulf addressed by name started, not realising that Eadulf had simply picked up the name from when his companion had called out to him. 'Tell me how you know Rechtabra.'

'Say nothing!' instructed the first man.

'But he knows our names, Cellaig. How—?'

'Shut up, you fool!'

Eadulf chuckled. 'Now, now, those of the Fellowship of the Raven should not fall out.'

The man called Cellaig could not hide his astonishment while his companion simply groaned.

'It seems there is a code of silence among the Fellowship of the Raven,' Eadulf went on, trying to encourage them to speak. 'However, it is not worth maintaining silence if Rechtabra has already confessed.'

'We don't know him,' asserted Cellaig, trying to recover the situation. 'What he says is his affair.'

'Oh? You come to his door in the middle of the night, and call on him by name. We know he was a member of your Fellowship. You said that your lord had a job for you all to do. What job?'

'Ask Rechtabra,' replied the man angrily. 'He seems to have told you most things.'

'Most things? Alas, not everything,' Eadulf mused. 'Sadly he is now dead to the world.'

'Drunk!' spat the man. 'So he betrayed the Fellowship in his cups!'

'I think you were meant to take that literally,' Eadulf said, hoping his voice sounded cold and threatening. 'He is, indeed, dead – to this world anyway.'

They stared at him uncertainly, and an expression of fear crossed the face of Duach. Eadulf could tell that he was the more malleable of the two. Still hoping that he appeared to be absolutely merciless, Eadulf reached over to the table, took up one of the short swords that he had removed from them and started to make a display of testing the point with the tip of his forefinger.

'Well, now,' he said, as if remembering something he had been interrupted about, 'I think you were about to tell me what your purpose was when you joined Rechtabra this night?'

'We were told to come here on Fellowship business,' Duach began.

'Enough!' scowled Cellaig, his voice rough. 'Remember that his reach is long and his vengeance certain.'

'Oh, so we are back to the power of this lord of yours.' Eadulf's tone was disdainful. 'Well, his vengeance isn't that certain. Twice I have escaped his attentions, even though he had Rechtabra kill his companion for not ensuring my death. It was Rechtabra who eventually met *his* death. So before you also start your journey to the Otherworld . . .' Once more Eadulf seemed preoccupied with testing the sharpness of the short sword.

'We know no more than we were to collect Rechtabra,' Duach began to babble, in spite of the efforts of Cellaig to silence him. 'We were then to ride to Cashel and attend the Great Fair.'

Eadulf tried not to show his excitement. He forced a disbelieving laugh. 'Your lord is so concerned for your welfare that he provides entertainment for you? I am growing weary of lies.'

'No, no!' the man shouted in a panic as Eadulf made a play of raising the short sword. 'It was for the business of the Fellowship. We had to seek out some performers . . .'

Cellaig began showering a torrent of abuse on his companion.

'I suppose you mean the *Cleasamnach Baodain*?' Eadulf's voice cut into the tirade.

It had the effect of stopping the flow of Cellaig's curses and causing a silence to fall.

'Who are you?' he finally whispered.

'I would say that perhaps I am your nemesis,' Eadulf replied jovially, 'except I doubt that you would know what that means. I am told your Fellowship is interested in the old gods. I don't suppose you know much about the old gods and goddesses of Hellas?'

'We don't know what you are talking about,' replied Cellaig in a surly tone.

'Well, I'd like to tell you about this goddess called Nemesis; she personifies the power of retribution, she is the punisher of evil deeds.'

Duach shivered. 'He has the knowledge, Cellaig,' he wailed. 'He uses strange words but he speaks of the Raven Goddess whose name must not be spoken – the Great Queen.'

'Shut up, you fool,' muttered Cellaig, but he did not sound as arrogant as before.

'The Raven Goddess? The Great Queen?' Eadulf's mind worked rapidly, trying to remember the stories he had learned from Fidelma. 'The Mórrigán, Goddess of Death and Battles.'

It was the girl who, having been silent for a while, finally spoke. 'I heard Rechtabra speak of the Raven Goddess of Vengeance, who feeds on the remains of the slaughtered on the field of battle and who creates strife between people and causes them to seek retribution on each other.'

'So this is all part of the Fellowship of the Raven? Mórrigán just means Great Queen, so what is her name that cannot be spoken?'

'Badh is her name,' said the girl, and the words caused Duach to shiver, groaning slightly. The girl went on defiantly, 'I do not care for the old superstitions. I am of the New Faith.'

Eadulf was interested. 'Are we saying that this Fellowship of the Raven is no more than people hanging on to the old ways and refusing the enlightenment of the New Faith? I have met similar folk before.' He recalled how Fidelma and he had been summoned to Tara when the High King Sechnussach was murdered in his bed and a plot was uncovered to bring back the Old Religion. It was a reminder that the Faith had not long been accepted in the country. It was scarcely more than two centuries ago that the High King Lóeguire, son of Néill, had accepted the New Faith. Eadulf knew that many places in the Five Kingdoms had not followed Lóeguire's acceptance.

He glanced appreciatively at the girl before turning back to the prisoners.

'Well, now we have been informed about your Fellowship, let us return to what you were meant to do when you reached Cashel and found Baodain and his performers.'

Once more it was Duach who answered.

'Nothing. We were told nothing. Only that once we were there, we would be contacted by someone of the Fellowship and must accept their orders.'

'How were you to identify and locate the contact? There are many people going to the Great Fair. You were to find Baodain's performers – and then what? How were you to announce yourselves?'

'What do you mean?'

Eadulf gave an impatient sigh.

'Were you to go to Baodain's performers and shout out "Here we are! What are we to do?"!'

Duach frowned, trying to understand. It was Cellaig who finally answered in a sour tone. 'We were told that the person we were to contact would know us and would reveal themselves to us when we reached there.'

'Nothing more? They would simply identify themselves to you and you were to do what they asked?'

'We all wear the emblem of the Fellowship,' was the uncompromising response.

Eadulf realised that they had told him all that he would ever get out of them. He glanced through the window; it was growing light.

'We will have to leave soon, Ríonach,' he said. 'Collect what you need but don't gather more than you can carry.'

She nodded and went into the bedroom. It was not long before she re-emerged with a small bag and Eadulf nodded approvingly. Meanwhile he had found a passable belt bag into which he put the emblems of the Fellowship of the Raven before gathering up all the weapons and placing them in one of the cupboards. He retained a couple of the knives as they might come in handy.

'Is there anything dangerous left in there?' he asked the girl, indicating the bedroom. 'Anything they can use?' She shook her head and Eadulf turned to the captives with a grim smile. 'I am getting slightly tired of heaving bodies around,' he told them.

'Here, what are you doing? You can't leave us like this!' protested Duach as Eadulf lifted him under the arms and dragged him into the bedroom, half-lifting, half-pulling him onto the bed.

'Oh, but I can,' he replied a little breathlessly before returning to repeat the performance with Cellaig.

'You are bluffing,' grunted the fellow. 'You are a man of the New Faith. You may be a foreigner but I see the tonsure on your head. You cannot leave us tied up in the middle of nowhere. We'll die. At least untie us.'

'Your so-called lord left me in more or less the same position – tied up and blindfolded somewhere in the middle of the marshland. I managed to survive. You are left in more comfortable circum-stances. At least I won't leave you blindfolded.'

'Please . . . please . . .' wailed Duach.

'Oh, and I shall be borrowing your horses,' Eadulf added. 'You see, your so-called lord borrowed mine when he left me to die on the marshland.'

He turned and shut the door behind him against their protests.

Ríonach was waiting for him in the main room of the farmhouse. She was clutching her bag of belongings.

'I don't understand,' she said.

'Simple,' he replied. 'We can make better time on horseback than walking. Can you ride?'

'I haven't been allowed to do so since I came here as Rechtabra's bride,' she replied, 'but yes, I can ride.'

'That is good. I don't like horses, but in these circumstances I shan't complain. All ready?'

The girl hesitated. 'But you can't really leave them like that,' she said, indicating the bedroom.

'I was left in a worse situation,' he countered grimly.

'But—'

'All right,' he interrupted. 'I have a kind heart. We'll get that shepherd you know to release them, when he comes to feed the animals. That is more than they did for me, so I am being generous. Does that make you happier?'

'I have enough on my conscience without more deaths,' she said quietly.

'Then give me your bag and let us go.'

There was a whimpering from the corner and the little terrier Rían was looking at them with a woebegone expression.

'You'll have to carry him,' Eadulf said. 'I don't think he'll be strong enough to run with the horses.'

She looked at him curiously. 'You are a strange man. You wouldn't hesitate to abandon your enemies to their fate, but you care for a little terrier.'

'You didn't think I would make you leave the dog here, did you?' he said gruffly. Then he turned and walked out of the door before she could answer.

The three horses that Cellaig and Duach had arrived on were certainly good ones, worthy mounts for warriors. As the girl had said, two of them were fully equipped with saddlebags. Eadulf took time to look through them in case they contained something of value. He discarded the clothes from both bags and tied the girl's bag in place on a dappled grey. He cradled the terrier, shivering in his arms, until she was mounted, then held the animal up to her. The little beast seemed happier once she had placed it comfortably across her saddle-bow.

Eadulf returned to the horse that he had selected, a chestnut, and mounted, taking the rein of the third animal to lead it.

'You'll not leave it behind?' asked the girl, indicating the horse.

He shook his head. 'It might come in useful. We could trade it.'

The sun was now rising and the countryside was becoming alive around them.

'You take the lead,' he called. 'We'll head for this Mountain of the High Fields – what was it, Sliabh Ard Achaigh?'

'And we will stop at the shepherd's homestead which is just

beyond the great highway,' she reminded him. 'He can release those men as well as feed the animals.'

Eadulf pulled a face. 'You do realise that they would not do the same for you?'

'That is no excuse to forget the teachings of the New Faith or to descend to their level,' she admonished. 'You sometimes speak strangely for one who claims to be a religieux.'

'Perhaps that is because I was a pagan until I reached the age of choice and fell under the influence of Christians from this country. Sometimes it is easier not to turn the other cheek because doing so often invites further injury rather than preventing it.'

'Do you believe in that goddess you were talking about – Nem . . . Nem . . . ?'

'Nemesis?' Eadulf gave the question some thought. 'An interesting point. Perhaps. I was a *gerefa* of my people. That is much like your Brehons. What is law and justice but retribution?'

The girl was uncertain. 'I do not think it is quite the same.'

'Perhaps you are right,' Eadulf admitted reluctantly. 'Don't worry. For the sake of both our consciences, we will alert the shepherd or someone else to rescue those men. However, I hope to be some way away from here before they are released.'

CHAPTER THIRTEEN

৵৩

They had been riding for some time, speaking little except when Ríonach gave a direction to Eadulf. They had crossed through a bordering forest to the main highway, which Eadulf realised must be the Slíge Dála, and joined a track on the opposite side. 'This way will lead us to the shepherd's homestead,' she told him. 'Beyond, you can see the Mountains of the High Fields where Brother Finnsnechta has his hermitage.' Eadulf was almost reluctant to leave the main highway as he knew that it was the quickest route to Cashel and the road that Fidelma and his friends must have joined after they left Rechtabra's farmstead. He wondered which direction they had taken; was it back to Cashel or on to Cill Cainnech?

They were moving to higher ground leading towards the foothills of the mountain range. They had not gone far along the path when, twisting through a small copse of beech and inevitable yew, they came upon a small homestead, where a dog started barking. At once, Rían, who had been lying quiet across the girl's saddle bow, stood up and began to bristle and snarl. Ríonach quietened him with a word of command, just as a man appeared out of the house and snapped an order to his animal to be still. The man looked familiar to Eadulf: a weatherbeaten fellow of middle years, with bright blue eyes. The man also seemed to recognise Eadulf.

'God's blessing on you, Brother,' he greeted, a moment before Eadulf realised it was the same shepherd whom he had encountered down in the marshland before he had reached the deserted homestead and was attacked.

'And to you, my friend,' Eadulf said, bringing his horse to a halt.

The shepherd said, 'You are dressed differently to when I last saw you.'

Eadulf gave a shrug. 'I had an accident in the marshes. My robes are not fit to wear.'

'And your horse is different, too.'

'My horse and I also parted company. I had to borrow this mount.'

The shepherd then turned to Ríonach with a frown. 'Aren't you Rechtabra's woman?' he asked.

'She is,' Eadulf intervened before the girl could speak. 'In fact, there has been an accident at the farmhouse and we are on our way to find Brother Finnsnechta and then a Brehon.'

'An accident, you say – to Rechtabra, you mean? How bad an accident?' the man asked thoughtfully.

'As bad as that which means we need to seek out a Brehon rather than a physician.'

The shepherd let out a low, whistling breath. 'I see. My sorrow for you, Ríonach.' The words were automatic and did not seem to convey any sorrow at all.

Eadulf allowed himself to add, 'I am afraid he has been killed.'

The shepherd's eyes widened for a moment.

'That is bad,' he muttered. 'But why go to seek Brother Finnsnechta? There's more chance of finding a Brehon along the great highway.'

A thought occurred to Eadulf. 'Do you see much traffic along the highway? I believe some companions of mine were on the road yesterday.'

'If you turn to look down the hill, you'll see that my homestead overlooks it, and sometimes it amuses me to watch people on their journeys.'

'I don't suppose you saw a lady with two warriors on the road.' It was a faint chance but to his surprise the shepherd nodded at once.

'Yes, I saw them. They were heading towards Cill Cainnech. I noticed her companions because they were wearing the golden collars of the King of Cashel's Bodyguard.'

'They rode towards Cill Cainnech?' Eadulf was almost exultant. 'Then we cannot delay. But should you wish to help us, we have had to leave the farmstead abandoned.'

The girl added: 'There are cows, pigs and fowl that need attention. If you, or someone, could go to the farmstead to attend to those matters, I will ensure that you receive recompense.'

The shepherd stared at her for a moment. 'I will do this, but not out of respect for Rechtabra, for I had little respect for him. It is out of sadness for you, Ríonach, for your suffering. My sons are tending our flock at the moment. I'll take them with me and we will put things to rights on the farmstead until you return with the Brehon.'

'I thank you on my behalf,' replied the girl. 'Will you also go *inside* the farmhouse, for—'

'We are concerned that some of the animals might find a way inside,' interrupted Eadulf, his features expressionless. 'We would not like to see any damage done.'

The shepherd looked puzzled for a moment and then nodded. 'We will see to the security of the place.'

'As a guarantee of a recompense for your neighbourliness, my friend, let us leave this horse with you.' Eadulf tried to dismiss the thought that the horse was not his to give away. He wrestled only a moment with the moral dilemma.

'In distress are friends known,' quoted the shepherd, as if to dismiss the idea, but then he stepped forward and took the reins of the third horse.

With a wave of his hand, Eadulf cantered away, with the girl following his lead. It was some time before she spoke, having waited until they were well out of earshot of the shepherd's hut.

'You didn't tell him about the prisoners,' she complained.

'Isn't there a saying among your people that a lie often goes further than the truth?'

She was puzzled and said so.

'You didn't think I was going to tell that poor man the entire truth, did you? What would have been his reaction if I told him about Cellaig and Duach, or where we acquired the horse? God forgive me if I told a lie, but lies can pass away while the truth will remain.'

'I still don't understand you.'

'Expediency is often a better path than truth. You said that the only person you used to trust is this Brother Finnsnechta. Let us now go and find him.'

Ríonach sighed. 'It is hard to trust anyone after . . .' She did not end the sentence but Eadulf knew how she must view life after her years with Rechtabra.

'My only sorrow is that I had to fool that poor shepherd,' Eadulf said. 'But I shall reward him for his neighbourly actions.'

'He won't get into trouble?'

'Of course not.'

'I meant at the hands of those men you left tied up.'

'There is no reason why he should come to any harm. He and his sons will free them, that's for sure. So why should they revenge themselves on those who release them from their bonds? The only people they'll seek to harm is us – if they can track us down – and we are long gone, taking their horses.'

'The shepherd will probably tell them we are heading for the Mountains of the High Hills.'

'I have told you not to worry,' Eadulf said confidently. 'They won't catch up with us now.'

The girl did not look convinced but remained silent.

They were well into the foothills of the mountain range now.

'Do you know exactly where Brother Finnsnechta might have his hermitage?' Eadulf asked.

Ríonach sat back and stared up at the rounded peaks. 'I was told that he dwelled in a place called Faill na mBan. Just above the edge of the treeline.'

Eadulf stared in surprise. 'Faill na mBan? Doesn't that mean "Cliff of Women"? A strange place for a religieux to have a hermitage. I don't suppose you know the way to it?'

'I know that one takes the path that leads up the hills to the place where two tall sandstone pillars are erected. They mark the start of the woods that cover the lower slopes of the mountains. They are also supposed to mark a pathway ascending through the trees to a spot below a cliff face where Brother Finnsnechta dwells.'

'Does Brother Finnsnechta know what sort of man Rechtabra was?' Eadulf asked.

'I don't think he knew Rechtabra. My husband told me that Brother Finnsnechta would not help me if I tried to run away from him – but that was because Rechtabra held all those of the New Faith in contempt.'

'So Brother Finnsnechta would not know anything about this Fellowship of the Raven?'

'I am certain of it. He was a friend of my mother's when she still lived, and he is a pious man.'

They couple rode on along the track which skirted the foothills. When it suddenly split in two, at that point they caught sight of the two sandstone pillars and turned to follow the path there, moving rapidly upwards through a thick barrier of trees. The track grew ever narrower and the trees seemed to hem them in. There was only room now for a single rider and horse to move along the pathway at a time. Eadulf decided to go first, following the tortuous path as it ascended through the foliage, climbing higher and higher. He was beginning to wonder if the girl had been misinformed, because he felt that the path was leading him so far up the mountain that he was surely going to cross the round peaks and descend the other side.

Then, all of a sudden, the trees thinned and finally came to an abrupt end before a flattened area of the hill. It was like a natural shelf on the side of the mountain. The first thing he noticed was that while on one side, it was open to the trees, the other side was blocked off by a curious cliff-like wall. Water gushed from it and poured down its greying sandstone face into a little pool below.

It was around this pool that a semi-circular wall, waist-high, had been erected, and within this wall stood a stone-built hut and some wooden outbuildings. They all looked of fairly recent construction. Smoke rose from the hut and the smell of cooking permeated the air. Attracted by a clucking sound, Eadulf identified a chicken coop and then a large hutch which clearly contained hares.

An elderly man emerged from the stone cabin and regarded Eadulf, who was still seated on his horse, with surprise. He then caught sight of the girl. The man who stood before the cabin was of indiscernible age. His head was completely bald, with a shiny pate as if it had been polished in beeswax. His skin was as pink and fresh as a baby's, with bright spots of red on either cheek. He was fleshy, the skin almost wreathed in folds around his neck. His eyes were a strange blue – a sort of violet – and his lips were red, thick and pouting. The plump cheeks swung to and fro as the man turned his head. He was dressed in simple brown homespun and wore a silver crucifix on a chain around his neck. Altogether, if this was Brother Finnsnechta, Eadulf decided that he was not a handsome man.

The hermit's eyes were penetrating, however, as he watched Eadulf dismount, hitch the reins over a nearby rail, take the terrier from Ríonach's hands and wait for her to dismount before he turned to greet the elderly man. By that time, however, the rotund religieux had recognised Ríonach. With an exclamation of pleasure, he hurried to meet her, with both hands outstretched. She put down the dog to greet him.

'Little Ríonach! How many years is it since I last saw you? Tell me how things are with you!'

He took her hands in both of his and she almost bobbed a curtsey to him, lowering her head and shoulders, but she did not say anything.

Brother Finnsnechta then cast a glance at Eadulf. 'This is surely not your husband, my dear? Rechtabra wears rough labouring clothes and yet I see a Roman tonsure on this man's head.'

'He is not Rechtabra,' replied the girl.

Eadulf spoke up. 'My name is Brother Eadulf.'

'By your accent, you are a stranger to this land?' the old man said, head to one side as if listening.

'I'll not deny it, Brother,' replied Eadulf. 'I am from Seaxmund's Ham in the Land of the South Folk.'

'Then you are a long way from home, my friend. But I have no understanding of it.' Brother Finnsnechta was frowning, as if trying to dredge up a memory. 'Eadulf of Seaxmund's Ham, you say?' Then Fidelma of Cashel is your . . . ?'

'I am husband to Fidelma of Cashel,' Eadulf confirmed.

Brother Finnsnechta stood puzzled for a moment and then sighed resignedly. 'I am sure there is a story to be told. Therefore, you must come away in, take a cup for your journey's sake and tell me what brings you to this mountain with my old friend's daughter, whom I last saw many moons ago before she married.'

The stone hut was dark inside, in spite of two openings for the light and a fire to keep out the spring chills. Brother Finnsnechta invited them to find seats and then poured some drinks. Rían the terrier lay down at the girl's feet, his eyes watchful on the old man.

'*Nenadmin*,' Brother Finnsnechta explained, handing them the wooden mugs. 'I make it myself from the wild apples that grow hereabouts.'

Eadulf took a sip and found the liquid cold and sweet; he complimented the old man on it.

'I think I do have a certain talent for brewing,' Brother Finnsnechta said modestly. 'I like to make *Fraechóga* – I distil it from the bilberry fruit which my friends bring me now and then from the heathlands.' He paused to sip his own drink and then looked from one to another. 'And now, my friends, tell me what brings you to this inhospitable mountain spot.'

It was Ríonach who said flatly: 'I have murdered my husband.'

There was a shocked silence.

'Oh, do sit down, Enda,' Fidelma snapped. 'Pacing up and down will not serve us to get out of this prison any quicker.'

Fidelma, Aidan and Enda had been confined in the small cell all night. They had been fed and taken for evening and morning ablutions, but no one had come near them to tell them of their fate. Their guards merely answered their questions in monosyllables and offered no conversation. Now it was well after dawn and Enda, in particular, was frustrated and angry.

'This might be Osraige, and we have heard stories of their plotting against Cashel – but this is no backwater,' Enda fumed. 'It is a township! It has an abbey up on the hill here, is on a trading river and the main highway runs through it. How can they dare to treat the sister of their King in this discourteous manner?'

'They seem to doubt that I am Colgú's sister,' she said philosophically.

'Idiots!' muttered Enda. 'Arrogant idiots.'

'Idiots or not,' Fidelma said, 'there is certainly something much amiss here.'

'And how are we going to find out what that is, locked away in here?' demanded Enda, kicking at the ground with his right foot.

'Certainly not by pacing up and down or by complaining,' Aidan told him.

Enda was about to answer back when Fidelma gave a loud exasperated sigh.

'We are wasting our breath, complaining and speculating about things. I am afraid we must wait until our captors decide to enlighten us.'

The three prisoners relapsed into silence for a while but it was not long before they heard movement and orders being shouted outside. The wooden bar was lifted and the key turned in the lock.

The man who had commanded their captors from the previous day stood framed in the doorway.

'Lady, I must trouble you to accompany me,' he said, his tone polite but firm. He beckoned with his hand.

At once Aidan sprang up. 'She does not go anywhere without us,' he said fiercely.

The man shook his head. 'Do you have a choice in the matter?' he asked with a cynical smile. 'Come, lady.'

Fidelma had seen two bowmen behind the man with their arrows already strung.

'You will have to wait here, Aidan,' she told the warrior quietly. 'Do nothing rash meanwhile.'

Aidan compressed his lips angrily as Fidelma stepped out of the cell. The jailer immediately slammed the door shut, locked it and pushed the bar into place.

'What now?' Fidelma asked coolly.

Her captor smiled. 'Now, lady? Why, we go for a little walk up the hill to see the Abbot.'

The answer surprised Fidelma but she kept her expression under control.

'The Abbot of Cill Cainnech?'

'There is no other abbey in this township,' the man said light-heartedly. 'Abbot Saran wants to know why you are making enquiries about the foreign wagon and its occupants.'

'I have told you who I am, and that should be explanation enough.'

Her captor grinned. 'On that matter, it is not I who shall be judge, lady. I simply obey orders.'

'And your orders come from Abbot Saran?'

'You ask too many questions.'

'That is the nature of a *dálaigh*,' she replied.

Fidelma was aware that another warrior had joined them as they walked from the *laochtech*. He marched behind them, one hand resting on the hilt of his sword. The authoritative young commander walked at her side, guiding her. There was nothing else for it but to accompany him as he indicated the way through the township. They passed the inquisitive stares of folk; some standing at the doors of their houses, others passing by on whatever errands they pursued.

'What do they call you?' she suddenly asked.

The man raised an eyebrow with a look of amusement. 'Yet another question?'

'Surely that is one that you are allowed to answer without being instructed to by your superior?' she commented.

'My name is Feradach.' His expression showed he did not care to be the recipient of banter even if he liked giving it.

'Battle-champion,' she chuckled.

'What?' The man was startled.

'That is the meaning of your name. It's fairly uncommon. Did your parents have high hopes for you as a warrior, or did you take the name yourself?'

Feradach almost glowered. 'It was my parents' choice – and my destiny,' he muttered.

'And if it is your destiny, who do you serve as battle-champion?'

He actually halted and turned to stare at her, saying, 'You are very clever, lady, but I have told you who I serve.'

Fidelma answered him with a bright smile.

'I was not trying to be clever, my friend. I merely wondered why someone who wishes to be a battle-champion is content to serve in this little township.'

The young man's eyes narrowed in annoyance. 'I am of Osraige, lady, and I serve my Prince.'

'Ah yes, Tuaim Snámh. But his capital lies north in the Sliabh Bladhma. Surely you should be in the bodyguard of your Prince and not protecting passing merchants?'

Feradach turned and strode on, muttering, 'I have said that you ask too many questions.'

'Well, Feradach,' she said, following him, 'if you do not ask questions, you do not gain any knowledge. Have you never heard what the great churchmen of Rome say – *scientia est potentia*?'

Feradach scowled. 'I know only a little Latin.'

'It means: knowledge is power.'

He did not answer and she was forced to relapse into silence as they moved away from the main township and walked up towards the new buildings of the abbey. The abbey was even more impressive as they grew nearer. It was built of blocks of reddish-coloured sandstone. Over the entrances were arches picked out in local black marble. Perched on the central hill, the complex was more like a fortress than an abbey.

There were plenty of men in religious robes milling about, each wearing the tonsure of the Blessed John which marked them as adhering to the forms and rituals of the Church of Colmcille rather than Rome. These religious scarcely bothered to look at the visitors as they went about their various tasks.

Feradach conducted her through the main gateway and into a large courtyard. A snort and whinny drew Fidelma's attention. She glanced to one side and saw a stable area and there, outside the stable doors, she saw her own horse, Aonbharr, impatiently nodding his large head and stomping at the ground as if he recognised her. A stable lad was expertly grooming him.

'Don't worry,' Feradach said, observing her scrutiny. 'Your horses are being well cared for. There is little room at the *Laochtech* to attend to such animals so we brought them here.'

'And our saddlebags and belongings?' Fidelma demanded.

'They are here as well,' smiled the warrior. 'Come now, the Abbot awaits us.'

He led the way through more iron-studded wooden doors and across another courtyard. To one side was a stone-built chapel. Opposite this was another small building with iron-studded doors and, to Fidelma's surprise, two warriors stood outside, seemingly to guard it. But straight in front of them was another building and it was to this that her captor led her. This opened into the main abbey buildings. He took her down a short corridor, paused before a strong-looking oak door and knocked.

It was opened at once by a tall religieux. He was gaunt and pale-looking. His eyes were dark and his features almost expressionless. He said no word to Feradach, whom he clearly recognised, but stood mutely to one side to allow them to enter.

The room within was large and rectangular, with a fire blazing at one end. Tapestries hung on the walls, covering its limestone blocks. The highlights in the room were picked out in black marble which, like the limestone, had been quarried locally. There was no sign of a crucifix or any other icons of the New Faith. In the centre of the room stood a large round oak table with handsome ornamental legs that had been expertly carved. Several chairs surrounded it, one of which was larger than the others – a high-backed chair, also carved to a high standard with creatures and figures which, to Fidelma's surprise, she recognised from ancient myth. There was a triple-horned boar; then a horse with a woman petting its newborn foal – was that Epona, the old Horse Goddess? She saw a carving of a cauldron with a figure that seemed to be putting a body into it while on the other side a man was climbing out of it. This was the symbol of rebirth. On top of the chair, overlooking everything, was the sinister carved figure of a crow or raven.

She peered around the large, high-ceilinged chamber, searching for some sign that she was in an abbey rather than a chieftain's feasting hall. There was nothing to show they were in a religious building rather than a secular one.

The young religious who had opened the door to them had moved to the fire and was putting another log onto it. There was a rope to one side of the fireplace and, after he had stoked the blaze, he tugged on this. Fidelma heard a distant, bell-like jangle and glanced at her guide, Feradach, who stood impassively just inside the door.

Time passed in silence and then one of the tapestries seemed to be moving of its own volition. Behind it was hidden a side door and through this a figure emerged.

The newcomer was short, rotund and bald. He had a pleasant face, but his hazel eyes were very watery, as if their owner had either been crying or was unused to daylight. There was neither humour nor malice in his expression, but rather a comical air of innocence and bewilderment. He hardly looked at Fidelma but crossed to the grand oak seat and lowered himself carefully into it. He then nodded to Feradach.

'Be seated,' Feradach instructed.

Fidelma looked at the seated figure in some amusement, but the rotund one's eyes were lowered. Shrugging she took the nearest chair.

The gaunt religieux, who had been standing near the fire, now came forward and cleared his throat.

'I am Failge, the *rechtaire*, the steward of the abbey,' he announced slowly, enunciating each word as if talking to someone who would find the language difficult. 'This is Abbot Saran.'

'And I am Fidelma of Cashel,' she replied strongly, and without pause went on: 'I demand an explanation of the extraordinary behaviour to which I and my companions have been subject!'

'Fidelma of Cashel is said to be Sister Fidelma, a religieuse,' replied the steward sternly. 'You are not dressed as a religieuse.'

'Fidelma of Cashel is said to be many things,' she shot back. 'Most of all she is a *dálaigh*, an advocate of the courts whose degree is *anruth*, and she can sit in the presence even of the High King if so invited.'

Brother Failge regarded her without a change of expression. 'You claim to be sister to King Colgú of Cashel . . .' he began.

'Not so,' snapped Fidelma.

The steward hesitated. 'What?' he gasped, looking in bewilderment towards Feradach. 'But you told us—'

'I do not claim it. I *am* his sister,' Fidelma said loudly and belligerently.

'Can you prove it?' went on the confused steward.

'If needs be. My Cousin Laisran is Abbot at Darú, which is only a short distance upriver.'

'But he is not here,' countered Brother Failge.

Fidelma did not stifle her impatient sigh. 'I notice my horse has been brought up to the abbey with those of my companions, who are warriors of the Nasc Niadh, the bodyguard of my brother. I trust you have searched the saddlebags that were still on the animals – or have you appropriated the contents?'

'Nothing has been interfered with,' Feradach said stiffly.

'Then I suggest that you bring my saddlebag here.'

Feradach looked quickly towards the still silent and almost immobile Abbot. But it was Brother Failge who made a motion with his hand to indicate that he should do as she asked.

A silence fell as the warrior hurried out, closing the door behind him. Fidelma sat with her eyes on the stout Abbot but he did not raise his head or let his eyes meet her own. So she turned to the steward, who stood motionless at the Abbot's side.

'I suspect that you have already searched the contents of the bags. So is this to check if I know what those contents are? I trust that you will be capable of recognising what it is that you are about to be shown,' she said with a malicious smile. 'Or is your knowledge also limited?'

The steward flushed. 'I studied for five years and my degree is *Sai*,' he said tightly. The degree was only one below the qualification that Fidelma held, although her degree had been taken in a secular bardic college and not in an abbey school.

'And where did you study?' She did not sound impressed.

'Across the river here and up to the Bhearú lies the Abbey of Fiacc—'

'I know it,' intervened Fidelma. 'It is at a place called Sléibhte.'

The young man hid what could have been surprise or disappointment that she knew the place.

At that moment, Feradach returned bearing her saddlebag. Fidelma took it from him and laid it on the table before her. From it she removed the golden chain, a symbol of the Nasc Niadh. She laid this to one side and then drew forth a small wand of white rowan, on which was fixed a figurine in gold. It was the image of an antlered stag, the symbol of the Eóganacht princes. The hazel wand emblem was the symbol by which Fidelma derived authority from her brother, Colgú, King of Muman, and with this wand she was able to command respect and speak as if she spoke with his voice. It was six years ago that her brother had handed that symbol to her when she went as his ambassador to Gleann Geis to negotiate on his behalf with a prince who had not recognised the New Faith. Six years ago since Colgú had made her a member of the élite order of the Niadh Nasc.

She held it out to Brother Failge, who took it carefully from her hand and put it before the Abbot.

'You do recognise these objects, don't you?' Fidelma asked cuttingly. 'This is the symbol which shows that I speak in the King's name and the emblem of my service to my brother, the King.'

There was a wheezy sigh and it took Fidelma a moment to realise that it was the first sound she had heard from the Abbot. A curious shudder shook the man's frame and he raised his head and looked at her with dark, impenetrable eyes. Then he began to speak. His words came out in a grating sound, as if something blocked his throat and prevented him from breathing properly.

'Your credentials are impeccable. Why is the sister of Colgú here in the Abbey of Cainnech and making enquiries about a particular wagon?'

'I am here in my capacity of a *dálaigh*, investigating two murders.'

The rotund face of the Abbot did not show any emotion.

'Murders? I was told you wished to find out about a particular wagon that may or may not have passed through this township.'

'Since you have accepted my credentials, there is something I must ask before I discuss my business further, Abbot Saran. I suggest that my two companions are now released from their imprisonment. I am sure that you have also examined their saddle-bags and found the golden torcs, the symbol of the Nasc Niadh, my brother's bodyguards.'

The Abbot turned towards Feradach and made a tiny motion with his pudgy hand. The warrior went to the door, opened it and whispered instructions to the warrior outside. Then he closed the door and returned to his former position.

'It is being done as we speak,' he said, but whether he was addressing Fidelma, Failge or the Abbot, Fidelma was not sure.

'Now, you may tell us why you are here,' the Abbot said slowly.

'Tell me why I was imprisoned when I informed this warrior who I was,' she asked next.

It was the steward, Failge, who answered. 'Fidelma of Cashel has a reputation – but as *Sister* Fidelma. You do not appear in the robes of a religieuse, nor do you introduce yourself as Sister Fidelma.'

'That is because I have left the religious,' she replied.

This finally brought a response from the Abbot.

'You have abandoned the New Faith?' The simple question seemed to imply a deeper question hidden within it.

Fidelma remembered the answer she gave to Abbot Ségdae, her brother's religious adviser.

'I said that I have left the religious, not that I have left the religion. I am a *dálaigh* by training, profession and inclination. I have accepted the position as legal representative of my brother, the King. I have not lived in a religious community since I left the Abbey of Cill Dara many years ago.'

There was another wheezy sigh and the Abbot slumped back in his chair.

'We were concerned that you might not have been who you said you were,' Brother Failge told her, as if that explained everything. 'And you were asking questions about that wagon and its occupants.'

'I have already said that it is a *dálaigh*'s place to ask questions.'

'True enough, but we were suspicious, especially when you said that the wagon was expected in Cashel.'

'Why should you be suspicious?' she asked, baffled.

'Firstly, why are you interested in this wagon?'

Fidelma made an impatient gesture. 'The wagon of which we speak arrived in Cashel with two dead bodies. A young male religious and a young girl. Both had been murdered.'

She was completely unprepared for the impact her words caused.

There was a sharp exhalation of breath from Feradach at one side, and Brother Failge's mouth opened as if to say something and remained agape. The Abbot, who had been toying with Fidelma's willow wand of office, jerked back in his chair as if someone had jabbed him with a sharp instrument. His small eyes widened and his mouth formed an almost perfect 'o'.

'They are both dead? Are you sure?' the steward asked urgently.

Fidelma studied them all with interest. 'So you know about this wagon and its occupants?'

The Abbot regained his composure first. 'Let us assure one

another that we are speaking about the same wagon. Describe it, if you please.'

'It is a foreign wagon. I have only seen them abroad and never in this country for they are built by no wainwright of the Five Kingdoms. The name the Romans give it is a *rheda*. I was told that it is a Gaulish word and that the Romans borrowed the design from the Gauls. It is large enough for six people to travel in comfort, is entered through a door and has windows, which in this case had a canvas covering over them. It is roofed as well, and the roof is curved so that any rain simply falls off. It has four wheels, iron-rimmed, and this one was drawn by a team of two oxen.'

She nearly mentioned the brand-mark but held back, for she felt she should not volunteer all the information at her disposal.

The Abbot leaned forward anxiously. 'And the occupants of the wagon?' he asked. 'You say that you are sure they are both dead? How did they die?'

'Both by poison. The male died before the girl. She also died of poison, but a few days after the male. She had joined the wagon train of a group of performers travelling to the Great Fair in Cashel. It seems likely that they passed through this township . . .'

'We have had quite a few performers through here,' intervened Feradach.

'Baodain's Performers.'

The Abbot sighed impatiently. 'Yes, they passed through the township not so many days ago. But the foreign wagon, with its occupants, had vanished some days before.'

'What do you mean, it had vanished?'

Abbot Saran glanced nervously at his steward. Again, Brother Failge replied for him.

'The wagon that you spoke of, with the man and girl, left our township at least two or three days before Baodain and his performers passed through here.'

'Two or three days?' Fidelma stopped to think. 'It was about that time afterwards that the girl drove out of the marshes and came upon Baodain's wagons. She asked if she could follow them to Cashel. However, it was not long before she was overcome and died. The wagon and bodies were brought to Cashel and hence became the concern of my brother, the King, and myself as a *dálaigh.*'

There was a lengthy silence while everyone digested the information. Finally, Fidelma spoke. 'You obviously are acquainted with the wagon and its occupants, so I would request that you now share that knowledge with me. Also, perhaps you will explain why my asking about it caused the imprisonment of my companions and myself.'

There was a pause. Then Abbot Saran, with a dramatic gesture, loosened the robes at his neck with a nervous tugging gesture, as if they had become too tight.

'Come and stand by me, Fidelma of Cashel,' he said in his grating tone. 'I need to show you something.'

Fidelma was puzzled but she rose from her chair and walked round the circular table to where the Abbot was seated. The steward stepped back to allow her to move closer.

'You have heard from my voice that I find it uncomfortable to speak. Now regard my neck.'

The Abbot opened his robe to reveal the bare flesh of his neck. A strange red wound was running around it. Not the kind of wound that implied an attempt to cut through his throat. It was more like a scorch-mark of a rough hempen rope having been pulled tight against the flesh.

'That is a grievous wound,' she observed quietly.

'Grievous indeed, for I nearly died. I still feel that there is something swollen and dislodged in my throat,' grunted the Abbot, pulling his robe back into place.

'My condolences at your having sustained such an injury, but I am at a loss to understand why you are showing this to me.'

'It is straightforward enough. The young man whose wagon you are enquiring about, tried to murder me by strangling me with a rope.'

CHAPTER FOURTEEN

Brother Finnsnechta was staring at Ríonach in bewilderment. He looked from her to Eadulf and then back again as though he hadn't understood.

'You did *what*?' he asked finally. His tone was one of shock.

'Perhaps I had better explain,' Eadulf volunteered, 'for I have some knowledge of your laws and I do not think Ríonach is her best advocate.'

The elderly hermit sat back and made a movement with his hand as if to invite Eadulf to speak.

Eadulf felt that it was best if he was sparing with the details. He confined himself to saying that he had been lost in the marshes, had come across Rechtabra's farm and was suddenly imprisoned by the farmer. Ríonach had freed him during her husband's absence. Eadulf emphasised that it was obvious that the farmer ill-treated his wife and that she was in great fear of him. Rechtabra had come back suddenly, lunged at him with a knife with the intention of killing him, and verbally threatened Ríonach, saying that he would deal with her afterwards. Fearful of her life, Ríonach had seized a *scillead* and hit him on the head in self-defence. Rechtabra had fallen to the floor and was dead. Eadulf added that he had immediately suggested they go to find a Brehon to report the matter, but the girl had been desperately fearful that she would not be believed, since her husband

219

seemed to have many friends locally. She had suggested that they come to find Brother Finnsnechta and seek his advice first.

Eadulf also decided to add that, while they had been discussing matters, two armed and aggressive friends of Rechtabra had called and he had been forced to trick them into becoming prisoners while he and the girl had escaped. It was a very sparse account of the reality, but Eadulf felt that it was enough for the time being.

Brother Finnsnechta's first question was about the welfare of the two prisoners.

'Don't worry,' Eadulf told him. 'I was also concerned with the livestock on the farm, and not far from the farmstead we found a shepherd. I told him about the livestock and the death of Rechtabra. He promised to go there with his sons and will have doubtless released the men by now.'

Brother Finnsnechta stared long and hard at Eadulf as if he found the story hard to accept.

'So you came looking for a Brehon?'

'As I said, Ríonach wanted to speak with you first. She recalled that you had been a friend of her mother's when she was alive, and felt you would be able to give her protection and counsel.'

The religieux looked sadly at Ríonach. 'I will not disguise the fact that this is a serious matter. What you have done, child, is a grave crime in the eyes of the Faith. For such actions there are undoubtedly consequences.'

The girl gave a protesting sob. 'I had no other choice.'

'There are always choices, child, when confronted with right and wrong.'

Eadulf was surprised at the old man's immediate condemnation.

'I think we should examine the matter in the light of the law rather than as a matter of religious faith,' he quietly advised.

'Ah, the law. For someone who bears the tonsure of Rome, you will know that some of the Faith are trying to amend the lewd, pagan laws of this land.'

'You mean those who adopt the Penitentials?' Eadulf asked in surprise. 'I am surprised you even speak of them. They only apply to certain religious communities and not to the countryside beyond.'

Brother Finnsnechta's eyes narrowed. 'Are you condemning the Penitentials, Brother?'

'Since coming to this land I have learned much from the laws of the Fénechus,' Eadulf replied flatly. 'One thing I did learn was that, when your High King Laoghaire set up his commission to revise the laws of the land, he involved three leaders of the New Faith – Patrick, Benignus and Cairneach. They sat on the commission with the leading Brehons of the day as well as three Kings, including the High King. It is even written in the *Senchus Mór* that what did not clash with the word of God in the written law and in the Gospels, or with the conscience of Christians, was confirmed as the laws of the Brehons. There should be no difference between the law of the people and the laws of Christianity. So it is the Penitentials who are in error and *not* the law of the Brehons.'

Brother Finnsnechta smiled – a smile without any humour in it. 'Very well, we will talk about the laws of the Fénechus and whether the girl is answerable to them. Remember that if a wife circulates a false story about her husband, if she vilifies him in any way, she has to pay compensation and can be cast out by her husband.'

Eadulf was annoyed. 'The husband is dead and I can bear witness to his cruel behaviour.'

'It could be argued,' the old man said, with a sideways glance at Eadulf, 'that your role is questionable. You could have been trying to alienate the girl's affections, and when the husband discovered this, it was the cause of his attack on you.'

Eadulf tried to control his temper. Brother Finnsnechta chuckled as he saw the expressions crossing the young man's features.

'I am merely suggesting what a Brehon might argue,' he added.

The girl suddenly rose to her feet, turned away from them and ripped off her tunic, exposing her bare back. She said nothing. She did not have to. There was a criss-cross of scars on her back, the result of many beatings.

'Put your tunic back on,' Eadulf told her gently. 'You have made your point.'

The girl did so, still without saying anything, and returned to her seat.

'Now Brother Finnsnechta, I trust you are satisfied?' Eadulf asked.

'Not exactly,' replied the man, to his surprise. 'We are dealing with murder here – the killing of a husband. Ríonach, you say your husband ill-used you, and you show us proof that someone has beaten you. Very well. Let us accept that it was Rechtabra. Why did you not leave him and seek a divorce or separation under the law, to which you are entitled? There are seven categories of divorce in which either side may end a marriage, and no penalties or special compensation are incurred. Furthermore, there are also seven other categories where a woman may leave her husband, demanding compensation from him and the return of her dowry.'

He turned to Eadulf. 'You may be able to correct me, Brother. But one of those categories states that any woman who has been beaten by her husband, especially having been struck a blow which causes a blemish or mark on her skin, has an immediate right to have her marriage declared void.'

'I have heard this is so,' agreed Eadulf. 'Nevertheless . . .'

'Nevertheless, the girl shall answer why she did not report her husband's behaviour,' the religieux said sharply. His tone caused the little terrier to come to its feet with a curious whining snarl. The girl calmed it with a gentle word.

'I was too scared,' she replied awkwardly. 'Out there in the marshes, who could I run to before Rechtabra would overtake me? I ran away only once; was caught and beaten. Rechtabra told me no one of the New Faith would protect me. Where would I go?

Who would believe me? Even you do not believe me – and I thought that as a friend of my mother and as someone who knew me as a child, I could trust you.'

Brother Finnsnechta thrust out his jaw aggressively.

'Trust does not come into a matter of law! Even Brother Eadulf here will know that. A crime has been committed. You have killed your husband. Even the Fénechus law accepts that the most serious crime is that which deprives a person of his life – and the worst of the crimes of murder is that of *fingal* – kinslaying.'

Ríonach looked helplessly at Eadulf and he felt a growing anger at the religieux.

'There is the matter of self-defence,' he said.

Brother Finnsnechta sniffed. 'For one who wears the Roman tonsure, I would refer you to the old scriptures that have been translated for us. Is it not written in Exodus: *Sin autem mors eius fuerit subsecuta reddet animam pro anima, oculum pro oculo, dentem pro dente, manum pro manu, pedem pro pede*—?'

'I don't understand,' the girl said miserably.

'It is in Latin, from one of our religious texts,' Eadulf explained gently, 'which says that one should take a life for a life, an eye for an eye, a tooth for a tooth, a hand for a hand, a foot for a foot. Brother Finnsnechta forgot to add that it goes on to say . . . a burn for a burn, a wound for a wound, a bruise for a bruise. The girl has plenty of burns, wounds and bruises from her husband. Doesn't that give her the right to seek similar compensation?'

Brother Finnsnechta snorted indignantly. 'The text is clear.'

'The text is from the Old Testament of the Hebrews which I thought we did not follow? If we did, then let us proceed with the next sentences, for does it not also say that if an ox or bull kills someone by accident, then not only is the animal to be put to death, but the owner of the animal also? Thankfully, the laws of the Fénechus are more enlightened than those which people adhered to in another land and in another age.'

'You are clever, young Brother. You have acquired a honeyed tongue.'

'Not so. I am a plainspoken man. I know the law recognises the circumstances in which the killing of another is justified. I have studied the *Cairde* law texts in which it states *diles gac frithgiun* – every counter wound is free from liability. In other words, self-defence is a defence – and the perpetrator is absolved from any consequence.'

Brother Finnsnechta was silent for a moment. Then he rose and, appearing to be chuckling with amusement, took up a jug and replenished their drinks.

'Wonderful, wonderful,' he beamed. 'I have not had such a stimulating exchange for many years. I congratulate you, Brother Eadulf.'

Eadulf took his mug of cider automatically, totally bewildered.

The hermit then turned to the girl and patted her on the shoulder, saying, 'You must forgive me, young Ríonach. I had to be cruel to you. I do accept your story and I am truly sorry for the plight that you have been in. But it seems you have found a worthy advocate in Brother Eadulf here.'

'But . . .' began the baffled girl.

'Killing and the killing of one's husband is a grave matter. I had to make sure of the circumstances.'

'I still do not understand,' Eadulf said frankly.

Brother Finnsnechta turned to him. 'It was not my role to sit here and simply be sympathetic. I had to know how your story would stand up to a serious examination by a Brehon. You have put the case very well and, as you say, it seems a clear case of self-defence. It is Rechtabra who stands as a *fer coille cáin* – a violator of the law – and, as such, no punishment is due to the one who takes a life in defence of their own.'

The tension in Eadulf's body eased a little. 'So you were simply testing us?'

Brother Finnsnechta nodded in amusement. 'Will you both forgive me? Now what is it you intend to do? Remember, I am merely an old man dwelling on the mountain. I have chosen a hermit's life. There is little I can do.' He turned to Ríonach. 'What is your wish, my child? To go back to the farm?'

The girl shook her head swiftly. 'I never want to see it again.'

'Yet you have the right to it and the value. As I recall, Rechtabra was without kinsmen and . . . ah, he did hold his lands under tribute to the Lord of the Marshes.'

'That would be Coileach?' Eadulf queried. Brother Finnsnechta made an affirmative gesture. 'I heard a rumour that he was dead. If so, who is the new Lord of the Marshes?'

Brother Finnsnechta seemed surprised. 'Coileach dead? I heard a story from one local man that he had gone to pay his respects to the new High King in Tara. He was always a reclusive man but not a bad lord. His own brother serves as his Brehon; that is Ruán. I think he had a son in service with the Prince of Osraige.'

'Whether Coileach is alive or dead, he is welcome to the farm,' the girl interrupted.

'But surely you would want some recompense?' asked the old religieux of the girl.

'I'd rather beg by the highway than have anything more to do with Rechtabra or his farm,' the girl said vehemently.

'That will not be necessary,' Eadulf assured her. 'I have already suggested that I could find you some employment in Cashel.'

Brother Finnsnechta raised his brows a little as Eadulf fell silent. 'But you have to sort out the legal situation first. You must inform a local Brehon, just as you have told it to me.'

'Now that we have had this discussion with you, I am sure that Ríonach will be less anxious about having the matter legally sorted out.'

'It is a comfort to know that I am not to be condemned,' the girl agreed. 'I feared no one would listen to me.'

'Eadulf here is a good advocate,' Brother Finnsnechta assured her.

'You should have nothing to worry about. However, the matter must be reported. On the road to Cill Cainnech you will pass the Hill of Ruán, the place where Brehon Ruán has his homestead. It will be easy to call in there and report this matter. There's no finer man than Ruán. I know him well. He is also a fair and just lawyer. You may safely place your case before him. Then he can record the circumstances and you will be free to leave the territory as you will.'

'Why should she be confined to the territory anyway?' asked Eadulf, suddenly cautious again. 'She will be accompanying me to the capital of Muman, to the court of the King.'

'Ah, you forget, young Brother. This is Osraige. We have our own prince here, and while we currently bend the knee to Cashel, it was not always so. It is the curse of being a tiny principality caught between two big kingdoms – Muman to the west of us and Laigin to the east of us. We are betwixt and between, my friend. And being so, we tend to keep ourselves to ourselves and rely on what is best for us in all circumstances.'

Eadulf could see the logic in what the man was saying.

'So you believe it is best for us to make sure the matter is cleared with the local Brehon before leaving the territory?'

'Exactly so,' the religieux replied. 'Trust Brehon Ruán, trust him with all the facts.'

'Very well.' Eadulf gave a smile of encouragement to the girl, who remained silent but was clearly anxious.

'Excellent. Hold nothing back.' He turned to Ríonach. 'You must know the way to Tulach Ruán?'

'When I was little, my father used to take me on the road that runs by there. It was whenever he had a bull or a cow to sell at Cill Cainnech.'

'So it is on the way to Cill Cainnech?' asked Eadulf, remembering that the shephered had said he had seen Fidelma riding in that direction.

'When you leave here, you have to return to the bottom of the mountains, onto the marsh plain, and then turn north. There is no other easy route around the Mountains of the High Fields. As you proceed north you will find yourself in a narrow valley that swings to the east. As the valley opens to the southern plains you will see a hill, called Tulach Ruán . . .'

'Tamhlacht Ruán?' Eadulf frowned, for the words sounded similar when pronounced.

Brother Finnsnechta chuckled. '*Tulach* Ruán. *Tulach* is a hill while *tamhlacht* is a graveyard. The Hill of Ruán is where the Brehon dwells. It dominates the great road to the east that leads directly to Cill Cainnech.' He glanced to the window. 'Ah. The clouds have blown away and you still have time to reach Tulach Ruán before nightfall.'

Eadulf was thankful, as he did not fancy spending a night at the old hermit's stone hut. The sooner he could move on and be reunited with Fidelma, the better.

'Then we shall disturb you no more,' he said, rising.

'Disturbance?' beamed the religieux. 'It was no disturbance to engage in a battle of wits and knowledge.' He turned to the girl. 'I am sorry I put you through that, Ríonach. I had to ensure the truth.'

'So long as the truth is known,' the girl replied, also rising.

'Truth is great and will prevail. Is that not a saying of our Brehons? Anyway, the least I can do is ensure you fill your water bags and take some baked bread and some cheese that I have produced with the help of my goats.'

The old man seemed in a good humour now.

As they were leaving his cabin, Brother Finnsnechta suddenly exclaimed, 'Wait! I know another way in which I can assist you. As I have said, I have known Ruán since he qualified as a Brehon. We both respect one another. I shall write him a note to declare that you come to him with my blessing. Just a moment.'

He turned back into the hut. They heard him moving around

inside and eventually he reappeared with a piece of folded papyrus. He handed it to Eadulf.

'Put it straight into your beltbag, my friend. It merely says that we have talked and that I support all that you and Ríonach have to say.'

Eadulf took the note and put it in his bag which he had taken, with some distaste, from Rechtabra's body.

'We are grateful, Brother,' he acknowledged. He went towards his horse as Ríonach had already mounted, picked up the little terrier and handed it to her. Once more it settled across her saddle bow. Then Eadulf was in the saddle and following the girl out of the small clearing and descending slowly between the trees. He glanced back and saw the elderly religieux standing watching them depart. He raised his hand in a gesture of farewell and received an answering wave.

For Eadulf, who never regarded himself as a horseman, and much preferred any other possible means of transport, it was not the most comfortable of journeys. He felt that he was going to slide over the horse's neck several times as it plunged down the steep incline of the mountain track. He wished that he still had his steady cob. This was a stallion, more a warrior's horse, and he was not used to handling the beast.

He was glad that he had allowed the girl to ride ahead, leading the way down the small path through the trees, for his horse seemed content to follow her. Ríonach appeared fairly comfortable on a horse as most people were who were raised on farms. Even with the added burden of the little terrier, she rode with an assured and confident attitude. So Eadulf allowed his horse its head. The animal needed no guidance, treading with sure feet behind its fellow. Eadulf's sole concern was to keep his seat, and so focused on this task was he, that he was surprised to find himself coming out of the trees and on to the verdant plain again.

Ríonach had halted and waited until he brought his horse along-side her.

'We proceed in that way,' she said, pointing ahead. Then she
added: 'Once more, you did not tell the whole truth.'

'In what way?' Eadulf wanted to know.

'You did not mention the Fellowship of the Raven to Brother
Finnsnechta,' she said. 'He might have heard something about the
mysterious lord whom Rechtabra was serving.'

'That is true, but . . .'

She frowned. 'Why do you say "but"?'

'Your people have a saying: there is danger in an open laugh.'

'I don't understand you.'

'I just thought it strange that Brother Finnsnechta started off
being so vehement in his condemnation of you, then suddenly
changed to the opposite view.'

'He explained that he was testing us,' she replied.

'I think it was more than that. Why should he change to being
so friendly and smiling?'

'That is easily understood,' replied the girl. 'Having assured
himself of the truth, he resorted to his normal pleasant self. He was
a friend of my mother, don't forget.'

'Perhaps I worry too much,' Eadulf said, before turning with a
smile to the girl. 'Let's get on. The sooner we get there the better
as there is less than half a day before nightfall.'

Once again the girl led the way, but this time Eadulf hung back.
His mind was still turning over Brother Finnsnechta's behaviour.
The hermit had indeed been helpful, but there was something
niggling at the back of his mind. Had he been *too* helpful? While
the girl rode on ahead, Eadulf reached into his beltbag and extracted
the piece of folded papyrus which Brother Finnsnechta had given
him. Holding the reins with one hand, he peered at what the religieux had written to Brehon Ruán.

If he had hoped to understand it, he was disappointed. It was
written in Ogham, the ancient form of writing which, it was claimed,
had been given to the people by Ogma, the God of Learning and

Literacy in the time before the coming of the New Faith. Eadulf had never mastered it and it was difficult to deduce what Brother Finnsnechta had written.

He refolded it with his one hand and thrust it back into the beltbag. Now his suspicions were deepened. Of course, there was a logical explanation. Brother Finnsnechta was an educated man and so was Brehon Ruán. Why should they not write to one another in the ancient form? Yet, if the note was simply saying that the old religieux was introducing Eadulf and Ríonach to him, and that he approved of and supported them, why disguise it in Ogham? Why not write it out in plain form which all understood? Was there something to hide? He wished Fidelma was here to decipher it.

Fidelma! He suddenly felt guilty. He had not thought about her for a while. Then his mind turned to the Fellowship of the Raven. What did it mean? What was its purpose? Was it just a group dedicated to the Old Religion? But the Fellowship definitely had something to do with the mysterious wagon and the deaths of its two occupants.

He was a bit put out that they had to pause in their journey to report to Brehon Ruán. He stared around. The Mountains of the High Fields still rose on the right side of the road while, to their left, the verdant marsh plains with little islets and clumps of trees and bushes spread as far as the eye could see. The two of them were approaching a small stream that came down the mountains and gushed like a waterfall over the grey sandstone rocks to cross the track and bubble on to feed the marsh.

'This might be a good place to pause for food,' the girl suggested.

Ríonach, who was clearly better at the task, watered the horses, while the terrier sat and watched her intently. Eadulf found some rocks to sit on and cut up the bread and goat's cheese, which they ate with some wild apples. The meal did not take long, nor did they exchange much conversation before they moved on again.

The path followed the contours of the hills before turning eastwards into a narrow valley, just as Brother Finnsnechta said it would. A distance away, Eadulf could see the main highway which led from Cashel to Cill Cainnech. He spotted it by virtue of the fact that he could see a group of wagons moving along it, going in the direction of Cashel. The girl saw him gazing at the sight.

'Merchant wagons,' she said with confidence. 'They are probably taking goods from Cill Cainnech to Cashel.'

Eadulf nodded. So that would have been the route that the foreign wagon might have taken if it had first arrived at Cill Cainnech. Brother Finnsnechta was right. Any wagon would have passed through the valley they were about to enter and would have had to pass the Hill of Ruán, which guarded the far end of the valley. He wished he did not have this suspicion about Brother Finnsnechta niggling away at him.

The day was already gloomy and clouds obscured the sun when they reached the far end of the valley; before them was a rounded mound of a hill in the centre before the valley widened onto the tree-filled plains beyond.

'That is Tulach Ruán, Ruán's Hill,' Ríonach said.

They were still some distance away but Eadulf could see that around the distant mound were uneven groups of trees, mainly birch and yew and some oak. Most of the surrounding area seemed to have been cleared for grazing and he could see cattle and even a string of horses in large fenced areas.

'If all those are his, this Ruán seems to be a wealthy Brehon,' he observed.

'I suppose the location of his homestead is a good one,' Ríonach replied. 'It straddles the main highway and maybe travellers feel obliged to pay deference to him.'

'That would be highly unusual,' Eadulf said disapprovingly. 'I have read some of the laws pertaining to highways in the *Book of Aicill*. There is a public right of way along such highways without a toll being extorted. If the main highway passes by Ruán's land then it is up to him to ensure its maintenance because he benefits by the trade it brings.'

'I know nothing of such things,' the girl responded.

They had crossed to the north side of the valley to join the main highway running on harder ground along the skirts of more high hills. The highway would twist across the valley again to pass close by Brehon Ruán's homestead. They had descended from the brief elevation of the highway and were starting to cross through the meadows where cattle were grazing. Eadulf began to feel more comfortable since they were well away from the marshland, and the cattle were a sure sign of the firmness of the ground.

Among the meadows was a fenced area where a number of horses were grazing. Eadulf and Ríonach were passing along the fence as the highway came nearer to the complex of buildings on the hillock. Eadulf glanced absently at the collection of a dozen or more animals beyond the fence. Among the roan-coloured stallions he spotted a grey-white animal, stoutly built with strong bones. He was not a great horseman and could hardly tell one horse from another, but he felt a chill run through him as he saw the familiar black patch on the little cob's forehead.

Reining in, he called sharply to the girl: 'Follow me! Quickly – back towards the cover of the trees!'

She was startled at his tone. 'Why?' she demanded.

But he was already moving, turning his horse as best he could and digging his heels in its sides so that it broke into a canter.

It was not until they were back on the north-eastern side of the valley, under the shelter of the tree-lined hills, that he eased the pace. The girl came galloping up alongside him as he finally halted.

'Whatever is wrong?' she panted. 'What made you turn back?'

Eadulf turned to her with a worried expression. 'Because that white cob in the field is the horse that your husband and his companion stole from me on the marshland!'

CHAPTER FIFTEEN

Fidelma examined the face of the portly Abbot in surprise.

'You say that the young man tried to murder you? Tried to strangle you? But for what reason?'

Abbot Saran sighed deeply. 'We shall try to answer your questions, lady.'

There came a knock on the door and Feradach went to answer it. There was a hurried conversation with the guard outside before he came back into the room.

'Your companions, Aidan and Enda, have been released and are now outside.'

It was Abbot Saran who answered for Fidelma. 'Then bring them in, now that we are certain of their identities.' He turned to his steward Brother Failge. 'Organise some refreshments, for we seem to have treated our guests badly but,' he added hastily to Fidelma, 'through justifiable suspicion and not through deliberate malice.'

'Your apology will be accepted – once you can explain how this suspicion came about and why you were attacked by the couple about whom we are enquiring.'

While Brother Failge hurried off through the side door behind the tapestry, Feradach opened the main door and ushered in Aidan and Enda. Aidan immediately crossed to Fidelma's side and examined her with an anxious look.

'Are you all right, lady? You are not harmed?'

'I am fine, as you see, Aidan,' she smiled. 'Aidan, Enda, this is Abbot Saran, the Abbot of this abbey. We are invited to take refreshment with him while he tells us the story of why he has been so wary of strangers asking questions in this township.'

'You are welcome, warriors of Cashel,' intoned the Abbot, in his wheezy voice. 'Be seated at the table. You also, Feradach.'

'It seems that Abbot Saran was attacked by the young man who died in the foreign wagon. He tried to strangle him,' Fidelma informed them. 'That was why they were so suspicious of us.'

Aidan and Enda exchanged a glance of surprise. It was Aidan who asked the Abbot bluntly: 'Was it you who killed him then? The man was given poison and was found dead in the wagon. We are told it took him three days to die. The girl died a short while later.'

Fidelma was about to admonish the warrior for his rudeness but the Abbot did not appear insulted. His expression was, in fact, one of sadness.

'I am a man of peace, my friend. I can assure you that they left here in good health, in spite of their actions. May their souls, if they still exist, rest in peace.'

'So who were they?' asked Fidelma.

'They came as visitors from the north to this abbey.' The Abbot settled himself back in his chair. 'They gave their names as Ultan and Ultana. These were probably not their real names, although, as you may know, these names signify the male and female forms of people who originate from the northern Kingdom of Ulaidh. They came to the abbey just over a week ago, driving the foreign wagon that you have described so accurately.'

'In what manner did they arrive?' Fidelma asked.

'By the main highway and across the river by ferry.' It was Feradach who supplied the answer. 'The man, Ultan, introduced the girl as his sister. They claimed to be members of the religious.'

'Did they say where they were from exactly?' asked Fidelma.

'Brother Ultan, as he called himself, said that they had travelled from the Abbey of Clochar,' Abbot Saran replied. 'That is in one of the northern petty kingdoms.'

Fidelma contained her interest by asking in a casual tone: 'Clochar is in the territory of Caipre Gabra, part of the Kingdom of Tethbae, isn't it?'

Abbot Saran showed no surprise at her knowledge. 'I believe it is.'

'By ox wagon, that would be a journey of several weeks,' Aidan pointed out.

'You are right, warrior. It would be a long and exhausting journey, indeed,' agreed the Abbot. 'The journey appeared to affect the girl more than the man. She had recourse to our apothecary.'

'What was wrong?' asked Fidelma.

'Exhaustion – although our apothecary told me that he suspected the girl was with child. After some rest, she recovered and seemed well enough.'

'Your apothecary was right,' Fidelma confirmed. 'She was bearing a child.'

Abbot Saran stared at her for a moment, apparently shocked. Then he lifted his hands in a helpless gesture but made no other comment.

'What was the purpose of such a journey?' Fidelma went on after a moment or two. 'Did they tell you?'

At that moment Brother Failge returned with two members of the abbey, bearing various dishes and jugs of wine and mead. The table was laid and the food placed accordingly. It was clear that the abbey was wealthy and took full advantage of the fact that it was perched at a busy river port with goods arriving from all corners of the world, especially the red wine which, after a hurried blessing from the Abbot, Fidelma and her companions sipped at appreciatively.

'The wine is from Gaul,' Brother Failge offered. He had not spoken in a while. 'This comes from an amphora shipped here only a few days ago.' He joined them at the table and was about to point to the various dishes but became aware that he must have interrupted a conversation.

'We were talking about Ultan and Ultana,' explained the Abbot, answering his unasked question.

It seemed a cue for Fidelma to return to her previous question. 'You were about to say whether they explained the purpose of their journey all the way from the north to here?' she reminded Abbot Saran.

It was Brother Failge who, after a quick glance at the Abbot, answered for him.

'The man who called himself Ultan claimed to be a scribe. The girl was his assistant. He said that he had been asked by his Abbot to collect details of the lives of some of the most influential churchmen of the land. He had come here to learn about the life of the founder of our abbey.'

'I would have thought that Cainnech's major foundation was north of here at the Field of the Ox?' interposed Enda, who knew a little about the area. 'Surely that abbey would be where records of his life and work are kept?'

Brother Failge cast a quizzical look over the warrior before relaxing with a smile. 'I do not think we need take the story that this man gave us literally,' he assured them. 'When I pointed out that our library held a copy of the Blessed Cainnech's great work, *Glas-Choinnigh*, "The Chain of Cainnech", Brother Ultan did not seem particularly impressed and scarcely bothered to look at it.'

'"The Chain of Cainnech"?' queried Fidelma. 'I am not too knowledgeable about Cainnech's work.'

'It is our blessed founder's commentaries on the Gospels,' explained the Abbot. 'It is of great importance for us.'

'Was it his lack of interest that caused you to suspect that Brother Ultan and Sister Ultana had some other motive for being here?' asked Fidelma.

'Let me tell you from the beginning,' Abbot Saran offered. 'Ultan and the girl, whether his sister or not, I do not know, arrived here with this story. We accepted them both and gave them hospitality. We are not a *conhospitae*, a mixed abbey, but we do have a small section for the female religieuses which connects with these buildings. We provided shelter for their oxen and their wagon, and food and drink for them both.'

'The girl had to rest from the journey on the first day and see our apothecary,' the steward reminded him.

'I have explained that matter,' the Abbot said.

Brother Failge went on: 'On the second day they became interested in exploring the abbey and particularly our central chapel.'

'Then on the third day this Brother Ultan began to ask questions about the Blessed Cainnech, especially whether he had left any writings concerned with how he had come to this place and founded his church here,' continued the Abbot. 'He seemed particularly interested in learning about the building of the chapel and the abbey here.'

'And that would be as you would expect, if he was writing about Cainnech's life and achievements,' Feradach said reasonably.

'Exactly so,' agreed the Abbot, 'We had no suspicions of anything at that time.'

'So, how did these suspicions subsequently develop?' Fidelma asked.

'Later, some members of the brethren reported some curious incidents to my steward.'

'Such as?' Fidelma prompted, when the Abbot paused.

'They reported seeing both the man and the woman wandering at night in the chapel, tapping the flagstones and appearing to listen to the echoes.'

'This was at night?' queried Aidan.

'In the dead of night,' confirmed Brother Failge. 'These complaints . . . well, not complaints exactly, more reports, I suppose, came to me. I then informed the Abbot.'

'So what did you do?' Fidelma asked.

'What else should I have done but seek an explanation from Brother Ultan and his sister.'

'Did they explain their strange behaviour?'

'I have to say they did, but not to my satisfaction. They claimed that they had heard a story that the Blessed Cainnech had left a written account of the foundation of the abbey and hidden the manuscript in a safe place in the chapel.'

'Were you told where – and who had given them this story?'

'They said that they had promised not to reveal their source, but they thought it was true.'

'You found this story unsatisfactory?'

'I certainly did,' the Abbot agreed.

'So you did not accept their explanation of what they were doing in the chapel at night. What did you think that they were up to?'

'I believe they had been trying to discover where the treasures of the abbey are kept.'

Fidelma raised her eyebrows. 'And *does* the abbey have treasures?' she asked him.

Abbot Saran spread his hands, a curious gesture from the wrists only.

'You have seen that there has been much building here in recent years. Not so long ago, this was a poorly built township whose strategic position was ignored. The abbey was no larger than a church on top of the hill, with a few huts for the brethren to eat and sleep in. I take pride in the fact that during the ten years since I was appointed Abbot, I have instigated the developments that have brought wealth to the people of the township as well as to the abbey itself. One day I hope to persuade our prince, Tuam Snámha, to locate his principal city here away from the northern mountains.'

'That does not explain how you brought about this miracle,' Fidelma observed.

Abbot Saran shrugged. 'If it matters, I am son of Faelchair, cousin to Tuam Snámha. With my family's support I managed to build up the quays along the river and encourage this township as a centre of trade. Soon we were able to build and expand the ecclesiastical buildings, and we are still expanding.'

'So does the abbey have any physical treasure?' She re-phrased her question.

'You have only to look around. *This* is our treasure. Stonework from various quarries surrounding the town has gone into the buildings, black marble, dolomite, as well as red sandstone and other materials. In disturbing the earth, we have found large quantities of red gold. Our craftsmen have excelled in creating great works of art – chalices, crucifixes, book shrines – and gold, silver and semi-precious stones have also been found in the vicinity. We trade in such artefacts to other abbeys and churches.'

'So you think that this was what Ultan and his companion were really after – your red gold and the items you make from it?'

'What else could it be?' Brother Failge intervened.

'Is that the only treasure within the abbey?' Fidelma asked him, ignoring the question. She held up her hand as she saw the wary expression on Brother Failge's face. 'I do not want to be shown it. Perhaps I should just ask if you truly believed that this Ultan and Ultana were simply thieves?'

'We do have a treasure chamber,' the Abbot replied solemnly. 'We have become a wealthy abbey.'

'So when you challenged them about what they were really doing in the chapel at night, and then told them that you did not accept their explanation, what was their response?'

'Response? I told them that I could no longer give them hospitality. If I did them an injustice, then at least they had seen the abbey and knew there was nothing here that could help them with what they claimed they sought. I suggested that they travel north to the Abbey of the Field of the Ox where they might receive a better reception. I did not tell them I suspected they were common thieves just looking for the abbey gold.'

Fidelma sighed. 'Was this the point where this man Ultan tried to murder you – when you told him to leave?'

'No, no.' The Abbot was momentarily disconcerted. 'They made the plea that it was too late in the day to start out so could they spend one more night in the abbey and set forth at daylight?'

'And you agreed?'

'I am a fair man, so yes, I agreed – what else could I do? I granted them one extra night's hospitality on condition that they left the next morning.'

'So the attack on you happened that night?'

'I was restless,' the Abbot admitted. 'I had summoned Feradach from the town and asked him to double the guard on our treasure chamber.'

Fidelma sniffed critically. 'I saw your treasure chamber and guards as I entered here. If the pair were after your treasure, they must have been blind to miss it.'

The steward looked shocked. 'We do not try to hide our wealth but merely keep it safe.'

'So you were restless,' Fidelma went on, ignoring the steward and prompting the Abbot to continue.

'I was unable to sleep and decided to get up and have a look round. I saw the guards were at their posts in the courtyard outside.'

Feradach added: 'The Abbot approached our guard-post well before first light. He asked me if all was secure. I answered that we had not heard a sound and that all was quiet.'

'Yet I was not reassured,' confessed the Abbot. 'I felt something was happening but could not understand what. Something drew me to the chapel. As I paused outside the door, I saw a light flickering in the interior.'

'Did you call the guard?' asked Aidan.

The Abbot gave a quick shake of his head. 'Foolishly, I did not. I opened the door, stepped in and saw Ultan standing against the holy altar with a metal bar in his hand. It was one of those bars with a sharpened end that builders sometimes use or farmers use for digging out reluctant tree roots. What I could not believe was that the man was trying to shift the plinth of the altar. I was outraged.'

Fidelma was puzzled. 'You mean he was trying to destroy the altar or that he was trying to move it?'

'I presumed that he was trying to destroy it.'

'Why? He had claimed to be looking for some documents written by Cainnech. Did he have cause to believe that they were under the altar? You believed he was trying to find the abbey's treasure. So what use would the destruction of the altar be?'

'He must have been looking for the treasure,' declared the Abbot. 'There was nothing else. He was probably misled.'

'So what did you do, having thus confronted him in this act?'

'I demanded to know what sacrilege he was about, disturbing God's holy altar. Then the next thing I knew, there was a blow across my shoulders that sent me flying. I landed on the stone floor. I did not pass out entirely because I heard the man whisper, "Leave him to me. Get the wagon ready." I remember the words very distinctly but I did not see to whom they were addressed. I presume they were to the girl. She must have been hiding behind the door with a cudgel or some heavy stick.'

'Go on,' pressed Fidelma, when he paused.

'There is little else to tell. I was barely conscious and trying to get to my hands and knees when I felt a cord around my neck. I struggled, but had no breath to cry out. I knew I was being strangled. Then all went black. The next thing I remember, I was waking in my chamber with one of the brethren bathing my face. There was a blinding light. In fact, it was daylight. I was still alive and had been unconscious for some time. I could not speak from the constriction in my throat. I was told that Brother Failge had gone with Feradach and his warriors to track down the culprits. When they returned that evening, they said they had lost their trail. As I could hardly speak, Brother Failge brought me a wax tablet and stylus; he asked me questions and I wrote down the answers.'

Brother Failge took up the story. 'I think it is clear what happened. The man had made one last attempt with his companion to find the treasure and was searching the chapel, believing it to be there, but was discovered by the Abbot. The girl knocked him down while her companion tried to strangle him. They then both fled empty-handed.'

'Why didn't the guards stop them leaving?' Fidelma asked.

'It was only after this event that we decided to have more than a few guards,' Brother Failge explained.

'It seems the thieves had prepared their wagon the previous night, ostensibly to leave in accordance with my wishes,' the Abbot said. 'So it was standing ready for the oxen to be yoked. After the attack, the man and girl slipped out of the side door in the chapel and along to the rear of the stables, and left in the darkness.'

'It was when I went to the chapel at first light that I found the Abbot, unconscious and barely alive.' Brother Failge took up the story. 'I had him taken to his chamber and attended by our apothecary before I went to fetch Feradach. We searched the abbey, but the man and girl had gone, together with the wagon and team of oxen. It was clear who was responsible.'

'I alerted my men and we chased after them,' Feradach said sombrely. 'I was sure that we would overtake them quite easily. You cannot travel fast in an ox-wagon. But they seemed to disappear into the air itself.'

'Which way did you go?'

'I split my men up, as there were several ways they could have gone. We did find some tracks heading for the western mountains, but after a while we lost them.'

'So you returned empty-handed that evening,' concluded Fidelma. 'The couple and their wagon had disappeared entirely?'

'As if they had been swallowed up in the marsh,' confirmed Feradach.

Fidelma sat back with a deep sigh. 'This presents more questions than it does answers.'

'Such as?' Brother Failge wanted to know.

'Why were they trying to remove the altar slab when I think they would have been well aware that Feradach and his warriors were on guard outside the building in the courtyard? Logic would have told them loud and clear that *that* was where the treasure was kept. That is, if the treasure was what they wanted. Why try to kill the Abbot, after he was rendered incapable, and then flee the abbey? And an ox-wagon is neither the most silent means of transport in which to escape, nor is it the fastest. One cannot get very far in an ox-drawn wagon if there are mounted warriors in pursuit! So how did they disappear? And where did they hide?'

'You raise some good points, lady,' Feradach said. 'But what else could these people be after, other than the treasure? There is nothing else of value here.'

'Perhaps you are right,' she said. 'Still, this raises one more sinister mystery that we must look into.'

'Sinister mystery?' repeated the Abbot, looking apprehensive.

'The man called Ultan and his companion Ultana left the abbey in the wagon. They were last seen to be fit and well, fleeing towards the Mountains of the High Fields or the great marshlands beyond. Would you agree that this is a fair assessment?'

'After I was attacked, I was in no condition to observe anything,' Abbot Saran replied distantly.

'My men believed the tracks of the wagon went westward – that is all,' confirmed Feradach. 'Then those tracks disappeared. It seems obvious they reached some shelter. Why do you think this is sinister?'

'Because in the day or so after leaving here, the man called Ultan was dead. He had died from poison. The girl Ultana had also been poisoned but she lasted a few more days than the man. The wagon had been in the marshes and then emerged on the marsh road to Cashel, where Ultana joined the Cleasamnaig Baodain, whose wagons were travelling to the Great Fair at Cashel. This was where she died. At that time someone also tried to set fire to the wagon but it was quickly put out.'

'I don't understand any of this,' said Abbot Saran in bewilderment. 'I trust you are not implying that they were poisoned before they left here, lady.'

'I never imply things,' Fidelma replied in an even tone. 'If there is an accusation to be made, I make it. I am merely asking questions. Since the couple were here, this is obviously the place to start our investigation. The fact remains that they left here and were both dead within a few days. We must try to find the answers to certain questions in order to get to the bottom of this mystery. The first question is, what brought them here: what were they looking for? The second question is, what happened between the time they left here and when they were found dead? I do not believe they were treasure-hunters, at least not in the sense you believe.'

Brother Failge swallowed nervously. 'I understand why you must ask these questions. But I can assure you that no one in this abbey poisoned them.'

'It is not assurances that a *dálaigh* seeks,' Fidelma replied coldly, 'it is facts. Give me facts – because I do not have any that make sense.'

Abbot Saran spread his hands; the same curious gesture without moving his arms, just a motion of the hands themselves. 'Then we can supply no further facts other than those we have told you. When these two would-be thieves left here, they were certainly alive and well. They disappeared before our warriors could catch up with them.'

'Apart from their names, which sound false, and their mention of coming from the north, from Tethbae, you say that you found out nothing more about them?'

'It is as we have said.' The Abbot sounded tired.

There came the nearby sound of a tolling bell and Brother Failge coughed anxiously, saying, 'It is the last service of the day . . .'

The Abbot rose and they all followed his example. 'The hour

grows late,' he said. 'You and your companions are offered the hospitality of the abbey for the night, lady, and you are welcome to join us in the chapel for the service.'

'We will accept both your hospitality and the invitation to join you in the chapel,' Fidelma replied politely. She did not add that it was the chapel she wanted to see rather than a wish to attend the service.

The warrior, Feradach, had important duties that summoned him back to the township, so he took his leave of them.

Brother Failge said, 'I will request one of our brothers to take your saddlebags to our guest chambers and I will escort you there after the service.'

Fidelma glanced at Aidan and Enda. 'We will get an early night's rest. It may be that the answer to our question lies back in the direction from which we have come.' She said the words pointedly in front of Abbot Saran and his steward.

It was Enda, who had hardly spoken since arriving at the abbey, who now articulated what was troubling her.

'What of Eadulf, lady? Cannot we find men who will volunteer to scour the marshes for him?'

In fact, she had been thinking about what she should do. Now she turned and explained the situation to their hosts.

'We seem to have learned what we can here,' she concluded. 'So tomorrow we will retrace our steps to the marshes in search of my husband.'

Brother Failge immediately offered assistance. 'If your companion is lost in the marshes, then we must speak with Feradach. I am sure he can send his men to Brehon Ruán, who dwells on the edge of the marshes and will advise on how and where to scour the most likely places in search for your husband, lady.'

Fidelma thanked him solemnly as the bell clamoured with a new urgency to summon them to the chapel.

✤　✤　✤

Amidst the darkening woodland, well screened from the Hill of Ruán, Eadulf and Ríonach finally reined in their horses. Eadulf was breathing heavily, as if it was he who had just galloped across the plain rather than his horse! The girl meanwhile was bewildered and trying to calm the little terrier, Rían, who was clearly fretting about the sudden burst of speed.

'I don't understand,' she said, also out of breath. 'Why did we flee from Brehon Ruán's homestead? You say that you saw your horse in his field – but what significance does that have?'

'Do you remember me saying that I was captured by Rechtabra and his companion?' Eadulf said. 'I was with my horse at the time, the little white cob with black markings on its forehead. I was blindfolded and the man, this mysterious lord for whom your husband and his friend were working, came to question me. I am sure he took my horse away with him when I was left alone in the marshland to perish there.'

'You told me that, but how can you be sure that the horse you saw was your cob? You have told me that you are not a very good horseman.'

'I can be sure because I still have the use of my eyes,' he snapped. 'Did I not see the dark mark on the beast's forehead? I have ridden that horse enough times to know it. It was the same mark. It means that my suspicion about Brother Finnsnechta was right. He was sending us directly into the arms of the man your husband served.'

'You mean he is a member of the Fellowship of the Raven? I cannot believe it of him.' The girl looked horrified.

Eadulf had been peering back along the path through the trees. 'I think that you had better believe it,' he said flatly. 'I can make out two riders crossing the plain from Ruán's homestead; they are riding fast in this direction. I think we were spotted as we rode away.'

The girl took one glance and confirmed his observation.

Eadulf looked desperately around. It would soon be dusk – but

not quickly enough for the darkness to conceal them from their
pursuers.

'When I was a little girl, my father brought me this way to avoid
highway thieves,' Ríonach reflected once again. 'There is a small
track up the hill which eventually leads to an abandoned ring fort.
We might try to hide there . . . we'll never outrun them on this
path.'

'Lead on,' Eadulf ordered, 'and let us pray that they are not good
trackers.'

The girl urged her horse forward with Eadulf close behind. It
was but a little distance before she turned sharply left through what
seemed to Eadulf's eyes to be just a tangle of overgrown bushes
and shrubbery. It turned out to be a steep, hidden path. Ríonach
brushed through, leaning low over her horse's neck as the upward
path rose precipitously through the densely growing vegetation. It
was even more difficult than the climb to Brother Finnsnechta's
hermitage.

Behind them, Eadulf imagined he heard the sound of pursuing
horses, blowing and snorting at their heels. He felt an uncomfortable prickling sensation in his back spine. It was a feeling of utter
vulnerability as he waited for the shout that would say they had
been spotted. He shivered.

The pathway came to a curious ledge on the hillside. It almost
appeared manmade for, under a large overhanging rock, there was
a fairly substantial cave with rocks and boulders forming a natural
protection around it. Eadulf saw that the path actually passed on
and upwards, but Ríonach had halted. She slid from her mount,
holding her terrier under one arm, and led her horse into the cave.
Eadulf had no option but to copy her.

She turned and leaned close to him, whispering: 'They will hear
the noise of our passage if we go any further. It's best to stop here
and remain quiet.'

Eadulf felt a quick sense of admiration for the young girl's courage and presence of mind. He whispered anxiously, 'I hope you can keep the dog quiet.' However, she had no time to respond before the sound of horses on the path below them became audible. Without consulting each other, they found themselves crouching behind the rocks as if it would assist their camouflage. Then, to their horror, the horses progress suddenly halted – almost directly below them. A voice cried out in annoyance: 'Why have you stopped?'

To Eadulf's ears, the voice seemed familiar.

'Because I don't believe they are stupid enough to head towards Cill Cainnech over these hills. That foreigner is quite intelligent. He would know that we would assume he was heading there. So I reckon he has doubled back the other way – back along the road towards Durlus or even Cashel.'

'Why do you think that?' demanded the familiar voice.

'Because, Duach, I am not a fool like you.'

Eadulf felt the girl start as she, too, recognised the two men. He pressed a finger against her lips.

'I have a score to settle with him,' Duach snarled.

'We both do. With him – and with that traitorous little bitch. Rechtabra was a good comrade and died a terrible death. Come, it's no use wearing ourselves out going further. We'll pick up their tracks along the marsh road.'

'Should we not tell Dar Badh what we are about, Cellaig?'

'And waste time? I doubt she will appreciate that! Did she not scold us enough for allowing ourselves to be tricked into captivity? Had that gullible shepherd and his son not arrived, we'd still be trussed like a pair of idiots.'

'True enough, and thank the powers they had horses, or we would not have been able to come back to forewarn him. She'll tell him, and the only way to redeem ourselves is by getting hold of Rechtabra's woman and the man.'

'Come – we are wasting time,' commanded the man they recognised as Cellaig. 'Let us be on our way.'

Eadulf and Ríonach listened to the sound of the horses cantering off back down the track towards the main highway. They waited until the sounds faded completely before allowing themselves to relax and breathe deeply.

'I hope nothing has happened to the shepherd and his son for offering to feed the livestock,' the girl fretted.

Eadulf was thinking the same thing. 'Who is Dar Badh?' he asked. 'Have you heard the name before?'

'It means Daughter of Badh, the Raven Goddess.' The girl shuddered. 'I don't think I want to meet her.'

'The sooner we can find Fidelma and my companions, the better. There is much here that I do not like.'

'It will soon be dark now.' The girl was practical. 'We cannot ride on along this path in darkness. And even if we had a lantern, which we do not, it would be seen at a distance and the track would still be dangerous.'

'Have you a suggestion?'

'Let's continue up to the abandoned ring fort. We can use it to make the horses comfortable and we can rest the night there. Then we can move on to Cill Cainnech at first light.'

'Won't our pursuers realise by then that we did not double back? Won't they turn round and try to overtake us again – and it will be broad daylight then.'

Ríonach shook her head. 'Even if they do, they will think we have joined the main highway into Cill Cainnech and will attempt to overtake us there. It is best to stick to these deserted tracks. Because my father always used them, I am sure I can remember the way.'

'Very well,' Eadulf acknowledged. 'Your advice has worked well enough so far. Lead on, Ríonach.'

Fidelma, as exhausted as she was, found herself unable to sleep. After she had returned from the chapel, she was shown to a small but comfortable chamber by Brother Failge. It was one of several chambers provided for visiting dignitaries and where women could stay. Aidan and Enda were given an adjoining chamber to share. As Fidelma lay on the bed, her mind was in turmoil; filled with concern for Eadulf and what unimaginable events could have befallen him. Then came the agonising sense of duty, that she had a task to complete as a *dálaigh*. She had always had a strong sense of duty which often forced her to overrule her personal feelings. That had certainly been put to the test for the first time when her close childhood friend and *anamchara*, her soul friend, to whom she would confess intimate secrets, became suspected of murdering her husband and her own child. Fidelma had pursued the case relentlessly and felt no remorse when she realised that her friend was indeed guilty and had conspired with her lover in the terrible affair. Duty forced her to bring her friend to justice.

Try as she might, she could not banish Eadulf from her thoughts. She knew that she had to concentrate on trying to resolve the murder of the strange couple. She had to discover their motivation for their search of the abbey chapel, and moreover, find out who had poisoned them. Yet every time a thought occurred to her, it was wiped aside by her fear for Eadulf's safety. So she tossed and turned restlessly on her bed.

It was a slight noise – the scrape of leather on the stones outside the door and then a moment of silence – that caused her to raise her head to listen. She heard a handle turning slowly and realised it was the door to her room. She began to swing down from the bed, her body tensed and ready to defend herself.

CHAPTER SIXTEEN

❧

Eadulf came awake, cold, stiff and aching in every joint. He groaned, blinked and tried to ease himself up into a sitting position. He had been lying on the damp grass by a stone wall with only his saddle and horse blanket for comfort. A short distance away Rían, the terrier, was seated looking at him almost with a quizzical expression; his tail thumping the ground. On the grass before it lay the bloodied, long-tailed remains of a wood mouse that had obviously been the terrier's meal. Eadulf turned and examined his surroundings. Ríonach was filling the goatskin water bag from a nearby spring. The horses were munching steadily from tufts of grass in a corner of the large stone wall enclosure. The sky was clear and blue, but the sun was barely above the distant eastern hills; it was pale and without warmth.

'Have I slept long?' he asked, getting to his feet and stamping them to eliminate the cramp.

The girl came over and offered him the water bag to drink from.

'I thought that you deserved to sleep a little longer,' she said kindly.

He thanked her and then gestured at the horses. 'I don't suppose we have any oats or other grain for them?'

'There were some berries that wild horses seem to like,' she said, indicating some bushes with her head. 'I picked some and gave them to them and made sure they had a drink.'

'Is there any of Brother Finnsnechta's bread left?' he asked hopefully, knowing that they had eaten most of it for their meal on the previous evening.

'A little.'

'Have you had some?' When she shook her head, he insisted that they divide the remaining bread and cheese between them.

'How long do you think it will be before we reach Cill Cainnech?' was his next question.

'We should be there well before midday,' she said confidently. 'If we avoid the direct route and keep to the higher ground, it's a longer way but safer. It reaches the river well north of the township and then we can head into it from there.'

Eadulf smiled at her. 'It sounds like a good plan.'

'This way is also through woods for much of the journey, which gives us cover, and the path is not too arduous.'

Eadulf glanced at the sky for a moment. 'The sooner we start out, then the sooner we shall arrive.'

He packed up the saddlebags and secured them. Then he stretched, looking around at their temporary shelter.

'Was this really a fort?' he asked, his gaze on the circular stone walls.

'Probably not,' the girl shrugged. 'These places are more likely to be old cattlepens or places where other livestock were kept. But some people think of them as forts.'

He was glad now that he had spent time with the warriors of the Nasc Niadh, for he knew that without the knowledge they had imparted, he would not have survived thus far. Thanks to them, he was able to approach and saddle his horse, albeit with a little difficulty. Ríonach scarcely needed any assistance at all. They mounted their horses and Ríonach began to lead the way eastward along a level track on the far side of the stone-encircled area. Eadulf was pleased that he did not have to re-negotiate the overgrown steep path again, to go back down to the track that they had left. His thoughts turned to his wife. Where was Fidelma now?

At that precise moment, Fidelma was on her hands and knees examining the base of the stone altar in the chapel while Feradach, with Aidan and Enda at his side, stood looking on. Over an hour before that, she had been disturbed before first light by a man's sudden, shadowy appearance at the door of her chamber.

'Do not be alarmed, lady,' he whispered. 'I need to talk with you.'

It was dark, apart from a faint glow from the ashes in the fireplace.

'I cannot talk to you in darkness, Feradach,' she replied calmly, recognising his voice. 'Can you light the lamp which is somewhere over there?'

The warrior felt his way over to the small table and picked up the oil lamp. She could make out his shadow as he moved across the room to the door. A lamp was still alight in the corridor, and Feradach had no problem in transferring its flame to the wick of the oil lamp. He came back, closing the door behind him, set down the lamp and then looked round. There was a chair against one wall and he lowered himself into it. Fidelma had thrown a robe around herself while he had gone into the corridor and now she sat on the bed and regarded him gravely.

'What business is it that you must come and disturb me in the middle of the night?'

Feradach actually chuckled. 'Not quite the middle of the night, lady. The birds will start to sing in the dawn fairly soon.'

'It is too early or too late to play semantics, Feradach.'

The warrior became serious. 'My apologies, lady. Something is worrying me. I do not think Abbot Saran was volunteering the whole truth.'

She stared at him for a moment in surprise. 'About what?' she asked, bemused.

'About the treasure of the abbey.'

'You mean there is no gold treasure taken from the local quarries?'

'Oh, indeed there is. The Abbot has, in the last ten years or so, built up a very respectable treasure. The abbey has used some of it to become involved in trade through its strategic position on the river here. You have seen where the treasure is kept.'

'But he admitted as much,' Fidelma pointed out. 'In what way has he been frugal with the truth?'

'It is said there was another great treasure and I believe that this is what the young man and woman were seeking when they were discovered.'

Fidelma was silent for a moment. 'That is quite a presumption, my friend, unless you have precise information. Perhaps you had better explain? But first tell me why you come to me with this story and at such a time? After all, you are a warrior of Osraige, as you have told me quite clearly. You serve the Abbot. Isn't your duty to the Abbot or your Prince?'

Feradach gave a grimace as if to dismiss the suggestion. 'It is true that my duty is to Tuam Snámha, Prince of Osraige, and the Abbot is his cousin. But you reminded me that the law stands above duty to princes. Anyway, Tuam Snámha has a binding treaty of peace and friendship with your brother, Colgú of Cashel. He pays tribute to the Kingdom of Muman. So my duty should be to your brother as well.'

'A fair enough argument, although I often find that the duties of a warrior of Osraige sometimes conflict with loyalty to Cashel,' she replied cynically.

'In this case, not so,' said the warrior. 'I think there is something more at stake here than the riches the abbey has acquired in recent years.'

'You intrigue me,' Fidelma said frankly. 'Very well – continue.'

'Do you know the story of the foundation of this abbey?'

'I have vaguely heard of it.'

Feradach inclined his head for a moment. 'Let me start at the time Cainnech came here. That was in my grandfather's time. This was one of the last great centres of the Old Faith. The defenders of the old gods and goddesses had been forced to retreat before the enthusiastic advocates of the New Faith. Everywhere, the old sanctuaries were being destroyed, rebuilt or converted to the New Faith, or even abandoned. From every corner of Ireland the Druids were leaving. Many were even converting to the Faith of Christ.'

Fidelma was a little impatient. 'This is basic history, my friend.'

'Indeed. But seventy years ago, this very mound on which this abbey was built was regarded as the last sanctuary of the Old Religion. The man who claimed the title of Chief Druid, together with his followers, had retreated here, and here they sought sanctuary, clinging to the beliefs that our ancestors had followed from the time before time.'

'So I have heard,' Fidelma nodded.

'Cainnech took this as an affront to the New Faith. He declared that the adherents of the old ways should be eliminated, and this spot consecrated to the New Faith, even as Pope Gregory had commanded. Cainnech was certainly no man of peace. He gathered an army and marched on this hill. I am told that he was an old man at that time for he died not long afterwards when he was eighty-four years old.

'My grandfather was still a young man when Cainnech and his army surrounded this hill. They were merciless: men, women and children who had adhered to the old gods and goddesses were destroyed. The hill ran with blood, every building was stained red. Fires then cleansed what was left. And finally, Cainnech ordered a church to be built to honour his victory. He blessed it and consecrated this hill, which had once been the sanctuary of the Druids, to the New Faith. Cill Cainnech is now the chapel of this abbey.'

'I have heard the tale roughly told, without as much detail,'

Fidelma said. 'But is it worth disturbing a night's sleep for? I thought you came to tell me about a treasure.'

Feradach's expression was serious. 'I was not telling you this story just to disturb you, lady. Legend has it that during those last days before Cainnech's army overwhelmed them, the Chief Druid and his followers had managed to hide a sacred treasure. It was hidden on this very hill and no one has ever discovered it after the citadel fell to the New Faith.'

'So you are trying to tell me that there is some pagan Druid treasure buried under the abbey?' Fidelma raised her voice in apparent surprise. 'And that *this* was the treasure that Ultan and Ultana came searching for?'

'And never found,' affirmed the warrior. 'But lower your voice, lady. The abbey walls carry sound and we must be circumspect.'

'You suspect that Abbot Saran knows all about it and, moreover, knows where it is hidden?' she said, just as loudly.

Feradach cast a nervous glance around. 'I do, but we must be quiet, lady. We don't want anyone to hear us.'

'And are you saying that *he* ordered Ultan and Ultana to be pursued and poisoned?'

Feradach gave an exaggerated shrug. 'I cannot make that claim. But it might be worth examining the chapel. The story among many people is that the treasure was put there – where the chapel now stands. That was where the sanctuary to the old gods and goddesses once stood. Would that not be the most likely spot to hide a treasure? It would explain why that couple were caught searching there.'

Fidelma was dubious. 'If Cainnech had no compunction in wreaking such destruction here, I doubt whether he would have left a treasure intact and built over it.'

'True,' agreed the warrior, 'unless it was so well hidden that he missed it. We know that Ultan and Ultana were not interested in the gold, silver and other precious artefacts that the abbey has acquired from the quarries and from trade over recent decades. So if they were not searching for those riches . . . what, then, *were* they searching for?'

'Let us presume that they were searching for this pagan treasure . . .' Fidelma paused as a thought occurred to her. Feradach waited for her to break the silence into which she had fallen. Then she raised her head. 'You might be right. Do you know much about this abbey and its history?'

The warrior smiled grimly. 'There's not been much history in a hundred years apart from the founding of this abbey and the growth of trade.'

'The Abbot implied that he had built the abbey?'

'That's right. Until he came, this was just a small church. In ten years things have altered drastically.'

'So he rebuilt everything?'

'Not everything. I am told that he left the chapel as it was and built his grand abbey around it.'

'Where did you get your knowledge of this matter?' Fidelma suddenly asked.

'My grandfather came from nearby. I heard tales from him. Seventy years ago is not so long in the minds of some people. My grandfather used to tell me that those adherents of the Old Religion who settled here possessed great wealth.'

'Those who settled here?' Fidelma repeated the phrase softly. 'Does that mean they were from elsewhere?'

'He said that those of the Old Religion had retreated here from many places all over Ireland. The Chief Druid, for instance, had fled here from one of the northern kingdoms.'

Fidelma looked up, alert. 'Did he know which one?'

'If he did, I do not remember.'

'So what are you suggesting, Feradach? What is the point of all this?' Her voice rose again, although she had hither to kept to a fairly normal speaking level.

'I thought we could take advantage of this darkness to go to the chapel and see if there was a purpose in Ultan trying to move the altar stone. Perhaps he was right and the pagan treasure does lie beneath it. If we go now, then the abbey is still asleep and we will not be disturbed.'

There was a movement outside the door and Aidan's voice came to their ears. 'Are you all right, lady? I heard voices.'

'Come in,' Fidelma called out. When Aidan entered, glancing with surprise at Feradach, she said: 'Feradach was suggesting that I go to the chapel with him to see if there is something hidden under the altar stone. Perhaps that is a good idea. We shall all go. Take Feradach and wake Enda and meet me outside. I must get properly dressed.'

Within a few moments all four were making their way to the chapel.

'What do you think happened to Ultan and Ultana after they fled from here?' Fidelma asked as they entered the gloom of the abbey sanctuary.

'It is hard to hazard a guess, lady,' Feradach replied. 'They just disappeared, as we told you. Great marshlands lie to the west of here, beyond the mountains. They say that many people dwell there who do not acknowledge the New Faith.'

'You think that Ultan and Ultana went to hide there?'

'Perhaps, although they spoke with northern accents for I have heard the same accents from emissaries from the northern kingdoms. But perhaps they were part of some fanatical group sent to find whatever it was that the Druids hid here.'

'So you believe Abbot Saran knew what they were looking for, surprised them when they were trying to move the altar; they attacked him and then they fled.'

'Something like that,' the young man agreed. 'But I am merely a warrior and not a *dálaigh*.'

'Did you discuss this with Brother Failge? He says he is qualified in law and therefore could perform the duties of a Brehon until a more senior and qualified judge was summoned.'

'I hesitated. Brother Failge is a good man but he is very supportive of the Abbot. I suppose he would be, being the steward here. However . . .' Feradach sighed. 'It is difficult to accuse the Abbot without proof.'

Fidelma looked round the chapel. She glanced through the window and saw there was a softening in the darkness of the sky. The birds were beginning to orchestrate their chorus to the coming dawn.

'We will not have long before the morning prayers,' Feradach urged. 'They will ring the bell soon. We have spent too long in talk.'

It was, indeed, only moments before a bell started tolling and there was the noise of the members of the community moving through the stone corridors of the abbey towards the chapel. Feradach's face was a picture of disappointment.

'We will wait until after the service,' Fidelma said. 'Let us take our position at the back of the chapel.'

It seemed that Abbot Saran favoured some of the new Roman usages of Latin and instructed the recitation of the declaration of belief with '*Angelus Domini nuntiavat Mariae . . .*' instead of the Greek forms which were generally used in many of the Irish abbeys. It had been in Greek that the word of the New Faith had initially been spread among the Five Kingdoms. However, Saran celebrated the service behind the altar and facing the congregation. Fidelma knew that most Roman Church clerics celebrated their services facing the altar with their backs to the worshippers.

It seemed an age before the service concluded and everyone disappeared about their daily tasks. The four waited until the chapel was abandoned and silent. It was so quiet that they could almost hear the sound of one another's breathing. Fidelma led the way to the altar, a solid-looking rectangle made of black marble. There were two candles still burning on it and these were removed at her request.

'Abbot Saran was attacked when he came into the chapel having discovered Ultan and Ultana trying to move this,' she stated.

Feradach nodded agreement. 'I think they suspected there was a means of moving the altar stone to reveal whatever it was they were looking for.'

'Do you mean that there might be a mechanism?' she asked.

'It seems logical,' the warrior said. 'Look at those carvings. Any one of those could act as some kind of handle.'

She knew the black marble was quarried locally. The craftsmanship was fairly crude. It looked like a simple table until one examined the base. Around it were a number of carved figurines marking a type of border where it rested on the flat limestone flags of the chapel. Fidelma went down on her knees and began to examine each figurine carefully, touching and pulling at it, watched in mystification by Aidan and Enda.

'I am sure that there *is* a movement in this somewhere,' she announced eventually. 'I think Feradach is right. I believe the altar is meant to be pushed to one side.'

She bent again and, using her fingers, carefully explored each figure once again.

Suddenly there was a hoarse cry from the chapel door. Abbot Saran was framed in the doorway, a look of shock on his face.

'This is sacrilege!' he croaked.

Fidelma rose to her feet and brushed the knees of her garment. 'Not sacrilege, no,' she replied calmly. 'I am performing the duty of a *dálaigh*.'

A moment later the figure of the steward, Brother Failge, appeared behind the portly Abbot.

'What is happening?' he boomed, looking from Fidelma to Feradach and back again.

'Ultan and Ultana were looking for something here. It was not the wealth you have laid up in your treasure chamber. They knew well where that treasure was kept – and ignored it. No, they were after something else.'

'And so?' The Abbot coughed. 'Does that give you the right to profane the altar of Christ?'

'You found Ultan in this chapel, trying to move this altar. Then you were attacked . . .'

'After which they fled,' Brother Failge said bitterly. 'Had there been anything worth finding, with the Abbot lying unconscious, they would have had time to carry out their task.'

'Perhaps they were in too much of a panic to stay,' Fidelma commented.

'This is outrageous!' Brother Failge exclaimed. 'Sister of King Colgú or not, you have no right . . .'

Feradach silenced him with a discreet cough.

'I have to point out, Brother Failge, that a *dálaigh* has many rights. One of them is the right to ask questions and expect answers.'

The Abbot turned to him with a surly expression. 'Your duty is to Osraige, Feradach, and the welfare of this abbey.'

'Feradach is right,' Brother Failge said. 'I do not like to admit it, but the law is not restricted by borders. The Law of the Fénechus is for *all* the people of the Five Kingdoms.'

Abbot Saran swallowed painfully. For a moment it looked as though he would argue with them, but Brother Failge reached forward, laid a thin hand on the Abbot's arm and said gently, 'Let the *dálaigh* ask her questions and let us resolve this matter.'

Fidelma smiled briefly at the steward. 'Thank you for your wisdom in this matter. I am told that this chapel stands as it was originally built after Cainnech destroyed the Druid sanctuary that was previously here?'

'The workmen whom the Blessed Cainnech ordered to build it did their job well,' conceded the Abbot in his grating voice. 'It is of good limestone, as you see, and they made excellent use of black marble.'

'Later you authorised the abbey to be built around it?'

Abbot Saran shrugged. 'I knew enough to let good work alone. We did not disturb the chapel.'

'You are aware of the stories that were told about this hill on which we now stand?'

'Stories!' snorted the steward. 'Tales for children to tell at bedtime.'

'You may be right, although it is said that there is many a truth in a fairy story,' replied Fidelma.

'I am aware of all the stories,' conceded the Abbot in a weary tone. 'Indeed, most of our abbeys and churches are built on the remains of the places where our people worshipped the old gods and goddesses. Seventy years ago, Gregory – the first of his name to be Bishop of Rome – wrote that the temples of the idols should *not* be destroyed. He ordered that holy water should be sprinkled over them. New altars dedicated to the Christ should be erected and the places converted to the worship of the True God. He was wise, for people who had attended such places of worship for thousands of years would continue to go to them. What better way to convert people to the New Faith?'

'Then you might have heard of the Golden Stone?'

They had been expecting a question about treasure but not the specific subject, and Fidelma's words brought strange expressions to the faces of the Abbot and his steward. Expressions that passed so fleetingly that Fidelma could easily have missed them.

'Golden Stone?' Abbot Saran grimaced. 'That is a story from some ancient myth. What has it to do with this abbey?'

Fidelma waited a moment, looking from one man to the other. Brother Failge remained silent.

'Perhaps we should see?' she mused. 'Ultan and Ultana were trying to push this altar stone aside when you entered the chapel. Is that not correct, Abbot Saran?'

'Push it aside? I thought they were trying to destroy it!' rasped the Abbot.

'I have been examining the base and there are signs of it having been moved a fraction.'

'What of it?' Brother Failge said fussily. 'The man and woman had succeeded in moving it a little when they were surprised by the Abbot. That is what caused the damage.'

Fidelma smiled thinly. 'They didn't know about the mechanism which would have allowed it to swing back the whole way to reveal what lay underneath.'

'There was nothing there and that is why they ran off,' protested the Abbot.

'I think we know better than that. I had just discovered something when you entered,' Fidelma went on, her voice still pleasant in tone. 'Feradach, will you assist me? Aidan, Enda, have a care of the Abbot and his steward. We would not like them to injure themselves.'

The Abbot and his steward stood almost frozen as Fidelma bent to the base of the altar stone and felt amongst the carvings which depicted figures dancing around the base. They were odd figures to put on a Christian altar. They watched as she moved her hands along, the figures . . . then she was turning one. There was a scraping sound and the altar stone gave a slight judder.

Fidelma stood up and glanced almost in triumph at the Abbot before turning to Feradach and saying, 'Will you help me push it aside?'

Together, observed by the others, they put their shoulders against the stone altar. After a few moments of resistance, it began to move, swinging on a hidden pivot. Fidelma stared down.

'A trapdoor!' she exclaimed. She reached down and grasped a small iron hoop and pulled. The hoop had been inlaid into the wooden trapdoor in such a way that it lay flat. It was not easy, but after a few hard tugs the wooden trapdoor lifted. Fidelma laid it carefully back. They all crowded round to peer down. A flight of narrow stone steps had been carved into the rock, leading down into darkness.

'I need a candle or a lamp,' Fidelma said.

'You do not mean to go down there, lady?' Aidan protested.

'That is precisely what I mean to do,' she asserted.

'Then I shall go first,' he told her.

Enda had seized two candles from an alcove at the side of the chapel and using his tinderbox had them alight in no time.

'I protest!' cried Abbot Saran. 'Those candles were to be used for the holy altar.'

'They are now to be used to see what is *under* the holy altar,' quipped Enda, handing one candle to Aidan and the other to Fidelma.

It was clear that Abbot Saran was inwardly raging at what he saw as desecration; however, Brother Failge stood in silence, his hands folded before him. There was no expression on his face.

Aidan started to descend the narrow steps.

'Watch your step, lady,' he called up as she prepared to follow him. 'There is much moisture down here seeping through the walls. There is moss on the steps, and it is very slippery.'

At the base of the stone steps was an underground chamber, its roof no higher than the height of a very tall man. It was a rectangular chamber, stone-lined, and many of the stones had faces carved on them. Fidelma had seen the like before. Horses' and birds' heads, and stylised faces with torcs at their necks. There were even solar symbols. There was no doubt in her mind that this had once been dedicated to the Old Religion.

'It seems empty,' whispered Aidan, drawing her attention back to their main purpose.

'Empty?' Fidelma turned, holding her candle high, and peered around. It was not a large chamber but there was an alcove at the far end opposite the steps. It was clear that it had been designed to hold something – possibly a small statue. A stone plinth had several markings on it which showed that it had been used as the base for a statuette, which had since been removed.

'Perhaps the man and girl did have time after all to remove what they had come for?' suggested Aidan.

'I doubt it,' Fidelma replied. 'You saw how difficult it was for me and Feradach to move the altar stone. Well, we are talking about a young man and a pregnant young girl firstly doing that, then trying to remove and transport a statue or heavy stone.'

Aidan sighed. 'I don't understand any of this.'

'Come on,' Fidelma said. 'There's nothing further we can do here.'

She climbed back up the steps into the chapel. The others crowded forward expectantly as Enda helped her out. Aidan followed close behind.

'Well?' demanded the Abbot. 'What was in there?'

Fidelma examined his anxious features carefully. 'You have no idea? You did not know about the hidden chamber?'

He shook his head quickly, then winced, his fleshy cheeks wobbling in indignation. 'Of course I did not!'

'Whatever was in there has been taken,' Aidan muttered.

'By that thieving pair?' raged the Abbot.

'I doubt it. They did not have the time or the capability to even open the way into the chamber. I believe they were looking for a sacred relic of the Old Religion which had been left here when the chapel was built. Many people would give much for that, even two centuries after the New Faith has spread through the Five Kingdoms.'

Abbot Saran looked startled. 'What sort of sacred relic? You mentioned a Golden Stone.'

'I don't know much about the old ways,' Fidelma confessed, 'but I do know that there were sacred stones which were connected with the old beliefs. There is the Lia Fáil at Tara. I have seen it. It is our tradition that the High King must take his oath at it. There are various other stones on which all our kings must take their oath – by placing one foot on the stone. The belief was that at the touch of a just and true king, the stone would shout in joy, while at the touch of an illegitimate ruler, one who was evil and corrupt, the stone would raise its voice in protest!'

The Abbot shivered. 'This is the House of the True Faith. We should not be speaking of such matters here,' he said in horror.

'Nevertheless, your chapel stands over a chamber which was devoted to the Old Religion and in which one such sacred stone reposed.'

Abbot Saran looked at them with his fleshy features moulded in a grim expression. 'Then we must reconsecrate this place, although it was done seventy years ago. We must cleanse the pagan chamber with fire and then drown it with holy water.'

'We still have to find out what happened to the man and the girl after they left here, and who poisoned them,' Fidelma reminded her companions.

'If there was some pagan object – a golden stone, you say – well, if there was such an item, then they *must* have taken it,' pointed out Feradach. 'For if they did not, who did?'

'And for what purpose did they seek it?' added the Abbot.

'After a few moments when no one spoke, Aidan asked, 'So what now, lady?'

'Now?' she responded brightly. 'It is nearing midday and I think the middle meal will be most welcome after all our exertions.'

This time they were not invited to eat with the Abbot, who had retired to his own private chamber. Instead they were shown by the now surly steward to the *praintech*, or refectory, of the abbey and seated at the end of one of the long wooden tables. Brother Failge issued instructions to the servers and then stomped away.

Feradach, who had joined Fidelma, Aidan and Enda, pulled a wry expression. 'He is not happy, especially at my support of you.'

'He has reason to be unhappy and so has the Abbot,' Aidan replied. 'Imagine finding a pagan shrine under the altar of your chapel.'

'An abandoned one,' pointed out Enda.

Fidelma paused as bowls of vegetable soup and fresh bread were placed before them by the silent servers. 'Abandoned – but how long ago? The scratch-marks on the plinth where we believe the object stood were fresh.'

'So the man and woman, whoever they were, did take it after all?' Feradach said, confused.

Fidelma shook her head. 'I am sure they did not, and for the reasons I have given. Someone else had got there first.'

Just then, the door of the *praintech* swung open and one of the members of the community entered. He paused, searched the room and saw them.

'Your pardon, lady. I am told you are Fidelma of Cashel.'

Fidelma looked at the religieux and said: 'I am.'

'There are a man and woman at the door demanding to see you. A madman, I am thinking.'

'What do you mean?' Fidelma was puzzled.

'He wears poor clothes like a farmer, but has a Roman tonsure and he speaks with a foreign accent.'

Hope suddenly sprang at her heart. 'Bring him forward then,' she said.

The religieux hurried back to the doors. A little while later, they swung open again and a familiar figure entered the room with a young woman trailing behind him. She too seemed familiar to Fidelma.

'Well, Eadulf,' Fidelma smiled broadly, 'where have you been all this time?'

CHAPTER SEVENTEEN

‌‌⟨image of decorative ornament⟩

When the excitement had died away, when the embraces, back-slapping and handshakes had ceased, Eadulf drew forth his companion, an embarrassed-looking Ríonach. She was still clutching the anxious terrier, Rían, in her arms.

'The story is a long one,' Eadulf said immediately in answer to the shower of questions. 'To save my life – indeed, to save her own as well – Ríonach had to kill Rechtabra. He was one of the men who held me captive and he would have killed me, had she not struck first.'

This prompted more questions from the group, each drowning out one another in their attempt to ask first. Eventually Fidelma managed to raise her voice sufficiently to restore order. Eadulf told the story as succinctly as he could, pausing to answer the occasional brief enquiry from Fidelma.

Then Ríonach added to the story from her viewpoint and was met with expressions of sympathy, especially from Enda who surprised Eadulf by his solicitude for the girl and sympathetic attitude.

'So now we know there is some curious secret organisation at work here that is devoted to the Old Religion,' Fidelma summed up. 'What did you call it – the Fellowship of the Raven?'

Eadulf nodded. 'Yes. And it looks as though the couple we found dead were part of it. The girl had their symbol on her wrist – as do the others, including Rechtabra and his friends.'

'You could not identify the man whom they called the "lord" and who came to question you?'

'They kept the light in my eyes while he spoke to me. However, I think I would recognise his voice if I heard it again.'

'When he looked at you, he said that they had captured the wrong person. Obviously your abductors had been looking for this man Ultan as well as the girl Ultana. But if they had already poisoned the couple, it doesn't make sense.'

'You believe that they picked me up by mistake simply because I was dressed as a religieux.'

'As soon as their leader saw you were not Ultan, you were blind-folded again and he left, is that correct?'

'Yes, but not before he ordered Rechtabra and his companion to kill me. It was only the fact that Rechtabra's companion, who apparently was in charge, was so superstitious that he thought the Eóganacht gods would curse him if he laid hands on me, which prevented my immediate death. His plan was just to leave me bound and gagged, to perish like that.'

'Was it this leader who took your horse?'

'Since I found my cob in the field of this Brehon Ruán, he must be the person who gave them their orders. I am told he is Brehon to the Lord of the Marshes, Coileach. But we have heard rumours that Coileach is dead or that he has gone on a journey to Tara.'

'You say that the hermit who dwells on the Mountain of the High Hills instructed you to go to this Brehon Ruán with your story, and that only by recognising your horse did you escape capture?'

Eadulf nodded. Then, suddenly remembering the note that Brother Finnsnechta had given him, he drew it out and handed it to Fidelma.

She glanced at it. 'It is in Ogham.'

Eadulf grimaced. 'I suspect that he presumed – and rightly so – that I would not know this ancient form of your language. Perhaps the message contains secret instructions. Do you know what it says?'

'I know enough to translate it,' she confirmed. 'It merely says "I commend Eadulf and Ríonach to the mercy of your hospitality. Brother Finnsnechta".'

Eadulf was disappointed. 'Nothing more incriminating than that?' he asked. 'Although even that could have been a message – "the mercy of your hospitality" could secretly mean that this Ruán should take care of us and not in a nice way. He would know me, if he *was* this "lord" who questioned me. He would also know that Ríonach was wife to Rechtabra.'

'It could be interpreted that way,' Fidelma agreed. 'Yet there is one thing in your story that I don't understand. This "lord" left you to be dealt with, but you were spared from immediate death because the man told to do it feared the retribution of the old gods of my ancestors. But when this same "lord" found that his instructions had not been obeyed, he or Rechtabra killed the man who had disobeyed him and then he came back to kill you. Why didn't Rechtabra turn on his companion before, when he knew the man was not obeying the orders? It seems illogical.'

Eadulf glanced apologetically towards Ríonach before saying, 'I don't think Rechtabra was too bright. He was one of those people who obey orders and do not stop to work things out for themselves. The other man was in charge, so Rechtabra accepted the situation until this mysterious "lord" gave him specific orders to the contrary. I have encountered individuals like that. They have the minds of brutes and just follow orders. This poor girl will attest to that. As I said, Rionach saved my life. I am greatly in her debt.'

There was a silence and, once again, Enda made some sympathetic remarks to the girl.

'It was lucky that you recognised your cob in Brehon Ruán's field before you reached his homestead,' Feradach commented to Eadulf, entering the conversation for the first time.

'And luckier still that Ríonach knew a place where we could escape from the pursuit of Duach and Cellaig, who had been sent after us. I just hope they did not take their revenge on the shepherd

and his son, whom we sent to free them.' Eadulf glanced question-
ingly at Feradach.

'Feradach is the commander of the guards in this township,'
Fidelma explained, realising that she had not introduced him.

'I have heard much of the husband of the lady Fidelma,' the
warrior said pleasantly.

Eadulf nodded absently. 'Then you have the advantage of me.
Have we met before?'

'Your comrades have spoken much about you,' replied the warrior.

Fidelma summed things up for everyone again. When all is said
and done, it seems that the link is still with this abbey, and this is
the reason why Ultan and Ultana came here. I believe the link
is this sacred pagan treasure or stone, and the secret chamber under
the chapel. Perhaps they were members of this Fellowship of the
Raven, or had been and were trying to extract some recompense.'

'What happens now?' Feradach wanted to know.

'We will have another word with the steward and the Abbot,'
Fidelma decided. She smiled at Eadulf, still clad in the farmer's
rough garb. 'Perhaps we can arrange for baths and a more suitable
change of clothing.'

When they found the steward in the main hall, he greeted them
in an unfriendly fashion.

'Have you not bothered the Abbot enough?' he demanded in
answer to Fidelma's request. 'He is gravely disturbed by your revelations of the secret chamber.' His eyes fell on Eadulf and Ríonach;
and with distaste on the terrier that followed at the girl's heels. 'We
allow no animals in the abbey,' he snapped.

Fidelma answered, ignoring his protest: 'This is my husband,
Eadulf of Seaxmund's Ham, and another companion.' She was not
specific about Ríonach's role. 'They have just escaped from the
very pagan group I believe is behind these troubles.'

Brother Failge glanced in surprise at Feradach. 'Are they here
with your approval?'

The commander of the Osraige warriors gave a quick assurance, upon which Brother Failge moved off with some reluctance to find Abbot Saran. A few moments later, the Abbot entered and seated himself. There was a frightened expression on his rotund features.

'Why have you come again to disturb the peace of this abbey, Fidelma of Cashel?' he greeted, clearing his damaged throat.

'The peace of this place was disturbed many years ago, Abbot Saran,' she told him. 'And the consequence of that is why it remains disturbed today.'

'I have told you that I knew nothing of that secret chamber,' protested Saran. 'I knew nothing either of the man and woman who tried to desecrate my chapel.' Unconsciously, the Abbot raised a hand to massage his throat as if reminded of the attempt to kill him. His steward, prompted by his duties, stood up and went to a side table to pour water from a jug and returned to hand it to the Abbot.

Eadulf had been watching Brother Failge curiously. Without any warning, as the steward was reaching forward to hand the drink to the Abbot, he grabbed the man's hand, causing him to drop the mug, which smashed, showering its contents on the floor. The steward gave an astonished yelp and everyone looked on in shock at the tableau formed by Eadulf and Brother Failge.

Eadulf was tugging something from the steward's wrist. The man was struggling, and he let forth a stream of profanities at Eadulf. No one else seemed capable of movement. Then Eadulf released his hold on the steward. Taken by surprise, Brother Failge staggered back. Ríonach meanwhile was trying to calm the excited terrier, who was growling and barking at everyone.

'I seem to have become quite an expert on collecting such baubles in recent days,' Eadulf commented in triumph, holding up an object for the rest of them to see.

It was a piece of twisted hemp from which a small brass disc was dangling.

Brother Failge gave a curious snarl and his hand went beneath his robes and withdrew from them a wicked-looking dagger. Before he could launch himself at Eadulf, however, the dagger had been knocked from his hand by the flat of Aidan's sword, and the point of that same weapon was now at the steward's throat.

Abbot Saran was staring at his steward as if he had never seen him before. 'What does this outrage mean?' he gasped.

Fidelma had taken the round metal disc from Eadulf and examined it.

'Well spotted, Eadulf,' she said. 'So this is the symbol of your Fellowship of the Raven?'

'You'll recognise it, I am sure,' Eadulf acknowledged with a smile.

Fidelma turned to Feradach who stood uncertainly by. 'I would ask that you restrain this man, for we will need to question him. He is obviously a member of this conspiracy and possibly the one person who can answer our questions about the deaths of Ultan and Ultana.'

Before the Osraige warrior could respond, Enda had removed a piece of cord from his belt and had expertly bound Brother Failge's hands. Then he pushed the steward onto a nearby seat. Feradach had scooped up the dagger that had fallen from the steward's hand.

'I understand none of this,' the Abbot croaked, looking from one to another as if in search of an explanation. His expression was almost comically woebegone.

'Perhaps we should all be seated,' suggested Fidelma. 'Then Eadulf can explain what he has told me.'

After they had seated themselves, and looked expectantly at Eadulf, he took the brass disc from Fidelma and placed it in the centre of the round table. Then from his belt bag he extracted firstly the disc he had taken from the dead man in the marsh, who had been his captor; then the similar disc he had taken from Rechtabra, followed by those from Cellaig and Duach. As he placed each disc alongside that which had been worn by Brother Failge, he recited where they had come from. Then he turned to Fidelma.

'I believe that you have another one to contribute?'

Fidelma felt in her comb bag for the metal disc and placed it with its fellows.

'That was taken from the wrist of the murdered girl we now know as Ultana,' she stated.

There was a silence before Eadulf began to speak. 'All these little brass discs have the image of a bird on them. Specifically, the image of a raven. Now the raven was a potent symbol of the Old Religion of this country, so I am told. It is the symbol of death and battle, of blood and vengeance, and is personified by the Triune Goddess Badh, Mórrígan and Macha . . . who collectively take the form of a raven. You will remember the story of the hero Cúchullain who, dying at the Pillar Stone, had the Goddess of Vengeance, in the form of a raven, perch on his shoulder to triumphantly drink his blood.'

Abbot Saran managed to summon a snort of uneasy indignation. 'Such superstitions should have no meaning in the New Faith.'

'Oh, but they do continue to have meaning in the minds of many people,' replied Eadulf. 'This has become the symbol of the Fellowship of the Raven, which is a group of people who still adhere to the Old Religion of this country. Ríonach's husband was one of them.'

The girl lowered her head in mute agreement.

'What is their purpose?' bleated Abbot Saran.

'Perhaps we can ask Failge?' replied Fidelma.

The steward gave her a sullen glance. 'I found the emblem. It is not mine. I – I found it on the wrist of the man Ultan.'

'That explanation seems reasonable enough,' the Abbot said quickly.

'Reasonable?' repeated Fidelma. 'Then kindly explain what is reasonable about drawing a knife to attack Eadulf, accompanied by language that does not belong in a marketplace, let alone in an abbey!' She paused and then said: 'I believe that they have chosen the Triune Goddess in order to wreak vengeance for the destruction of the Old Faith, and to seek the death of the New Faith.'

The rotund Abbot blinked bewilderedly. 'You mean they want revenge for what Cainnech did here when he overthrew the last of the Druids seventy years ago?'

'Something like that,' Eadulf agreed, his mind latching on to Fidelma's line of thinking.

'And you believe that Ultan and Ultana were part of this conspiracy?'

'It seems likely, but we need more facts.' Fidelma turned to Failge, who was sitting hunched up, his hands tied, glowering at them. 'You will answer some questions now.'

The steward gave a contemptuous snort. 'That I will not.'

'I think you will.'

'And I *know* that I won't. Threats will not force me to speak to you.'

'Who mentioned threats?' Fidelma said mildly. 'I do not make threats,' she went on. Then she sighed. 'Is it your last word that you will not speak further of this Fellowship of the Raven?'

Brother Failge raised his chin defiantly and sneered, 'I will answer nothing. I will speak no more to you. I will endure all physical pain you can inflict on me. I shall *never* betray the blessed raven.'

'Physical pain?' Failge had actually used the word *branndán* – torture. 'Why would you think that we would resort to torture?'

'Because that is the way with you – you of the New Faith. It is well known that you are spreading new laws called the Penitentials in place of our ancient laws. Mutilations, hangings, drowning . . . they are used by many abbeys who have adopted foreign ways, where wrongdoers are physically punished instead of being forced to compensate their victims. I have seen it written in *Di Astud Chirt agus Dligid*, On the Confirmation of Right and Law, that it was Patrick who first introduced such vicious punishments into this island. So do your worst. I shall not talk.'

'If you are part of a group seeking vengeance, is that no better than the vengeance of the Penitentials?' queried Fidelma.

'The New Faith has taught us the weapons we must use to overcome them,' replied Failge stubbornly. 'When a forest burns, one often has to light another fire to stop it destroying the entire forest . . . "burning for burning" as your teaching goes.'

Fidelma paused thoughtfully for a moment before addressing Feradach and Enda, saying, 'Go into the chapel and open the underground room again.'

They looked surprised, but she made no further comment and so they left to fulfil her instruction.

'What do you intend?' Abbot Saran asked anxiously.

'I intend to explain the difference between our law system and the rules that certain communities of our religious have misguidedly adopted – these rules called the Penitentials which incorporate foreign laws of punishment.'

Failge laughed aloud. 'Are you saying that you can uphold our old laws and values while accepting this New Faith from the East?' he challenged.

'Do you say that we cannot?' she countered.

'I do. Have you not read the justification for torture that these so-called Penitentials would inflict – such as the call for us to mortify our flesh in order to gain an afterlife? In our religion, when we die, we are simply reborn in the Otherworld, the parallel world. When we die in that world, we are reborn in this one. Our stations in both worlds depend on how well we have lived our lives. While we dwell in this world, on the eve of Samhain, the Otherworld becomes visible to us – and those whom we have wronged, who have passed there, can return to exact their vengeance.'

'I know of that belief,' Fidelma assured him. 'But you claim the Penitentials expect us to indulge in mortification of the flesh to obtain an afterlife?'

'The Gospels of the New Faith declare it,' Brother Failge spat.

'I have not heard it said,' she declared.

'It is so said by Paul in his letter to his followers in Rome: *si enim secundum carnem vixeritis moriemini si autem Spiritu facta carnis mortificatis vivetis . . .*'

'If you live according to the flesh you will die, but if by the Spirit you put to death the misdeeds of the body, you will live,' muttered the Abbot.

'So you are interpreting this as an exhortation to inflict punishment on the flesh to deaden natural functions and desires in order to gain an afterlife?' Fidelma was appalled. 'That is nonsense.'

'Then many who follow this New Faith have no sense.'

'What are words but labels that can be misinterpreted?' Eadulf said.

'I am not the one doing the misinterpretation,' returned the steward. 'It is the clerics who maintain these Penitentials.'

'I don't doubt that many will have sympathy with your cause, Failge,' Fidelma mused, ignoring the disapproving look of the Abbot. 'I myself feel saddened at the loss of some of the moral concepts from the old days. But I have to remind myself that I am a *dálaigh*. I am an advocate of the law of the Fénechus and not that of the Penitentials, and it is to the law of the Fénechus that I must turn.

'I am not judging either the New or the Old Faith,' she went on, 'but the crime of murder. I am investigating the deaths of this young couple whom we are now calling Ultan and Ultana. Then there is the capture of Eadulf here, and the attempt to murder him – which resulted in other deaths. This, from the evidence that has been shown, is the responsibility of the Fellowship of the Raven. You appear to represent this Fellowship, Failge. Under the law of the Fénechus you have a right to present your defence.'

But Brother Failge shook his head, saying, 'I see what you are trying to do, but it will not work. I shall say nothing.'

Fidelma rose as Feradach and Enda returned.

'We've opened the entrance again, lady,' reported Feradach.

'Bring him along then.' She nodded to Brother Failge. Then she glanced to Ríonach, who was still sitting with bowed head. 'It is not necessary for you to come, my dear. You may remain here with your dog. Enda – you may stay with her.'

Feradach and Aidan hoisted the steward to his feet, each supporting one of his arms. Fidelma led the way to the chapel, Eadulf and Abbot Saran following along behind her. 'I don't understand,' muttered the fat Abbot; this had become a phrase that he was repeating again and again, almost as a religious prayer.

Fidelma walked to the top of the steps and pointed downwards into the underground chamber. Her face was a mask.

'At least you will pass to your Otherworld surrounded by the images of your Old Faith, Failge.'

The steward's eyes went wide. 'Surely you do not intend to incarcerate me down there?' he breathed.

'But you told me that I can.' Fidelma actually smiled. 'You expect little else from the New Faith. Do you not claim that we not only mortify our own flesh but ensure the mortification of others?' She spoke to Feradach. 'Untie his hands and give him a candle, Feradach . . . not a large one, just a stub so that he can quickly look on the images of the old gods and goddesses, who will doubtless sustain him in his dark vigil.'

There was a silence. Then the horrified voice of the Abbot cried: 'But you are a *dálaigh* . . . I protest! You cannot bury a man alive, no matter what he has done. This is not the true way of the New Faith!'

'Did Brother Failge not quote from one of the sacred texts to prove it so?' demanded Fidelma. 'What was the quotation?'

'Punishments should be life for life, eye for eye, tooth for tooth, hand for hand . . . burning for burning . . .' conceded the Abbot. 'But—'

'Exactly,' she interrupted grimly. '*Animam pro anima*. Untie his hands, but Aidan, keep your sword at his throat. Try not to kill him

278

if he refuses to descend – he might need some persuasion. Where is the candle stub I asked you for? Light it and give it to him, and light another one for me.'

Feradach reluctantly did as he was told. Fidelma took the candle that he had given to her, placed it on the altar and took from her comb bag a pin. To their surprise, she measured down the wick with her thumb and then thrust the pin into the candle at that point. Then she turned back with a glance of impatience. The men moved reluctantly, as if they could not believe her order. Brother Failge took the lighted candle stub from Feradach with a defiant smile and began to descend the narrow stairs. He paused for a moment and stared malignantly at Fidelma. 'My vengeance is to come, Fidelma of Cashel. Look for me on the eve of the Feast of Samhain. Look for me . . .'

She signalled to Feradach to push the altar stone back in position. Even Eadulf was looking at her in dismay. Like Aidan, he found her action entirely out of character and was unable to believe the scene that he had just witnessed. It was almost impossible to accept this new callousness in her.

'Now, Aidan, go and tell Enda to prepare our horses. We must soon be away from this place.' When Aidan hesitated for a moment, as if he wanted to say something, she added, 'Don't forget to ensure that Eadulf and the girl's horses are also ready for the journey. Ríonach will accompany us to Cashel in fulfilment of Eadulf's promise, and Feradach will also be joining us. Tell Enda to make haste.'

'Are you leaving?' Abbot Saran asked, aghast. 'Leaving after . . . after . . .' Words seemed to fail him as he gestured to the closed slab hiding the secret chamber.

Fidelma turned back and regarded his outraged expression as if in amusement.

'You will not object to our departure? I thought you would be rejoicing.'

The Abbot pointed to the floor at the base of the altar. 'You have exacted a terrible punishment. This abbey will not sit quietly with the grave of an unbeliever under its chapel.'

'What better place would you have an unbeliever resting for eternity?' Her voice was cold.

'It will be my Christian duty to open the chamber as soon as you have departed,' declared the Abbot, angrily leaving the chapel. 'I pray I am not too late.'

A moment later, Aidan returned. 'Enda and the girl have gone to the abbey stable to get all the horses prepared.'

'Very well. I am afraid, Aidan, you have the most tedious task of all – to watch that candle here. Come and tell me when the pin falls out.'

'It shall be done, lady,' the warrior replied.

Fidelma turned to Eadulf. 'Now let us join the others and I'll tell you my plan.'

Eadulf was smiling as he had finally guessed what she was about. 'I still don't approve,' he commented. 'You don't really think that you will scare a man like that into talking.'

'Scare?' Fidelma voice was almost innocent as she led the way back to the hall.

'You mean to frighten him by pretending to bury him alive; allowing him to go mad with fear in the darkness so that when you release him, he will start babbling his confession to you.'

Fidelma merely smiled broadly but did not reply. As they came into the hall, Enda and the girl were re-entering.

'The horses are all ready. I persuaded the stableman that this was on the express order of Feradach and Abbot Saran.'

'Excellent. I think we shall soon be embarking on the last phase of our investigation.'

'You mean that Failge will tell us where to find this mysterious lord who leads the Fellowship of the Raven?' Eadulf was still trying to make sense of her actions.

'And now,' Fidelma did not answer him but turned to Ríonach, 'are you content to come to Cashel?'

The girl looked very happy indeed. 'I would like nothing better, lady.' Then a cloud crossed her features. 'But don't forget I killed my husband. I have to do penance . . .'

'Penance?' Fidelma made the word one of disgust. 'We will relate your story to the Chief Brehon of Muman and I will represent your case. Even as Eadulf has done in theory, I shall do in practice, and all shall be well. And should you want to stay in Cashel, then we shall find you some means of security.'

'You can rely on Aidan and me to do what we can to help Ríonach, lady,' Enda added enthusiastically.

Eadulf saw Fidelma smile to herself and knew he was missing something.

At that moment, Aidan hurried into the hall. 'The pin has fallen, lady.'

Fidelma stood up with a decisive motion. 'Excellent. Let us now see if I was right.'

'Right?' queried Eadulf curiously, but she was already striding after Aidan. She had reached the door of the chapel when Eadulf and the others started to follow.

'Aidan, give Feradach a hand with the altar.'

The two muscular warriors leaned their weight on the heavy altar stone after removing the catch and were soon pushing it in the curious motion on its pivot to reveal the entrance to the underground chamber.

'You've been here the whole time?' Fidelma asked Aidan.

'All the time, watching the candle-grease dripping,' he assured her.

'Very good. The candle if you please, Aidan.'

She was peering down into the darkness. Aidan took a new candle, lit it from the one which had been burning, and joined her.

'Right, give it to me,' she instructed.

'I shall go first again,' Aidan said. 'He might be ready to pounce on you. Just because his stub of candle is out, it doesn't mean to say that he is unconscious.'

Without waiting for a response, Aidan was descending the narrow stairs into the subterranean chamber.

He had hardly got to the bottom of the steps when he gave a cry.

'He's gone, lady! He is not here!'

chapter eighteen

(ornament)

'I thought as much.' Fidelma seemed completely unperturbed; in fact, she was smiling at their staring faces. Then she called down to Aidan. 'Stay there! Feradach and I will join you.' She turned to Eadulf. 'I want you and Enda to take all the horses and meet us on the main highway on the western side of the township. Enda, do you recall there is a point where a track leads off to the rear of this hill towards an isolated group of buildings? It looks like a smith's forge. I pointed it out when we came here.' When Enda nodded, she went on: 'Wait there with the horses because I am sure that Failge will be heading in that direction.'

Eadulf was shaking his head. 'You knew all along that there was a secret exit? You incarcerated him, knowing he would get out and maybe lead us to this mysterious "lord"?'

She shrugged. 'I saw the scuff-marks where a stone had been removed from its base: they ended at the wall. Now even the most superstitious would find it hard to believe that the stone could be dragged through a wall, so my conclusion was that there must be a secret door through which it was taken. Whoever stole the Golden Stone forgot that stone scraping on stone leaves marks. Yes, Failge *is* going to lead us to this "lord" of the Fellowship of the Raven and also to this pagan icon. I believe the passageway will come out on the western side of this hill.'

Eadulf wasted no time but left the chapel with Enda and Ríonach, with Rían the terrier trotting after them.

Fidelma said to Feradach, 'You go first and I'll follow.'

The Osraige warrior grinned wryly at her. 'So you knew about the secret passage while you were pretending to entomb Brother Failge alive? There was I, thinking you had a merciless heart, lady. You must be very clever.'

'No, I am merely logical. I was sure that he knew the secret way out and gave him time to leave. And now he will lead us to the lair of this conspiracy – to the very heart of it. The sooner we start after him, the sooner we can catch up with him.'

With a shrug, Feradach started down the narrow steps into the gloom of the secret room.

'What now?' Aidan was holding his candle high and examining the walls.

'Straight ahead,' Fidelma said. 'See the alcove in which the stone stood? I think the back of it is actually the secret door.'

'I can't see any means of opening it,' replied Aidan.

'Perhaps you are wrong, lady,' Feradach said.

Fidelma moved forward with her candle and examined it. 'I noticed something that might be the mechanism when I was down here before. Ah, yes . . . Whoever built this place knew all about secret mechanisms.'

There were carvings of mythological beasts and icons throughout the small underground room. But to one side of the alcove was a bird image with extended wings. Fidelma began to prod the stone icon. There was a subtle change of texture about the head. She realised that it was fashioned of metal, a smooth brass, whereas the rest of the body was stone. With a grunt of satisfaction, she pulled and twisted the head and, after a few moments, she felt it give and heard a click. There was a moment of disappointment, for nothing happened: the wall was still in place. With a frown, she moved forward and pushed against it. Then it swung backwards easily. It was a surprising piece of craftsmanship – a wooden door but with the front covered by a thin layer of stones. From the interior of the room, it gave the impression of being solid stone.

Beyond it was now revealed a narrow, dark passageway.

'You lead the way, Feradach. We'll follow,' Fidelma said, trying to keep the triumph out of her voice.

The Osraige warrior said nothing but set off into the passage holding his candle aloft. Fidelma followed, leaving Aidan to come behind.

The passage was an old one, for the odours of the earth were stale and the floor was well-worn. It seemed to twist and turn a little bit. This worried Fidelma because she had estimated that it would lead through the hillside on which the abbey had been built to emerge west of the township where she had seen the smithy. It had been on that basis that she had instructed Eadulf, Enda and Ríonach to wait for them there with all the horses. Now and then the roof of the passage dipped so that they had to duck and, at one point, wade through a flooded area where the water rose above their ankles.

It seemed as though they had been walking for quite a while before they entered a small cave. They could hear the nearby sound of metal ringing against metal. A faint light trickled through an exit sealed off by a wooden door. Feradach went ahead and drew the door open, for it was not locked. They emerged at the rear of a small complex of buildings that obviously constituted a smith's forge. A fire was roaring in the forge itself; the smoke and fumes were all-pervasive. Fidelma experienced a moment of satisfaction as she realised that her guess had been correct.

A burly man who had been in the act of hammering metal over an anvil had noticed them and he turned in their direction. There was surprise on his face as Feradach led the way forward.

'My lord,' gasped the man. 'What . . . ?'

'You recognise me as the commander of the guard in this township?' snapped Feradach. 'We are following a religieux who has just come from this tunnel and need to know where he is gone.'

The smith stared from Feradach to Aidan, and then to Fidelma. He seemed to be trying to gather his thoughts.

'Come, man,' prompted Aidan harshly. 'We know he came this way, so you must have seen him.'

'That's right,' Feradach added. 'Speak the truth and nothing will happen to you.'

The smith nodded reluctantly. 'The man came by and took a horse.'

There was a small paddock next to the smithy containing several animals. Nearby was a track which must lead towards the main highway, as Fidelma had observed on their journey into the township.

'I presume that links up with the great highway, west to Cashel?' she demanded.

'It does, lady.'

'How long ago was it when this man left?'

Once again the smith looked helplessly from one warrior to another before returning to Fidelma. 'Not very long, lady.'

'It's not the best place to site a forge,' she commented, looking around. 'You are very isolated here.'

'I get by,' mumbled the smith. 'The forge has been here for as long as I remember.'

'As has the secret tunnel into the abbey?' she replied without humour.

'Remain here, smith, for when I return I will have questions for you,' Feradach warned him. Then he said to Fidelma, 'It will take some time to reach the main highway. I fear we have lost Failge.'

Aidan then stepped forward and, without explaining, took his hunting horn from his belt and blew several curiously timed blasts on it.

'It will save us a walk,' he told Fidelma, and smiled grimly. 'A member of the Nasc Niadh will know what is to be done.'

Only moments passed before they saw a rider leading three horses – one of them Fidelma's mount, Aonbharr – cantering along the track towards them. It was Enda.

He halted, grinning. 'I heard the old signal, Aidan.'

'Well done,' Fidelma approved as she mounted up. 'Did you see any sign of Failge?'

'As we approached the junction with this track, lady,' Enda replied at once, 'we saw him on horseback, heading towards the Mountains of the High Fields. We were too far behind to catch him and he was going at some speed, but I marked his passage.'

She pointed to the gate of the paddock. 'You'll find tracks of a horse coming out of that paddock a short while ago. Observe them and see if there is anything that sticks in your mind that you can track if the need arises, but I am sure I know where he is heading.'

Enda, who was famed for his ability to track, swung off his horse and made a quick examination of the ground. Then he smiled and remounted.

'The shoe on the left foreleg has a bent nail,' he replied. 'He should be easy to track.'

'Then let us go,' replied Fidelma, urging her mount forward.

'Where to?' Feradach asked as they began to trot towards the main highway. 'Where do you think he is going?'

'Where else but to the homestead of Brehon Ruán?'

With no further explanation, they rode towards the junction where Eadulf and Ríonach were waiting impatiently for them.

'Westward?' called Eadulf unnecessarily, for Fidelma had already turned and was heading along the road towards Cashel.

'Westward, indeed,' she affirmed as she passed him. She kept the pace at a canter. It was no use tiring the horses to try to overtake their quarry.

No one spoke as they moved in a single body along the highway towards the distant mountains. Now and then Enda rode on alone to observe the tracks in the dust of the road. Eventually, as the hills drew nearer, Fidelma slowed the pace to a walking speed. Eadulf was grateful and managed to manoeuvre his horse alongside her.

'If we are to confront the thugs of this Fellowship it would be better to approach carefully,' he advised. 'We don't know how many are involved in this Fellowship of the Raven. Apart from Failge, there are Duach and Cellaig and that woman called Dar Badh – and there may be others. After all, two of them are already dead, I mean the farmer Rechtabra and his companion.'

Fidelma nodded absently and glanced at the sky. 'It will soon be dusk. It might be wise to come upon the place at nightfall.'

Feradach overheard and called: 'People in these areas usually loose their hounds at nightfall. The wolves are still plentiful and they need to protect their livestock. Better to ride up while there is still light and chance how many men he has. I am sure that they won't be expecting us to follow so soon.'

It was a point to consider.

'Very well,' she agreed reluctantly. 'There are six of us and three warriors among our six. If we are on our guard, we should be safe enough. We'll go directly to confront Ruán.'

They had come to a small pass with hills on either side. Fidelma called a halt for a moment to rest the horses. Enda had already said that he had passed along this route before, and now he pointed at a small hill to the south.

'There is an ancient fortress up there. You should be able to see across the plain to Tulach Ruán where the road turns north between the mountains before turning west again through the marshes and on to Cashel. From up there, we could see the lie of the land and check that the way ahead is clear.'

'That might be a good idea,' Fidelma agreed.

'I don't think it will help us,' Feradach disagreed. 'Even if the way *is* clear, we can still be spotted from Ruán's Hill as we approach.

I suggest we move on immediately and reach Ruán's homestead before dusk.'

'It's always best to be prepared,' Fidelma decided. 'You, Feradach, and Aidan, wait here with Eadulf and Rionach. I'll go with Enda up that hill and scout the terrain ahead.'

Eadulf and Aidan exchanged an anxious look, but they knew that Fidelma never did things arbitrarily or without forethought.

They rested their horses and allowed them to drink at a small roadside stream while Fidelma and Enda climbed the hill. The two returned after only a short while and pronounced that the way ahead was all clear as far as they could see. Then they all remounted and moved off.

The homestead of Ruán had been built atop a small hillock and seemed to be a converted *rath* or fortress. It was still as intimidating as when Eadulf had first seen it, dominating as it did the pass through the mountains. Close up, he saw various buildings around the main structure. There were several field enclosures, including the one in which Eadulf had spotted his cob. As they approached, they could see that many of the buildings were actually deserted. Feradach moved closer to Fidelma.

'Allow me to go first in case there is danger,' he suggested.

'We already know there is danger,' she replied firmly, 'so it will not be necessary.'

Feradach made to protest but decided against it.

'I think he is right that we should approach more cautiously,' Eadulf advised quietly. 'We don't know how many belong to this Fellowship. But we do know that they are prepared to kill any that they see as enemies. Being a *dálaigh* and the King's sister will mean nothing to them.'

'Trust me, Eadulf. I am not underestimating my enemies,' she replied.

They moved up a broad path to the main gates of the fortified building.

'I'll let you announce our presence, Feradach,' she invited. 'You have a powerful enough voice.'

The Osraige warrior gave her a curious glance, followed by a half-shrug, and then lifted his voice and thundered: 'Open the doors! It is Feradach of Osraige with Fidelma of Cashel, who seeks the presence of Ruán, Brehon to Coileach, Lord of the Marshes!'

There was a pause and then the gates opened. To Eadulf's surprise, it was a portly woman who had opened them. They rode into the courtyard and she shut the gates behind them. Now she stood glaring at them as they dismounted. Fidelma threw a quick glance around the enclosure but there was no sign of anyone else.

'The horses can be left here,' Feradach said, as if he had taken command. 'Go, woman, and announce our presence to your master, Ruán. Tell him we come in search of Brother Failge. Understand?'

The woman seemed to be staring at the warrior with a surprised expression. Then she gave a bob of her head and hurried off.

Feradach followed her, hand on his sword hilt, as she entered the main door of the building on the far side of the courtyard.

'Be careful,' Eadulf warned him.

'This is my job, Brother Eadulf,' the warrior assured him.

They had entered into a large hall with three doors leading off from it. It was an austere sort of place with a few tapestries and trophies of the hunt displayed around it, and a central circular table with a few chairs but no ornaments upon it. The portly woman seemed to have disappeared. They stood undecided until one of the doors suddenly opened and the woman reappeared.

'Brehon Ruán will receive you now,' she said, addressing Feradach with lowered eyes.

The warrior turned quickly to Fidelma, drawing his sword. 'This may be a trap, so I will go first with Aidan and Enda. We will make sure all is safe before you follow.'

Led by Feradach, the warriors stepped through the door that the old woman had indicated. There was a sudden grating sound, and although the door to the room still stood wide open, it was as if a sheet of iron had dropped behind the door. Fidelma, Eadulf and Ríonach could hear the shouts of surprise and anger from the warriors trapped beyond.

The woman, still standing in the room with them, was chuckling and making no attempt to run from her duplicity.

Even as Eadulf moved forward to see if he could locate the mechanism of the door to release them, a cold voice shouted: 'Stay still or you will die now.'

They froze for a moment.

'Well, Brother Failge,' Fidelma turned calmly, 'it seems you have outsmarted us.' The former steward of Cill Cainnech stood in one of the other doorways.

'I believe that I have,' returned Brother Failge, his laughter harsh and cruel. 'You came like lambs to the slaughter.'

'There is only one of you,' Eadulf snapped. 'You have made me angry enough to try your mettle. I handled a bow and a cudgel before I accepted the way of the religieux.'

'Then you had better turn around,' Failge replied coldly. 'After that, I advise you to take your weapons and place them on the table.'

Eadulf recognised Duach and Cellaig immediately. They had emerged through the last door and were holding in their hands weapons that were not common among the warriors of the Five Kingdoms.

'Stay still,' repeated Failge 'for, as you see, my men are armed with crossbows. They are deadly accurate at this range.'

Cellaig looked proud as he held his weapon a little higher. 'Some years ago we had the fortune to join the Ulidians when they fought the Cruithin at a ford across the Lagan up in the north country. The Cruithin were generous. They not only left their dead on the field but also these weapons. We took them as spoils and learned their use. Interesting devices. I am told they were much favoured in Ancient Rome. I think they are called *arcubalistae.*'

Fidelma knew that the warriors of the Five Kingdoms preferred longbows, for they had a greater accuracy than the crossbow, although she was aware that the Romans and Greeks had introduced these weapons among the Britons. The Cruithin, in the north of Britain, certainly favoured them. However, at such close quarters there was no argument about accuracy. The little bolts the weapons propelled were deadly. It was clear that Cellaig and Duach knew how to handle them.

'Now, weapons on the table!' ordered Failge.

'We do not have any weapons.' Eadulf replied.

'But you doubtless have knives or daggers. Place them on the table and do not try to conceal anything.'

'They are in our saddlebags,' Fidelma replied. 'And since you have separated us from our warriors, we are defenceless. So what now?'

Brother Failge addressed the still simpering woman who had led them into the trap. 'Search them, Dar Badh, to ensure that they don't lie.'

The portly woman shuffled forward and quickly, though not expertly, ran her stubby hands over them and peered into their belt bags. 'No weapon on them, lord,' she sniffed.

'Then you may return to your kitchen,' he ordered. He then addressed Fidelma. 'Your ruse to entomb me alive showed some imagination, lady. I will have to see if I can do better with my plan for your own exit to the Otherworld. It is a comfort to know that you have failed to prevent the fruition of our plan.'

It was Eadulf who responded. 'Your plan? What plan would a band of fanatics such as you have that we need fear?'

Brother Failge gave him a look akin to pity. 'I seem to have given you credit for knowing that which you do not know. It is sad that you will die in ignorance.'

'If we are to die,' Fidelma replied evenly, 'I would much rather not die in ignorance. Perhaps you could enlighten us? After all, you believe that we shall be reborn in the Otherworld when we die. Let us have the knowledge of why we have been despatched there before our time. What good would such knowledge do in the Otherworld? Otherwise, according to your belief, we might have to come back and visit you on the eve of Samhain, as you promised to visit me.'

Brother Failge smirked. 'You have a good sense of humour, lady. It is a pity that you chose the wrong side. Your passing will not be as simple as a quick rebirth. When your earthly flesh perishes, Donn, the feared Lord of the Dead, will come in all his terrible splendour to claim your souls and take you to Tech Duinn, the House of the Dead. That is the great assembly place of the dead before they begin their journey to the Otherworld.'

Fidelma replied grimly, 'I know the ancient legends.'

'Legends? We know them as reality. Do you realise that there are many places which we collectively call the Otherworld? For some there are the dark, brooding purgatories of the Fomorii Islands, such as Hy-Falga or Dún Sciath, the Lands of Eternal Shadows. For the true believers there is Tír Tairngiri, the Land of Promise, or Tír na nÓg, the Land of Eternal Youth. Alas, you are not destined for the lands of happiness. You will probably be lost forever in Magh Da Cheo, the Plain of the Two Mists, designed to wander for eternity, seeing nothing, hearing nothing.'

Eadulf shivered, for he had been raised with the gods and goddesses of his own people before converting to the New Faith.

'It seems then that you are able to dictate to the gods what they should do with us,' returned Fidelma dryly, not daunted by his solemn recital of the legends she knew well. 'But so far, you have told us nothing more than what we knew already. We know that you and the so-called Fellowship of the Raven are just a group of fanatics trying to live in the past with the Old Gods.'

A muscle in Failge's cheek twitched.

'We know the story,' went on Fidelma, outwardly oblivious to his anger. 'The hill which is now Cill Cainnech was where those last members of the Old Religion retreated a hundred years ago. I presume many of them fled from the north and brought the Golden Stone with them. It came from Clochar, the Place of the Stone. I am told that it was regarded as a sacred stone through which the gods and goddesses spoke to the servers of the Old Faith.'

Brother Failge bent his head forward in unwilling agreement.

'It was hidden in the hill,' he said softly. 'That was before Cainnech and his Christian marauders attacked and slaughtered most of our people. A secret chamber had been made in the hill and the entrance was disguised. It was symbolic because the Christians were driving all our old deities into the hills, the *sidh*, and when they could not entirely eradicate our beliefs the Christians pretended that the old gods and goddesses were sprites, elves, goblins and fairy creatures in order to denigrate them. We, who remained loyal, knew the truth, and we waited for our time to come again.'

Failge wore the gloating expression of a fanatic. 'And now our time *has* come! We are emerging throughout the Five Kingdoms. Sechnussach the High King was the first to feel our wrath. Oh yes, I have heard how you and Eadulf overcame our followers on Hag's Hill and discovered the truth of Sechnussach's assassination. Therefore it is just that you have both fallen into our hands.'

'It is certainly interesting that we have found more of you fanatics here,' Fidelma agreed calmly. 'But because you have nearly managed to get away with disrupting the Five Kingdoms once, it does not mean you will do so again, nor that you will be able to persuade the people to rise up with you.'

Failge was unruffled. 'I am sure that you have heard the news from the north these last six months? The revenge of Badh has started.'

'Ah, Badh the Raven Goddess,' Eadulf sighed, following Fidelma's unconcerned attitude. 'And what innocent souls has *her* vengeance claimed?'

'Innocent?' Failge repeated angrily. 'You must have heard that

Ard Macha was burned, and Beannhoir and even the Abbey of Telle on the edge of the High King's own territory.'

Certainly Fidelma had heard of what had been thought to be local unrest during the previous months, with attacks on the great abbeys to the north.

'So your Fellowship of the Raven is a northern group?'

'Northern? Of course not! It is found in all the Five Kingdoms. When the Golden Stone is raised as our battle emblem to drive the New Faith from this land, we will be joined by all the clans in all the kingdoms.'

'Ah yes, the Cloch Ór, the Golden Stone. You have successfully moved it from under the abbey?'

'You are intelligent, Fidelma of Cashel.' Failge grinned apprecia-tively. 'Yes, indeed. We have moved it, ready to take it on its journey to rally our followers before we march on the High King Cenn Faelad and replace him with his cousin Niall, son of Cernach.'

'Niall?' Fidelma frowned. 'The grandson of the High King Diarmait, who died of the Yellow Plague? But he is a mere boy. He is scarcely at the age of choice.'

'A figurehead is all we require – not someone who can think for himself.'

'Like the inanimate stone that you worship?' Eadulf was fed up with the sneering face of the man.

The former steward turned and suddenly struck Eadulf across the face, causing him to stagger a little from the unexpectedness of the blow.

'You mock what is sacred, Saxon!' snarled Failge. 'Well, soon you will be sorry. Badh does not take sacrilege lightly.'

Eadulf recovered and smiled. Through the blood on his lips, he said, 'What is she waiting for, then? I would have thought a Goddess of Vengeance would be as quick to temper as you have been, Failge. Or is it that she is powerless to strike without someone like you having to do it for her?'

Failge took another step forward, raising his hand, but Fidelma moved into his path.

'Before you proceed with your vengeance, let me just get one more thing clear and then we can all depart to the Otherworld with a good conscience.'

Failge hesitated and then shrugged, lowering his arm. 'What more is there that you want to know?'

'You say that the Golden Stone was taken from Cill Cainnech. I assume you removed it from the secret chamber and that it is now here?'

'Yes, lady, you have guessed correctly. It was brought here and is ready to be transported north to join our people.'

'Was it to be transported by Ultan and Ultana?'

For a moment Failge stared wide-eyed at her and then he roared with laughter.

'Now you ruin your reputation, lady. It was *because* of the arrival of that couple that we had to move it before we were ready.'

'So who were they?'

'Truly,' Failge was still trying to control his mirth, 'I have no idea who they were. I suspect that they were sent to find out the whereabouts of the Golden Stone.'

'So what happened to them?'

'Abbot Saran discovered them in the chapel, as I have told you, and was about to raise the alarm. That would not have been good for our plans. Unbeknownst to him, I had actually followed the Abbot to the chapel, and it was I who knocked him unconscious. I told the young man, Ultan, that it was the Abbot who was the keeper of the sacred stone and that he would never allow them to escape the abbey. I said that I was a friend and urged them to leave at once. I told him to take the girl and his wagon and head west to Tulach Ruán, where they would find supporters. I would follow them, and explain everything.'

'This they did?' asked Fidelma thoughtfully.

'Yes. After they left, I used a cord to nearly strangle the Abbot. I did not mean to kill him, merely to injure him enough so that he would be out of action for a while. Leaving him in the chapel, I then told one of the guards at the stables that the Abbot was missing and that a search should be made, knowing that he would soon be found. I also said that I was taking a horse to look for the couple who I had seen fleeing the abbey. Being on horseback, I easily overtook the ox-wagon before they reached Tulach Ruán, and guided them here.'

'So when Abbot Saran recovered, he thought it was Ultan and Ultana who had attacked him in the chapel?'

'Yes. And Ultan and Ultana were received here by the leader of our Fellowship . . .' went on Failge.

Eadulf said heavily, 'I'd like to meet him.'

Failge grinned mockingly. 'You have already met him.'

'In the dark, with a blindfold over my eyes – and when it was lifted, a light was shone into my face, so that I could see nothing,' returned Eadulf.

'Never mind,' replied Failge. 'He might allow you to see him again before . . . Ah well, to return to the young couple. Hospitality had been offered them. We did our best to discover exactly who they were and where they came from. What we learned was that they were working for the New Faith and would be a threat to our plans.'

Fidelma sighed. 'So how did they meet their deaths? I presume you forced them to drink hemlock?'

'Forced? No, not forced; they drank it of their own accord, although I confess it was administered by stealth and they did not know what they were drinking. They thought they were among friends.'

'So you did poison them?'

'That sounds so dramatic, but essentially, it is true. We offered them hospitality for the night, believing that they would never wake in the morning. At that point, Dulach and Cellaig were supposed to take the bodies to the Raven House.'

'The *what?*'

'We are the Fellowship of the Ravens,' smiled Failge, 'the raven being the potent icon of our Goddess Badh. We have built a special caged house here in her honour, where we make offerings to her. They are voracious scavengers, these birds of ill-omen. We have to provide them with small mammals, reptiles – even eggs – and they will also devour corpses. I have known them to attack anything with fresh blood on it.' He glanced at Ríonach, who was cowering behind Eadulf, her terrier still in her arms. 'That little dog you hold will make a tender morsel for them.'

The girl suppressed a scream and clung fiercely to the animal, which seemed to know it was in some danger for it began to whine softly.

Eadulf laid a hand on her arm. 'Don't worry, Ríonach. He won't be carrying out that threat.'

'You are mistaken, Saxon, if you think I will not do so,' replied the former steward.

'You planned to take the bodies of the man and girl to be consumed in this Raven House, as you call it,' Fidelma intervened hurriedly to distract him.

'That was the idea,' agreed Failge, almost reflectively as if he was trying to understand what had gone wrong. 'Unfortunately, I left the task in the hands of Duach and Cellaig, who imbibed too much that night. When they awoke, not only had the two fled, but they had taken their wagon.'

'That must have been a nasty moment for you and your leader,' commented Eadulf with grim humour.

'Cellaig and Duach set off on fast horses but lost their trail.'

'They are not too good at tracking people, are they?' Eadulf said, with a glance at the two men, who still stood with their crossbows cocked and ready to fire. 'They soon lost our trail when they tried to chase Ríonach and me.'

'Listen here, Saxon . . .' began Cellaig angrily but Failge waved him to silence.

'And that was the last you saw or heard of them – of Ultan and Ultana?' Fidelma asked.

'Until you turned up and reported the good news that they had both died of the poison and had been unable to report the where-abouts of the Golden Stone.'

'The girl tried,' Fidelma told him. 'She had written it in Ogham but I did not understand it until now. She was dying and not able to concentrate. She wrote "the Golden Stone at the graveyard of . . ."' Her eyes suddenly lit up. 'Of course! It was not a graveyard at all. She put down *tamhlacht* when she meant to write *tulach*. The Hill of Ruán. The words sound similar and she made a slip of the pen. The Golden Stone was at the Hill of Ruán.'

'So near, eh?' Failge replied with a careless smile. 'Well, it shows that Badh is with us and guides us with her hand.'

'It shows that the hemlock was with you,' Eadulf snapped. 'It took that poor girl more than three days to die.'

'It does not matter.' Failge was complacent. 'It was frustrating not to have known where she and her companion had disappeared to. My men did search the marshes. We put the word out for our people to be on the lookout for them. Baodain's Players were passing on their way to the Great Fair, so when they stopped in Cill Cainnech I ensured the word was passed among the travellers.'

Eadulf was startled. 'So Baodain and his group played a part, after all?'

Cellaig, who had been silently waiting with his crossbow, suddenly stirred and said, 'I grow weary. Enough of these speeches and explanations, Failge. Let us get rid of them. There are more important matters to attend to.'

'Indeed,' Failge agreed. 'We have talked far too long.'

'But surely your leader, your mysterious lord, will want to say his farewells to us first?' Fidelma said.

'Yes – where is your lord, Ruán of Tulach Ruán?' demanded Eadulf. 'I think it is high time that he received us.'

Brother Failge stared at him for a moment and then started to chuckle. Cellaig and Duach too grinned at one another.

'I suppose we should take you to him. He will be probably pleased to see you.' Catching sight of Eadulf looking at the still closed metal door, Failge added, 'Don't worry; your companions are safe for the time being. They shall join you in the Otherworld soon enough, so you will have company when Donn comes to collect your souls.'

They were taken through a stone corridor to a stairway in the building. The steps led down to another iron door. With Failge leading the way, they were followed by the two men menacing them with their crossbows. Failge opened the door with a flourish and motioned them all inside.

There was a lantern hanging centrally in the underground room. Directly beneath it was a chair on which an elderly man sat slumped. His white hair was bedraggled, his face was bloody, bruised and swollen. He was bent forward, his shoulders moving as he breathed rapidly. Only the fact that he was tied to the chair prevented him from falling to the floor. He stirred fearfully as they entered.

'Have you come . . .' he mumbled, blinking as he tried to focus. 'Have you come to torture me again?'

Failge chuckled. 'Torture you? Indeed not. We have brought you some companions who will now share your journey to Tech Duinn, to the House of Death.'

'Cut me free but a moment and I will take *you* to Tech Duinn as my companion, Failge.'

'That you never will,' answered Failge gently. 'There is no place in this world for pious people like you. You have outlasted your usefulness anyway.' He turned to Fidelma and saw that she and Eadulf were staring at him with incomprehension. He laughed and waved his hand in a grandiose fashion at the constrained old man. 'Allow me to present Ruán, Brehon to the late, unlamented Coileach, Lord of the Marshes.'

Eadulf was shocked. 'So Ruán is not . . . ?'

'The Lord of the Fellowship of the Raven?' smirked Failge. 'Now whatever gave you *that* idea?'

'I know from your voice that you are not the one,' replied Eadulf angrily. 'So when are we to be graced with his presence?'

'Right now, I believe,' Fidelma answered grimly. 'Come in, Feradach.'

chapter nineteen

Framed in the cellar door was the commander of the Osraige warriors.

'I warned you, my lord,' Failge said to the newcomer before turning back to his captives. 'I warned you that this woman was very clever. We should have dealt with her immediately instead of wasting all this time. However, as the pompous Abbot Saran would have said – *praestat sero quam nunquam* . . . better late than never.'

Fidelma did not seem perturbed. 'Poor Abbot Saran. I presume he suspected nothing of your involvement, nor your plans?'

'Abbot Saran is a self-important fool. He thinks only of making money from trade to build up the riches of the abbey, not knowing that beneath it lay a symbol through which he could have ruled the Five Kingdoms if he had wanted.'

'It was just a stone,' Eadulf pointed out.

'Just a stone?' Failge's voice rose slightly. 'It is much more than that. It is a powerful symbol of faith, an icon that will scatter the enemies of the Old Religion and cause a rebirth, a new dawn. But first Badh will have her vengeance on those who would seek to destroy her.'

'Well, we have a better quotation for you to learn by, Failge, rather than the one you have just quoted,' Fidelma said quietly. '*Praemonitus praemunitus.*'

302

A look of uncertainty came over Failge's features.

Duach gave him a nervous glance. 'I don't understand all this foreign business. What did she say?'

'I said, forewarned, forearmed,' Fidelma translated.

As she spoke, Feradach suddenly came sprawling into the room and fell on the stone flags of the floor. At the same time Duach gave a yelp as his crossbow splintered and fell from his bloody hands.

'Drop it or I shall run you through,' came Enda's voice. Cellaig stood in indecision for a moment with the tip of Enda's sword at his throat, pricking a tiny speck of blood from it. He then dropped his crossbow on the ground and held his hands away from his sides. His companion was now cradling his broken wrist, moaning and cursing, as Aidan also came into the room behind his companion.

'I would not try anything stupid, Failge,' advised Fidelma in a cold tone.

However, the former steward seemed incapable of movement, shocked to the core by the unexpected reversal of fortune.

Feradach was groaning and trying to get up from the floor.

'Lie still, Feradach, if you want to live, or you will die at our feet where you fell!' Aidan ordered. 'I am in no mood to be lenient with you after what you had planned for us.'

Feradach still tried to move but the tip of Aidan's sword was at the back of his neck and he stopped. Meanwhile Aidan had also drawn his dagger and menaced the wounded Duach with it while keeping his sword on Feradach's recumbent form.

'Eadulf, take the weapons from those two.' Fidelma indicated Duach and Cellaig. 'Ríonach, if you will put your dog down for a moment and cut Brehon Ruán's bonds, it would help.'

It was neatly done in a matter of moments, and then Fidelma instructed Eadulf to use the bonds that had tied the old man to bind the hands of Duach and Cellaig, adding that he need not bind their feet together as they were all going back to the main hall.

'When can I get up?' groaned Feradach from the floor.

'Once Eadulf has secured your hands behind you.'

'How did you know?' was the man's next question.

'How did I know that you were the mysterious lord and leader of this group of fanatics? Easy enough,' replied Fidelma. 'Eadulf thought he recognised your voice though he could not definitely swear to it. The smith made a slip and addressed you as "lord", an odd title for a *cenn-feadh*, a commander of a hundred warriors of a township guard.'

Aidan was puzzled about how she had been able to forewarn him about Feradach. 'But, lady, it was Feradach who showed us to the underground chamber. How could you come to suspect him after that?'

'That was the very point at which I started to suspect him,' Fidelma explained. 'He came to my room at night when it was dark and tried to incriminate the Abbot as the person who knew where the secret chamber was. It was actually his intention to accompany me to the chamber and then by a ruse, like the one he tried on you just now, he would have incarcerated me inside it. Then he planned to claim that I had left the abbey and would have sent you on a wild-goose chase in search of me.'

'But we all went together,' Enda pointed out.

'Only because Aidan heard the voices in my chamber and came to investigate. I had deliberately raised my voice several times, hoping to attract his attention. Fortunately, it worked. I suggested we all went to the chapel together. Feradach was forced to improvise, but not very well. He tried to distract us as we followed Failge from the chamber. Suspicion is nothing without evidence. When we stopped on the road, Enda suggested going up the hill to see if there was any danger on the plain before us. That was the perfect opportunity for me to share my suspicion with him. I did so, and he then warned you, Aidan. Both of you were to stick closely to Feradach's side. Sure enough, Feradach used a trick to try to separate us. It worked . . . except that he was not expecting that you would be on your guard against him. He either planned to stab you in the back or use the same ruse to escape through another door and leave you both as prisoners.'

'That is exactly what he did try, lady,' Enda said. 'But we were ready for him. We disarmed him and persuaded him to lead us here – just in time, it seems.'

'I said that she was clever, lord,' wailed Failge, now completely revealing his almost subservient role to the warrior.

'With Badh on our side, who can prevail against us?' Feradach's tone was venomous. 'These unbelievers have but a temporary victory. Already our people are waiting in the north. One by one, the lordships will come over to us and soon Tara will be no more. The Raven Goddess will triumph. Have no doubt.'

Fidelma shook her head sadly. 'I think you will find that doubt is the beginning of wisdom, Feradach. It is the essential starting point to knowledge, to question and to learn.'

'Then you will soon learn that no one can withstand the might of Badh.'

'If that is so, how is it that she and all the other gods and goddesses of the ancients have almost vanished during these last two centuries? If none can prevail against them, where are they now?'

With a sudden cry of anger, Feradach tried to launch himself at her. But his cry of anger ended in a scream of pain as Aidan's sword plunged into the Osraige warrior's right shoulder in a swift stroke. The man fell to his knees cursing, as blood coursed from the wound. Even though he was wounded, Eadulf immediately secured his wrists behind him. Only then did he inspect the damage Aidan's sword had inflicted.

'A flesh wound,' he said. 'Lots of blood but not life-threatening.'

'Let us move him to the hall where we can bind his wound,' Fidelma said. 'Ríonach, will you help Brehon Ruán?'

The Brehon smiled with a tired expression. 'I think I shall be able to manage. They did not tie me up for long. I have been kept prisoner for the past week or so. They brought me down here just before you came.' He glanced down at Feradach without pity. 'He is my own nephew,' he said sadly. 'The son of my dear brother, Coileach, Lord of the Marshes – and the murderer of his own father!'

They stared at the old man for a moment of two in surprise.

'So Coileach is dead?' said Eadulf. 'Feradach is the new Lord of the Marshes as well as lord of these fanatics?'

The elderly Brehon sighed. 'He takes after his grandfather, my father, who witnessed the massacre of those who followed the Old Religion. He fed the boy stories before he died and it seemed Feradach was lost to the New Faith from then on.'

'Time for explanations later,' Fidelma intervened gently. 'Ríonach will help you. You go with them, Eadulf. Next these two.' She nodded to Duach and Cellaig. 'Watch them carefully, Enda.'

After they left, Fidelma turned to Failge and Feradach. 'Aidan will be behind you both, so do not try anything further. We'll look at your wound when we reach the hall, Feradach. But you brought your injuries on yourself.'

Failge went first, trailed by the now grim-faced Osraige warrior, whose blood was drenching his clothing. Aidan's sword had penetrated deeply. Aidan followed them both, sword in one hand and dagger in the other. Fidelma was close behind him. Rían, realising that his mistress had already gone on, let out a series of worried barks and went scampering up the steps between their legs and along the corridor to catch her up.

Ahead of Aidan, the former steward of the abbey seemed to understand his position now. His shoulders were slumped in defeat and he turned pleading eyes back on his former leader.

'Save me, Lord!' Failge cried. 'You have the power. You said that Badh would protect us.'

'Save yourself and Badh will sustain you,' Feradach retorted angrily, the blood still seeping from his wounds and dripping on the stone floor of the passage. They moved slowly along the corridor back towards the main hall. On the left side was a large open window looking out onto the yard, where it seemed some of the domestic livestock was kept. Feradach hesitated slightly as he came abreast of the window. Aidan's sword touched him lightly on the shoulder.

'Don't even think about it,' advised the warrior.

Feradach attempted to shrug, winced at the pain in his shoulder but moved on. There was a wooden door just beyond the window that appeared to give access into the yard. Aidan was momentarily off-guard, having thought the man would have tried to escape through the open window and not through a closed door. He was thus unprepared for what happened next. The door apparently opened outwards, a fact known to Feradach. With his arms still pinioned behind him, Feradach suddenly kicked it open with one foot, leaped through it and evidently used his body to slam it shut behind him. They could hear the flapping of wings and repeated shrill cries.

'What's in there, a chicken coop?' demanded Aidan, shoving at the door. It gave only slightly but held fast. Feradach's body must be holding it closed.

Failge had turned and was staring in shock at being deserted by his lord.

While the group stood uncertain for a moment, they became aware of the strange gurgling croak of ravens. Then came the sound of repeated screams – rising from a human throat.

Aidan tried again to push against the door, but it gave no more than the space of a finger or two. Even with Fidelma's help it could not be budged.

'No use,' Aidan grunted. Then with a curse he handed his sword to Fidelma. 'Watch this one, lady,' he said, indicating Failge, before grabbing one of the lit lanterns in the corridor and launching himself through the open window. The sound of flapping wings and shrill cries continued.

'What is it?' Fidelma demanded. Failge was trembling; his face was pale and taut with shock. He seemed unable to make any sound.

Then Eadulf came running back with the elderly Brehon limping after him. The old man glanced at the door.

'That used to be my hen-house, There's another door at the far end of it. He can escape through it into the grounds.'

Fidelma shook her head. 'I don't think so. Something is in there and it is not chickens. Eadulf, your turn to watch Failge.' She handed him the sword. Then, taking another of the nearby lanterns, she followed Aidan's example by climbing through the window.

She found Aidan standing, his lantern held high, gazing in horror at the sight before him. A chicken shed had been built with one side against the main building and could be entered by the door through which Feradach had escaped. The sides were covered in a wire mesh which allowed air and light in for the birds. Another door at the far end remained closed. Their lanterns revealed what was inside. The creatures within were certainly not chickens. A grisly debris of black feathers, blood and torn flesh covered every surface. The bloodied corpse of Feradach lay crunched up against the door; it was the weight of his body that had blocked it. And on his bloody form were perched a dozen large black ravens, harbingers of death, crouching in their shiny plumage, their tiny eyes glinting wickedly. One glance was enough to know that Feradach was beyond all help and Fidelma turned away, feeling a terrible nausea.

'I thought they were just scavengers,' she said weakly. 'I thought they didn't attack human beings . . .'

'There was blood on him, and his arms were tethered so he could not defend himself.' Aidan gave a philosophical shrug. 'These birds do usually prefer to scavenge, but if they are starved, as these birds have been, who knows what they will do.'

'It is justice in a way,' Fidelma sighed, resolving her emotions.

'I am not sure I understand,' Aidan queried.

'He called himself Lord of the Fellowship of the Raven, believing in the vengeance of Badh, the Raven Goddess of Death. Isn't that what all this business is about? It's what he believed in. Well, it looks as though Badh, the Raven Goddess, has claimed her own.'

Back in the main hall, Fidelma surveyed their prisoners grimly. The portly woman who called herself Dar Badh sat resigned on a chair, her hands also tied now. Duach and Cellaig were bound to the legs of the main table, and to one side Failge was placed bound in another chair. He looked pale and shaken by what had happened to his leader.

Fidelma and the others went into the kitchen where Ríonach volunteered to prepare a meal for them. Eadulf had examined Brehon Ruán's chafed wrists and had cleaned the cuts and bruises on his face. He found some salve in the kitchen and gently rubbed it into the affected areas. Then the old man was invited to tell his story.

Brehon Ruán could summon no sorrow for his nephew's fate. The boy had always been wayward. His grandfather, as he had already told them, had been a bad influence on him. When Coileach had become Lord of the Marshes, he had sent his son to be trained as a warrior at the fortress of the Prince of Osraige. It was thought this would help the young man to mature. Neither Ruán nor Coileach heard much of him until Feradach had reappeared a few months ago as commander of the guard at Cill Cainnech.

It was not long afterwards that Feradach and Failge, with some men that Ruán thought were members of the brethren of the abbey, appeared at Ruán's homestead. They escorted a wagon which was carrying a curious stone. They explained that it had been excavated from a local quarry. Failge requested that the wagon be kept in Ruán's stables. The old Brehon was not particularly interested in such things, but he agreed. Nothing further happened for a while.

Then a week or so previously, Feradach and Failge had arrived with a young man and woman who drove a strange-looking wagon drawn by an ox team. It was that same evening that Feradach made his Uncle Ruán a prisoner in his own room.

'What about your own servants?' asked Eadulf.

Ruán gestured to the portly woman. 'I kept only this one as my house servant, for my needs are not great – and now I find that she has betrayed me.'

The woman scowled and said nothing.

'But you have a large farmstead and stables. What of those who helped you there?'

'It is true that I usually have at least three local folk working for me when help is needed. But the last major work on the farmstead was last month, which we sometimes call "the month of ploughing". Since then, little help has been required. It is not until next month that our seasonal labours will start again. However, I have found that two of my regular workers are no longer here. Failge has replaced them with his own men. There are others, but I don't know what has happened to them.'

'Others? Probably those who met their death on the marshes,' muttered Eadulf. 'But three men to run such a farmstead as this are surely insufficient?'

'It can be done with good men,' returned the Brehon. 'But I am sure Feradach commanded more.'

'What about your brother, Coileach – Feradach's father?' Fidelma asked.

'I did not realise anything was amiss until I found myself a prisoner of my own nephew,' the old man said sadly. He went on to explain that some of the local farmers had arrived to seek his advice as a Brehon. Ruán was brought from his room with Duach and Cellaig at his side. The farmers were concerned that Coileach, Lord of the Marshes, had disappeared, and that his fortress and farmstead were being controlled by strangers. Ruán was instructed to reassure the farmers by pretending that his brother had gone to pay his respects to the new High King in Tara and would not be back for a while. Duach and Cellaig warned him that if he refused or betrayed them, death would be instant. After the farmers left, he was again imprisoned in his room. It was then he realised that Feradach must have killed his own father who, like Ruán, was a strict and moral man and an adherent of the Faith, unlike their own father, Feradach's grandfather.

It was also then that Ruán understood that he was only being kept alive to serve the purpose of allaying fears about the disappearance of Coileach.

'You were going to tell us about the curious wagon and the young couple,' Fidelma urged gently.

'Oh yes. As I said, after they arrived, I was imprisoned in my room. My woman servant came to give me food. I asked why she had betrayed me and she would only say that she was a true believer in Badh. I did hear shouting and movement on the morning after the young man and woman arrived,' he added.

A short time before Fidelma and her party had arrived today, he had been taken from his room to the cellar, handled roughly by Duach and Cellaig and tied to a chair. He had known that his time was now limited.

Fidelma was thoughtful. Then she said: 'This curious stone that Failge brought here . . . I presume that it is still here?'

'It is, as far as I know.'

'Then I desire to see it,' Fidelma announced, rising.

'I will take you to the stables,' Brehon Ruán replied, exhausted as he was. 'It is my house and I want to reclaim it,' he added after she protested.

Fidelma instructed Aidan and Enda to watch the prisoners carefully and then signalled Eadulf to follow her. She picked up one of the lighted lamps on the way as darkness had now descended.

Outside, the horses were still standing in the gloom of the courtyard and stamping a little fretfully at being deserted for such a long period of time.

'We will have to attend to the horses. Is that the stable?' she asked, pointing to a building in the gloom.

'That is my main stable,' Ruán agreed. 'That is where Failge put the wagon with the stone in.'

They crossed to it and opened the doors. A sturdy farm wagon of the type called a *baighín* stood inside. Holding her lantern in one hand, Fidelma nimbly climbed up on it.

The wagon contained a large object, about the length of a short man, lying on its side, covered with sailcloth. Watched by the others, Fidelma drew back the cloth, revealing a stone, similar to the standing stones that Eadulf had often seen about the country, placed as memorials, and sometimes carved with words in the ancient Irish form called Ogham.

'Is this the Golden Stone?' he asked incredulously. 'I expected something more imposing.'

Fidelma pointed to the stone. 'See the flecks of gold? Once it was covered in gold. Yes, this is what lies at the root of all this death and deceit. You are right, Eadulf. It doesn't look very impressive, does it? I was just wondering how Feradach and his followers managed to drag it from the hidden chamber though the passageway to that smithy.'

'Where there is a will, there is always a way,' Eadulf remarked philosophically. 'So this is the famous Golden Stone. If I placed it by the roadside, folk passing by would not give it a second glance.' He was clearly still disappointed as he peered at it. 'I just thought it would be a little more spectacular. There is not even any ancient writing on it.'

'No, none,' replied Fidelma. 'Yet it was believed, according to the Old Religion, that the gods and goddess spoke through this stone to the Druids, who would interpret their words to the people.'

'Maybe it is the mind of the beholder and not the eye which makes the stone so sacred,' remarked Eadulf sagely.

'Well, it is now important enough for us to take it to Cashel.'

'It is only a stone,' Eadulf protested. He had made the remark before and this time it was Brehon Ruán who corrected him.

'It is an icon of the Old Faith and, as such, has the power to motivate people. It motivated my father, but he was from that generation where the Old Religion and the New Faith were in conflict. Worse is the fact that it motivated my own nephew to murder. That is an example of the mesmeric power of the stone.'

'Icons always seem important to people,' Fidelma agreed sadly. 'We of the New Faith venerate the symbol of the fish and the cross, although the cross is now more potent since the end of Roman repression of the Faith. Yet it is not the icons themselves but what we see in their symbolism that is the real source of power.'

'I've never understood why the members of the Faith adopted the image of a fish as a symbol,' Eadulf remarked. 'I can understand the use of the cross – the old Roman method of execution on which we are told the Christ was executed. But why the fish?'

'In those early days, when Christians were being persecuted by Rome, in order to distinguish friend from foe a secret sign was needed; just as Feradach and his fanatics used the raven symbol for their belief in Badh.'

'But a fish?' pressed Eadulf.

'The early language of the Faith was Greek.'

'And so?'

'*Ichthys* is the Greek work for fish. The Greek for "Jesus Christ, God's Son, Saviour" is *Iesous Christos Theou Yios Soter*. Take the first letters – I, Ch, Th, Y and S of the word and you have *Ichthys* – fish.'

They replaced the cover over the stone and closed the stable door. Eadulf stared glumly at the fretful horses in the courtyard. 'We shall need to become stable lads tonight.'

'True enough,' Fidelma agreed. 'Also, we must watch the prisoners throughout the night, for we can do nothing before first light. We'll take it in turns with Aidan and Enda. Tomorrow we shall be faced with the problem of getting these prisoners and the Golden Stone back to Cashel. There are others of this Fellowship about. For example, that smith who guarded the secret tunnel will expect

Feradach to return. Then Ruán here says his brother's fortress and farmstead are occupied by Feradach's men.'

'Perhaps we could send to the township for help?' Brehon Ruán offered. He still looked exhausted, having been kept prisoner for so long. 'Surely some of the Prince of Osraige's warriors there will help?'

'I would not trust anyone now,' Fidelma said soberly. 'Don't forget, Feradach commanded those warriors. Perhaps he fooled them and they are genuine adherents to the Prince of Osraige, or maybe they are all part of this Fellowship. I would not trust anyone in Cill Cainnech unless I had the company of two-twenties of Nasc Niadh at my back.'

'Then we seem to have a choice of abandoning the prisoners or the stone,' Eadulf declared.

'I'd rather not abandon either,' Fidelma replied firmly. 'But I could do with more warriors to keep an eye on the prisoners. At the moment Failge is in shock. I must admit that I can understand it. I have never known ravens to attack like that. I don't trust Duach and Cellaig either. They are well used to arms and might have some tricks up their sleeves.'

It was an exhausting night. Failge seemed to have retreated into his own world and it was clear that he had not recovered from the death of his leader and by such a vile retribution. He sat with eyes closed, unmoving and not responding even when offered a drink or food. The portly woman was also fairly uncommunicative but her mood did not impinge on her appetite. It was clear that she was not very intelligent, nor a moving force in the curious Fellowship of the Raven. Duach and Cellaig were clearly not fanatics. They seemed to have little interest in any religion. This fact made their role worse, in Fidelma's eyes. They were mercenaries and she swiftly came to the conclusion that they would cheerfully serve and kill in the service of whoever paid them the most.

Although exhausted, Fidelma was glad to welcome the eventual coming of the dawn. Only the little terrier seemed to have slept soundly through the night. Ríonach went to busy herself in the kitchen with the dog trotting happily after her. Enda immediately volunteered to fetch water from the well for her. Fidelma noticed that the young warrior still seemed keen to help the girl at every opportunity. Fidelma had spoken to Ríonach during the hours of waiting for dawn and heard more details of her sorry story and her account of what had happened at the farmstead. She tried to reassure the girl that, under her knowledge of the law, she had little to fear. Eadulf, she noted approvingly, had already given her the correct advice on her defence.

Aidan had been despatched to take a position on the lookout tower at the gates of the homestead as a precaution in case any of Feradach's warriors approached from the township. It was only after everyone had eaten that Fidelma recalled that there remained one distasteful task to be carried out.

Leaving Eadulf and Ruán to watch over things, she took Enda with her into the backyard. The evil-looking inhabitants of the hen coop seemed quiet enough now; crouching darkly, the rising sun reflecting on the shining black of their feathers, eyes glinting with that strange malignance. Now and then, they let forth a grating sound from the back of their throats – a sound that was far more intimidating than the shrill cry of their feeding. There was still quite a lot of Feradach's body left. Fidelma screwed up her face and turned away for a moment.

'Lady, you don't have to do this,' Enda told her sympathetically. 'I can handle it.'

She shook her head. 'It is my responsibility as a *dálaigh*,' she said. 'Had I not ordered his hands to be bound, he might have fought his way out of the shed.'

'Had he not attacked you, had he not done this or done that . . . wishing things were different is no consolation for what has happened. If wishes were cows, then every farmer would have a wealthy herd.'

Fidelma caught herself and realised that Enda's old saying and his comment were valid. She thanked him.

'We must be careful then,' she advised. 'These birds are vicious. Grab those *scúap* and give me one.'

The *scúap* were yard brooms made from bundles of reeds. Gripping them firmly, they approached the door of what had once been the hen coop. Fidelma slipped the catch and threw the door open wide. Then they both retreated either side of the coop and began to bang on the netting and yell. At first the ravens seemed resentful, staring beadily at their tormentors, but then they started to hop through the dried and bloodied remains on the floor of their prison towards the open door. At first they did no more than hop onto the earth outside and then, as Fidelma and Enda carried on thwacking the side of the coop with their brooms, yelling loudly, the birds flapped their large black wings, took a few experimental hops into the air and then were suddenly away, soaring upwards into the morning sky. They circled a few times as a flock before disappearing on towards the distant marshlands.

The next task for Fidelma and Enda was even less pleasant.

Fidelma had first returned to the house and asked Ruán for something that she could use as a winding sheet for his nephew's body. Realising what they were about, Ruán, as frail as he was, had taken a spade and gone to a field behind the outhouses and begun to dig a grave for the remains. Enda quickly took over the task; then dragging the sheet with the remains wrapped in it, he pushed it into the hole.

Once the last spadeful had been thrown over to cover it, Fidelma drew a sigh of relief.

'I suppose I should offer a prayer for his soul but I don't think he would appreciate it. You could say Badh took him. So, as he believed, let us hope that Donn has gathered his soul and taken him to Tech Duinn on his voyage to the Otherworld.'

Enda muttered that, in itself, it was prayer enough.

'There is a stream just behind the trees there,' volunteered Ruán, pointing in that direction. 'I bathe there myself. I'll fetch *sleic* and towels to dry ourselves.'

They came from a society that was highly conscious of keeping the body clean and healthy, and bathing was a daily occurrence, although it generally took place in the evening. However, after the efforts of clearing the ravens and their victim, it was essential, according to the old physicians, to wash themselves clean. The *Crith Gablach* insisted that foulness must be washed away with *sleic*, soap, and the body dried with fresh linen.

When they finally rejoined the others, it was mid-morning, and Fidelma realised that it was time for a decision. They could delay no longer before setting out for Cashel.

'Would we find horses in your field strong enough to pull the wagon containing the stone?' she asked Ruán.

'I should think so,' replied the Brehon. 'Although I have not had a chance to assess my stock since being made a prisoner.'

'I presume that you have a plan?' Eadulf asked Fidelma.

'We could put the prisoners in the wagon with the stone, ensure the team is strong enough, and the rest of us will ride our own horses as an escort, After that, all we can do is hope that our road to Cashel will be a safe one.'

At that moment Aidan, who had been at his lookout post, burst into the hall, slightly out of breath. 'Now we have real trouble,' he gasped without preamble. 'Riders, a score or more of them, are coming along the highway. They will be here in a few minutes.'

CHAPTER TWENTY

'This is not good,' Aidan was whispering, although there was no reason to do so. The approaching riders were still some distance away. He and Fidelma had climbed up to the watchtower next to the wooden gates of the homestead. The others waited anxiously below.

'Can you identify the riders?' Eadulf called up to them.

'I make out twenty horsemen, and from their demeanour they are not amateur warriors,' Aidan responded. 'We won't be able to defend this place if they are hostile.'

Fidelma too was observing the column of riders. 'At least they are not coming from the direction of Cill Cainnech. We might be lucky. But even if they are loyal to Feradach, we might be able to fool them. We have not achieved this much to be overcome now by this fellowship of fanatics.'

'I doubt we can fool them.' Aidan was pessimistic. 'The only alternative will be to fight.'

'One thing at a time,' Fidelma replied, although she silently agreed with him. 'Let's wait to see if they are merely passing. They might simply be on their way to Cill Cainnech.'

They did not have long to wait because the column of horsemen soon turned off the main highway and followed their leader up the short track towards Ruán's homestead. A little way from the main gate, their leader halted his men before coming on alone at a trot to rein in before the wooden gates.

Even before he drew close, Aidan let out an astonished gasp. 'I recognise that man.'

Fidelma was already smiling in relief. 'Open the gates,' she called down to Eadulf. 'Let Luan and the Nasc Niadh in.'

An astonished Luan was still shaking his head in disbelief when Fidelma and her companions surrounded him with shouts of welcome.

'Now tell us, what brought you here?' she demanded when things had quietened and the rest of Luan's troops had been assured that all was well.

'A young man, the son of a shepherd from these parts, rode into Cashel with a strange story,' Luan explained. 'There was a lot I didn't understand about his tale of a farmhouse, a dead farmer and two men who had been made prisoners there. The shepherd and his son had released these two men, who thanked them by promptly stealing their horses and galloping off, cursing and swearing about giving chase to a man and a woman.

'The shepherd had already spoken to the man and woman. He described the man as a foreigner wearing the tonsure of Rome. The man sounded remarkably like friend Eadulf, but the woman did not appear to be you, lady. Anyway, it worried the shepherd and so he sent his son on his remaining horse to Cashel to report the matter because the man had mentioned Fidelma's name and he thought the King should be informed directly.'

'That shepherd should be well rewarded,' Eadulf declared.

'Indeed. Well, the King ordered me to take a company of men and ride here to make enquiries. We followed the tracks to a hermit's place in the mountains. The hermit was called Brother Finnsnechta. He confirmed that it was Brother Eadulf and told us that he had advised him and his companion to come to Brehon Ruán at Tulach Ruán. And so here we are.' Luan ended by raising his arms in a helpless gesture. 'I have no understanding of any of these events, lady.'

'No matter,' Fidelma said cheerfully. 'All will be explained in due time. For the moment, the Fates have smiled on us. We have prisoners and a wagon to transport back to Cashel. We were going to have some difficulty with the journey, so your arrival is fortuitous.'

'Is it a heavy wagon?'

When Fidelma took him to the stable and showed him, Luan was doubtful. 'With that large stone in it, I would say it will take several days to haul that wagon to Cashel, even with a strong team of horses. Why do you need to take the wagon and stone, lady? On horseback, we can return to Cashel in half that time.'

'But it is the stone in the wagon that is important,' Fidelma pointed out.

Luan looked at the wagon and scratched his head. 'What's so special about it? It's just a bit of old rock.'

Eadulf chuckled and clapped the warrior on the shoulder. 'I'll explain all about that "bit of old rock" later, Luan.'

Fidelma was standing, thinking. 'Now that your men have arrived, we can get them to round up some of Brehon Ruán's horses. We'll select a good team for the wagon. Half your company can act as escort for the wagon back to Cashel, if you command them. The rest of us can escort our prisoners on horseback, assisted by the other half of your men.'

'Very well, lady,' Luan agreed.

'We can then give a full report to my brother before the arrival of the wagon. Were the *Cleasamnaig Baodain* still under restriction in Cashel when you left?'

'They were, lady, although the King and the Chief Brehon did not seem too pleased about the situation.'

'Has the Chief Brehon returned to Cashel then?'

'He has.'

'So the sooner we return, the better.'

Six days later, the council chamber of King Colgú was crowded with sombre-faced people.

The arrival in Cashel of Fidelma and her party had been met with curiosity and much excitement. People knew that the party included prisoners. When, some days afterwards, Luan and his warriors had arrived, accompanying a wagon containing an object that looked like a small standing stone, which was hauled up to the King's palace, there was considerable speculation and animated gossip.

Fidelma and Eadulf were met by her brother, the King, on their arrival. Colgú was with his Chief Brehon, Fíthel. The new arrivals gave a brief account of their experiences in Osraige, and it was agreed that a *dál* or court should be convened on the following day. Cerball, Lord of Cairpre Gabra, who was still at Rumann's inn, would be summoned to attend, as well as all the adult members of Baodain's Performers.

In agreeing to this, Colgú regarded his sister with some resignation.

'Are you sure that all the mysteries can be explained? Will you be able to enlighten us about what happened when the girl's wagon was set on fire on the marsh road?'

'Have I ever let you down, brother?' Fidelma replied, with one arched brow.

Her red-headed sibling grinned at her. 'You have caused me much worry and anguish, but you have never let me down in the end.'

Fidelma's response was a disdainful sniff as she left.

So now the council chamber was packed. Colgú of Cashel sat with his Chief Brehon Fíthel on his left side. His heir-apparent, Finguine, sat on his right. Next to Finguine was seated the dour, autocratic Cerball, Lord of Cairpre Gabra. Ségene, Abbot of Imleach and Chief Bishop of Muman, was seated on the other side of the Chief Brehon. The elderly Brehon Ruán was seated next to him. Ready to present their report, Fidelma was placed with Eadulf at a table at the left side of the chamber. Nearby sat Ríonach, who had had to leave her dog in the palace kitchens with Dar Luga, the housekeeper. Next to her sat the elderly Brother Conchobhar, the physician and apothecary.

To the right of the chamber stood the prisoners – Failge, Duach, Cellaig and Dar Badh. The entire adult group of *Cleasamnaig Baodain*, Baodain's Players, had been brought in and given a place facing the King. Warriors of the Nasc Niadh were stationed at strategic places around the council chamber.

Brehon Fíthel waited until a hush had descended before officially opening the proceedings. As was custom, he acknowledged and welcomed the distinguished guests by name. Finally he turned to Fidelma.

'Are you ready to make your submission on the matters before this *dál*?'

'I am.' Fidelma quickly outlined the circumstances of the conspiracy.

'The matter began with a curious fire on the marsh road, the death of a girl dressed as a boy, and the discovery of her companion several days dead in the wagon. It was the second death that led Eadulf and me, and our companions, into the lake of fire and evil that we subsequently encountered. Indeed, we found an evil that threatened the peace of all Five Kingdoms and the New Faith itself. With her companion dead from poison, the girl, also dying from poison, was trying to make for Cashel to meet someone – someone to whom she was determined to make a report even though she must have known she was dying. She knew how important the information was that she carried.'

Fidelma turned her gaze to Cerball. 'That report was meant for you, Cerball, Lord of Cairpre Gabra, was it not?'

Cerball stirred uncomfortably. If some in the council chamber were expecting an indignant denial, they were disappointed, for he merely inclined his head in agreement but said nothing.

'We are told that the girl was called Ultana and her companion was Ultan. Were they emissaries from Cairpre Gabra, or from Tethbae?' queried Fidelma.

'Cairpre Gabra will suffice,' Cerball replied without emotion. 'We owe allegiance to Tethbae, so it makes little difference. I should add, for your record, that their names were, in truth, Ultan and Ultana.'

'Were they sent here by you?'

This time Cerball shook his head. 'They were sent by Febal, Abbot and Bishop of Clochar, to whose community they belonged.'

'Then I presume that you also come here at his request?'

Cerball shrugged indifferently.

'We'll take that as confirmation,' Fidelma observed. 'By the way, did you know that the girl, Ultana, was pregnant?'

Cerball started visibly in his chair. Then he said quietly: 'I knew they were married and had decided to undertake this mission together. But we had no idea that the girl was with child. She did not mention it. Abbot Febal would never have allowed them to go on the mission, had he known this. He would not have endangered her and the soul of the unborn child.'

'The child was only a few months in the womb,' piped up Brother Conchobhar, from where he was observing proceedings. 'I doubt whether the soul had entered into it.'

The laws, which all physicians had to obey, differentiated between aspects of an unborn child when considering abortion. There was the establishment of the foetus, then the forming of the flesh of the unborn, rising to the point when it was finally considered that a soul had entered the child.

'I did not know,' Cerball repeated softly, his face showing a terrible sadness. 'She was my niece, the daughter of my own sister.'

'I believe that they were sent to discover something,' continued Fidelma in a more gentle tone. This time he did not respond at all. 'They were sent to discover the location of the Golden Stone, which your people call the *Cermand Cestach*. It is one of the sacred stones of the Old Religion, through which superstitious people believed that the ancient gods and goddess spoke to their Druids. Will you tell us its story, Cerball?'

The Lord of Cairpre Gabra leaned back in his seat, a resigned expression on his face. 'The story is well known in the north,' he countered.

'But we are now in the south,' Brehon Fíthel intervened pointedly.

'Very well,' Cerball continued, after a moment's hesitation. 'Our kingdom at the time of the coming of the New Faith was ruled by Cairpre; hence Cairpre Gabra is the name of our territory. Cairpre refused to give up the Old Religion. He and his people guarded this sacred stone of which you speak – the Cloch Ór or the Golden Stone. The immediate guardian of the stone was a noble called Cairthinn. He was loyal to Cairpre. However, Cairthinn's son, Aedh, met with Blessed Patrick and became converted to the New Faith. Afterwards, he became known simply as the Son of Caithinn, Mac Cairthinn. When he took over his father's land and became guardian of the stone, he founded his church at the very spot where the Golden Stone rested. Oh, he had the stone sanctified with holy water and symbols of the New Faith, of course, and eventually built his abbey around it. The place was still called Clochar, the Place of the Stone.'

He paused, looked round and found he had an attentive audience.

'Well, as you know, the Old Faith and the New Faith were in conflict for many years. Many of the Old Faith tried to protect their holy relics. That was when the Golden Stone was taken – stolen from the very cathedral of Clochar. For many years no one knew where it had gone. Then stories circulated, stating that a hundred years ago, the Druids with some of the Old Faith had retreated to the south, down the River An Fheoir, to a hilltop where they tried to continue worshipping in the same way their ancestors had in the time before time. Then a man called Cainnech led a Christian army to that spot, destroyed the Druids' sanctuary and then set up his church there.'

'Cill Cainnech,' muttered Colgú uneasily. 'We know the story.'

'It was rumoured that the Golden Stone had been taken there with other symbols of the Old Faith. But after the destruction of the Druids it seemed to disappear. Indeed, all word of it had vanished. Then recently a new rumour began to circulate among the people, saying that the stone survived. It had been hidden, it was said, under the very church that Cainnech had built, and protected by a small group who remained loyal to the ancient beliefs. Of more concern was the unrest among those who claimed that soon the stone would be revealed and those who remained true to the Old Religion would rise up and drive out the Christians.'

'And was that why you sent the couple called Ultan and Ultana there? To find out whether the stories were true?' Fidelma asked.

'Indeed. They were to pretend to be looking for material to write a life of Cainnech. I charged them to report to me if they discovered that there was any truth in the rumours. To stop any suspicion, they were to meet me here during the time of the Great Fair of Cashel.'

Colgú leaned forward a little. 'And if they had discovered the location of this Golden Stone, what did you intend to do with it? Surely these pagan icons mean nothing to those of the New Faith?'

'They are beginning to mean more,' replied Cerball. 'There is currently much unrest in the north. You already know that the High King Sechnassach was assassinated as part of a conspiracy by those loyal to the Old Faith. Your sister played the prominent role in uncovering this.'

There was a muttering of agreement, for the story was well known.

Cerball went on: 'Groups of those who still cling to the ancient religion have continued attacking communities of the New Faith.

the Abbey of Ard Macha was burned recently; the Abbey of Beannchar and that of Telle – all attacked and burned down within a short period. The word was that the sacred stone would soon be produced and a great Druid would interpret the word of the ancient Goddess Badh, who was demanding vengeance on those who preach the New Faith.'

'Your emissaries had discovered that a secret group guarded the whereabouts of the stone,' said Fidelma, taking up the story. 'A group of fanatics called the Fellowship of the Raven, who held Badh, the old Raven Goddess of Death and battles, as their divine inspiration. They each wore a symbol tied on their wrists by a piece of hemp cord; it was a brass disc with a raven depicted on it. The girl Ultana had found one and tied it to her wrist for safekeeping.'

'So, if your emissaries had found this Golden Stone,' Colgú turned to Cerball, 'what then? What was to become of it?'

'It was our intention to return it to the Abbey of the Stone, to Clochar, to be sanctified again in the New Faith and placed in the porch of the cathedral. In this manner, it could be shown to the populace that the old ways had perished. We felt this would dissuade people from returning to the Old Faith.'

'A laudable intent,' Brehon Frithel acknowledged dryly.

'As I have explained,' Fidelma continued, 'Ultan and Ultana believed that the stone was hidden beneath the chapel in the oldest part of the Abbey of Cill Cainnech. They did not realise that the Golden Stone had already been removed to another place by the Fellowship, who now suspected them. Ultan and Ultana in turn suspected Abbot Saran, but it was the steward, Failge, of whom they should have been wary. When the Abbot went to confront the pair, Failge entered the chapel behind him, and knocked him unconscious. He then persuaded the young couple that he was their friend and that they should flee to Tulach Ruán, where they would find safety from the Fellowship of the Raven. By this time, Ruán had been made a prisoner in his own homestead. Feradach was his nephew and had even killed his own father, Coileach, Lord of the Marshes. Feradach was more fanatical than his comrades, for kin-slaying is considered the worst crime of all.'

She paused a moment before continuing. 'It seemed that Feradach and Failge were able to maintain their deception of being supportive of Ultan and Ultana. A meal was given to the young couple and during that meal they were surreptitiously fed a powerful distillation of hemlock.

'What the murderers had not considered is the fact that hemlock does not act immediately. The couple had been given a room in Ruán's homestead for the night, the idea being that by the next morning they would be dead and their bodies would then be disposed of. It is an unpleasant fact that this bizarre Fellowship even kept half-starved ravens, to which they sacrificed offerings to Badh, the Raven Goddess, according to their beliefs. I will allow you to imagine the fate they intended for the young couple.'

She had to wait patiently for the cries of disgust to die away.

'Feradach and Failge could not stay away from the abbey for long and so they had to return so as not to raise suspicion. Therefore they left their accomplices, Duach and Cellaig and the woman, Dar Badh, to finish their evil work and dispose of the bodies the next morning.'

The portly old woman, standing with hands bound next to Failge, screwed her features up and actually spat towards Fidelma. 'Badh will come for you soon, my fine lady,' she cried, her voice trembling with curses.

Aidan started towards her but Fidelma held up her hand. 'She can do no harm now,' she said. 'Her words are as powerless as the goddess she is named after.'

'What happened then?' Brehon Fíthel asked.

'The couple were young and strong. Sometime during the night, they must have realised that they had been poisoned and were in danger. It was dark and I think the household had probably fallen into a drunken slumber. Ultan and Ultana managed to escape in their wagon. We may never know the exact circumstances. They knew they had to reach Cashel to pass on the information to Cerball.

'It was Ultan who succumbed to the poison first. In desperation, Ultana drove the wagon into the marshlands, where she found a deserted farmhouse and stopped, no doubt seeking sanctuary in order to nurse her husband. Perhaps she hoped he would recover. Sadly, she had to watch him die. Knowing she could do no more, and aware that her own strength was ebbing, the girl determined to drive on to Cashel to find Cerball.'

The Lord of Cairpre Gabra sat with his head bowed.

'Abbot Ferbal and you should both be proud of her,' Fidelma told him. 'She knew she might not make it and so she wanted to pass on the information. She had discovered the emblem of this secret Fellowship, the brass disc that was found on her wrist. She also laboriously wrote a note in Ogham, explaining that the Golden Stone was at the Hill of Ruán. But her mind was confused, and instead of *Tulach*, she miswrote *Tamhlacht*, meaning the *grave* of Ruán and not the hill. In the same confusion, she thought she would disguise herself as a boy to avoid recognition, forgetting that her wagon was distinctive enough. The poison had that effect. Indeed, when she met up with Baodain's Players on the marsh road to Cashel, it was thought she was drunk or ill. The poison was over-coming her senses.'

'Ah, now we are approaching the matter before us!' Brehon Fíthel exclaimed. 'That matter is the events on the marsh road, the fire and the deaths of these emissaries from the Abbot of Clochar. You have already told us that they were poisoned by the order of this man Feradach, now dead, and of Failge who sits before us. Yet, having been poisoned, they managed to escape and the girl, at least, managed to reach the road to Cashel.'

Baodain abruptly stood forward, unbidden. 'We have heard that the girl was poisoned before she joined my wagons. She wasn't thinking straight, so that was why she set her wagon on fire by accident. I said so all along. That fire and her death have nothing to do with us. We have nothing to answer for. We can go!'

'I'll say when and if you can go!' Brehon Fíthel shouted angrily. 'Return to your place.' He addressed Fidelma. 'Do you have any comment on this?'

Fidelma acknowledged that she did. 'Failge admitted that Baodain's Players had passed through Cill Cainnech after Ultan and Ultana had managed to escape from the clutches of the Fellowship of the Raven. Failge had asked them to be on the lookout for the couple, saying that they must be eliminated to protect the secret of the Golden Stone.'

Baodain was on his feet again, protesting, 'We were not told anything of the sort! True, we saw the steward of the abbey. He sits there before us and I recognise him. But all else is a lie.'

Brehon Fíthel looked troubled. 'Did Failge actually tell you that he asked Baodain to eliminate the couple?' he asked.

'His words were that he asked Baodain's Performers to be watchful for Ultan and Ultana.'

'That does not mean that the performers were part of this conspiracy, nor that they sought to harm the couple,' Brehon Fíthel stated.

'It does, because there is more to it,' Fidelma argued. 'Duach admitted to Eadulf that he and Cellaig had been instructed to come to Cashel to seek out someone in the *Cleasamnaig Baodain* who would give them further orders. Eadulf asked Duach and Cellaig how they would recognise this person as a member of their Fellowship. Cellaig managed to silence Duach, but not before he told us that all members of the Fellowship wore a distinctive badge – the brass disk with the raven symbol.'

'So you are saying that someone among the players is a member of the Fellowship of the Raven?' Brehon Fíthel clarified.

'I am saying that two members of the Fellowship were among

Baodain's Players. Not realising that Ultan had already perished and that Ultana was near death, their intent was to stop them reaching Cashel. So they decided to kill the girl, secure the doors of the wagon, so that anyone inside could not escape, and set fire to it. Thus it would look as though the girl had set fire to it by accident.'

'But I don't see how anyone could set fire to the wagon with impunity while the wagons were moving along the highway,' Brehon Fíthel objected.

'I was initially misled by the *picc* that was splattered on the wagon. True, some of it had caught alight and was difficult to extinguish until it was beaten out. But it could not have been the means of the fire. *Picc* has to be heated and give off fumes before it becomes combustible. As it was already on the wagon, it was too dry. No,' Fidelma said, 'it was alcohol that was the incendiary. The two conspirators worked in harmony. They would stop their wagon while one rushed back to kill the girl while the other secured the doors in case her companion was inside. In fact, only one door needed securing and this was done with a quick bowline knot. Then the incendiary material was thrown over the girl and wagon with the bucket of *picc* placed nearby to mislead people as to the cause of the fire.

'That was when they found that Ultana was already dead. The poison had finally worked. Time was of the essence and in their panic they decided to carry on with their plan. Having secured the door, the jug of alcohol was thrown towards the driver's seat, catching the girl's body on one side. They ignited it. The girl's body, however, fell from the wagon and the flames of her clothing were extinguished. Improvisation was called for. One of them dragged the body a little way away; giving the impression that she had jumped from the wagon to avoid the flames.

'The other wagons were still proceeding, with no idea of the drama being enacted behind them. Again, time was against the murderers. They should have let matters take their course once they found Ultana dead. Had they done so, they would not have been implicated.'

Baodain had turned, a look of anxiety on his face. 'But the only people in a position to do this without being seen were . . .'

'Ronchú and Comal,' agreed Fidelma.

'It is lies!' Ronchú took a few steps forward, his voice raised in angry rebuttal. 'All lies and speculation. Let this woman prove it.'

'The speculation is endorsed by one eyewitness,' Fidelma replied calmly. 'Echna, the equestrian performer whose wagon was just in front of the wagon of Ronchú and Comal, told me something that continued to worry me. Comal had said that they were proceeding along the highway when her husband alerted her to the flames from the wagon behind them. She blew the alarm horn. She said that she had not seen the body of the girl lying near the rear wheel of her wagon until she looked back. But Echna told me that she had happened to glance back to see Comal climbing onto her wagon before she blew the warning. She presumed that she had heard or saw something, went to investigate, saw the flames and then issued the warning. She, too, thought that the girl had leaped from the driver's seat, run forward to the rear of their wagon and collapsed.

'Comal stands convicted out of her own lips. As to the knot securing the door of the wagon, it is a knot few people would use. Ronchú, however, is a conjurer who uses such clever knots for his act. Ronchú had tried to convince Eadulf that it was the *picc* that was the source of the fire. He implied that he had been the one who warned people of this, and it was he who claimed that it was impossible to put out with water. But Tóla, the groom, mentioned that it was he, not Ronchú, who had started to use a broom to smother the flames, with others following his example. I subsequently examined the area and clearly smelled alcohol, which alerted me to the possibility that it had been used to start the fire. Who had easy access to strong alcohol? I was told on the journey here that Comal had the ability to distil *braccat*, the malt alcohol. Ronchú and Comal said too much when they should have remained silent. Eadulf and I were suspicious from the start about their involvement

. . . but involved in what? Before we could present the case against them, we had to find out what that involvement was – and what motivation.'

Ronchú and Comal were being voluble in their defence and the Chief Brehon had to order them to remain silent before turning to Fidelma.

'Very well,' he said. 'It seems that you have sound arguments, but you still need verification as to their part in this conspiracy. You say that the prisoners Duach and Cellaig were to make contact with someone in Baodain's Players, who would be recognised only by this emblem of the Fellowship of the Raven, So, have you seen this emblem on Ronchú or Comal's wrists?'

'I have not,' replied Fidelma, causing him and the assembly some surprise. 'I do remember that Ronchú has a nervous habit of massaging his wrist when speaking to us; the piece of hemp that usually tied the emblem to his wrist was obviously causing him soreness.'

'That is certainly not confirmation,' Brehon Fíthel declared.

'I understand that. So, while Baodain's Players were being brought here to this chamber, I asked Eadulf to search the wagon of Ronchú and Comal. Eadulf, show the emblems to them.'

Eadulf rose, his face expressionless, and from his belt bag he took a couple of the brass discs threaded on to hemp rope. He had hardly approached Ronchú and Comal, holding them out for them to see, when Ronchú turned to his wife with a curse. 'You mindless *Gast Gaoithe*!' he cried, using a contemptuous term for a woman. 'Didn't I tell you to hide them well? You—'

Comal started to scream back at him. 'It was your stupid plan, you foundling spawn of a bastard! We should have left well alone.'

The screeching pair were eventually removed from the chamber, still shouting abuse at one another. Order and quiet was eventually restored.

Fidelma turned to Brehon Fíthel with an apologetic smile.

'I confess to the court, I have just played a trick. The emblems displayed by Eadulf were not those of Ronchú and Comal. I did not *say* they were. And while I said that I had asked Eadulf to search their wagon, I did not say he had actually done so. They thought the brass emblems were their own and it was their guilt that convicted them.'

Brehon Fíthel looked shocked at her sleight of hand. 'That is most unusual, Fidelma. I am not sure that I can allow this as evidence . . .'

'You can allow a confession,' she replied, unperturbed. 'And I am sure a leisurely search of their wagon will now reveal the items. Anyway, there is something else.'

'Something else?'

'After Ultana and her wagon had joined the *Cleasamnaig Baodain* while they were watering their animals, Baodain told me that Ronchú had trouble with his harness and had to pull out of the third position in the line of wagons. He was able to rectify the problem in time to rejoin in sixth position. That placed his wagon directly in front of Ultana's wagon. Why would he do that? It meant that he and Comal realised who Ultana was and already knew they had to kill her and destroy the wagon. By making that manoeuvre, Ronchú and Comal's wagon became the only vehicle immediately in front of Ultana. They had to be the culprits.'

'So it was no great mystery,' Colgú remarked, hiding a humorous smile. 'It was simply a matter of commonsense.' Fidelma swung round, a touch of fire flickering in her eyes, before she realised that her brother was being ironic.

Brehon Fíthel, however, was serious. 'What you have discovered is a repulsive story of religious fanaticism.' The man shifted his weight and peered around at the prisoners. 'Two centuries ago, a New Faith came to this land. Many found it an alien creed. Others merged it in with the old ideas and values. But in that interval, between the decaying and disappearance of the Old Faith and the formation and establishment of the New Faith, there was always a period of danger. Some people would become uncertain; others confused or even frightened. Emerging on both sides, there could be a wild fanaticism as each tried to protect their own beliefs. Unfortunately, claiming one deity as an ally for partisan values leads to the worst fanaticism of all. It is a step towards barbarism which destroys our humanity.'

There was a silence while the Chief Brehon continued to gaze towards the prisoners.

'Certainly the case seems clear to me now. Failge, one-time steward of Cill Cainnech, will be handed over to the care of Abbot Ségéne, as Chief Bishop of Muman, until the punishments are decided. I believe Failge took sacred vows to one faith while holding allegiance to another.

'The two men Duach and Cellaig seem willing to sell themselves to whoever will pay them. I shall ask King Colgú for permission to take a company of the Nasc Niadh to Cill Cainnech and the two prisoners will come with us to help identify any remains of these vermin called the Fellowship of the Raven. You have told us there are some at the fortress and farmstead of Coileach. I am sure that Duach and Cellaig will be most willing to do this for a promise that they will face lesser sentences than the ones they deserve.

'As for the woman who calls herself Dar Badh, this evil and twisted creature must be taken to a secure place where she can do no harm.'

'One point more,' Fidelma spoke up. 'What of the Golden Stone? As you know, we have brought it for safekeeping to Cashel. It was taken to Osraige nearly a hundred years ago from Cairpre Gabra when the Druids retreated to what became Cill Cainnech. Is it the property of Osraige, who now pay tribute to Cashel, or is it the right of Cashel to hold it? Or is there a third choice?'

'The law would say that it is now up to the King of Muman to dispose of it,' Brehon Fíthel answered. 'He is overlord of Osraige.'

Colgú sat back thoughtfully for a few moments. 'The one thing we must ensure is that it is never used by fanatics again. That was the purpose for which the two young people came from the Abbey of Clochar to retrieve it for their Abbot.' He turned towards Cerball, Lord of Cairpre Gabra. 'Come and stand before me, Cerball.'

The Lord of Cairpre Gabra rose hesitantly and came to stand before Colgú.

'My decision is that the stone be handed over to you, that you may transport it back to the place of its rightful origin so that it may be sanctified once again to stand in the gateway of the abbey at Clochar,' said Colgú. 'To stand there so that people of the New Faith shall see it as merely a symbol of our ancient history and of a new hope for our future under the guidance of the New Faith.'

The Lord of Cairpre Gabra bent his knee before Colgú in traditional respect. 'It will stand as a memorial to the wisdom of Cashel and the talent of the King's sister,' he averred.

'Better still,' Fidelma suggested gravely, 'may it remind people of the sacrifice of two young people – Ultan and Ultana – who gave their lives and that of their unborn child to stop such fanaticism.'

There was a pause and then Brehon Fíthel was rising. 'I think the business of this court is now completed.'

'What about judgement for Ríonach?' It was Enda who called out, causing everyone to turn in surprise.

Brehon Fíthel was astonished, for the warrior had no authority to address the court once the Chief Brehon had risen. A look of annoyance was forming on his features. Fidelma took a quick step forward.

'Enda means the girl Ríonach whose case I mentioned to you last night,' she explained hurriedly. 'Perhaps now is a good time to clarify her situation?'

'Is the girl here?' the Brehon demanded.

Fidelma motioned for the nervous young woman to come forward. Enda approached to stand at her side.

Brehon Fíthel gazed sternly at her.

'It is claimed that you killed your husband. Is that so? Do you plead guilty to the charge?'

The girl lowered her head unhappily. 'Yes, I killed him,' she admitted in a faint voice.

'There are mitigating circumstances,' Eadulf intervened, moving forward to join them.

'I have been made aware of them,' replied Brehon Fíthel coldly. 'Nevertheless the girl killed her husband and therefore there is a penalty. There is no action without consequence. Even in your circumstances, Ríonach, the law is clear.'

The girl visibly tensed as several moments of silence passed before the Chief Brehon continued.

'The evidence is that you were treated unlawfully, firstly by your father in forcing you to marry for mercenary purposes. Then you were unlawfully treated by your husband, Rechtabra. Had you been able to make a complaint before a Brehon, such as Ruán, he would have ordered the return of your full *coibche*, your dowry, a *smacht* fine and an *eric* fine, and you would have had the choice of divorcing or separating. Is that not so, Brehon Ruán?'

He had looked for confirmation to the elderly Brehon who had now also come forward. 'That is so,' he confirmed. 'But the girl was prevented from doing so.'

'She continued to be abused,' Eadulf added stoutly. 'It was to protect me, as well as in self-defence against the loss of her own life, that she killed Rechtabra. The man was hardly better than a beast. He was one of those who did the killing for this Fellowship of the Raven.'

Brehon Fíthel addressed Eadulf reprovingly. 'I did not ask you to provide evidence, Eadulf of Seaxmund's Ham.' Then: 'In balancing the two matters, you, Ríonach, must pay a body fine of twelve *screpalls*. But you will be allowed to keep the farm, livestock and all other goods as constituting your husband's fine and penalties for his treatment to you.'

'But I don't want them,' blurted out the girl.

The Chief Brehon smiled grimly. 'Then I am sure you will find someone who will purchase the farmstead from you.'

'Meanwhile, Ríonach's fine will be paid by me,' Fidelma said. 'I am sure the farmstead will be easily disposed of.'

'Then the matter is dismissed,' announced the Chief Brehon. 'And that, I hope, finally concludes the business of this court.'

Enda turned to the girl with a broad smile. 'Come, we'll go and discuss how best we may dispose of your farmstead, since you no longer want to return to it. And, of course, we must find a way of compensating that shepherd and his son. From what Eadulf tells me, things might have turned out very differently, without their intervention.'

Fidelma and Eadulf exchanged a knowing smile as they watched the warrior and the girl leave the council chamber. 'I hope Enda also likes highly strung little terriers,' Eadulf remarked, and they both laughed.